# SOULLESS Saint

KINGS OF KILBORN UNIVERSITY
BOOK ONE

KINGS OF KILBORN UNIVERSITY
BOOK ONE

Petal and Thorn Books is an imprint of Thorn House Publishing Inc

Copyright © 2023 Elena Lawson



**This is a work of fiction.** Characters, incidents and dialogs are products of the author's

imagination and are not to be construed as real. Any resemblance to actual events is strictly

coincidental.

**Cover design & formatting:** Pretty In Ink Creations

**Edited by:** Jennifer Jones @ Bookends Editing

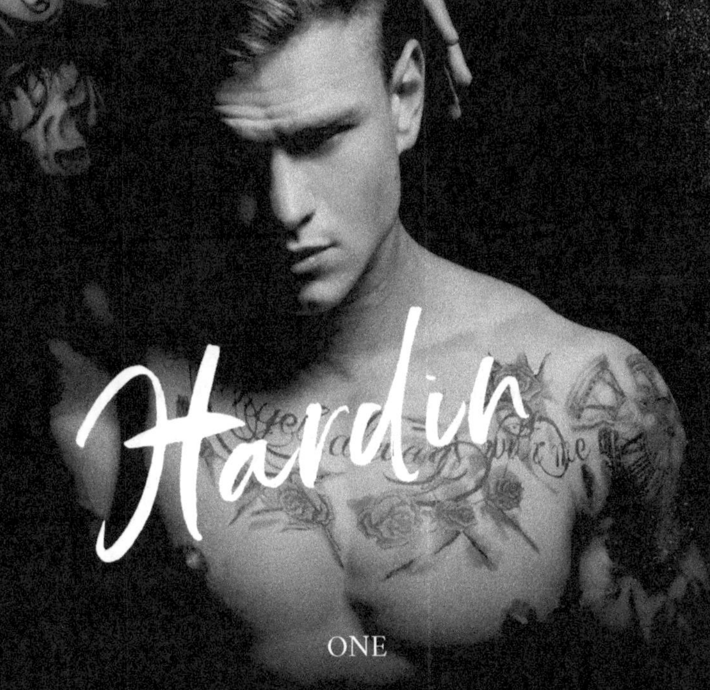


## ONE

*Where the fuck are you, Kaleb?*

The early morning sun glared angrily through the open top of the Bronco, heating my already boiling blood as I barreled down the Sunday streets of Santa Clarita.

I craned my neck to check oncoming traffic before blowing another red light and hanging a sharp right onto Grove St.

*I swear to fuck, if your ass is at Minty's...*

My tires spat gravel onto the road as I pulled into our old dealer's driveway, lifting myself out of the Bronco by her roll bars. The squat white house near the edge of Canyon Country stared out into the day with dark eyes. Quiet.

Not for long.

I took the steps three at a time, landing my fist on the

front door once, twice, three times. Rattling the window panes.

"Christ!" Minty shouted somewhere inside and the sound of pills scattering over the floor met my ears.

I knocked again, twice, louder.

The dirty once-white blinds covering the window to the right of the door crinkled, beveling back and forth. "*Shit,*" Minty cursed, and I listened as no less than three locking mechanisms unlatched before the door swept open.

I shoved past Minty's gaunt frame, into his kitchen, where something that smelled like acid simmered in a shallow blackened fry pan on the stove. Pills popped and crunched under my boots.

"Hardin, man, what the fuck—"

I spun, leveling the full weight of my stare on him, a tremor of heat coiling up my spine, heating my cheekbones where they flared out.

*Don't fuck with me, Minty.*

He reared back a step, hands raised. "No harm done."

"*Kaleb,*" I growled, eyes tracking the airspace behind him, scanning the two caved-in sofas in the living room and the darkened doorway of the bedroom beyond it.

"Kaleb?" Minty repeated as I stormed past him through the living room and into the bedroom, flicking the light on.

"Minty, it's too early..." a scratchy feminine voice mewled from beneath the covers, her pale foot retracting beneath their warmth with a shuddering sigh.

I slammed my palm against the wall, the release from

the sting licking down the length of my body like salve applied to a wound. I tipped my head to the left, cracking my neck, shaking out my tight muscles as I made my way to the bathroom, Minty blathering something unintelligible in my wake.

Empty. I threw back the shower curtain to be sure, but he wasn't here.

"*Hardin*," Minty said, and I guessed it wasn't for the first time by the exasperation in his tone.

I turned to him.

"Kaleb's not here, man. I haven't seen him in months."

I felt my face twisting.

*If he was fucking lying to me...*

"I swear," he added, normally hooded eyes wide and red with his promise. "If he shows his ass here, you're my first call."

My gaze narrowed on a black slip of fabric by Minty's feet.

He saw it the same time I did, and paled.

"Hardin..." Minty said warily, already backing away.

I bent to retrieve the sweater, turning it over in my palm. The fabric fell to one side, revealing the shining silver Saint emblem on the right breast. Kaleb had been wearing it when he left around midnight.

I crumpled it in my fist, deciding to give Minty exactly three seconds to explain before—

Nope.

I launched at him, the sweater abandoned in favor of the front of his t-shirt as I coiled my other arm back and swung, vision tinted red. Minty's head knocked back, mouth slack, eyes wide and blinking as blood spurted from his shattered nose.

"When?"

He spluttered for a response, trying to pry my hand from his shirt as he came to.

"Minty?" the girl from the bedroom said groggily then screamed before I heard the door shut behind her. Smart bitch.

"When?" I repeated, hitting him again.

He gurgled, blood coating his tongue, mixing with the saliva to dribble down his stubbly chin. "Around three, man!" he managed after a good hard shake before lifting a trembling hand to his busted nose.

I released him and he doubled over, falling into the side of the sofa.

I stepped toward him, and he fell back on his ass. He knew what I wanted. He'd better start talking.

"He didn't buy nothin', okay?"

My chest vibrated with a growl.

"*He didn't.* It's why I said he wasn't here. He came. Drunk as fuck. Hung out a while, talked some shit about getting high like old times. I-I told him you'd have my head if I sold to him. Bastard pulled his gun on me, but then he just laughed and said my shit wasn't worth it. Took off on his bike."

I swiped the sweater from the floor, deciding whether I believed this fucker after he just lied to me once.

"I *will* call you if he shows up again. You have my word, man."

Because that shit's worth so much?

I shook my head, staring at Minty as I walked past him right out the still-open front door, slamming it behind me so hard that the window to the right of the door shattered. The gratifying sound ringing in my ears all the way back to the Bronco.

As soon as I had the engine started, I lifted my phone, jamming Kaleb's name on the recent calls list and putting it to my ear, pulling back out onto the street.

I needed to head back to the house, check and see if he was back.

The call rang eight times before hitting voicemail.

The robotic voice finished her spiel, and I let the voicemail record nothing but the sound of the wind as I sped back through Santa Clarita toward home.

Damien would lose it if he knew Kaleb was out alone, piss drunk in the night. There was a new player in town and our father had been grim as he'd explained how we were to keep a low profile, stick together, and never leave the house unarmed.

The Saints *owned* the city of LA with my father at the helm. My brother and I took care of Santa Clarita as part of that territory as soon as we turned eighteen. We'd ruled both without incident, side by side, for going on five years.

And I'd never seen him as on edge as he was right now.

Whispers in the matrix of smaller gangs my father allowed to operate in his territory said the new player was an Irishman. His gang known only as the Sons of O'Sullivan. The twist of the knife? Apparently this foreign implant had strong ties to the new senator.

If those ties were stronger than the ones we had, it could mean a whole goddamn shitstorm was headed our way and there was absolutely no fucking warning when it would make landfall.

The fact that the Sons of O'Sullivan hadn't come to my father was a threat in and of itself. You didn't move in on the king's territory without first bending the knee, offering to pay tribute. Play by the rules.

My phone buzzed in the cup holder and I snatched it up, the wind eating up the sound of the voice on the other end of the call. I hit the brakes, forcing all traffic behind me to come to a grinding halt.

Tires screeched and a couple horns blared. Idiots who didn't recognize my vehicle.

"Hardin?"

Sam's voice came through more clearly, but it was still hard to hear over the damn horns blaring behind me. I lifted from my seat, drawing my gun from the back of my waistband to lift it overhead. I fired once and fell back into my seat, laying the Taurus 1911 across my lap. The horns silenced.

"Speak."

"Hey man, so, *uh*, Kaleb's here at the bar. I told him I was shutting down at five but he wasn't ready to leave."

I was already turning around, heading east toward campus and the Copper Crown. I didn't consider the bar hidden above the bookshop on the Row mostly because like Sam said, he closed it down around three usually. Maybe four in the morning if it was a Saturday. But for a King of Kilborn he'd keep it open as long as needed.

*Damn.*

Of course that was where he took his drunk ass to.

I sighed.

At least the bastard was all right, at least until I got my hands on him.

"Don't worry. Already nicked his keys so he isn't going anywhere, at least not on his bike. Want me to try to—"

I hung up, pushing the Bronco faster as I weaved through the lazy traffic, carving an almost straight line to the Copper Crown.

The nondescript black metal door was already unlocked for me when I pulled up, leaving the Bronco to idle on the street. The narrow stairwell was cleaner than I'd ever seen it and I knew Sam had to find ways to busy himself while my brother drowned himself in whatever was Sam's best scotch.

My phone went off again in my pocket and I jerked it out, finding two messages waiting for me there. One from my father with an order to meet him at the shop later today.

The other in a group chat from Rook, one of our cousins from the Thorn Valley chapter of the Saints.

**Rook: Have you seen her yet? Ghost says she's staying at some motel nearby. Mind checking it out? Make sure it isn't a shithole?**

My hand tightened around the device.

Why the fuck we'd agree to keep an eye out for their girlfriend's best friend here in SoCal was beyond my ability to comprehend right now. We had enough shit to deal with.

I started a reply message, stopping halfway through to take a steadying breath, erase what I'd written and start fresh.

**Hardin: Have some shit to deal with today. Might have time later.**

His reply was immediate.

**Rook: Thanks, bro. I can tell Ghost's worried about her.**

I sighed at that. Both the fierce and virtually unkillable Ava Jade—aka, Rook's *Ghost*—and her best friend had been through some fucking shit over the past year. They had matching scars over their hearts to prove it. Against the odds they'd somehow both survived the gang war and the sadistic fuck who'd wanted to make Ava Jade his own personal perfect doll.

Unlike her best friend though, Becca didn't know all the ways to kill a man. She was a mostly innocent bystander that got mixed up in the fight. No doubt she had some mental scars to match the one over her heart after that shit.

Her scholarship to CalArts here in Santa Clarita meant Ava Jade couldn't keep an eye on her friend as closely as she'd like, but it wasn't the woman herself who asked us to check in on Becca. It was her three boyfriends. Our cousins.

To them, if Becca was important to Ava Jade, she was important to them, too. Never mind that the threat against Becca and her bestie had already been handled...

But I understood, to an extent. Becca was a known ally of the Saints now. Someone important to the woman who was now known as the Saint's Dagger. Which meant that she could never truly be safe ever again.

I scrolled back up the pages of messages, pausing just before Becca's photo could light up my screen, shutting it off instead. I remembered what she looked like. Her image burned into my retinas the instant it glowed over my screen for the first time.

Something about those eyes...

I clenched my jaw, casting the image from my mind. Rolling my shoulders back, I settled the rattle of nerves going up my spine as I pushed through the door at the top of the stairs.

A gust of scotch and cherry cigar scented air slapped me in the face as I entered. The music that'd been muted in the stairwell was louder now that I was inside, but not so loud that I couldn't hear Sam rearranging the stock behind the bar running along the left side of the attic-like space.

Sam lifted his chin in greeting, his blond hair loose around his shoulders instead of pulled back in its usual leather tie. He inclined his head to the back of the space, and I peered through the haze of smoke to find my brother. The only soul who appears to be left in the Copper Crown besides its owner.

Kaleb's tatted arms rested lazily over the back of a dark sofa facing the other way, his sun-stained brown hair messy. His head lolled back, hands fisting the leather.

I stalked toward him, hearing a sucking sound, followed by a gag and a low female moan. Kaleb's eyes were shut as the little brunette knelt between his thighs, her head bobbing up and down on the head of his cock as she worked the base with a manicured hand.

My brother's lips parted on a silent exhalation of pleasure, and I kicked the couch.

He jerked, but didn't open his eyes, moving a hand instead to the back of the girl's head, guiding her to take his thick cock more deeply into her throat. She gagged on him again, but she didn't fight him, even as he fisted a hand into her hair and held her there, thrusting up into her throat until her cheeks turned red.

I kicked the couch again.

"What the fuck, man..." Kaleb slurred, letting the girl get a gulp of air. She gasped as her lips popped off his dick, and he cocked his head at her, reaching forward to run a thumb over her glistening lower lip. "Did I tell you to stop, Poppy?"

"It's Pippa," she corrected.

"That's what I said."

"*Kaleb*," I hissed, heat fizzling across my back as I stepped around the sofa and gave the girl a hard stare. Her reddened, watery eyes met mine with a bolt of fear.

She disentangled herself from Kaleb's grip and held a slip of red fabric over her naked tits, keeping her head bowed as she rose to her feet, collected her purse from the low table, and muttered a *Sorry, Hardin,* as she fled.

"Bro, what the fuck?" Kaleb said, fumbling an empty pack of cherry cigars from the small pocket on the front of his tank. "Shit, I'm out."

I kicked his leg.

His face twisted into a sneer as the empty pack drifted

to the floor to mingle with the empty scotch glass and beer bottles there. "What are you doing here?"

I lifted a brow at him. Was he fucking serious?

He lifted a brow right back. "What? The silent treatment? As fucking usual."

It was my turn to sneer. He knew damn well why I wasn't talking. My heated gaze darted to Sam behind the bar and back again.

"Shit, man," Kaleb groused. "Sam doesn't care if you have a—"

I dragged him from the sofa before he could finish, hauling his drunk ass onto his feet before he could say something he wasn't able to take back.

Kaleb cursed as I towed him along with me, my fist in the back of his tank the only thing keeping him on his feet.

"Okay, okay, Christ, I'm *going*," Kaleb grumbled as Sam nodded his thanks and farewell.

I kicked the door to the stairwell open ahead of Kaleb, and stepping out, he immediately gripped the handrails on both sides and swayed on his feet as he looked to the bottom.

"Shit."

The door shut behind me, and I growled low. "I got you, just move your fucking ass."

"He speaks!"

"*Kaleb*," I warned, my stomach twisting, the shriveled thing in my chest aching for my brother.

As much as I fucking wanted to, it was hard to be pissed at him.

To everyone else, this was just how Kaleb sometimes got, but I knew the truth.

I knew why he needed to drown himself in expensive scotch, push himself to the edge of oblivion. But after the last time, nearly nine months ago now, I thought it was finally over.

Now I doubted it ever would be.

Some trauma stuck with you and Kaleb's had fused itself to his bones like a demented shadow. Rearing its ugly head whenever it got hungry, feasting on whatever stability he'd managed to regain since its last meal.

I helped him down the stairs, practically having to lift him to get to the bottom, otherwise we'd have been there for a fucking hour.

He slipped on the bottom step, coughing, hunching over to one side to vomit onto the cement landing. I shut my eyes on a hard sigh, waiting for him to be finished retching before I lifted his left arm over my shoulders, hauling him onto my back in a fireman's carry.

The sun scalded my overtired eyes as I used my brother's ass to push through the door back out onto the street. The students milling around looking for hangover food and coffee scattered from my path as I carried Kaleb to the still-idling Bronco and all but tossed him over the side into the back seat.

If he puked back there, the fucker was going to clean that shit himself. I twisted my neck to get out the kink there and pushed my black hair away from my eyes, spitting the lingering cigar smoke flavor onto the pavement.

And there she was.

Becca Hart.

She stood perfectly still on the sidewalk a few shops up, frozen as our eyes locked together. Hers wide and wild, fearful and hungry as her thighs pressed tight beneath the curve hugging black dress she wore. Her full lips parted. Powerless to look away until I released her.

My cock twitched in my jeans, and I wired my mouth shut, hating how my body reacted to her. I'd had my fair share of women, but they were a means to an end. And *none* got me hard without a considerable amount of work.

Her chest rose and fell rapidly and I knew if I rested my callused palm over the mounds of her tits, I'd feel her heart racing.

My upper lip curled and her fear intensified.

Good.

If she were smart, she'd stay the fuck away from me. The Saint's Dagger wouldn't like what I wanted with her best friend.

The need to claim her, mark her, *break her*, seared through me like white fire.

I ground my teeth, breaking eye contact, sending her stumbling back into a bench. I lifted myself over the passenger door, slinging my body into the driver's seat, rocking the Bronco with my weight before I shifted her into drive and peeled away from the Row.

Forcing myself to leave before I decided to throw her into the backseat with Kaleb and take her with me.

# Becca

## TWO

"Rough night?"

The balding man next to me on the city bus leaned in, lowering his voice to a conspiratorial whisper. "Don't worry, darlin'. We've all had them."

I shot to my feet before he could pat my thighs. The man lifted his hands in a plaintive gesture at my cutting glare, letting out a strained chuff of a laugh.

My teeth ground noisily in my jaw.

I was dead once. For a full two minutes. This was a walk in the fucking park. It didn't matter that I had barely two hundred dollars left in my wallet. Or that I'd had to spend the night in a seedy motel, jamming towels against the base of the door to make sure no one could shove a coat hanger under it and force their way in.

Nope. Didn't matter at all.

. . .

I clutched the top rail as I made my way to the front of the packed bus, grimacing as I squeezed through the other people along for the ride.

My nose wrinkled at the menagerie of foreign scents, leaving me wondering if the mothball and harsh detergent stench clogging the back of my throat was from one of these people or the stiff floral motel comforter.

Dipping my head, I gave my shoulder a covert sniff and gagged. Yep. The motel had fused its decaying essence to my Loro Piana dress.

Taking a centering breath, I reminded myself my sour mood was more than likely due to the acute lack of caffeine in my system. I wasn't about to touch the oxidized single cup brewer back at the motel.

Checking the map on my phone again, I made sure the bus still headed in the right direction. I missed the first one, even though I was waiting at the stop promptly at 8:52 am like the online schedule said.

My phone buzzed, a message dropping down from the top of the screen, making my fist clench around the device.

**Dad: There's still time to change your mind. The dean of admissions is waiting for my call. There's an apartment in the city with your name on it. I've already put a deposit down. All the amenities, everything you could...**

I didn't bother tapping it to read the rest.

This time, I wouldn't be bought. Not after all the shit I'd lived through this past year. As if on cue, the scar over my heart throbbed and I hunched against the bone-deep ache until it passed.

It was a miracle I was alive at all after being shot in the chest at close range. I wasn't about to waste this second chance at life doing absofuckinglutely *anything* I didn't want to do. And if that meant living the broke girl life, then so be it. I'd loved art since I was old enough to soak my stubby fingers in plastic paint cups, smearing rainbows over the white-washed walls.

This scholarship to CalArts was the opportunity of a lifetime, and if I didn't at least try to take it, then I was an idiot.

Oh so cliché, but it was true: money couldn't buy happiness. I was living proof. I still went looking for it in all the wrong places… which was what got me a backstage pass behind the dark curtain of Thorn Valley in the first place. Once I'd seen it, I couldn't unsee it, but that wasn't why I stayed.

She was.

My lethal bestie, Ava Jade. She needed me, and I wasn't the sort of bitch who left a friend in the dirt. Not anymore.

"Excuse me," I muttered as the bus rolled to a stop and the other students on board shuffled forward, jostling everyone in their path. I followed in their wake, stumbling from the step down to the sidewalk.

I righted my footing, taking a long breath of fresh air, closing my eyes at the feel of warm sun on my cheeks.

"Watch it," a growl sounded behind me before a body

knocked into my shoulder, shoving me out of the way while the bus drove off.

I lifted my purse back onto my shoulder, a hot coil of rage shooting up my spine, leaving me wishing for one of Ava Jade's blades as I watched the woman who almost knocked me over storm away.

I shook my head.

Coffee. I really needed a fucking coffee before I attempted murder.

My heeled boots clacked against the smooth sidewalk as I lifted a hand to shield my eyes against the sun, getting my bearings.

I rushed through here yesterday on my way to the administrative office at CalArts, but I was only really *seeing* it for the first time. The strip of shops and bars where I stood lay stretched out in the middle of a wide green space. Far off, over the rooftops of the shops to the left, Kilborn University stood proudly, with its stately columns and reaching spires. A marvel of red brick and Grecian inspiration that could give Harvard a run for its money.

To my left, in the distance, down a winding path through the gardens rested CalArts. Modern, done up in all white with warm brown wood accents.

The two universities shared this common green and the shops between them.

My stomach growled and I cleared my throat to conceal the sound, an old habit I'd never completely managed to break.

"Sorry," I sighed, moving out of the way of a group of

women linked arm in arm as they strode down the street. The smell of cloying gardenia perfume and… was that coffee?… clung to them as they passed.

I whipped my head around, searching the windows of the shops the way they'd just come, my mouth already watering. A few shops down, a black door burst open and the few students who'd been walking past scattered, hurrying to get out of the way.

Wary, I paused, scanning the street for danger as my pulse pounded in my throat.

A tall man in a leather jacket exited the building, dragging another man with him. I spotted the idling Ford Bronco on the street right outside and noticed that not a soul came anywhere near the two men as one dragged the other to the modded vehicle.

The top was removed and a light bar clung to the underside of the brush bar on the front grill. Wide-eyed spotlights perched above the windshield on the roll bar. It looked like a beach wagon and backcountry hunting truck had a shockingly attractive baby.

The guy in the leather jacket unceremoniously tossed the half-dead one over the side of the Bronco into the back seat, earning himself a slur of curses.

That's when it hit me, the smell of stale liquor and cherry cigars. My nose wrinkled as the nondescript black door shut with a metallic clatter.

The man in the leather jacket rolled his shoulders back, twisting his neck this way and that as he pushed inky hair back from his face with tattooed fingers.

He snorted loudly before turning to spit into the street, giving me a full view of his face.

He was paler than a man living in SoCal ought to be, but it didn't take away from his cruel beauty. I swallowed, following the long line of his tatted neck up to a sculpted jawline, black brows, one with a tattoo arching over it in sharp script I couldn't read from this far away.

*Turn around,* I chastised myself, every alarm bell in my body ringing. *Just turn around. Walk away.*

I shuffled a foot back, but before I could spin on my heel, his head whipped around, piercing dark eyes meeting mine. A muscle in his jaw ticked as he took me in, upper lip curling with something like disdain as he drank up every inch of me. Those black eyes holding me hostage until he was finished.

The instant he looked away, I felt my body sag, catching myself on the rough wood of a light post. Old staples dug into my palm.

Dark and gloomy gripped the top bar of the Bronco and launched himself over the side like he wasn't hiding two hundred pounds of pure muscle under the dark jeans and jacket he wore.

Spoiler alert: I was pretty fucking sure he was.

*Scorpio,* a tiny, scared voice whispered in my mind. *Definitely a Scorpio.*

He revved the Bronco engine, eyes fixed to me through the windshield, and I stumbled back as he floored it, foolishly afraid he was going to hop the sidewalk and run me down.

My purse rang loudly, and I cursed as he sped past,

digging into the abyss to find it. Ava Jade's ringtone, the live version of one of her duets with Primal Ethos blared into the morning air, slicing through all the angst of a minute before.

As soon as I lifted it from my bag, it slipped from my fingers onto the sidewalk and I yelped as someone walking by stepped on it.

"Shit. Shit, I'm so sorry," the guy said, bending at the same time as me to pick it up. I snatched it from his fingers with a growl on my lips.

"Watch where you're walking," I barked, making him reel back with a snide remark on his lips as he walked away and I answered the call *just* before it could go to voicemail.

"Aves?"

Something sharp bit into my finger as her voice came through and I suppressed a cry of pain, pulling my phone back from my ear to see the screen was good and smashed.

"Hey, Becks!"

I clenched my teeth.

"Becks?"

I lifted the phone back to my ear more carefully, hating how my eyes instantly watered with frustrated tears. "Hey, girl, how's the tour?"

"It's a tour," she said. "Being stuck in a tiny ass bus with this fucker isn't exactly the glamourous rock star life you're picturing."

"You fucking love it," I heard Corvus grumble

somewhere near her and, I could practically feel the sexual tension coming through the phone line.

"*Mmhmmm*," I joked, agreeing with Corvus, though I knew she probably missed her other guys. While she was off on tour with Corvus, Rook and Grey were helping Diesel take care of shit back in Thorn Valley. Making sure no other gang would ever so much as lay a toe in their territory again.

"Whatever," Ava Jade said with a laugh on her lips and I could see her eye roll as though she was right here with me. Fuck if I didn't wish she was. "Enough about the tour. How's SoCal? When do you start classes again?"

"Tomorrow."

"How's that Airbnb you found?"

I cringed at the lie. Aves knew my dad cut me off, but I made it sound a lot less desperate of a situation than it really was. Just because she inherited a buttload of money from her aunt didn't mean I was going to let her pay my way, no matter how many times she insisted.

"Uh, I wound up at a motel," I said with a swallow. "The Airbnb fell through."

It wasn't entirely a lie. I *had* been looking into an Airbnb the last time we talked, but they wanted over a grand for the week. The motel cost me fifteen bucks a night.

"A motel?" Her tone changed.

"It's really not that bad," I lied again, trying to make it true. "It's in a nicer area and the bed's cozy. There are locks on the door."

I was sure she'd slept in far worse places and didn't complain at all.

Though she also knew how to incapacitate a man a hundred different ways. I didn't, but it was something I'd decided to become committed to learning if it meant being able to sleep through the night again after what happened.

"That's it, I'm cash apping you."

"*No*," I all but snapped, inhaling deep through my nose to regain control, a caffeine deprivation migraine forming behind my eyes. "Sorry," I muttered. "I just… I feel like I need to do this myself, you know?"

A long silence filled the other end of the line, punctuated by a soft sigh. "Yeah. I know. Just promise me that if you get stuck or you need help, you'll call?"

"Promise."

"Because you know you would do the same for me if the situation was reversed. It's not charity if it's between friends."

I cringed inwardly at the insinuation, even though I knew she didn't mean it that way.

"Right." I chewed my bottom lip, thinking about the not quite two hundred dollars left in my purse and how long it would last me between the nightly rate at the motel and food. Could I even afford a latte?

Before I could cave in and accept her help, I spotted the cafe I'd clocked the first time I walked this street yesterday.

"Any job prospects yet?"

The sign read *Death before Decaf*, and my heart leapt.

Just *one* latte. Then I'd use the shitty single cup brewer in the motel room from now on.

"Becca?"

"What?" I shook my head, trying to tune back into the phone conversation as I narrowly missed getting hit by a late model BMW while rushing across the street, inhaling the intoxicating aroma of a freshly pulled espresso shot and warm frothed milk as if I could taste it already.

"Have you had any job interviews?"

Right. The other part of living the broke girl life. I needed a job. Yesterday.

I'd scanned the wanted ads in the local paper that'd been placed outside my motel door like an actress out of a nineties movie, but there wasn't much to find. The online ads had more options, but almost everything required either some kind of degree or a minimum X amount of years of experience. I had neither.

Thanks to my wealthy upbringing, I'd never worked a damn day in my life.

"Uh… there wasn't much that I think I'd have a shot at, but I'm working on it."

I stepped out of the way as a nauseatingly touchy couple stepped from the coffee shop hand in hand, nuzzling each other like they were cats instead of human beings.

The door swung closed behind them before I could grasp the handle.

"You'll find something," Ava Jade was saying on the other end of the call. "Just don't give up."

A flyer posted on the outside of the door caught my

eye, and I stopped, my lips parting at the simple message printed in black serif on the otherwise simple slip of white paper.

*Part-time Barista Position Available. Inquire Within.*

"Actually, Aves, I do have an interview. Right now. Can I call you later?"

"You fucking better. And you're coming to the Lodi show next month, right? We miss you."

I nodded as though she could see me and then laughed at my space-cadet ass and strolled into the shop. "I'll be there. Love you."

"Love you."

I hung up and dropped my phone back into my purse, taking in the coffee shop that looked huge from the outside but somehow managed to feel small once you were swallowed up inside it.

The brick walls were painted a flat black and artwork of several different, yet distinct types adorned them in each separate cozy little nook area of the long space. On closer inspection, it was obvious that each nook featured artwork by a different artist. Likely rotated out every few weeks or months.

A girl with curly blonde hair at the counter helped the couple of customers in line, while a guy with a shock of white hair and *killer* eyeliner frothed milk in a stainless steel pitcher at a monstrosity of an espresso machine down the line.

It put the little Rocket Apartamento machine I'd had installed back at Briar Hall to absolute shame.

I couldn't wait to get my hands on it.

"Can I get you something?" the girl with the blonde hair called, finished with the other customers in line. She cocked her head at me curiously, taking in my Loro Piana and Stuart Weitzman boots, an envious but also leery expression creeping onto her heart-shaped face.

I swallowed, trying to channel my inner confidence, aka, my inner Ava Jade, as I strolled to the counter. "Hi, is the manager available?"

A crease formed between her brows. She hadn't been expecting that.

"Is he expecting you?"

"No. I, *uh,* I just saw the job posting outside. I want to apply."

Her brow lifted, but she turned, hollering toward the back of the cafe, her name tag catching the overhead light. Kate.

"Logan!"

"He'll be right out," she said, her blue eyes finding the person behind me, hinting that I should move out of the way.

I didn't. "Sorry, could I also get a latte? Large, three shots of espresso?"

She nodded, keying it into the register.

Were lattes always seven fucking dollars? Jesus.

I handed over a few bills with a cringe, forcing myself to drop another dollar and change into the tip jar because *first impressions* and all.

"Thanks," I said, strained, as a man pushed through a swinging door from a back room and came down the serving line to the front.

"Thought we talked about the shouting thing, Kate. What is it?"

Kate indicated where I stood and I lifted to my full height, holding out a hand to the man with the messy brown hair and six o'clock shadow that gave him an *I'll escort you to the fires of Mordor* quality that was really working for him.

"Becca Hart," I said with more confidence than I felt.

He narrowed his eyes. "Logan," he replied, giving me a once over as he took my hand, giving it a firm yet short shake. "How can I help you?"

"Your latte," the guy with the white hair said, pushing a tall cup across the counter to me. I didn't miss the look he gave me or the fact that he'd put my latte in a to-go cup even though I never specified whether I was staying or not.

This wasn't going well.

*Stop overthinking it, Becks.*

I cleared my throat, taking the cup with a smile. "I'm here for an interview."

The manager's brow furrowed. "I don't have any interviews today."

A good sign. The position wasn't filled yet, then.

"Have you submitted a resume?"

The better question was whether I'd even written one. Answer: no.

No fucking idea where to start.

I scoured my brain for a sharp reply, but came up empty.

Shit.

"No," I answered, deciding the truth was probably the best place to start if I was going to have any chance at working here. "But if you have five minutes, I promise I'll make it worth your time. I know my way around an espresso machine and I'm a people person."

At least the first part was true.

He scrutinized me in a new light.

"Do you have a resume with you?"

*"Umm..."*

"Look, Becca, was it? Why don't you come by tomorrow with a resume and I'll take a look—"

"I'm here now, and so are you. There's nothing a piece of paper can tell you that I can't in person."

His eyes popped wide at my insistence, something like interest sparking in their hazel depths.

"All right," he acquiesced after a moment's hesitation, jerking his chin in the direction of two vacant armchairs near the front of the shop in an alcove of rainbow abstracts. "You have five minutes."

He lifted a section of the counter and stepped through, brushing past me, untying his apron as he went.

I followed behind him, my nerves on fire as I watched him toss his apron over the back of his armchair and flop down onto the cushion.

The pressure of knowing this job could be the difference between me surviving on ramen and motel coffee or real person food and free lattes threatened to crush me.

My palms were slick with sweat as I slipped into the seat opposite him and brought the latte to my lips. That first sip feeling helped ease the nerves enough to let my shoulders drop.

"Four minutes, thirty seconds," Logan said, cocking his head to one side. "Tell me why I should hire you instead of one of the forty other applicants who actually bothered to drop off a resume."

I inhaled, and readied myself to exhale the most bullshit list of job experiences and strengths I probably didn't possess.

After my four minutes and thirty seconds were almost through, I knew he wasn't convinced. He leaned forward over his knees, steepling his fingers as he considered me. "Was any of what you just told me true? Or was it all bullshit?"

My stomach dropped.

I wasn't *that* bad of a liar.

But I also had no idea what I was talking about when it came to explaining job duties and experience. Fuck.

"Okay, look, I—"

Logan stood up with a sigh, reaching for his apron. I beat him to it, scooping it from the back of the armchair. I pulled it over my head and knotted it at the back of my black dress.

"What are you doing?"

"Working. Give me a shot. I'll work the rest of the day for free, and if by the end of it you still don't want to hire me, then I'll leave."

He pinched the bridge of his nose. Behind him, I noticed the guy with the white hair cocking his head at me with a grin while he whispered to the blonde. At least I was providing some entertainment.

"I wasn't lying about knowing my way around an espresso machine," I pressed. "Let me make you a latte."

His hazel eyes met mine, lips pressed in a tight line. He wasn't saying no. I grabbed onto that life raft with both fucking hands.

"Please," I changed tactics. "I need this job."

"Fine," he said, giving me a sharp look before I could jump for joy. "But I don't tolerate liars, Becca Hart."

"Right. I'm sorry."

"You have four hours. Impress me."

# *Kaleb*

### THREE

I sucked in a breath as cool water poured over my head in the shower, balling my hand into a fist against the tile.

*"Fuck."*

Dipping my heavy head, I let the water roll down my back, cooling the sun heated flesh there.

Hardin left my ass in the back of the Bronco, parked in our driveway to sleep off the booze in my system.

The fresh air probably did me some good, but the reddened skin of my right arm and the side of my neck begged to fucking differ. I felt like a damn pot roast left too long on broil. My ass deserved it, but that didn't dilute the sting.

My eyes unfocused, and I opened my mouth to gulp down some cool water before deciding cold showers were absolute bullshit. I cranked the lever and sighed as warmer water gushed down from the rain head.

There was a very good chance I was still drunk, but I could taste sobriety on the horizon.

...and the inevitable hangover that would no-doubt tag along with it like the ugly red-headed stepchild it was.

Already the drumbeat echo of my heart was starting to pound in my skull, mounting the pressure behind my eyes.

I leaned into the tile, reaching down to stroke the length of my cock, knowing that a good orgasm would stave off the inevitable at least long enough for me to get some coffee in my system.

Of course, I'd have rather been allowed to finish with the perky-titted brunette at the Crown.

What was her name? Persephone? No, maybe Percy?

I wondered if she gave me her number. If I'd been sober enough to ask for it.

I pressed my forehead to the tile as I worked my hand up and down my shaft, rubbing over the head. I reached for the shower oil and dumped a load of it onto my swiftly hardening cock, shuddering at the slippery feel of my hand, remembering in fuzzy imagery the way perky-tits' tongue had slid expertly on that little spot just... there...

Picking up speed, my muscles tightened, remembering the sound she made when my tip pushed past the dam at the back of her mouth, filling her throat.

I wondered what her pussy would've felt like. If she was just as skilled with that as she was with her dirty mouth.

My core tightened, and I grunted, chasing the sensation only to lose it.

*"Dammit."*

I racked my brain for a clearer image, but when the memory of the girl with the perky tits lifted her head, her lips popping free of my cock, she wasn't little miss perky tits anymore. She had haunted eyes with flecks of gold in their mahogany depths. A long mane of shining dark hair and lips made for sinning.

She was the girl in the picture my cousins sent us last week.

I came hard, grunting into the stream of water as I poured out into the shower drain.

*Holy fuck.*

Outside the shower, a loud thud pounded against the door.

Hardin's not so subtle warning to hurry the hell up.

"Hold your fucking panties," I hollered over the spray of water, sighing into the steam as I rushed to finish showering.

"What the shit did you do with my clothes?" I shouted, stepping out a few minutes later to find the floor covered only in the Turkish bath mat Ma had replaced the old one with last week.

It wasn't like I was going to put the cigar-scented shit back on, but still, what the fuck? I was *showering*. The least he could do was stay the fuck out of the bathroom for five goddamned minutes while I nursed my wounds after leaving me out to dry in the sun.

"Hardin!" I pushed when he didn't reply, feeling that headache now.

I wrapped myself in one of the oversized towels that matched the bathmat and left the bathroom still dripping wet, uncaring that I was soaking the tile and hardwood.

A wad of black fabric smacked into my face the instant I exited the bathroom and I snarled, catching it in a fist before it could fall to the floor.

"You left that at Minty's."

So *now* we were speaking. Great.

I chucked the sweater into the hamper next to the bathroom door, finding all my other clothes there, the pockets turned out. "*Relax*," I hissed. "I didn't buy anything."

I would've if Minty had let me, but that was besides the fucking point. His shit was trash anyway and I could've found what I was after in a hundred other places if I'd wanted to. No one would deny a King of Kilborn, let alone a Saint. I went to Minty because I knew he'd say no.

See? I still had a half a brain, even if my brother was looking at me like I'd chucked the whole damn thing out with Saturday's trash. I'd long since accepted my role as the family fuck-up. Why couldn't he just let it go?

"Relax?" He threw the word back at me with enough venom to give a snake charmer necrosis. "We're supposed to be keeping a low profile, Kale. What fucking part of that is hard to understand?"

Sometimes I wished my brother didn't talk to me either, but alas my parents and I were the only ones he was more than comfortable mouthing off to whenever the mood struck him.

I pinched the bridge of my nose, trying to breathe through the skull piercing ache just behind the flesh and bone there.

"What the fuck do you want me to say, Hardin?"

"It's not what I want you to say," he growled. "The Sons of O'Sullivan are—"

"You're right. Is that what you want? Can we be done with this conversation? I can't do this shit right now."

I turned on my heel and went to the kitchen, leaving wet footprints all over the dark hardwood and even darker tile.

It wasn't like I fucking planned to be out all night, but when I woke up covered in sweat with the taste of ash and blood in the back of my throat, I just...

I grabbed the coffee pot, dumping the remaining dregs of old java into a mug to shove into the microwave.

A shuddering breath left my lungs as I braced myself on the counter. I was only going out for a couple drinks. The last party we had here cleaned us out of liquor and I knew I wouldn't get back to sleep without its sweet, sweet oblivion.

Hardin's slow sure-footed footfalls entered the kitchen behind me. He didn't speak.

"It won't happen again."

We both knew it was a lie.

I thought I was done with this shit. If anyone had the right to be angry about it, it was me. He suffered the worst of it when we were kids, why didn't he still suffer like I did?

Why was his only scar the inability to talk to anyone he wasn't bonded to through blood? And that shit wasn't a fucking weakness at all, but a strength. Hardin had only to look at someone in that way he had and he could scare the literal shit out of them faster than anyone could with words.

He wielded his silence like a weapon, and whenever he did open his mouth to speak, everyone shut the fuck up and listened. A single word from him was like the drop of a guillotine blade. Final. Inarguable.

Like this conversation.

"We're meeting Damien at the shop in an hour," he grumbled, ignoring my false promise. "Clean yourself up and take some aspirin."

I spied my phone next to the sink and lifted it, remembering I left it behind when I grabbed my bike keys and took off. Which meant that perky-titted brunette from the Crown had definitely *not* put her number in it. A waste.

"Hey, did Sam—"

"Yeah. He nicked your keys."

My bike would be around back in his garage then, safely away from anyone who might mess with it. At least Hardin wasn't giving me a hard time about driving that shit less than fucking sober last night. Though I figured that was only because he had bigger issues swirling in that thick head of his.

I tapped my phone and messages lit up the screen like

I'd been gone a damn week instead of a few hours. Missed calls and voicemails from Hardin filled a page of notifications, along with nudes from the two freshmen I'd shared my bed with last week. Nice.

There were some new messages in the group chat with our cousins, The Crows. I scrolled past all the other shit and tapped them, licking my desert dry lips.

"Hey, Hardin, you find the girl yet?"

The microwave beeped, and I jerked the door open to stop it from squawking again, putting the piping hot coffee to my lips.

My brother's back stiffened, and he paused in the living room, turning so I could only see the side of his face. "She found *me*," he said in a low voice.

"What?"

"On the street outside The Crown. Watched me dump your ass into the back of the Bronco."

I winced. Not the best first impression. But I could fix that.

"So, she's here then?"

He heaved an annoyed sigh.

Okay, obviously she was here. I didn't pretend to be the smartest motherfucker, but give me a break, there was a bottle's worth of Aberfeldy still filtering its way through my abused kidneys.

*Where*, was what I meant to ask.

"What about the motel?" I thumbed back through the messages in the group chat as I continued to burn my tongue on the steaming coffee.

Hardin wiped a palm over his face and turned back to

face me. "There are over fifty motels in Santa Clarita, Kale, the girl could be at any one of them."

"Shouldn't be hard to narrow down."

"We have our own shit to deal with before we can take a goddamn babysitting shift."

I cocked my head at him, taking note of the firm knot between his brows. The way his dark eyes shifted over the floor. He really didn't want jack shit to do with this girl.

His loss.

My fucking gain.

"Don't worry about it, I'll make some calls."

No problem, big bro, I'd handle it, make sure we kept our word to our cousins. Hell, I might even enjoy it. I scrolled back up to the photo of the girl from earlier in the group chat.

"What's that?" Hardin asked, stopping just shy of shutting himself into his room, which really would've been the best thing to happen all morning.

My brows pinched as I followed his sharp gaze to the front of the house, hearing what he heard. The echo of footfalls against the flagstone path leading to the front door.

Hardin drew his weapon, and I set my coffee down on the coffee table, my shaky fingers upturning the whole damn thing on the floor, scalding my bare feet.

The front door crashed open, and I whirled around, my towel falling into the coffee on the floor.

"Fuck, Ma!" I grumbled as Hardin put his gun away, opening his mouth to speak before he saw who was following our mother into the house. Gillian *fucking* DeLuca.

She made no secret of her obvious approval as her beady brown eyes zeroed in on my member. Ma on the other hand.

"Ugh, Kaleb," she cried, rolling her eyes as she hefted three Costco bags into the house. "Put some clothes on."

"Then I wouldn't be the heathen you raised."

She scoffed in disgust, and I didn't move to lift the coffee soaked towel, wondering if Gillian was going to move from the door any time this week or if she truly planned to stand there gawking like a mutt before a feast of bones.

Hardin tossed me a pair of dirty gym shorts from the hamper, and I grudgingly put them on if only to stop Gill from soaking the welcome mat with drool.

"Better," Ma said with an approving smirk as she made her way into the living room to draw me into a hug, her long graying black hair brushing over my shoulder. She pulled away, getting a better look at me. "You look like shit."

"You know you can pick up the phone and call before you just show up? That way you might not get a show you didn't want a ticket to."

Her eyes crinkled and she gripped my chin, giving it a shake. "I like to keep you on your toes."

I jerked my chin out of her grasp. "The fuck is all that?"

Hardin was already in the kitchen, studiously ignoring Gill as he went rifling through all the bags. She regarded him with a wary eye, keeping a constant minimum of three feet between them at all times. If only I commanded the same fear, maybe she'd leave me alone, too.

As it was, Gillian DeLuca was what my father liked to affectionately call a Saint's Sinner. One in a chain of many women who venerated us not with prayers or tribute, but with hands and tits and lips of both varieties. All in the pursuit of becoming a permanent fixture. The wife of a Saint.

Gillian made it clear who her target was, but to be fucking frank, I'd rather fuck a goat. And it wasn't her dull brown eyes, small and spaced too far apart, or her nonexistent ass. Hell, it wasn't even the fact that I was pretty sure she'd sound like Miss Piggy if I ever porked her. No.

Her relentless, at times almost stalkerish pursuit of me was what kept her firmly in do-not-fuck territory. I'd play nice, though, because for some incomprehensible fucking reason, Ma'd taken a liking to her.

Probably all part of her master plan. Get close enough to Ma, you could also have Dad's ear, and I knew for a fact Dad would heartily condone the idea of me settling down with a steady lay.

The idea made my skin itch.

One pussy for life?

Might as well get me a prescription for limp dick meds at twenty-three because there was no way the same pussy could tempt me on the daily.

Monogamy was overrated.

Marriage, not even a word in my fucking vocabulary.

"Last time I was here there was exactly one slice of moldy bread and two empty mustard bottles in your fridge."

"Not true," I corrected her. "There was also beer."

She fixed me a hard look, going to help Gillian fill our cupboards and fridge with so much goddamn food I wouldn't be able to squeeze a beer in there if I tried.

"We picked up some more of those Turkish towels, too," Gillian said, her nasally voice grating against my nerves and still-tender brain tissue. Her eyes fell to the still semi-swollen ridge of my cock clearly visible beneath the gym shorts and then to the towel by my feet. "Good thing since it looks like you already ruined one."

Ma scowled at the towel and I picked it up, glad for any excuse to leave the room. "The coffee'll come out," I said on a sigh, making for the laundry room. "Since you're here, make yourself useful and put on another pot, would you?"

"Kaleb St. Vince—"

Ma started but Gillian was quick to cut her off. "I'll do it, Sloane."

"Don't pander to him. That boy needs to–"

I shut myself into the laundry room, chucking the towel into the wash basin before exiting out the door on the other end into my bedroom. I flopped onto my bed, smelling my own sweat, dried on the sheets now. Ignoring it.

The maid would be here in a few hours, hopefully after Ma left since she had no idea we hired one the instant she stopped coming around to bitch and moan and ultimately clean everything we didn't want to.

Propping my head up, I brought up a new browser window, needing to distract myself from the onslaught of imagery from last night's unconscious brain dump. In the search bar I typed in *Rebecca Hart*, and settled in to spend the next hour learning who exactly I would be *'babysitting.'*

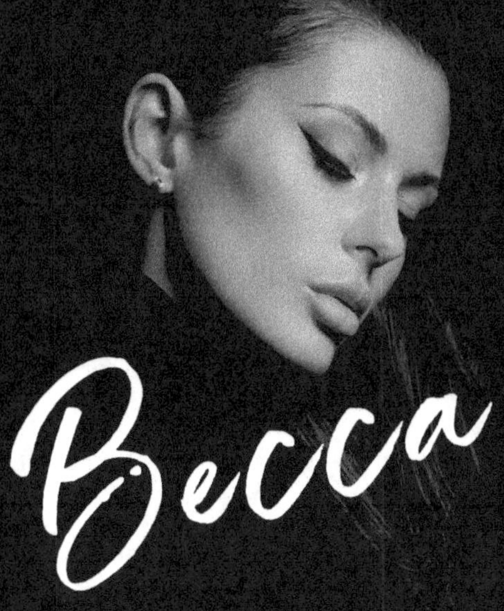

# Becca

FOUR

"This is us."

Kate sighed as she jiggled the key in the lock and shouldered the old wooden door open. It was the only apartment on the top floor of the converted gothic style mansion, which seemed to be a major plus since the common areas downstairs were filled with students lounging in nests of their own post-binge-drinking filth.

"It isn't the Ritz, but it's the nicest apartment in the building," Kate went on to explain, ushering me into the space. It smelled like Kate's magnolia perfume and Toby's smooth musk cologne.

Both employees from Death Before Decaf shared the apartment set barely six blocks away. The location was probably the best thing about the place. I did my best not to cringe at the decor. To my left, it looked like a rainbow barfed over the low furniture in the living room. There were even pink utensils in a teal bucket on the kitchen counter off to the right.

Kate kicked off her shoes and slung her purse over the side of the couch. I bent to unzip mine as she crossed the creaky floorboards and gestured to two doors on either side of a hallway.

"That's me." She indicated the room on the right. "And that's Toby." The one on the left.

She continued down the hall and I rushed to catch up. "Sorry to say you get last pick, but it *is* the closest to the bathroom."

"Anything's better than where I'm staying right now."

"Where did you say that was again?"

Kate fought with the handle, using it to lift the door slightly to be able to push it open. She gave a shrug and a smile that looked more like a grimace, holding it open for me.

"A few miles up the highway."

"Not The Bedrose?"

I winced. "That's the one."

"Jesus, girl. What the hell are you doing there?"

A sigh passed my lips. "It was the cheapest and it had a room."

Oh how the mighty had fallen…

A bed with a black metal frame sat with a bare mattress that was definitely older than I was at the center of the wall on the far side of the room. A little pedestal nightstand perched next to one side. Late afternoon sunlight cast gothic shadows over the floor from where it streamed in through the single tall arched window on the left.

I crossed the room, holding my breath as I opened the double doors on the opposite side of the room, praying for closet space.

A small smile tugged at my lips, finding a closet much deeper than I'd anticipated. It wouldn't fit even half of what I brought from home, but I could make it work.

"Rent's five hundred all-in."

My smile faded, and I remembered the barely two hundred dollars I had in my purse. I was now twenty richer from splitting tips with Toby and Kate for the morning, but it still wasn't even half.

I chewed my lower lip, the idea of spending even another five minutes in that dingy motel alone making my skin crawl and that familiar feeling of anxiety crush my lungs.

"You don't have it, do you?"

I turned back to face her, shaking my head, waiting for the slap of rejection. "Are you looking to rent it right away?"

There were cobwebs in the corners of the ceiling and a good layer of dust on the floor. It looked like it'd been empty for a while. Maybe they could wait until I had the cash.

Kate opened her mouth to answer when the front door creaked open and shut heavily. "Kate? You guys here?" Toby called from the living room.

"Back here!"

He appeared in the threshold next to Kate, tossing his white blond hair back from his eyes to lean against the weathered wood. "So, what do you think?"

"I think it's perfect," I answered honestly. I didn't know either of them outside of the four hours we'd just spent working together. Well, them working, me floundering to figure out how to wear a fake smile, and learn a menu I didn't know, and a cash register that spoke a foreign language. But I already knew I'd feel a hundred times more comfortable here, with other people, *other students*, around than I would in the motel that seemed to only cater to greasy men on motorcycles and Ted Bundy types in station wagons.

I wrung my hands in my dress. "But I can't afford it right now. I was just asking if you were looking to rent it right away."

Toby lifted a brow, eyeing me up. "Is that a Loro Piana?" He indicated my dress with the tip of his head.

Surprised, I grinned. "It is. I had to wait in line for it at her trunk show in—"

"Look, babe," Toby said, interrupting with a breathy laugh. "I don't know what your story is and I won't ask unless you want to share, but if you're short on cash, then I have a pretty good idea how you can make some in a hurry."

Kate, seeming to catch on, nodded her head. "You have more fancy shit like that dress?"

They didn't mean...

"If I put that baby up online right now, someone at

Kilborn will buy it within five minutes flat," Toby supplied, confirming my worst fears. "What's it worth, like twelve hundred? I could probably get you six or seven for it. Minus my fee for facilitating the sale of course."

I rubbed the luxe fabric between my fingers, reconsidering the room.

*Fuck.*

I swallowed past the razorblades in my throat, resisting the urge to whisper sweet nothings to the Loro Piana. She'd been the last size small on the rack and I'd almost taken a lady's eye out to get her. I wore this dress the first night I'd taken Ava Jade to the Docks back in Thorn Valley.

We'd been through some shit together.

Steeling myself, I lifted my gaze to Toby and nodded. "All right. Do it."

He whipped out his phone without another word and guided me to stand over near the window. "Shouldn't I take it off?"

"Nah. You rock it like it was made for you."

Way to twist the knife, dude.

"Besides, the listings with pictures of people wearing the clothes always sell better."

"You've done this before?"

"I'm not this well dressed by accident, babe."

Sure enough, I took in the outfit he'd been hiding beneath the Death Before Decaf apron, finding designer denim and a stylish t-shirt from last season's Cuccinelli collection.

"Those are six hundred dollar jeans."

I thought of the wage Logan from the cafe explained to me when he'd offered me the job this afternoon, trying to do the math. He'd have to work something like forty hours to afford them.

"Try eighty bucks," he said with a wink, snapping the first few photos of the dress.

My lips popped open.

"Thrift shop, baby. Stand to the side, lift your chin."

"Actually, could you just crop my head out of those?"

He nodded his understanding, probably thinking I didn't want people to know I was selling my designer clothes but in reality I didn't want my bestie finding out. It would only make her worry. Or my dad. It would make him smug as fuck.

"Toby will probably have that sold within a couple days. You can stay in the meantime," Kate offered and I felt a three ton weight drop off my shoulders in relief.

"Are you serious?"

"Yeah. I got to admit, I thought you were some snooty stuck up bitch when you first walked into Death today—"

"Yup," Toby agreed, popping the 'p' with a cheeky smirk in my direction. "*High class* bitch."

Kate rolled her eyes. "Ignore him. Anyway, you're definitely not what I had you pegged as. And I mean, you're in two of my classes at CalArts, so we can share notes."

Toby chuckled. "Totally thought she was a Kilborn girl."

"Are they that bad?" I asked, wondering if anyone I saw out in the Row this morning was from there. Though I supposed an artsy cafe with a name like Death Before Decaf would draw the more easy going crowd from the university I was attending.

"Not all of them," Kate replied. "But most are what Tobes and I like to not-so-affectionately call the Kilborn Karens."

"Make their skim milk, half-sweet sugar-free caramel flat whites even a little bit wrong and they'll refuse to pay."

"And don't even think about getting a tip."

"Oh no," Toby agreed with mock drama in his eyes. "Tipping is strictly off-brand for Kilborn Karens."

Toby finished with the pictures and we all found our way back into the living room, where Kate put on the kettle to make us some fresh pressed coffee. Seeing the tall glass pitcher with the chrome details and plunger top made me want to cry with relief after considering the use of the machine in the motel room this morning.

I dug around in my purse for my last two hundred bucks while Kate poured the boiling water over the perfectly coarse coffee grinds, letting them bloom like a pro before adding water all the way to the top and giving the whole thing a gentle stir.

If I swung the other way, I might've fallen in love with her there and then.

"Here." I handed her seven slightly crumpled twenties and a ten dollar bill that looked like a rabid racoon got at it. "At least let me give you a little something until Toby can sell the dress for me."

"Already got two bites," the man himself called from

the living room sofa. "Baiting the line now. I'll have your first month's rent in two shakes, baby doll."

I let out a little laugh.

"So she does know how to smile," Kate joked as she poured us each a cup of coffee. "I was starting to worry you only knew how to bare your teeth."

I remembered trying to force my lips wide to smile at all the customers in the cafe and my face heated. "Oh god, was it that bad?"

"Any worse and you would've curdled all the dairy." She scooped a lump of sugar into her mug and gestured to mine. "Sugar?"

"Just one."

"Boom, baby!"

We both turned to Toby in the living room, who jumped up from the couch, pumping his fist in the air. He pocketed his phone with a triumphant grin, showing off a row of straight white teeth behind his full lips. "Less than an hour is a new personal record. Seven hundred and twenty bucks. After my finder's fee that's six-fifty for you. Rent is paid and this guy's bringing a bottle of Dom to the party tonight."

"Dom?"

"Okay, so, like a really good prosecco, whatevs. Same shit."

I snorted. "Thanks. I really appreciate it."

"Get naked, love. I need to wash and hang dry that beauty before I meet the buyer in a few hours.

*Um...*

"She's straighter than an arrow, and I'm more gay than two dicks touching, but if you want some privacy, use the bathroom down the hall."

"I'll loan you something to wear for now," Kate offered. "Though I don't have much that's black."

"Oh, I do!" Toby offered. "I have this black sheer Armani button down that would look killer if you're wearing a black bra under that."

Kate perked up. "I have a little suede skirt that should work with that."

"Done."

"Uh…" I trailed off, unsure what to say. Anything other than thank you would be rude. "Thank you. I should probably try to go get my stuff from the motel. Do you guys have any idea where the nearest bus stop is?"

Toby put a hand to his chest, looking absolutely scandalized. "As if any roommate of mine is going to take the bus."

"Because your rust bucket is so much better?" Kate teased.

"At least I have wheels Katie-poo."

Kate clucked her tongue in reply, sipping her coffee.

"Let's get that Loro Piana through the wash," Toby said, pushing me down the hall to the bathroom. "And then I'll drive you, 'kay? Let's be quick, I've got a party to get to and a man to woo."

"Ugh, give it up, Tobes!" Kate shouted after us. "Kaleb bats for the other team."

"Did you think you'd like matcha smoothies before

you tried them, Kate? No. But now they're your favorite. Don't crush my dreams."

He leaned close to whisper into my ear, "Such a buzzkill that one," and shoved me into the bathroom.

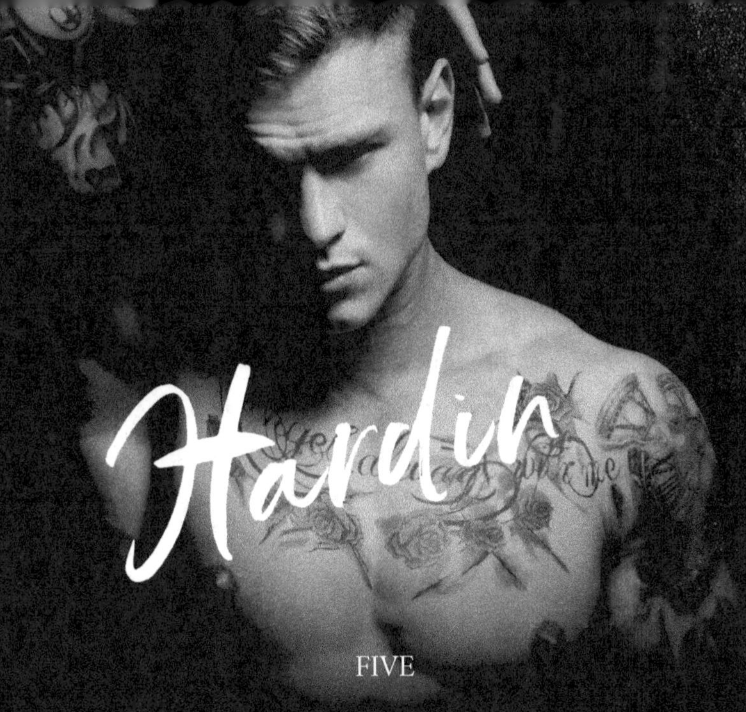

# Hardin

## FIVE

When we pulled up to the front of Saint's Autobody, Dad's truck was already parked near the entrance. Kaleb sighed heavily, pale under his sunburnt skin as he considered the meet we were about to have with our father inside. I snatched the sports drink from the cup holder and slapped it against his chest before climbing out the driver's side.

Normally Kaleb drove us everywhere, the clear choice as the better driver, but by the look of him, he was still drunk. Probably would be until tomorrow if he partook at the party later tonight.

I knew I should cancel it, but Sundays at the Saint's had become something of a tradition in Santa Clarita. Gave our congregation a place to gather for worship. Strengthened and solidified our place among them as gods. To be revered and feared.

"What do you think this is about?" Kaleb asked, wincing as he shut the passenger door behind himself and rushed to catch up to me.

I gave him a hard look. "What the fuck do you think it's about?"

The Sons of O'Sullivan. It had to be. When Dad wanted to meet about smaller matters, we'd meet at his place so Ma could cook us all a big dinner and then force us to clean the kitchen after. When it was important—when he wanted his main crew there for the meet—we met here.

Bells atop the door rattled as we entered and I tipped my head to Pope behind the counter on the right.

"Hey, Pope," Kaleb called. "You get that last order sorted?"

"Stripped clean and put away wet," Pope called back, indicating the two vehicles we'd brought him the week before, stolen from a flatbed while in transit headed someplace east, had been stripped of all useful parts with the rest sent away to be destroyed beyond any recognition.

"That's my man. How's my baby?"

"Almost ready. Hooking up the NOS this week."

"As long as she's ready by next weekend for the race."

"Would I leave you without a ride?"

Kaleb kissed his two fingers and threw them in Pope's direction. I shook my head, feeling the spark of heated frustration attempt to ignite in my blood and fail. My muscles heavy and bones leaden from a night spent chasing my brother all over this godforsaken city without so much as a lick of sleep.

"Kaleb. Hardin," our father said as we entered the back room through the weathered oak door to find him standing over a table and open laptop. "Glad you've both decided to grace us with your presence."

His slate gray eyes jerked between us, made to look even lighter with the way his black hair fell over them, unkempt and still damp from a recent shower.

I cleared my throat, giving him an inclined head in apology, my gaze unconsciously shifting to Kaleb, laying the blame where it was due. Damien St. Vincent's eyes snaked to his other son and narrowed before trailing back to me. I shook my head, warning him not to question Kaleb's state. His lips tightened.

Archer and Zade cleared the area nearest the head of the table for Kaleb and me to take our seats to the right and left of our father.

Dad took a sharp inhale and I could see the moment he reset from father back to gang leader. "As I was saying before your asses showed up twenty minutes late," he began, spinning the laptop around with two fingers so the screen was visible to the group of Dad's most trusted Saints at the table. "We still haven't made contact with our Irish neighbors. They've evaded us at every turn."

I squinted to see the images on the screen, finding grainy footage of a group of men in leather jackets. The first our father has been able to capture as proof that they are in our territory. "Anyone recognize the location?"

My jaw flared as I took in the familiar area, a residential street. Dad took us there a bunch as kids to have dinner with the police chief and his wife and their son, Danny.

"Chief Andrews died of a heart attack last night."

Fury rolled up my back, locking every muscle. My nostrils flared as I let out a hot breath, clenching my jaw and my fist atop the table.

"A heart attack?" Kaleb pressed, asking the question all of us wanted to know the answer to.

There was no way the Sons of O'Sullivan were within a block of Chief Andrews' house—at 8:53 pm by the timestamp on the footage—for him to die of natural causes a few hours later.

No. Fucking. Way.

"That's what the coroner said."

The coroner? Why hadn't Dad just asked Maggie, his wife.

My dad caught my stare, and the flash of pain he hid from the others only intensified my need for blood. Chief Andrews wasn't just some cop we paid off to run our business. He was fucking family. He and Maggie both. For fuck's sake, his son, Danny, went to Kilborn with us. He was in one of Kaleb's classes.

We'd find out the truth of what happened. One way or another.

"This is an act of war," Zade said, his gravelly voice rumbling through the small room.

Damien was nodding, but his brows were drawn as he leaned into the table, palms flat against the wood. "It might be."

"*Dad*," Kaleb said, indignant as he leaned back in his chair, more torn up about Chief Andrews than he was letting on. Dad wasn't much for throwing a ball around when we were kids. But whenever we had dinner at the Andrews' place, the Chief would always take time to toss a ball with Kaleb and Danny in the backyard while Ma and Mrs. Andrews gabbed over wine. Dad and I would watch it all from the deck.

Like I said, the man was fucking family.

Kaleb sat up straight, reaching into the pocket of his jeans for his phone. "We need to talk to Maggie."

"Maggie doesn't want to see anyone right now," our Dad said sharply, glaring at Kaleb.

"Too fucking bad," Kaleb hissed back, but Dad lifted his torso just to slam his palms back down on the table, shaking the long pane of wood.

"*Kaleb*," he warned. "The woman just lost her husband. The least we can do is respect her enough to give her space while she grieves."

Kaleb's gunmetal eyes flitted to me, an unspoken agreement passing between us. Dad was wrong here. If the Sons were to blame for Chief Andrews' death, we needed to know. We needed to know *now*. Dad was letting his emotions where the Andrews' were concerned cloud his judgment.

Something that'd been happening a little too often lately if you fucking asked me, but nobody did.

I gave Kaleb a slight nod and he sniffed, pocketing his phone once more.

"Fine," he said, crossing his arms. "But if it was the

Sons and we don't do jack shit about it then they're going to think they can get away with worse and you damn well know it."

Our dad bowed his head, taking a breath deep enough to make his back expand to damn near twice its natural size. "We give her a couple days. Then I'll get your Ma over there to talk to her. If Maggie knows something, my Sloane will be able to get it out of her."

Finally. Some fucking sense.

But we didn't have days if this was an act of war against us. We needed to retaliate, and quickly. With no fucking mercy.

"In the meantime," Dad continued, addressing the rest of the Saints in attendance around the table. "We have the meet with our Eastern neighbors in a few days."

"And?" Archer pressed, lifting a brow. "We're all set for that. Location's prepped. Time is set. Cash is in hand for the buy. We're good."

Dad's jaw flexed. "Nah. Something's off. The Warden's being squirrely as fuck. We spoke to confirm the meet last night, and he was trying to get out of it."

"Why?" Kaleb asked, like his head was thick. Obviously the 'why' of it was why Dad brought it up. The lack of an answer to that question the problem. "We've done all our arms deals through The Warden for three years. There's never been a problem before."

"Exactly," Dad confirmed. "I don't like it. I'm going to need you and your brother there with me."

"Take Zade and Arch," Kaleb complained, and I kicked him under the table to shut him up.

He winced, jerking upright to rub the new tender spot on his shin with a sneer in my direction.

I nodded to Dad, confirming we'd be there.

If The Warden was trying to back out of a deal with us, there had to be a good reason, and I wanted to know what it was.

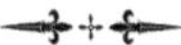

Twenty minutes after hammering out the details for the meet with the Warden, Kaleb and I were back in the Bronco. He cut me off and slung himself into the driver's seat before I could protest.

"So should we go to the Chief's place now or after lunch?"

He pulled out of the lot, lifting a hand to wave at Dad as he exited the shop, on his way to break the news about Chief Andrews to Ma. I didn't envy him. In the last few years Ma'd taken a passive role among the Saints, but it wasn't always that way. Once, she was known as the Queen among Saints, even more bloodthirsty than Dad.

Now she was everyone's Ma. But you still didn't cross her. Not if you wanted to keep your most vital organs intact.

"*Hardin.*" Kaleb elbowed me as he pulled out onto main street.

I turned off the radio, jerking my head for him to continue straight instead of turning right, back to Santa Clarita. "We do it now. And it ain't the chief's place anymore. It's Maggie's now."

Kaleb's smirk fell from his lips, replaced by a sorrowful scowl as his fingers tightened on the wheel until his knuckles turned bone white.

"If it was them, they'll pay," I promised him, the rushing wind doing little to cool the heat of fury still warming my cheeks. My fingers twitched, aching for destruction.

Beside me, Kaleb sniffed, and I did him a solid, pretending I didn't hear and keeping my eyes trained ahead.

Chief Andrews was like family, but he wasn't *blood*.

I was angry someone might've tried to take him from us. That the pain of his loss would affect Ma, Dad, and Kaleb. But anger was where it ended. It was where it always ended.

"Pull in over there." I pointed to the lot of the convenience store where Dad had no doubt gotten the footage, just down the street from the Andrews' place.

"Why?"

"Just pull in, park around the side there."

Not a minute after Kaleb pulled up alongside the back of the store by the dumpsters, Dad's truck rolled down the Andrews' street. He slowed in front of their house but didn't stop then sped off down the road.

Kaleb turned in his seat, a brow lifting.

"You really thought Dad wouldn't check to make sure we didn't come straight here?"

I shook my head when he didn't reply, stepping out of the Bronco.

Kaleb took something out of the dumpster, and when I

turned around to see what it was, I grimaced. He plucked a few browning flowers out of an otherwise still mostly-alive bouquet, wiping some debris off the patterned cellophane wrap.

"Really?"

"You got a better idea?"

"Yeah. Go inside and buy a fresh one, dumbass."

He twisted the bouquet this way and that. "There's nothing wrong with this one."

I rolled my eyes, jamming my fists into my pockets before I throttled him just for breathing. There was no mistaking that I was on edge. I felt sorry for the next bastard who pissed me off.

We took the stairs up to Maggie's front porch two at a time, stepping through the little sunroom to her front door where there was already a wide array of glass casserole dishes and bouquets sweltering in the sun. As Kaleb knocked on the door, I bent to peel back the foil on one of the dishes, finding a watery lasagna beneath.

It'd been there for a while.

It looked like it'd all been there a while actually.

I peered out the screened-in porch, craning my neck to double check that I did see Maggie's silver sedan in the driveway. I did.

Kaleb knocked again, but Maggie didn't come.

"Move."

Kaleb barely had time to jump out of the way before I booted the door down, the sound of splitting wood and metal rattling against drywall echoing through the otherwise silent house.

I drew my weapon and Kaleb followed suit, trailing me into the house. I jerked my head to the living room off to the left for Kaleb to clear as I made my way down the hall, my skin itching as I tightened my grip on my Taurus 1911.

"*Maggie*," I bellowed into the quiet and stopped dead at the sound of a soft sob coming from the other side of her bedroom door at the very end of the hall.

We hadn't been for a family dinner at the Andrews' place in years and my wide frame filled the narrow channel of space as I stormed down the hall and shouldered through the door, my gun arm raised.

I jerked right, then left, searching for a threat to obliviate, but I found only Maggie. The older woman with graying brown hair knelt near the end of the bed, clutching a picture frame between her small hands. Fat tears dropped onto the glass, and she sniffed as she tried to use the heel of her palm to wipe them off the glass, managing only to smear them around, obscuring the wedding photo trapped beneath.

"Maggie?" Kaleb hedged, shouldering past me and into the room. He went to Maggie, kneeling beside her. He tried to take the frame, a soft hand on her upper arm, but Maggie jerked it back from him.

"No," she hissed through the tears. "*Leave*, the both of you."

"I'm sorry, Maggie," Kaleb said softly, releasing the frame, his apology only spurring her to cry harder. Not the cry of a woman who tragically lost her husband to a heart attack. Anger etched dark lines into the tan skin of her forehead, creased the edges around her eyes and mouth.

"You need to leave now, boys."

"Let us help you, Maggie."

She leveled her red eyes on Kaleb and screamed into his face. "You can't help me!"

Kaleb paled at the pain and scorn in her hoarse voice, but he didn't budge. "Answer me one question, Maggie, and we'll leave. I swear."

Her face crumpled.

Kaleb put his hand on hers, still holding the frame in her lap. "Was it a heart attack?"

She shook her head, but she wasn't saying no. She just *wasn't saying*. "He's gone now, what does it matter?"

"You know why it matters," Kaleb replied.

Another tear streaked a path down her cheek, catching at the edge of her mouth. "I've got Danny to think about now," she croaked.

Something in her stature changed, her shoulders straightening. Stiffening. Her gaze hardening.

"So yes," she spat. "It was a heart attack that took my Shane from me."

Her watery blues lifted to me, and I found the truth I needed drowning in their depths. The fury just below the surface, begging to break free.

I swallowed, taking a steady inhale before speaking. "If you saw the man again, would you recognize him?"

The creases in her forehead smoothed at the sound of my voice and I realized I wasn't sure she'd ever heard it before. She blinked as something seemed to shake loose or maybe click in her mind. She knew what I was asking her. I wouldn't put her or Danny in danger by forcing her to give me a name. For all we knew her house was bugged and there was always a risk whoever did this would find out we'd learned who they were through Maggie.

No doubt a death sentence for both her and her son.

What I was asking was simply if *she knew* who did it.

Her chin quivered, and her lips pressed tightly closed, but her head dipped once in a nod.

*Yes.*

It was all I needed to know.

"Kaleb, let's go."

# Becca

## SIX

I barely managed to get my suitcases through the door to my new bedroom before Toby was rifling through them, digging for more items to sell… and something else.

He chose an emerald plaid skirt and ordered me to keep the loose fitted sheer black button up with it. He paired the outfit with my knee highs and the virtually indestructible tights with the seams running up the backs of the legs and declared I was his wingwoman for the evening.

I mean, how could I say no? The guy had just made my rent payment for me, and judging by the way he ooooed and awed over the other clothes in my suitcase, he was going to make me a lot more.

It hurt more than it should've watching him separate the items I was allowed to keep versus the ones he knew he could make me money.

By the time he was through, the *keep* pile was so small that I'd have to wear some of the same items more than once in the same week to make decent outfits.

But it was also somehow liberating. I never would've thought to sell my clothes or my heels or the collection of Hermes scarves I'd been building for the last two years.

It was a massive *fuck you* to my Dad, which, honestly? Felt fucking amazing.

*You'll never make it on your own, Rebecca,* he said with a tired sigh that night over New Year's dinner when I told him I'd accepted the scholarship to CalArts. *I give you two weeks. Three at best before you're right back here on my doorstep.*

I allowed myself a moment of pride as Toby drove us through the streets of Santa Clarita. It'd been a matter of days since I arrived here and already I had a job and an apartment. It wasn't without a bit of help, but still.

My fingers drummed the cool metal outside the passenger window as we sang along to a new Taylor Swift song on the radio.

The wind tangled my long hair, blowing it into an absolute fucking mess, but I found I didn't care.

I laughed as the song changed to one by Halsey, and Toby started drumming the wheel and wiggling his ass in the seat. How he was this happy all the time without drugs was beyond me.

Shaking my head at him, I tugged a joint from my purse. One of the last ones I'd rolled from my remaining stash last week. I put it to my lips, lifting a brow in question at Toby. "You mind?"

"Please," he urged. "As long as you're sharing."

I grinned.

We were going to be friends, I decided. He didn't have a choice.

I took a long inhale, trying to ignore the slight staleness of the pot from sitting in my purse for so long in an unsealed container, but beggars couldn't be choosers and this was my second to last one.

Toby took it from between my fingers only a second after I pulled it from my lips. He put it to his own and sucked, filling his lungs before coughing harshly, cutting me a pained look between spurts. He handed it back. "Fuck, babe," he wheezed. "You call that pot?"

"It's been sitting in my purse for a minute, sorry."

I took another drag, deciding he was right. It really did taste like shit. I put it out in the ashtray below the sound system dials in his old Toyota, waving the smoke out the window.

Toby drank greedily from a bottle of sprite in the cupholder, making a face before he set it back down and patted my thigh. "Don't worry, babe, I've got you. We'll get you some proper green."

I sagged with relief in my seat, putting my hand to my chest as I batted my lashes at him. "My hero. Saving my ass twice in one day... how could I ever repay you?"

He lifted his brows, jerking his chin to the street ahead.

I followed his gaze, finding an American Craftsman style house at the end of a cul de sac. But the large hunter green and deep mahogany home wasn't what drew my attention. It was the people scattered over the front lawn, filling the porch where the large carved door stood ajar.

The thrum of good bass and the smell of good booze beckoned us in a warm welcoming wave.

"You can repay me by helping me catch a Saint."

"A what?"

A flash of unease flicked up my spine, pushing me forward in my seat as Toby parked the car down the street from the house and checked his hair in the rearview.

He winked at me instead of answering, oblivious to my sudden apprehension.

*I misheard him.*

I must've misheard him.

He probably just meant that the guy was a saint, not a *Saint.* I shook my head, but still my throat was dry.

"Toby?" I prodded again, wanting to be certain, but he was already stepping out of the car, the body of the vehicle rocking as he shut the door behind him.

He tapped twice on the window, making me jump before I heard his voice call, "You coming, babe?"

I followed Toby up the street, jogging to catch up with him. He held his arm out, looping it through mine. "So, do you prefer tacos or hotdogs? Or are you more of a food is food type of lady?"

It took me half a second, but once I understood what he was asking, I laughed. "I'm fasting at the moment," I replied. "But when I'm not, I'm a hotdog girl. Though I've sampled some pretty good tacos, too, so…"

I shrugged.

He nodded appreciatively.

"Yeah, hotdogs can be vicious. I totally get the fasting."

"Don't underestimate tacos. They can be just as vicious."

"Speaking from experience?"

An image of Brianna comes to mind. She ran Briar Hall, my old high school, until my girl, Ava Jade, put her in her place. She'd burned off half Bianca's hair, forcing the self-titled queen bee to shave it bald.

I smiled, remembering the first day I saw her with a shaved head in class. One of the best moments of my life. She deserved everything Aves threw at her. It was her fault I lost the only real friend I had at Briar Hall. It was her fault Jenny Taylor was dead.

"Becca?" Toby stopped suddenly. "You good?"

I swallowed, refocusing on the present. Brianna Matthews was firmly in my past with every other horrible thing I left behind when I boarded the bus to SoCal. This, right now, was my present, and I intended to live in it.

"Fucking amazing," I replied. "Come on, let's go inside. I need a drink."

Toby hauled me across the lush green lawn, through groups of students smoking pot and drinking. Past a couple that was only one thin garment away from straight up fucking in the grass.

I found myself laughing, that familiar buzz in my blood awakening as we climbed the three steps to the front door and passed the threshold.

Toby led me by the hand through the student clogged front entryway, snaking a path through the house toward the kitchen.

My nose filled with the scents of hoppy beer and sweet liqueur. I could feel the bass from the music rattling in my chest .

We stopped next to a center island littered with empty plastic red cups, several bottles of different sodas and at least half a dozen bottles of booze in varying states of fullness. The refrigerator hung open across from us, two guys with red hair that looked like twins pulled fistfuls of deli ham and turkey from a crisper drawer, stuffing their faces.

"What the fuck?" I laughed, my voice swallowed up by all the noise just as the song changed to one I knew. Primal Ethos' newest hit single, Dark Duet, ft. my girl Ava Jade came blasting on through the speakers and a few students hollered, their bodies swaying to the opening beat.

I smiled, feeling a sense of pride as Ava Jade's haunting voice started at a breathy whisper and grew into a skin tingling siren call, Corvus' voice entangling with hers as they hit the chorus.

"I have you pegged as a whiskey girl," Toby shouted over the music, and I turned in time to grab the plastic cup he pushed into my hand. He raised a brow in question, and I nodded.

"You guessed right!"

He knocked his cup into mine before taking a long drink from his own. I stared down into the amber liquid, a shiver of unease scattering through my body.

"Don't worry!" Toby shouted, tipping his head in the

direction of my cup. "This is the safest place to drink in all of Santa Clarita. Scouts honor."

I licked my lips, nodding once before knocking back the whiskey, moaning quietly to myself as the burn seared a path down to my belly. My tensed shoulders relaxed, and I held my empty cup back out to Toby, giving it a little shake. "One more?"

He grinned widely, pouring us two more shots. I guessed we were *not* driving back to the apartment tonight. I hoped Uber was decent all the way out here.

With the first day of classes tomorrow, I'd allow myself a reprieve from all the stress of the last week, but I wasn't staying for the long haul. I needed sleep. *Real* sleep. Not the one-eye-open bullshit I'd been enduring at the motel.

"So, which one is the lucky guy?" I whisper shouted in Toby's ear as we leaned back against the kitchen counter to people watch and nurse our fresh cups of whiskey.

Even at over six feet tall, Toby went up on his tiptoes to see over the crowd, peering into the massive living room beyond the kitchen. The open floor plan allowed for you to see almost the entirety of the main floor.

The front door, still ajar as students passed in and out, was to our right, smack dab between the kitchen and living room.

All the way across the house, another door leading to what I assumed was a side garden was also open to the night.

To the right were two hallways that I guessed led to bathrooms and bedrooms. Oddly, no one went down those hallways, almost as if there were an invisible barrier keeping everyone penned in this front area of the home.

Toby tugged the sleeve of my sheer shirt, excitedly bouncing on the balls of his feet as he gestured across the room. "There, you see him?"

I set my drink down, branching my palms against the tall kitchen countertop to lift myself higher.

"There," Toby said again. "The guy with the light brown hair. In the dark gray long sleeve."

I scanned the bodies in the wide space, my gaze narrowing on the guy Toby called *Kaleb*. I felt my lips part as I drank him in. He threw his head back in a laugh at something someone was telling him, the line of his jaw somehow even sharper at that angle.

His eyes glimmered with mischief.

And that gray long sleeve? He wore it like a fucking model. The sleeves rolled up to the crooks of his elbows to reveal muscled, tattooed forearms. The tuck of the sleeves only serving to accentuate the fullness of his biceps above.

It hugged his chest like a glove, every crest and valley of his chest showing through the thin, distressed fabric, but fitted loose around a narrow waist.

"*Right?*" Toby trilled. "The man is a *King*."

I snorted, hopping back down from the countertop.

"I'd kneel at his throne," I joked, lifting my cup for another sip. "If I weren't *fasting*."

"More for me," Toby smirked, inclining his head to the living room. "Come on, let's go say hi."

We waded through the partygoers, and I clutched my

purse tighter to my side, half wishing I'd left it back in the car. Another couple of whiskeys and I was liable to set it down somewhere. Toby and I completed the sale of my Loro Piana dress on the way here and this little black purse now held the rest of the cash I needed to pay Kate the rent. But I wasn't a total idiot, the important bits, like my phone and driver's license were safely stowed in my boot like my bestie taught me. When I had a second, I'd stuff the cash into my other boot too, just to be safe.

"Hey, Kale," Toby called as we neared Kaleb and the small group of guys surrounding him. I flagged behind, trapped by a train of girls on their way out to the side garden, their cloying perfume making me gag.

"Toby, man, haven't seen you out in a couple weeks."

I stepped through and into the circle just as Kaleb and Toby slapped hands, grasping at the elbows for a manly embrace. I winced on Toby's behalf. That was not the move of a guy who was into him. It was the move of a guy who had firmly placed Toby in the *friend* category. But if my new roomie hadn't given up, I wouldn't be the one to crush his dreams.

"Yeah," Toby said, preening at the fact that this godlike man noticed his absence. "Went up north to visit the fam. Just got back a few days ago."

As Kaleb straightened, our eyes met and his easy smile faltered, replaced with a look of surprise. I remembered I'd just walked into a group of guys shooting the shit and wondered if he was put off by a taco encroaching on the hotdog party.

"*Uh*," I mumbled, ready to excuse myself for another

drink, shaken by the way Kaleb's gaze was still fixated on me, heavy and intent, but Toby curled his fingers around my wrist, dragging me forward.

"Kaleb," he said in a sweet drawl. "Meet my new roommate—oh! and co-worker, actually—Becca. Becca, this is Kaleb."

I licked my lips, casting my gaze away from his unwavering stare. "You have a nice place," I offered, hoping he couldn't hear the crack in my voice over the music. It was his place, right?

I thought I remembered Toby saying it was Kaleb's party.

"It's not usually so crowded," he said with a smirk pulling at one side of his lips, showing off a dimple in his cheek that I hadn't noticed there before.

My lips tripped over a reply, not really knowing what to say to that. I gave Toby a little shove toward Kaleb instead, remembering I was supposed to be a wingwoman tonight. And dammit, I was *fasting*. Not even a feast that gorgeous was going to tempt me.

"You two catch up," I ordered before turning to Toby, taking the still mostly full cup from his hands. "I'll get us a refill."

Relief rolled over me in a wave as soon as I walked away, though I could still feel Kaleb's eyes on me as I weaved my way back to the kitchen. What was his deal?

I shakily poured two fresh cups of whiskey, this time mixing it with a little ginger ale. Fingers of heat clawed up the back of my neck, and I couldn't be sure it was from the whiskey.

When I turned back around, I saw Toby and Kaleb laughing together through the bodies between me and the living room and knew I shouldn't interrupt.

Bathroom. I needed a bathroom. A good splash of cool water would fix me right up.

Despite Toby's assurance that this was the safest place to drink in Santa Clarita, I scooped up our cups and carried them with me, lifting them overhead to avoid spilling as I carved a path toward the corridors on the other side of the living room. I was careful to circle around the groups of people, keeping out of Toby's—*and Kaleb's*—lines of sight. Not ready to be drawn back in yet.

I half wondered if it was a mistake to come. When Kate declined Toby's request that she join him, I should have declined, too. But Kate had the excuse of being scheduled for the opening shift at Death Before Decaf the next morning. I had no such excuse, not scheduled for my next shift until tomorrow in the late afternoon after class.

The dark hallway swallowed me up as I slid past a few people, stumbling down its throat. "Shit, sorry," I muttered, almost spilling on one of the girls near its mouth.

"Do you know where the bathroom is?" I asked, but she continued her conversation, ignoring me as if I were invisible. I might as well have been. Aside from Kaleb and Toby, no one here had said two words to me. My stomach flipped with nerves, that grade-school desire to fit in still there even after I'd spent years working so hard to kill it dead.

It didn't matter, though. I had Ava Jade and the Crows

back in Thorn Valley. I had Toby and Kate now, too. Who the fuck cared if any of these jackasses paid any attention to me?

Not me.

*Not me.*

I passed the first door on the right, its narrow shape denoting it as likely to be a closet. The next one on the left, that had to be it.

"Fuck," I muttered, looking around for somewhere to set down the cups so I could open the door. But the hallway was entirely bare save for the doors.

No one was down here so I set them on the hardwood floor close to the wall and shouldered into the room.

Darkness enveloped me, and I squinted to make out the shapes you'd normally find in a bathroom but couldn't see anything more than a foot past my own face. I reached in, running my palm along the wall to find a light switch, a whispered curse tumbling from my lips.

The smell from within filtered out, strong enough to overpower the stench of alcohol and pot coming from the front of the house. I shivered at its intensity. There was no mistaking it. That was *man* smell. And not like old socks and gym shorts. No.

This was warm amber, leather, and musk with a woodsy undertone. Despite the fact that I was definitely fasting, I allowed myself half a second to close my eyes and breathe it in, letting out a sigh.

God*damn.*

I opened my eyes and reeled back, sensing movement

inside. I withdrew my hand, not able to find the light switch.

*This is not a bathroom*

"Sorry," I chirped. "I'm just looking for—"

Tattooed hands reached out from the dark, yanking me inside so quickly I barely managed a strangled yelp before the door shut behind me, sealing us into the darkness.

My back connected with the closed door and rough fingers snaked into my hair, gripping the back of my neck as a warm body pressed into mine.

"Wait—"

Lips met mine in a hard kiss. Something slumped to the floor and my hands that were one second ago pressing firmly against a bare, wide chest, started to slacken.

The monster in the dark stole all the air from my lungs, breathing me in until I couldn't feel my legs and I knew that if it weren't for the way he was holding me pinned I would fall right on my ass.

He tasted like honey and whiskey, and when his tongue swiped at the seam of my lips, I opened for him on instinct, a soft moan rattling up my throat.

He growled at the sound, his chest reverberating against my fingertips, making my toes curl.

His hand on my hip moved, snaking lower, reaching down between my legs, fiddling with the hem of my skirt.

*Oh fuck.*

Callused fingers brushed my inner thigh and my back arched, our lips parting as I threw my head back at the violent sensations making all rational thought flee my body.

*I'm supposed to be on a hunger strike.*

*No hotdogs allowed.*

*But... a girl's gotta eat.*

The sound of my tights tearing as he ripped out the crotch hit me like a bucket of cold water and suddenly his hot lips on my neck didn't feel good anymore.

My breathing turned shallow and vivid images of someone else's hands on me in the dark burst into my mind. I pressed my thighs closed, trying to extricate myself from the monster in the dark, my heart beating wildly against my chest. My head spinning.

He tried to force my thighs back open with a growl, but I shoved his hands away.

"No," I managed around the lump in my throat, trying unsuccessfully to find the door handle.

He caught my wrists and pinned them above my head, his hot breath trailing down my neck to my chest until his lips met the supple mound of my breast.

Despite myself, my nipples pebbled at his touch, but when he pulled back, I reflexively kicked forward. Ava Jade's words rang in my ears. *Always hit 'em where it hurts. You're not always going to have a weapon and there's nothing that'll bring a man to his knees faster than a good kick to the family jewels. Do it fast. Do it hard. Then run.*

A hard breath forced past his lips as my heel connected, and I watched the shadow of him crumple. His grip on my wrists slackened enough for me to pull free, and I whirled around, frantically trying to find the door handle, hot tears in my eyes.

My fingers brushed it, and I twisted, rushing forward.

But he was faster. His hand curled around my shoulder, spinning me in place while the other shoved the door back closed.

I opened my mouth to scream but the light flicked on, blinding me, striking me mute. I lifted my hands, sensing an attack and he knocked them away.

Forcing my eyes to adjust to the sudden brightness, I blinked, taking in over six feet of tattooed muscle. Familiar eyes bore into mine, confusion, shock, and lingering pain from where I kicked him glimmering over their dark surface. It was him.

The guy from outside of Death Before Decaf. The one I'd seen toss his friend into the back of a Bronco before staring me down and driving off.

Danger radiated off him in waves, and I swore I could see his skin damn near rippling with rage. He clutched his bits and piece in a protective fist with his other hand, a scowl forming on his lips.

I could tell immediately that I was *not* who he was expecting to see.

He released my shoulder, pushing back with a sneer, saying nothing.

"What the fuck?" I muttered, mentally kicking myself the moment the words left my lips, but I couldn't help it. Didn't care that he was massive and imposing and was giving off major I'll-kill-you-vibes.

Hadn't he heard me saying no? Regardless of the fact

that no more than three seconds before that my body was saying yes, yes, *yes*.

My body sang with still pumping adrenaline, my heart making its own bassline in my ears, louder than the music still pumping outside the door.

He said nothing, just stared at me, disgust twisting his features. Making his full lips flatten. His cheekbones flare. His deep brown eyes darken and the tattoo above his right eyebrow warp until the word was unreadable.

He released his junk and straightened to his full height, jerking his chin crudely at the door. I didn't need a bigger hint than that. He was telling me to fuck off.

"Fucking asshole," I muttered to myself, not able to leave the room fast enough. I slammed the door behind myself hard enough to rattle the wooden panels in the hallway outside.

# Becca



### SEVEN

I stormed back to the kitchen, all but shoving the people out of my way until I got to the sink. I filled a plastic cup with cold water from the tap and greedily gulped it down, trying to clear my mind, calm my nerves.

A light touch on my shoulder had me whirling, ready to use the cup as a weapon, a lot of fucking good that would do, but it was just Toby. "I thought you left!" he exclaimed, his demeanor changing as he read my expression. "Shit, are you okay?"

I chucked the empty cup onto the center island with the others and swiped the back of my hand over my wet lips. "Fine. I think I'm ready to take off, though. You good if I leave you to it?"

His eyes slanted sympathetically, but he nodded. "I'll order us an Uber. It's getting late, anyway."

"No," I urged. "Don't leave because of me. It's just…"

*It's just* what?

That I didn't like the way Kaleb was looking at me? Or that I maybe liked it too much?

That I just accidentally walked into the bedroom of someone who could probably kill me with his pinkie finger and nearly let him finger fuck me against his bedroom door?

God. What was wrong with me?

"Don't even worry about it. I have class in the morning anyway."

He tapped away at his phone screen, but I stopped him. "Seriously, I'm good. Just have a bit of a headache. Stay."

He frowned, but clicked off his phone screen and pocketed it. "Okay. As long as you're good."

I nodded, trying unsuccessfully to relax.

Toby pivoted so he was leaning against the counter with me. He stilled, letting out a little gasp as he popped his hip. "Do you see that?" he asked, and I could tell it was a struggle to keep his voice even. Maintain a straight face.

I followed his line of sight to where Kaleb was sitting in an oversized armchair facing our direction. The crowd was clear enough that he had a full view of where we stood, and he wasn't wasting it.

"Oh my god," Toby preened. "He's totally checking me out. *Act cool, Tobes.*"

Toby pushed his hair back and turned to me as though he didn't even notice Kaleb checking him out. Trying to appear flippant. But it wouldn't have mattered anyway.

Because Kaleb wasn't looking at Toby.

He was looking at me.

"I'm going to head out," I announced, wincing at the disappointment in Toby's expression. I was being an absolute shit wingwoman, but judging by the way Kaleb was watching me, poor Toby didn't have a chance with him anyway.

"Awe, okay, babe. Get home safe, yeah? I'll be right behind you."

He drew me in for a kiss on the cheek, and I ducked past him with a hasty *see you back at the apartment*, making a beeline for the front door.

I got about halfway, swallowed up by the throng of drunk students, when someone stepped in front of me. "*Whoa*," I said, sidestepping her. "I almost ran right into you."

She mirrored my step, blocking my path and I cocked my head at her, taking in all five foot five of slender body and pushed-up tits. She flicked her red hair back from her face and stared me down with eyes too small for her face. "Maybe you should stay in your lane, then, honey."

"Excuse me?"

"You don't belong here."

I lifted my brows, almost letting out a laugh, stopping only because I saw what was clipped to the front pocket of her jeans. A pocket knife. Too shiny and new to have ever been used, but I wasn't about to give her an excuse to dirty it.

"Good thing I was on my way out, then," I quipped, shouldering past her.

"Hey, valley-girl," she called after me, her nasally tone

like a lash against my last fucking nerve. I stopped, but didn't turn, too afraid I wouldn't be able to contain what came out of my mouth next.

"Forget this address. If I see you here again—"

I didn't let her complete the thought, rolling my eyes as I exited the house. She didn't need to finish whatever bullshit threat she was about to sling at me. There was no way I was coming back to this house again.

The instant the cooler outside air hit me, filling my lungs, the tension in my shoulders eased.

I walked quickly toward the road, eager to put space between myself and every lousy person at that party save for Toby.

Numbly, I fingered my phone from my boot before wrapping my free arm around myself. I flicked a finger over the screen, swiping until I found the Uber app, I got it open just a second before my phone lit up with a low battery warning, shut down the app, and the screen went black.

I tapped the screen, nothing.

"Shit."

I pressed down hard on the side button.

"No. No, no, *no.*"

I tapped again, uselessly before groaning loudly, not caring who heard me as I pushed it back down into my boot. The party raged across the street, and I considered going back in, asking Toby to order me an Uber, but I couldn't bring myself to do it.

I just wanted to go back to the apartment, wash off the warm leather and musk scent still clinging to my skin. Rinse the honey and whiskey flavor from my mouth.

The last thing I needed was to get involved with another *bad boy*. Because that worked out so well last time. I should've been learning from the mistakes that got my mom killed, not repeating them.

As if on cue, the scar on my chest, right over my heart, ached deeply, making me clutch at it, gritting my teeth.

"Want a ride?" The smooth, accented voice asked over the low rumble of an engine. Sitting in the driver's seat with his arm slung out the window was a guy I didn't remember seeing at the party, but to be fair, I'd been more than a little distracted.

I squinted past him, but there was no one else in the car with him. Just long leather seats that looked pristine despite the fact that the car itself was a classic. A black impala sleek enough to swipe the panties off any girl who dared step inside.

"Pass," I blurted. "But, thanks."

"I'm headed back to the Row," he persisted, that accent caressing my ears. What was that? Not British. Scottish? *No.* Irish. Yes, definitely Irish. "It's no trouble, and I don't bite."

His smile said differently.

"I'm waiting for a ride."

"No, you're not."

"Excuse me?"

I started to walk but he eased off the brakes, following alongside me as I moved further from the party.

"Do you even know where you're going?"

"Look, I'm not getting in the car with you. For all I know you could be a serial killer."

"Name's Aodhán," he continued as if I didn't just accuse him of mass murder, confirming my suspicion of his origin. Something in the way he said it. Not Aiden, though it was pronounced so similarly it would be an easy mistake to make. No. It was *Aodhán*, Irish. Traditional. And somehow... endearing?

No.

Not even a little.

I really needed to get laid. I promised myself I'd charge every single one of my *toys* when I got back to the apartment. This girl didn't need a beating heart and brain attached to her dicks. Just a remote control and rechargeable batteries.

"Cool name, why don't you go tell it to someone else."

He tipped his head back against the leather seat and laughed, the sound of his low chuckle barely audible above the chug of the muffler.

"Here," he said, and even though I tried to keep my gaze straight ahead I couldn't help but peek out of the corner of my eye to see him holding something out to me. I stopped, and he hit the brakes in tandem, the little plastic card between us held out by his first two fingers. "Take it."

I clenched my teeth, but I did, snatching it from between his fingers. It was his ID. And right there printed in black ink on the white card was his full name. Aodhán ó Súilleabháin. From Belfast.

"If you take a picture of it and send it to your pals then I can't very well kidnap and murder you, can I?"

I bit my lower lip, looking down the long, dark road ahead and realizing that I had no fucking idea how to get back to the Row.

"For all I know, you could be the one doing the murdering," he added with a wink. "Let me give you a ride. You look like you could use one and I wouldn't be the gentleman I am if I left a lady alone in the dark."

His green eyes sparked in the glow of headlights from an oncoming car, the twin beams painting his dirty blond hair with streaks of purest gold. Making the silver cross earring dangling from his right lobe reflect the light.

"Go on," he urged. "Take a photo."

I hesitated, my throat going dry. If Ava Jade knew I was even considering this she would have my head on a fucking platter. But Aves wasn't here and unless I planned on going back into the party…

Biting the inside of my cheek, I bent, retrieving my phone from the inside of my boot. I made a big show of 'taking a photo' of his license and sending a text, careful to make sure the phone screen stayed out of his line of sight. I even went so far as walking around to the front of the impala to 'snap a pic' of the license plate, committing it to memory instead.

ANRCHST.

I slid into the passenger seat, the supple leather brushing against the backs of my thighs as I shut the door behind me. Aodhán reached between us to twist the knob on the sound system, turning up the radio to a low hum, filling the silence with a classic rock song.

"I didn't catch your name, love."

A permanent smirk seemed fused to Aodhán's lips but it did nothing to make him seem happy. He was more... flippant? Slouching in the seat with an arm draped over the wheel as we drove through the quiet Sunday night streets of Santa Clarita. He lifted a chain from beneath his dark t-shirt, putting a silver charm to his lips.

"Becca," I told him, passing him back his license, wondering if it was even valid over here. "Do you go to school here?"

"Becca," he repeated, as though he didn't think it suited me. "I wouldn't have guessed."

"You didn't answer the question."

Aodhán deftly used a single hand to open the wallet on his lap and slip his ID back inside. "I do."

"Kilborn?" I guessed, trying to imagine him in my art class and failing. But then again, from what I heard about Kilborn, he didn't seem the type to fit in there either. I couldn't imagine him in a polo shirt, or a button up, or a blazer, attending classes on law or hedge funds.

He nodded. "Part-time. Also taking a couple open electives at CalArts."

Part-time?

Interest piqued, I couldn't stop the next question falling out. "So, you don't have a major, then? What's your plan? I mean, how will you get a job."

I heard my father's voice in every word out of my

mouth and cringed inwardly. Those were *his* worries. *His* hang-ups. Not mine.

Aodhán shrugged, that ever present smirk still in place on his lips. "Not planning to ever have one," he replied with a mischievous gleam in his eyes. "Not unless you count carrying on the family business, but I don't. It's more of a lifestyle than a *job*."

My lips pursed before I opened them to ask him what he meant, but he beat me to it. "What about you, love?"

"I—"

"No, wait, don't tell me. Artist, is it? You don't look much like the other girls hanging 'round Kilborn."

I bristled at his assumption, maybe because he was insinuating I was somehow different from other girls, or maybe just because he was right.

"You can just let me out around the block," I said instead of telling him so, considering myself in a new light. The clean lines of my black bra showing through the sheer fabric of the oversized men's button up I was wearing. The wing tipped liner on my eyes. I yanked down the hem of my skirt, remembering the tears in my tights hidden beneath the pleated plaid fabric.

I undid my seatbelt before Aodhán pulled up to the sidewalk just a block down from Death Before Decaf and only a few blocks from the apartment that I thought I could remember how to get to on my own.

"Thanks for the ride."

I stepped out of the car, faster than I needed to, careful to shut the door gently as I stepped up onto the sidewalk.

He leaned down in his seat, peering up at me through

his lashes, that silver charm he'd been working with his teeth now laid over the top of his black shirt. A four leaf clover with a diamond at its heart. "Anytime, love," he winked. "Now, get home safe. The streets at this hour are no place for a pretty face."

I got less than a block down the street, huddling against the sudden chill in the air when it hit me.

"*Fuck!*" I shouted, loud enough to wake anyone sleeping in the buildings around me, but I didn't care. I slammed my palm against my forehead, gritting my teeth.

I'd forgotten my goddamned purse.

# Kaleb

## EIGHT

Hardin glared at the sun baked blacktop on the way to campus like it personally offended him. When I turned on the radio, rolling down the window, preferring the fresh air to the icy air conditioning, he jammed the power button and rolled the windows back up, stewing in his usual silence.

"What the fuck crawled up your ass last night?"

He didn't reply, just pulled his phone from his pocket and flicked his thumb over the screen.

"That's it, isn't it?" I taunted. "Did Felicia—or whatever that blonde babe's name is—stick a finger in your ass? *Oh shit.* Did you *like* it?"

I put a fist to my mouth to cover the grin there and he twisted in his seat to glare at me instead of his phone. "Just fucking drive, Kaleb."

I dropped my fist, cocking my head at him. "Seriously, man, what's your deal? You didn't come out of your room at all last night. I figured when you were done with Felicia you'd at least show your face for five fucking minutes—"

"Fee didn't show."

I felt my brows lift. "She stood you up?"

My brother had been banging the blonde first year off and on for a few months now. There were very few women who could handle him in the bedroom, if the countless girls I'd seen fleeing from his room with their clothes balled against their naked tits was any indication. But the blonde one with the doll-like features and baby blue eyes, the picture of virginal innocence, was apparently the wildest sexual deviant he'd ever encountered.

She got bonus points for not wanting anything more from him than his dick in every one of her holes. She didn't even seem to mind that he never spoke a word to her.

"Man, that's shitty. Guess it's time to find a new playmate."

He shrugged, but I could tell it was bothering him more than he let on. He adjusted his position in the seat uncomfortably and I realized he was counting on Felicia to relieve some of the pent up pressure.

With all this bullshit going on with the Sons of O'Sullivan and my little stunt a couple nights ago, he was wound tighter than a top. And now he probably had a case of massive blue balls to top it all off.

I had to say I knew the feeling.

Rebecca Hart was in my house last night. Standing right in front of me. And she was even sexier in person than she was in her photograph.

The long dark hair, the even longer legs. The gentle arch in her back just above her peachy ass. The simple black bra I could see through the sheer shirt she was wearing, doing almost nothing to cover tits that I would happily suffocate in if given the opportunity. And those eyes…

No other chick in my house existed in that moment. Or any moment after she abruptly vanished. Sunday nights at our place were always a guaranteed lay. Sometimes I'd take two chicks back to my room after telling everyone else to get the fuck out, if it was an extra good night.

But last night?

Last night I jerked off not once, not twice, but *three fucking times* to her picture, which I now had saved to my phone. But it wasn't enough. I woke up with a raging hard-on and her image still scorched into my mind, but no amount of lube or tugging or fucking anything was going to get rid of it except the real thing. So I did what I imagined sad retirees did in the mornings. I threw a robe on to cover the stubborn wood in my boxers and threw my sorry ass in an ice cold shower, waiting the requisite fifteen minutes under the steady stream before it finally, painfully, deflated.

I'd found out which motel she was staying in yesterday afternoon, but the ornery woman at the front desk told me she'd already checked out. I'd missed her by a few hours.

Now, at least, I knew where she went. She was staying with Toby. *Working* with Toby. I didn't know where he lived, but I knew where he worked. Death Before Decaf. I'd have to come up with an excuse to pay her a visit soon.

Hardin reached wordlessly into the back seat of the Bronco, pulling something black and boxy from the floor. He discarded it on my lap like if he touched it any longer it'd burn him.

I pulled into the campus lot, turning the leather bag over in my lap as I drove to the very front, to the spot that didn't need a sign to be permanently reserved for us.

"The shit is this?"

Hardin sniffed, all but throwing the passenger side door open the instant I put the Bronco in park. "Belongs to the Hart girl. She left it in my room."

"She... *what?*"

"Get it back to her."

"Bro!"

I shot up in my seat, gripping the roll bar above me to lift myself higher, shouting after Hardin as he stormed away. "What the fuck was she doing in your room?"

He didn't bother giving me a reply, vanishing around the edge of the weathered red brick exterior of Kilborn University.

I fell back into my seat, considering the purse still clutched in my fist. I rolled the decision around in my mouth for an entire second before knocking it over on the passenger seat, upending its contents.

Inside there were the usual suspects; lipstick and some other makeup shit I flicked aside. Her wallet, stuffed with a healthy amount of cash. A name tag from Death Before Decaf. A joint that I pilfered to tuck behind my ear. A half empty bag of peanut M&Ms and… a miniature bottle of hot sauce?

I tossed the tiny red bottle back on the pile and ran my hand along the inside lining, checking for anything else, my fingers finding a little bump on one side.

It took some poking around, but I found the tiny slit in the fabric on the bottom right corner of the bag, just big enough to get my fingers inside and tug the little item out.

"That sneaky fucker." I smiled to myself, examining the tiny tracking chip in my palm before sliding it back in where it'd been hiding, stuffing the purse back full with all the other items, save for the joint, which was now mine.

I shot off a quick text to Hardin.

**Kaleb: Mind sharing the tracking data with the group, big bro?**

His reply came just as I was walking into the lab for advanced computer sciences.

**Hardin: The fuck you on about?**

**Kaleb: The tracker you planted in her bag.**

**Hardin: I didn't plant shit in her bag. I didn't even open it.**

**Kaleb: You think it was the Crows?**

**Hardin: How the fuck should I know?**

I rolled my eyes, moving to slide into the seat I'd claimed as mine last year, but there was already someone there, typing his credentials into the system, either oblivious to my existence or doing a damn good job of ignoring it.

"Hey man, shuffle down one, this seat's taken."

The guy tipped his head to peer up at me through a mess of choppy blond hair, a wicked curve to his lips. "Sorry, *bro*, I'm already logged in," he said, and something about the way he said it set me on edge.

I lifted my brows, realizing I didn't recognize this guy. He was probably new. Didn't know the rules.

I opened my mouth to tell him to move his fucking ass, but my phone chimed in my fist, and I caught the message lighting up the screen from the corner of my eye.

**Hardin: Just asked Rook if we should plant something on her or if they already had. They haven't. You sure it's a tracker?**

The blood in my veins ran cold.

If Hardin hadn't planted the tracker and the Crows didn't either, then who the fuck did?

I folded myself into the seat next to the new guy, the issue of dominance forgotten for the moment as I texted Hardin back.

**Kaleb: I'm sure.**

**Hardin: That's a fucking problem.**

**Kaleb: I'll handle it. Don't mention anything to the Crows. They have enough shit on their plates while Corvus and Ava Jade are on tour.**

Hardin didn't respond, but I didn't expect him to. The several messages we'd just exchanged were the most he'd ever held up a digital conversation with me. Probably with anyone.

It wasn't lost on me what the topic was, that he was so forthcoming because it had to do with *her.*

The ice in my veins thawed, replaced by something much *much* hotter.

I'd have been fucking lying if I said I wasn't still wondering why the hell Becca Hart was in my brother's bedroom last night. He might not tell me, but I'd make sure *she* did.

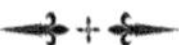

Hardin growled some shit about finding intel on what happened to Chief Andrews when we returned home after class, locking himself away in his room.

My brother was right about one thing: we didn't have a lot of time to be looking out for Rebecca Hart. We were under a lot of heat and the meet with The Warden for our arms deal was in a couple days. The man was still acting squirrely when Dad contacted him to reconfirm, trying to wriggle out of the deal.

Not a good fucking sign.

Then there was some shit that needed tending at Saint's Autobody. The shop was mine and Hardin's baby. Born of my need for speed and his love of old cars, but fuck if she wasn't a pain in my ass.

The main business wasn't fixing mufflers and souping up engines, though. It was the wealth of stolen vehicles we had our discreet staff of Saints pull apart and put back together, selling the aftermarket products to savvy buyers.

The last batch of *merchandise* was spreading thin, and one of the dumbasses in charge of 'scrubbing' missed a serial number in the last sale. Now, somewhere out there, a car we sent out was one accident away from landing us with a massive lawsuit and possible jail- time.

Jail time we would never have to serve, but I didn't want the fucking legal bills. At least when Hardin was finished getting his law degree he'd be able to identify the loopholes that could save our asses faster than a lawyer would return our calls.

I flipped the little tracking device around between my fingers as I left Saint's Autobody—crisis averted for the moment thanks to my quick thinking to bring the customer back in for a *free tune up*—and drove to the coffee shop.

Squishing the little device between my fingers, I racked my brain, trying to think of any way to reverse track whoever planted it, but coming up empty. These types of devices only *received* information, they didn't transmit it.

The Row was loud with the hustle of students running around, grabbing groceries and rushing to study dates that were really just booty-calls for smart people. I honked at a guy in a sweater vest who'd just pulled up to the last spot out front of Death Before Decaf.

He ducked back into his car with a nod and pulled back out, giving me the spot. I offered him a nod in return as he drove off, and I shut off the ignition, turning to look through the windows of the cafe.

It was getting near dark outside and the light within glowed warmly, or maybe it was just *her*. I wasn't sure she'd be working, but there she was, her face twisted with concentration as she pulled an espresso shot and frothed milk at the same time, slinging caffeinated beverages down the serving line like some kind of machine.

I pawed my dick, telling it to settle the fuck down in my head because no man in his right mind talked to his dick out loud in public, and got out of the Bronco, Becca's purse—sans tracker—in hand.

The bells above the door jingled loudly when I entered, but not a single head turned in my direction except hers. Her brown eyes snagged on me like you might snag your belt loop on a door handle. Jerking her to a complete and total halt. Frothed milk bubbled up over the side of the metal pitcher she was holding and she cursed, twisting off the dial for the steaming wand and setting the pitcher down hard.

"What happened?" the blonde girl at the counter asked, excusing herself from a customer to rush back to where Becca stood, now bouncing from foot to foot as she ran her hand under a stream of cold water from the tap. I grimaced.

Yeah. I had that effect on people, what could I say?

I got maybe two more steps before I noticed a familiar head of dark hair bent over an empty coffee mug in the corner. His back was to me, but I wouldn't mistake anyone else for my own fucking blood.

"Hardin?" I called, momentarily abandoning my stoic watch of Rebecca Hart to approach him. "Thought you were 'gathering intel?' "

He rose before I could plop my ass in the seat opposite him, his hard gaze flicking between me and his empty coffee as if to say he just stopped by for some java. My jaw clenched.

"If you were just going to come here anyway, why ask me to return her bag?"

His gaze narrowed and I could tell he was considering whether he'd answer me here, within earshot of all the other students in the nearby tables.

"That was before you found a tracker in her fucking bag," he said in a low voice and shouldered past me to leave, the few students seated closest to us gaping at the sound of his voice.

I shook my head, going to the counter where Kate was whispering something to Becca, who was drying off a very red hand. Her honey brown eyes met mine and she crooked a finger at me.

I turned this way and that, making a show of it as I arched a brow and pointed to my own chest, mouthing *me?* over the din of clacking laptop keys and students chatting.

Becca rolled her eyes before rushing around the front counter. I almost forgot I was holding her purse before she snatched it from my fingers. "What, your brother couldn't be bothered to return it to me himself?"

She glared at the spot Hardin just vacated as she dug around in the bag, checking that everything was still where she left it. Her body noticeably sagged in relief when she found all her cash still tucked into her wallet.

"Hello to you, too."

"He doesn't talk much, does he?" she asked, a twitch beneath her eye. "I tried asking him where my purse was and he just, like, grunted at me. What *is* that?"

I scratched the back of my neck, the fire of her indignation hot enough to scorch.

Cringing, I cleared my throat. This was *not* going how I imagined it would. "Yeah, he's not much of a talker."

"You think?"

"What was your purse doing in his room, anyway?"

Her cheeks flushed scarlet, giving her away before a single word left her mouth. "I was looking for the bathroom."

She pinched the bridge of her nose, sighing heavily as though the weight of the day was about to crush her.

"You look like you could use a break. Come on, let's go grab a drink."

She jerked her head up, looking at me like I'd grown a second head. "I'm *working*," she said, enunciating the two words like I must've been the stupidest person in the world.

"You don't have to be."

I flagged the other girl, now swarmed with more customers than she could rightly handle on her own, but maybe the jackass who owned the place would come out from his dungeon and help her out. "Hey, she's taking a break. I'll have her back in an hour."

"*Okay,*" the girl replied with a tight lipped smile, going

back to taking the next customer's order without missing a beat.

Becca looked between me and her co-worker, confusion turning to flustered in the blink of an eye.

I held out my arm, ready to wash away every tight line in her face until it was slack, her lips only able to form one word. One name. *Mine.*

She stepped back, her lips twisting. "Look, Kaleb, is it? I don't know who the fuck you think you are, but I'm not going anywhere with you, and you can tell your jerkwad of a brother that he isn't welcome here when I'm working. Not until he learns how to form enough words to string together an apology."

"*Uh—*"

"Thanks for bringing back my purse," she added, almost as an afterthought, already backing away from me. "But one of you owes me a joint."

I watched after her, stunned, not really sure what the hell just happened. Fuck, she was feisty. Just my type.

I remembered the tracker I found in her purse, still burning a hole in my pocket, and felt a knot form between my brows. Whoever put it there definitely didn't have her best interests at heart, and for whatever maddening reason, I wanted her protected. And not just because my cousins asked me to keep an eye out for her.

I wanted her safe.

A sense of responsibility settled in my gut like heavy metal, so strong I could almost taste it on my tongue. Responsibility for a person other than my brother.

Which was why I'd replaced the tracker that'd been

from unknown origins with one that was my own private stash, fastening it to the same spot the old one had been in her purse.

If Dad could see me now, he'd be so damn proud.

Becca adjusted her apron, going to the espresso machine to pick up where she left off making drinks for the steadily growing line of customers. When she noticed I was still standing here, she gave me a look and brushed her hand in the air, telling me not so subtly that I could fucking go.

Someone whistled low, and I spun, seeing that more than a few students had entirely stopped what they were doing to watch our little exchange. As soon as my attention was on them though fingers flew back over keys and heads bent over notebooks, all of them pouring over imaginary work to avoid my eyes.

All except one idiot, the one who whistled, who stared openly, at least until my eyes met his. Then he coughed, mindlessly tapping the spacebar on his new MacBook.

Heat fizzled up my spine. I wasn't my brother. His rage was renowned all throughout Santa Clarita and most of SoCal, but if there was one fucking thing I couldn't stand it was someone laughing at me.

Laughing at me like *he* did... before my brother killed him.

I snatched up the MacBook and bent it backward over my knee, dropping it to the floor before I could think too much about it. "*Oh shit*," I said, eyeing the fuck out of the guy who looked ready to piss himself while maintaining an innocent air as I picked the busted pieces back up and set them on the table. "So sorry, man, I must've slipped. Hope that wasn't too expensive."

"N-no, it's all good. A-accidents happen."

I smiled, patting his shoulder, watching his Adam's apple bob in his throat. "You have a good night."

### NINE

I should've trusted my gut.

Toby even *told me*, but I wasn't hearing him. Now, though, I was listening.

"I really don't know how you still have a head on your shoulders," Kate whispered, still scribbling notes down in her book based on the slides at the head of the auditorium style classroom.

When Kaleb came into Death Before Decaf yesterday, she'd told me he and *Hardin*—aka Mr. Dark and Gloomy, aka the monster in the dark—were brothers. But she failed to mention they were *fucking Saints—literally the* sons *of Damien St. Vincent*— until after I kicked Kaleb's ass out of here.

"I mean, I don't think Kaleb would ever actually hurt a woman, but I know he isn't above ruining someone's life for slighting him. You need to be more careful."

My nostrils flared, and I tried to refocus on the projected slides but the words seemed all jumbled. Illegible to my racing mind.

I'd been here for barely a damn week and already I'd managed to attract the attention of two of the most dangerous felons on campus. What was it about me that drew them in?

Was there something wrong with me?

Was I just a magnet for anything and everything self-destructive? Was I destined to become collateral damage like my mom? Ruined by the two sons of the same fucking man who ruined her? I couldn't let that happen.

But it didn't help that Kaleb was drop dead gorgeous. And it definitely didn't help that his jackass of a brother happened to be the best kisser I'd ever encountered in my nineteen years of life on this godforsaken planet.

*Ugh.*

I consoled myself with the knowledge that at least now that I *knew* who they were I could stay away from them.

And if they didn't leave me alone, I had an ace in the hole; Ava Jade, the Saint's Dagger herself. She may not have been a part of the SoCal chapter, but every splintered cell of the gang spread over this country was once part of a whole. If anyone could pull some strings and see to it that they left me out of their bullshit, it would be her.

But I wouldn't worry her unless I absolutely had to.

I was Becca 2.0 now. With an apartment that I paid for myself and a job I damn well *earned*. I could handle my own shit. I could be every bit as strong as my best friend.

Okay, well, maybe half as strong, but that was still stronger than any other person I'd ever had the honor to know.

"Becca?" Kate pressed, and I realized she'd been asking me something as I tapped the cap-end of my pen on the notepad in front of me. I met her worried blue-eyed stare and watched it bob between me and my empty notepad as class ended.

"Sorry, what did you say?"

"I asked if you wanted to come to hot yoga with me tomorrow. You look a little…"

"Stressed?" I supplied.

"Actually, I was going to say you look like you're going to murder someone, but stressed works, too."

I huffed out a laugh I didn't really feel. "That's just my face. You get used to it."

Kate grinned, gathering up her books. "Tatum's before next class?"

We only shared Art Foundations together since she was focused more on ceramics and I was firmly decided on painting. We strolled out from the main building, and I let Kate lead the way to the little snack shop cafe they had on campus. The coffee was absolute shit, but they had good muffins, if you were into carbs, and the smoothies weren't half bad, either.

"Two strawberry banana please," Kate asked the counter attendant once it was our turn, and I squinted at some art show posters on the wall while we waited, moving down the row of them.

I nearly tripped over a pair of black booted feet,

crossed at the ankles, pressing a palm flat to the wall to stabilize myself.

"Shit, sorry, I didn't mean to—"

Whatever I'd been about to say choked off as I jerked my gaze over a pair of dark wash jeans, past a loose fitted t-shirt with a wide stretched out collar, and up into a pair of familiar green eyes.

"It's you."

"Aodhán," he reminded me, setting his phone down on his lap. I noted the tattooed fingers, the word PRAY inked one letter per finger on his right hand.

I scanned the rest of him, searching for anything that could be considered gang ink in the myriad of tattoos running up his arms, but there were a hundred things that could've been gang ink. The trinity of crosses. The hourglass. The white dove. The reaper. Or the roses and thorns.

"Right. Thanks again for the ride."

"The pleasure was all mine, love."

That Irish accent should be illegal.

A friction formed in the air between us, charging it with static that only grew with each beat of silence that stretched too long.

"Two strawberry banana smoothies!" the counter attendant called and I jumped, relieved at the interruption.

"Well, see you around, *Aodhán*."

"How about tonight?"

I froze, turning to find him kicking back in the

armchair, his fingers pleated together, tucked behind his head, exposing his Adonis belt.

My gaze got stuck on a flowing script tattoo running down the sharp curve of his hip bone, vanishing beneath his jeans.

It was in a language I didn't understand but assumed to be Irish Gaelic and damn it if I wasn't about to drool.

"What do you say?" He adjusted his hips, breaking the spell with a smirk on his lips. He'd caught me staring.

I shook my head sharply, trying to cast off the flush I could feel heating my face. "No, I'm… I'm fasting."

"I'm not opposed to a liquids-only date."

My brows knotted. *What?*

"Oh. No, I mean, not *fasting* like that. I'm—"

"Not single?"

"Right," I agreed, leaning into the lie. "I'm already seeing someone."

"Lucky guy."

"Becca, we're going to be late for class."

Kate made no secret of openly gawking at Aodhán, her blue eyes darting between us with brows raised so high they vanished beneath her blonde curls.

"Right, I have to go. Thanks again… for the ride the other night."

*You already said that, idiot.*

"As I said, anytime, love."

Aodhán tipped his head, his caramel hair falling forward to cover his eyes as he fingered the four leaf clover charm from beneath his shirt to flip it over his fingers.

I couldn't leave fast enough, almost knocking into another table on my way to the door when Kate waited with two large smoothies in her hands. She leaned into my side as we exited. "Okay, who is that?"

"I was hoping you could tell me," I admitted, taking the smoothie from her and drinking several gulps of the cool liquid to calm the angry flush in my cheeks and the heat that'd built elsewhere, too. "He's not part of the Saints, is he?"

Kate shook her head, stopping where the curving walkway split off into two separate directions. One way leading to my class, the other to hers. "Don't think so," she said. "I've never seen him before."

Not that it mattered. I wasn't interested. Not even a little.

If I wanted a real dick, I'd find myself a nice dress-shirt-and-slacks, tattoo free fuckboy. No more bad boys for this girl. No fucking sir.

"Oh."

I bit my lower lip.

"But I'd like to see a little more of him though if you know what I mean…" she continued and I let out a little laugh. "I mean, as long as you aren't calling dibs."

"Off the market, remember? besides , he's not my type," I lied.

"Well, maybe if you see him again you can introduce me?"

Kate already started backing away down the path to her ceramics class, not waiting for my reply, skipping as she went.

The sunshine to my fucking raincloud.

I waved with my best impression of a smile, still feeling uneasy after the exchange in the snack shop with Aodhán ó Súilleabháin.

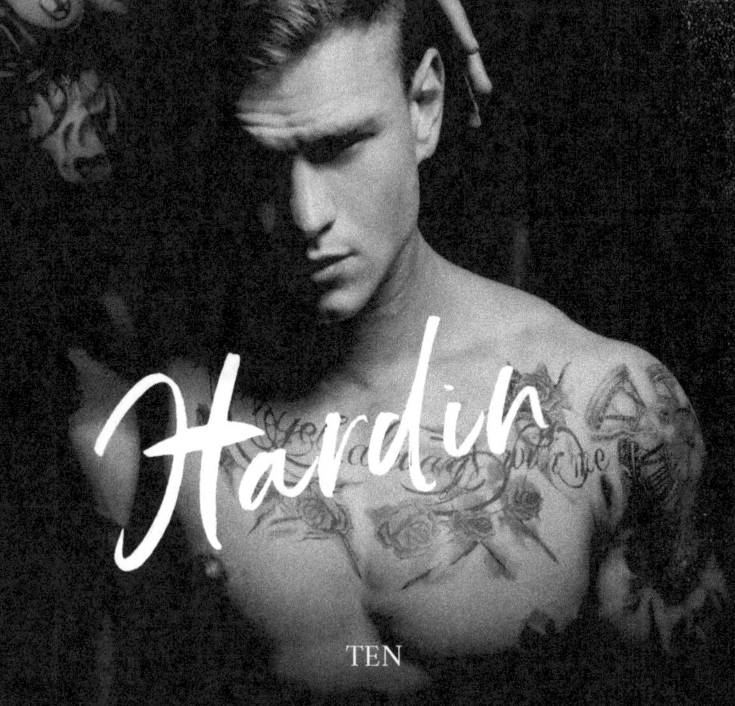

# *Hardin*

## TEN

Three days.

Three fucking days and I could still taste her in my mouth. Her scent still clung to me like a bad aura, as irrevocably fused to me as my own black shadow.

I knew what the therapist Ma made me see when I was thirteen would say. She'd used words like 'obsession' and 'unhealthy' and 'control.'

She'd tell me to try to shift my focus to something else, something important. Except I'd been trying to do exactly that since the first moment I felt the shift within—the hyperfixation lifting its ugly head after a long nap—and failing spectacularly.

I needed to be on my fucking game tonight. We were meeting with The Warden in fifteen minutes for our arms deal: the one we desperately needed to replenish our stock after a raid last month that couldn't be bought out.

A raid I suspected only happened because of a tip off. All of our storage locations were kept under tight lock and even tighter lips. The only way one of them could've been found was if we had a leak. And the only idiots dumb enough to mess with us were the new players in town.

The Sons of O'Sullivan.

If the shoe fucking fit.

"Where are you right now, bro?" Kaleb asked, sliding a clip into his Sig Sauer and checking the chamber before slipping it back into his waistband.

I mirrored his movements, double checking my clip with a shrug.

Zade and Archer chatted with our Dad near the front of the warehouse.

Archer chose the place for its location far outside Santa Clarita on the canyon road. Good for a private meet. Bad if anything happened that would require backup. It'd take our boys in black too long to get here.

I traced Archer's side-profile, sizing him up as he sniffed, lighting up a dart, still in conversation with Dad.

In the right light, everyone could be an enemy in the mask of a friend. And there was no one I wasn't considering as a potential liability save for Kaleb and my father. It didn't mean shit that Arch had been with us since I was barely out of diapers. That he was Dad's best friend.

Unlike the rest of them, I was under no delusions that loyalty was an automatic given once you were *in*. They may have passed the trials and that made them Saints, but it didn't make them blood. No matter how well Dad thought he knew them.

"Why this place?" I asked Kaleb in a whisper. "Why all the way out here in butt fuck nowhere? I don't like it."

Kaleb cocked his head at me, mulling over something, his brows drawing closer together. But his unease evaporated after only a second, replaced with that indifferent stare as he leaned against a stack of wooden pallets and crossed his arms. "We've used this spot before. Why so tense?"

I opened my mouth to tell him to stay alert—something I should've been reminding myself instead—but the sound of tires rolling lazily over gravel outside closed all the mouths in the warehouse.

Damien slapped the side of an old metal oil drum twice with his palm, standing upright. "Look alive, boys, The Warden's here."

My hard stare met Kaleb's, conveying to him what I feared without the need for words.

He gave a subtle nod before moving into place next to our father. I pushed into the space between Archer and my Dad, rolling my shoulders back and cracking my neck to not so subtly hint that he needed to step away, give me a wide fucking berth.

He did, giving me an odd look before settling into a wide-legged stance with his hands clasped at his front, chin up.

Outside, somewhere off to the right, out of view, one, two, three car doors slammed. Two from one car, one from a second vehicle, if I was right.

The heavy footed gaits of at least seven, if not eight of The Warden's men crunched the gravel.

The Warden was the first to appear, his thick silhouette blocking out the near picture perfect view of the gold dust landscape and the setting sun sinking below the canyon walls in the distance.

"Warden," our dad said, not so much a warm greeting as it was a grimace. "I have to admit, I was worried you might not be joining us on this fine late summer evening."

His lackeys trudged up behind him, a total of eight including the man himself. Eight to our five.

Nice odds. We could manage if it came to it.

My Dad's voice rang in my ear from earlier, but his words, meant to be comforting, only made me even more uneasy because they meant he wasn't prepared. He wasn't expecting a double cross.

*We've been working with The Warden for going on eight years now, Son. I know the man better than I know some of my newer recruits. We bring in eighty percent of his business. If he fucks this up, he's not just a shit business man but a fool.*

"*A dead fool,*" I'd countered.

"Would I ever stand you up, St. Vincent?" The Warden replied, coming to a stop just shy of entering the warehouse, keeping a solid five yards of distance between his group and ours. I didn't miss the surprise crossing his face when he noticed Kaleb and me standing alongside our father.

Clearly, he hadn't been expecting us to join this meet. His mistake. Maybe Dad wasn't as unprepared as I thought. But there were a few things different than expected on their side, too. The number of men he brought for one, but also the one man who was missing.

Weston. The Warden's nephew. He always joined The Warden for these tradeoffs, but he was suspiciously absent.

I elbowed Dad, jerking my chin in the direction of The Warden's men. Specifically, their empty hands.

He knew the drill. They brought the merchandise inside for us to examine before we'd pay them a cent. But not a single one of these fools was carrying a damn thing.

"Now, don't tell me you've come all this way empty handed," Dad prodded, and I could already see the gleam of malice in his slate eyes. The trademark look Ma always said I replicated perfectly from trying so hard to be just like him as a younger kid.

Now though, I'd wager my intimidation game was even stronger than my old man's, and I wielded it now, my nostrils flaring as I stared down each one of The Warden's men in turn. Daring them to fuck with us.

Craving the release that only came from the clean arc of sharpened steel or a cascade of bullets burying bone deep into flesh.

*Just give me a fucking reason,* I taunted wordlessly. The devil knew I could use the distraction.

The Warden cleared his throat, readjusting his stance on the gravel, the spurs on his custom black boots tinkering loudly against the crumpled stone. "There's been a slight change of plans," he said, and I watched his Adam's apple bob, noted the sweat beading on his forehead where the sun-reddened flesh met thinning brown hair. "We weren't able to source the—"

"Don't give me that bullshit," Dad interrupted, his tone even despite the murder etched into the lines of his face. "Two weeks ago you told me you had everything on hand or en route so quit fucking me around and give it to me straight. Where are my fucking guns?"

The Warden paled, but stood straighter, his mouth working as he reconsidered his next words before he finally settled on what I gathered was the truth. "They ain't coming, Damien."

"Keep talking."

"We, *uh*… we have ourselves a new client. One that would only partner with us if we offered them full exclusivity."

My Dad spat on the cement floor. "The Sons."

"I'm not at liberty to say, I'm afraid."

"So," said Dad, jabbing two fingers in the air between himself and The Warden. "You're telling me you're throwing away a fucking eight-year-long partnership? Kissing—*what?* —at least eighty percent of your business goodbye? And for what? To be exclusive to a new player you have no loyalty to?"

The Warden recoiled at his words, but my old man wasn't finished.

"Tell me that's not what you're saying, Warden. You do *not* want to make an enemy of me."

If it were possible, the arms dealer became even paler at Dad's threat. "It ain't that simple, Damien."

"Enlighten us, then," Kaleb piped up from Dad's other side. "Or we'll simplify it for you."

"This new player, they ain't messin' around, D. I've never seen a man so… so… *unhinged*. He wants this territory. *Your* territory and he's not going to stop until it's his."

*I knew it.*

We all did, but this was proof. The Sons of O'Sullivan were out for our blood. Our land. Our *home*.

Acid frothed in my stomach, burning its way through every one of my veins, engorging the muscle in my back like a fucking steroid injection. I shuddered at the buildup of unbridled rage, seeing through slitted eyes and a glossy red tint.

"He can fucking try," I all but seethed.

The man to The Warden's right jumped, actually fucking *jumped* at the sound of my voice, lurching back an entire step.

My Dad laid his hand on my shoulder, giving it a rough squeeze, telling me in his way to regain control.

I inhaled long through my nose, feeling my body quake on the exhale.

"And since when do you bend to the whims of terrorists, Warden?" my Dad asked, calmer than he had any right to be after the Warden's admission. "Why not come to me? Why not ask for my help?"

The Warden dropped his head, but not before I saw the flash of pain cross his expression.

"Where's Weston?" Kaleb asked, voicing the question I was thinking. A thousand scenarios rolled around in my head. The Warden said the new player, the leader of the Sons, was *unhinged*. What could he have done to make The Warden bend the knee?

It wasn't fucking rocket science.

I knew before he opened his thin lips to tell us.

"Weston's dead."

He didn't need to say anything else. The Sons had made their play. They offered The Warden a deal, likely with a lot of zeros attached to it, and when The Warden tried to refuse, they made a show of force. Standard practice.

Likely the Sons told The Warden that if he didn't take the deal someone else he cared deeply about would be next. A risky move, unless you had the force to back it up.

We didn't know enough about them yet to know that for certain, but by the rattled exterior of The Warden, I was starting to think we were about to have a big fucking mess on our hands.

"Sorry to hear that," Damien said, running his tongue over his teeth as he considered our next move.

We needed the guns we came here for, more now than we did just five minutes ago.

Dad held up a hand when The Warden opened his mouth to speak, cutting him off before he could spew even more bullshit. "However, I'm going to need our order, Warden. In full. You understand the precarious situation we're in, even more so now than before."

The guy to the Warden's right jerked his gaze to the Warden and back to us twice in quick succession. I fixated on him as my Dad and The Warden continued to talk in circles. It was clear we weren't getting our guns. Not as long as this other player was still on the board.

But there was something else keeping me teetering precariously on the edge of anarchy. Shifty Eyes clenched his jaw, a muscle ticking near his cheekbone. He looked away quickly when he noticed me watching him, his right hand twitching at his side.

Then it clicked.

Why come at all if they didn't have our guns? What good would that do other than piss Damien off and waste our time? If The Warden was now in the Sons' pocket, this whole fucking thing could be staged.

They were the lure.

The guns the missing bait.

And we were the clowns with hooks in our goddamn mouths.

I smiled.

Shifty Eyes looked up, realization dawning. He knew I figured it out. "Warden!"

The Warden drew his weapon, his eyes widening. "Now, boys!

I was already three steps ahead, my gun was out, and I'd fired three rounds before they managed to get off one. Three bodies crumpled to the gravel, identical wounds in their thick skulls.

I knocked Archer to the ground, out of the path of a bullet, before stepping across my father, knowing he was the one that needed to survive this exchange otherwise we'd all be royally fucked.

Damien pivoted on his feet, and I mirrored his

movements as the rest of The Warden's men scattered, pressing my back against his. I felt the reverberations from the kick of his gun against my own shoulder as he shot his weapon, lighting up the growing dark with a scattering of gun fire.

It rang through the canyons like a song, echoing louder than the screams that followed it.

Archer went down.

"*Behind!*" I growled, dropping to the ground in a roll, picking Arch up with me on the follow through to deposit him behind the stack of empty oil drums.

A broken war cry sounded behind me, and I drew my blade, clutching it in reverse at the hilt, the blade along my forearm arcing as I twisted my body.

Shifty Eyes gurgled as the slit in his throat—the thinnest seam—split open, pouring his life's blood down the front of his shirt. He went to his knees. To his face. Crimson spreading around his head like a demon's halo.

I lifted my face to the ceiling, inhaling deeply. The acrid bite of sulfur and sawdust in the air filled my lungs, settling the devil within.

"*Arch,*" Damien roared, and I blinked, coming down from the peak of my delirium to find my Dad pressing his bare hands against a wound in Archer's stomach. He'd been clipped on the right side. Too far right to have hit his stomach. Or his kidney.

He was a tough bastard. He'd live if we could get him back to the Shop.

"I'm good," Arch was saying through a snarl. "I'm good. Just get me up."

"Everyone else whole?" Kaleb called, stalking over, his gun still out, blood splashed over his high cheekbones like warpaint.

I nodded. He assessed our Dad and Zade before he tucked his weapon back into his waistband, bending to help Dad lift Arch from the cement floor. "What the fuck was that?" he asked, breathless as they shouldered Archer's weight, making their way out.

"Perimeter," Dad snapped at Zade and he nodded, a jump in his step as he rushed out ahead of them to check there wasn't anyone else waiting outside.

Archer sagged between my Dad and brother, passing out, making them carry the whole of his weight.

"Wasn't it obvious?" I asked in a husky tone. "The Sons have declared war."

# Becca

## ELEVEN

*How do normal people* do *all this?*

I was dead on my feet by four in the afternoon after spending all my soul energy on a watercolor painting that wound up looking far too much like an abstract homage to Dark and Gloomy for my liking.

A hot shower shared with Mr. Waterproof Eight Inch and a nap would have been fucking fab but no. I had to do my laundry, with Toby's help because I couldn't get the knobs to work. Then after that I needed to pick up some groceries because this bitch had to eat on occasion, *and then* it was time to drag my ass to my evening shift at the cafe.

My eyelids drooped heavily over my eyes as I sat slumped on a stool in the storage room, surrounded by the aromas of loose leaf teas and rich coffee for the two more minutes my break allowed.

I scrolled on my phone, the crack in the screen just another *fuck you* I couldn't afford to fix, laughing at me with each swipe of my finger.

At least I'd have some extra cash to pad my nightstand drawer soon. Toby was practically selling an item a day. At this rate I'd have to come to work in my satin pajamas because I wouldn't have anything left to wear. I snorted to myself at the mental image, my phone buzzing with an incoming message from my best friend.

**Ava Jade: I can't wait to meet your roomies. Are they nice to you? They better be being nice to you.**

My lip twitched up into a smirk. I'd finally filled my girl in on all the shit she'd missed since Sunday. Well, the shit that wouldn't worry her, at least. That I found an apartment and a job. That class was good but draining. That I was still vehemently single and planning to stay that way.

**Becca: They're great. You'd really like them.**

I typed out another message, but hesitated before sending it.

**Becca: When are you coming for a visit? I miss you.**

I erased it instead.

Aves had a lot going on right now. Between the tour and everything the gang demanded of her, it wouldn't be fair of me to make her feel bad about not being able to come. Besides, I'd see her when Primal Ethos made its way to Lodi for the show soon. That was good enough.

**Ava Jade: Are you carrying that taser I gave you?**

I shook my head, remembering when she pushed it

into my hands before I left Thorn Valley. *Go for the neck,* she'd said. *Or the balls. Either is fine.*

It was in my closet, tucked behind the little bin where I was keeping my belts. Truth be told, I was afraid to touch the thing. With my luck I'd tase myself before I managed to tase anyone else. But she was right. I should carry it with me.

**Becca: I promise I'll put it in my purse when I get home from work.**

**Ava Jade: Keep it there.**

**Becca: Stop worrying!**

**Ava Jade: Never.**

I clicked off my phone and slipped it into my jacket hanging from one of the hooks near the back wall. Break time was up.

Toby entered as I was leaving, removing his apron in favor of a light sweater, finished with his shift for the night. It would be just me and Kate till closing time, now.

"You good if I head out a few minutes early?" he asked.

I shrugged. "It's dead out there. We'll be fine."

He pushed his arms into the sleeves of his sweater with a sigh and leaned in to brush his lips against my cheek. "See you at home, then?"

"See you at home."

I followed him out into the space behind the long counter where Kate was helping the only customer currently in the cafe.

"Oh, wait!" Toby exclaimed. "I keep forgetting to ask: want to be my date again this weekend?"

I couldn't stop my expression from souring at the

thought of going back to that house at the edge of the cul de sac. *Their* house. "Another party at Kaleb's?"

*Please say no... then I won't have to.*

"No, no, but they *do* throw a party, like, every Sunday. It's kind of a thing. You get it, because they're *Saints*. It's like church but instead of taking a communion of bread and wine you get dick and hard liquor."

I laughed.

"No, I was talking about the race."

"The race?'

Kate finished pouring a latte with a perfect leaf design in the frothed milk, handing it to the customer before turning to join us near the milk fridges. "Tobes and me always go. You should come. I usually don't bother with a lot of the parties, but race night is worth the inevitable hangover, especially if you get chosen to ride shotty with a driver."

I lifted a brow at Kate, seeing her in a new light. I wouldn't have taken her for a thrill seeker. "Have you ever been chosen?" I asked.

She shook her head and a few curls came loose from her messy bun. "Not yet, but I have it on good authority that one of this month's racers has a thing for blondes. So, maybe..." She trailed off with an excited squeak, but there was something else I needed to know first.

Ava Jade made me promise I wouldn't involve myself in any criminal activity, at least not without her.

"Are we talking *legal* racing?"

Toby gave me a conspiratorial look. "Sure, if that's what you need to hear to say yes."

I licked my dry lips, the idea of being sucked back into a leather seat and hurtled down a winding road sounding almost… euphoric. Fun. Just watching the races would be fun, too, I guessed. And after the week I'd had so far, I was overdue for some.

"Okay, fine, I'll come. *If* I have anything left to wear by then."

"Knew we could count on you." Toby swatted my ass, winking before sauntering to the front of the cafe. "Laters, babes."

I shook my head, watching him go. "He really doesn't like to be told *no*, does he?"

"Nope. He's a yes man through and through, but if it wasn't for his pushy ass I'd probably never leave the five block radius around campus."

The evening wore on at an absolutely glacial pace, pulling equipment out to clean beneath, counting stock, doing basically every part of this job that made me want to gouge my own eyes out.

I shouldered the massive coffee grinder back into place on the sparkling countertop with a grunt, sagging against it once it was back where it belonged.

"Fuck," I breathed on a sigh, gaze lifting to the clock on the wall for what was probably the fifth time in as many minutes.

Still another forty minutes to go. Then I had the divine privilege of passing out face first on my creaky mattress before waking up to do it all over again tomorrow. At least I was off work tomorrow. The break would give me an entire evening to catch up on sleep and recharge before the race on Saturday.

*Silver linings, Becks.*

I swiped the back of my palm across my forehead and it came away damp with sweat, making me grimace. *Ugh.*

"Your face is doing that thing again," Kate singsonged from the cash register, where she cleaned the same spot she'd just cleaned thirty minutes ago.

I attempted to unknot my brows. Smooth the tension in my jaw. Kate's theory was that it was so dead in here because my *murder vibes* were scaring all the customers away.

She might not have been wrong. I was feeling extra murdery, frustrated that even after three—*yes, three*—triple shot americanos I could somehow still be this exhausted.

If Betty-loo-what's-her-fuck came in here right now asking for her usual eight-step latte, I was just as likely to throw it in her face as I was to actually make it.

"*Ugh,*" I sighed. "I can't help it. I never knew four hours could feel like four entire days."

"Welcome to the working class, roomie."

I rolled my eyes, regretting my decision to spill the beans to her over matcha smoothies at lunch today. She hadn't missed a single opportunity to make jokes at my expense since finding out I'd never worked a day in my life. Or bought my own groceries. Or done my own laundry.

"Go ahead, laugh it up."

"Awe come on, let me poke fun. It's like watching a baby take—"

"*Don't,*" I warned her with all of the ire but none of the fire, trying to keep my lips from turning up in a smirk. "Don't say it."

She looked at me through her lashes mischievously. "Or what?"

"Or I'll replace all the coffee in the house with decaf."

Her mouth gaped open, eyes round as she wielded the dirty rag in her hand like a weapon, whipping it in my direction. "Death first!"

I chucked a to-go cup at her, and she whipped it out of the air with a *'Ha!'* just as the bells over the door rang.

The pair of us dropped our makeshift weapons and straightened up, holding back laughter as a couple came in, going straight for the little nook near the very back, laptop bags slung over their shoulders. But if I'd learned anything in the last few days, it was that nook number nine was *not* for studying. Its placement, set off to the right of the main corridor, tucked away in a tight alcove, made it the perfect place for the covert spreading of something more vulgar than book pages.

"Not even going to buy something first," I chided in a whisper once they were gone.

"*Tsk, tsk,*" Kate added between bouts of quieted laughter when the bells rang again, but this time signaling the entry of someone I recognized.

Aodhán pushed damp hair from his face as he entered, as if he'd just gotten out of the shower before arriving. He paused mid swipe of his fingers through the blond locks, eyes meeting mine.

Surprise lifted one of his brows as he slowly approached the counter and somehow I was there. A thin slip of counter and a cash register the only things between us.

"You work here?" he asked, his head tipping to one side as he considered me, taking in the black apron, the name tag, my slick dark ponytail.

"Last time I checked. You aren't stalking me, are you?"

The question sprang from my grinning mouth as a joke, but once spoken, forced me to consider it myself.

Could it be total coincidence that I'd run into him not once, but three times in the last three days? A sinking feeling plummeted low in my gut, and suddenly it was a struggle to keep my expression even, the air rattling in my lungs.

Aodhán leaned against the counter with a wry smile that managed to both charm me and set me somehow back at ease. "You caught me. I just can't seem to stay away from you."

Behind me, Kate cleared her throat, and I jerked back from him, blinking rapidly. "Who's your friend?" she asked innocently, and I remembered she'd requested an introduction with the mysterious Irishman.

"This is Aodhán," I said, coughing before I could speak. "He, *uh*, he gave me a ride home from Kaleb's the other night."

"Such a gentleman," Kate said with a beaming smile, bending forward against the counter in a way that afforded Aodhán a full view of her perky breasts, but he didn't seem to notice. "I'm Kate," she offered. "Becca's my roommate."

Aodhán's green eyes gaze slid briefly to Kate before returning to me. "Could you make me a Red Eye, Kate? One sugar."

Her smile grew as she rose from her ass-out perch on the counter, clearly not taking Aodhán's request for what it was. A dismissal.

I swallowed. "That'll be five fifty," I told him, ringing up his drink. "Unless you want something else?"

"Is that a trick question?" he asked, and from the look he was giving me, I knew exactly what else he'd ask for if he thought I'd give it to him.

"Kate's single," I whispered, the whirr of the espresso grinder concealing her from being able to hear us. "You could ask her for whatever it is you want."

He frowned, something sharp slashing across his features before that panty melting smirk was right back in place. My skin prickled with gooseflesh, and I worked to swallow, my throat suddenly dry.

"It isn't her I want."

"Oh?"

Aodhán slid a ten dollar bill across the counter at the same time Kate returned with his drink. He wrapped his fingers around it, the tattoo, *PRAY,* on full display across his knuckles as he sipped the piping hot liquid without so much as a flinch.

"Becca, are you going to give him his change? Sorry, she's still learning."

I barely noticed Kate taking my place at the till, swiping up Aodhán's bill to deposit in the cash drawer and pull out his change.

"Keep it," he insisted and she blushed, dropping the change into the tip jar.

"And he's generous, too."

Aodhán glanced up at the clock. "Will your boyfriend be picking you up?" he asked me with a challenge in his stare. "I'd like to meet him."

"Boyfriend?" Kate laughed, and I gave her a hard look. "Becca doesn't have a—"

The bells rang again, cutting Kate off, thank fuck.

But I would not being thanking fuck for the fuckery it just deposited on the welcome matt.

Could this day get any more exhausting?

Hardin entered the cafe, his black eyes fixed on Aodhán, jerking between us as if he were accusing me of something, which was ridiculous because I barely knew him. Unless you counted an intimate knowledge of what his lips and fingers felt like when they were pressed to various parts of me.

Hardin approached the counter, pausing just shy of where Aodhán stood as if waiting for him to move out of the way.

Aodhán didn't budge, nodding to the empty slice of counter next to him where Kate would surely be glad to help him.

Still, Hardin didn't move. He stared at Aodhán in a way that made my skin prickle, second-hand fear for my new Irish friend making my blood chill with dread.

"Your usual, Hardin?" Kate asked, her tone light and hesitant, the way you might speak to a wolf to avoid being eaten alive.

His heavy glare didn't waver so much as an inch as he nodded once, slowly. Kate rushed away to pour him his plain drip, black. She grabbed a to-go cup, but Hardin let out the tiniest of growls and she paused with a little *"Sorry, Hardin"* before fingering a warm mug from the top of the espresso machine instead.

"I saw you talking to your brother in here the other day, so I know you're not mute," I found myself blurting, crossing my arms over my chest. "Which means you're fully capable of apologizing for the other night."

His dark irises slid to mine, a vein jumping in his temple where there was a smear of something red near his hairline. Was that… was that blood?

My lips parted, realizing the smear on his forehead wasn't the only place red stained on his skin. There was deep red in the cracks of his knuckles. Spattered lightly over the shirt he wore beneath his leather jacket.

*Oh god.*

I swallowed, struggling to pull my gaze free from Hardin's only to find Aodhán *smirking* at him. The guy must've had a death wish.

"See you around, Aodhán," I said, keeping my voice as level as I could while Kate returned with Hardin's coffee.

Aodhán's brows lowered, confused at my not so subtle hint for him to leave before they shot back up, as if he'd just figured something out.

"*Ah,*" he said, straightening from his leaning stance on

the counter, gesturing to Hardin with his to-go cup. "You must be the lucky guy."

"No, he's not—"

"It's okay," Aodhán interrupted, something about his speech sounding odd to my ears. Flat. He cast another wink in my direction. "I can take a hint. 'Night."

He saluted Hardin, taking his leave, the big oaf still just standing there at the counter, coffee in hand. Watching me.

Despite the fresh blood on his hands, I couldn't help the lick of indignant fury coiling up my spine, hot enough to burn away any remaining dread.

"What the hell are you staring at?" I all but shouted, my frame expanding with hot air. "You can't just walk in here and scare away the customers, okay? That's *my* job."

His teeth clenched behind his stupid lips.

"Are you really not going to say anything?"

"*Becca*," Kate called uneasily from somewhere off to my right. "*Just leave it alone*. Hardin, that's on the house. Sorry for my—"

"Don't apologize for me," I snapped, fully unable to keep myself on a leash anymore. I was tired and sore and just *done* with guys like Hardin and Kaleb thinking they could do whatever they wanted whenever they wanted just because of who their Daddy was. Who they were.

"I'm not sorry," I told Hardin, feeling my resolve strengthen with every word. "And Mr. Dark and Gloomy can pay for his coffee. Actually, you know what—"

I lurched forward, taking the mug from his hand. I spun on my heel, stomping to the stack of to-go cups near the coffee carafes, plucking one off the top of the pile. I poured the hot coffee from his mug into the cup and slapped a lid on it, not bothering with a sleeve even though it was hot enough to scald my palm.

"That'll be two ninety," I said, setting the cup down hard enough on the front counter for a spurt of black liquid to erupt from the drinking hole. "Cash or card?"

Hardin's upper lip curled back over white teeth and something in my stomach flipped.

"*Cash or card?*" I asked again.

The skin around his eyes crinkled, and for the first time, I was able to read the word scrawled in sharp scripted ink over his brow.

The word *SUBMIT* taunted me from its perch, and a defiant grin pulled at my lips. The word *No* ringing loudly in my mind. I'd submitted my entire life. To my Dad. To the jackass who used me to try to get to my best friend only to put bullets in both our chests.

I was *done* submitting.

I was done with this entire idiotic fucking charade.

When Hardin didn't move to pay or take the cup, preferring to stand there with hands balled into fists, I lifted it back up, unceremoniously tossing it into the large stainless steel sink down the line, drawing a gasp from Kate as dark liquid splashed up high enough to slosh onto the floor.

"We're closing," I slung at him. "You should leave."

His face twisted, the pain in his dark stare at odds with his violent expression, making the knot in my chest squeeze until some of my rage melted away.

*Haunted*: it was the only word that fit, and it had no right to be on a face so cruel.

Hardin left without his coffee, slamming a palm hard against the frame of the glass door as he exited the cafe. The resounding *crack!* like a gunshot in the quiet.

"Damn, girl, you got a death wish?"

I slumped once Hardin was fully out of sight, whatever chemical that'd been alive in my veins a second ago now fully and completely depleted, leaving me lightheaded and unsteady on my feet. But with a smile on my lips. That felt... *good.*

"No," I said, lifting my eyes to the ceiling with a sigh. Ava Jade would be so damn proud, right after she bit my head off for putting myself at risk. "But I think I finally found my spine."

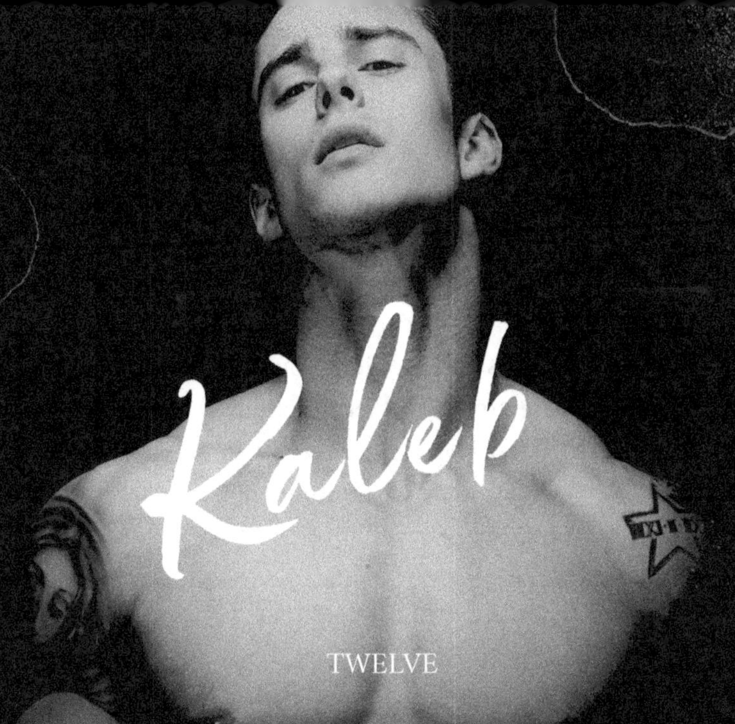



## TWELVE

With our lackeys from Kilborn on the job, there weren't many places Becca could go without our knowledge, but *here*? When I finally have five minutes to myself, aching to spend every one of them on her, *this* is where she's at?

**Kaleb: You sure this is the place?**

I fired off the text to Clay, a guy who shared my computer science class and wanted an in with the Saints.

If I was honest, I hadn't even noticed the place before now. A swinging sign hung from wrought iron hooks, jutting from the mouth of an alleyway. A curling arrow pointing down the clean swept cobblestone. It read *Oxygen - Hot Yoga Studio.*

Made sense since I'd seen the Row randomly filled with babes drenched in sweat carrying yoga mats from time to time.

My phone buzzed in my hand, and I checked the reply,

hitting ignore on two others that chased it onto my screen. Gillian DeLuca needed to take a hint. She'd been texting me nonstop since last Sunday night at our place, and it was starting to annoy the absolute shit out of me.

Just because Ma liked her didn't mean I was going to tolerate what I was sure could amount to a harassment charge if I were to pursue legal action. Hardin would know. Not that I'd waste my time pursuing a piece of paper when a few choice words and a gun could get the job done in half the time.

I ground my teeth, swiping past her message and one from Dad. I just fucking *left* the autobody shop and he was already on me. Hardin and I were to keep our asses glued to the Santa Clarita streets, using all of our eyes and ears to scour every inch of our turf for the Sons.

I was on it, or at least I would be, right after I was through here.

**Clay: I'm sure. Her roommate got her a trial week and she's booked for something called Modo.**

My ass may have been in more danger than Becca's with the Sons on the prowl, but that didn't mean whoever planted that tracker in her bag didn't have equally malicious intent. She needed to be watched. And I wanted to be the one to do the watching.

And the touching and the biting and the licking and the fucking, but that could come later.

I'd wait.

Not like she was giving me a fucking choice.

Unless I could slip through one of the cracks in her armor, my dick was going to get a little too well acquainted with my right hand. And since no other ass in Santa Clarita seemed to give me so much as a semi anymore, it was Hot Yoga or fucking bust.

Another message came in from Clay.

Clay: Better hurry if you want to catch her. The class is starting at 2.

It was already 2:01 pm.

Cursing to myself, I pocketed my phone and jogged down the cobblestone alley toward the wooden door set into the brick down near the end. I just needed to talk to her. I needed five minutes.

If I explained some things, maybe she wouldn't be so quick to dismiss me. To dismiss Hardin. I mean, I understood why she did, knowing her story, but not every gun wielding gang man in Cali was a replica of the sadistic fuckwad that shot her and almost killed her best friend.

Take our cousins, The Crows, for instance. They were good shit. Rook was a little unhinged—okay, fine, more than a little—and Corv a little neurotic, but I wouldn't want anyone else at my side in a shitty spot. Grey was loyal to a fault and would do anything, and I really meant anything, for their girl.

Was that not something to desire?

I reefed the door open and stepped through into a low ceilinged space filled with yoga gear available for purchase and a pocketed wood box system stuffed with outside shoes and bags. The lighting was so dim I had to squint into past the racks to see the guy lounging in a swivel stool at a desk, keying something into a computer monitor.

Where the shit was everyone?

"Hey," I called to him. You got a—"

"*Shhh*," he hushed me sharply, finishing whatever he'd been typing before he peeled his gaze from the screen to give me his attention, and promptly lost every drop of blood in his face.

He tugged at the collar of his long sleeve shirt, dropping his gaze. "I'm so sorry," he croaked. "There's a class in session just down the hall and our clients expect silence in the room."

I had no fucking idea what he was on about but the word *class* I focused on. "Modo class?"

He nodded, seeming confused.

"Wait!" he called as I brushed through the racks on my way to the hall. I figured I had about twenty minutes before Dad got really pissed at not hearing back from me. I needed to make this quick.

"What?"

The skinny guy hopped off his swiveling stool, rushing over. He stopped along the way, gathering a charcoal gray rolled matt from a pyramid of about thirty, peeling a pair of matching shorts from a rack. He handed me both, pushing them into my arms. "You'll need these. On the house for my rudeness when you walked in. Men's changing rooms are down the hall to the left. The studio is on the right. We're not meant to admit anyone to class late, but I'm sure Rosana won't have a problem with it in this case."

"Right," I said, looking down at the random shit in my

arms. "This all I need?"

His shoulders hitched as he thought of something else, rushing to the counter and back to bring me a bottle of water. "That's it. You're all set."

Maybe it was the guy's overeagerness to please or the fact that I didn't want Becca thinking I was even more of an asshole than she already thought from the other day at the cafe, but I decided I should at least attempt decorum.

"Thanks," I bit out, going in the direction he indicated, to the men's changing room. The space was almost entirely devoid of all life. Long wooden benches squatted low beneath empty hooks. Only a single hook appeared to be in use which meant I was going to be one of only two shlongs in a lipfest.

Normally, I'd have fucking preened. Not today. Today there was one and only one girl whose attention I wanted.

I fucking prayed that once I had her, and *I would* have her, whatever fixation I had on her would fade.

She had to see the commitment here. I mean, fucking *yoga*, just to talk to her. I'd never worked this hard.

I removed my shirt and pulled my Sig from my waistband, looking around for a place to put it. Dad would flip shit if he knew I was unarmed even for a second right now, but I couldn't risk scaring Becca away before I could get two words out. So, no gun.

"Fuck." Finding nowhere to stash it, I wrapped it in my shirt and peeled off the rest of my shit, piling it all on top of the bundle. The shorts the guy at the front gave me left little to the imagination, but that could work in my favor. I was more a shower than a grower and all eight flaccid inches of me were on full display in these tiny ass gray shorts. So was what I considered my best ink. The blue-eyed crow in flight painted over the mountain of my kneecap an homage to my cousins in Thorn Valley.

I grabbed the mat and the bottle of water, making my way shirtless, shoeless, gunless—might as well have been fucking naked—to the studio. Hot air slapped me in the face as I entered, and I braced against it. When they said *hot* yoga, they weren't fucking joking.

The woman sitting cross legged at the head of the massive room looked up with contempt in her eyes. She must've managed to recognize me even in the low lighting because she said nothing, just went back to breathing deeply with her head bent.

I squinted into the humid air, scanning over the thirty or so people lying like corpses on their mats. Eyes closed. Bodies limp.

My lips cracked into a grin when I found her, her chest rising and falling in deep, lengthened breaths, making her perky tits push hard against the containment of a plain black sports bra. Her dark hair fanned out to one side from the high ponytail she had it tied up in, and I wondered if she'd like my fist wrapped around it, using it as an anchor while I plowed into her from behind.

My cock quickly excited itself into a semi before I shook away the thoughts battering against my skull like a hailstorm.

The space beside her was blessedly empty, and I made my way to it, tripping over several sets of legs by the time

I got there. I struggled to get my mat unrolled and laid out as straight as hers, but it would have to do.

My gaze flicked up to the instructor at the head of the room, and she made a downward motion with her hand, encouraging me to join the others in the corpse position.

I clenched my jaw but sat backward on the foamy mat, lying on my back. It felt… wrong. Lying spread eagle with my eyes shut. All vital organs open and on full display.

I kept one eye peeked open as the instructor began to speak.

"Inhale deeply as you make your way out of shavasana, take a pause on your right side, breathe."

Becca turned away from me, and I followed her movement, turning onto my side, my eyes roving the length of her back down to a peachy ass. Fuck, she had a sexy back.

A *sexy back*?

What the hell was wrong with me?

"With your breath, let's move into child's pose."

She rolled onto all fours, her back bowing like a cat before she sank back in her hips, stretching her arms high over her head until she was pressed flat against the yoga mat, bowing as if in prayer to some ancient deity.

And fuck if I wasn't getting hard as all hell beneath these too-thin shorts.

I attempted to mimic her movements, but a tightness in my lower back and hamstrings made it all but impossible, so I floated somewhere between a crawling stance and an awkward bow over my mat, sweat already starting to bead at my hairline.

"Good," the instructor crooned. "Now, with your breath, lift up onto all fours for a round of cat and cow."

*What?*

Becca pressed forward on her palms, her movements fluid like a dancer. She arched her back, lifting her chin up to the ceiling, exposing a long neck that I wanted to taste with my tongue.

When she curled her back upward, bending her chin, her eyes opened. She did a double take when she saw me, her even breaths traded in for a few heavy ones. Everyone around us continued arching and bowing their backs while Becca mouthed to me *what are you doing here?*

*Thought she'd never ask.*

"I came to talk to you."

Even though I kept my voice low, I earned myself a few puckered lips and wordless grumbles from the other yogis who no doubt still had their eyes closed.

She shook her head, and we both followed the instructor from the mat to a standing position. Becca pressed her palms together at her heart and bowed her head, but there was a knot between her brows and tension in her forehead that wasn't there before.

"What do you want?"

Her whisper was so low I wasn't sure if I heard her right.

"Did I do something to offend you?"

The woman on my left shushed me sharply, and I turned to glare at her. She took one look at my face, bent to peel her mat from the floor, and left.

Becca sighed, lifting her arms high overhead before

bending to touch her toes, everyone in the sweaty ass room completely in sync except for my ass. Becca's palms skimmed the floor, but I could barely get past my damn knees in that position.

"Let's assume I *did* do something to offend you," I continued when it became clear she wasn't going to answer me. "What could I do to make it up to you?"

A few more grumbles from the throng, but I ignored them, keeping my attention solely focused on Becca.

"Nothing," she whispered. "There's nothing you can do because I'm not interested in knowing you."

"I'm not buying that."

I'd seen the way she was looking at me last Sunday, like she could eat me alive with her eyes alone. She'd looked at me the same way when I went to return her purse, even if the words coming out of her mouth didn't match the hunger in her stare.

"I'm not selling it," she retorted in a harsh whisper, continuing to follow along with the instructor. "It's the truth. I've had enough of gangs and guns to last me a lifetime."

"So I've heard."

She jerked upright at that, her brown eyed stare piercing in its intensity. "What do you mean?"

I smirked. "The new girl on campus shows up at my house and you think I don't look into her? I always know who's in my home, and if I don't, I make it my business to find out."

At least a part of that was true. I couldn't tell her the Crows asked us to keep an eye on her. I wouldn't hang them out to dry like that, not unless there was no other option. What she needed to know right now was that I didn't think she was safe, and I'd made it my business to ensure said safety.

She frowned at my words, likely regretting ever coming by.

"Well, I won't be coming to any more of your *Sunday Masses*. One of your friends made it very clear I wasn't welcome, not that I care."

My face pinched, and right away the urge to ring the neck of whoever made her feel that way pulsed through me like angry fire.

"Who?" I asked, but I barely got the word out before I realized exactly who would've said some shit to her. "Wait. Red hair? Bitchy face?"

"That's the one."

"Don't mind Gill, she's all bark, no bite." *...and I would handle her myself.*

Her brows lifted, but she said nothing. Why was she being so difficult?

The instructor guided us into some warrior stance, but while everyone else faced the right wall, I did the opposite, facing left so I could be face to face with Becca as she stretched her arms wide and leaned into her forward leg.

And *those thighs...*

I mimicked the move in reverse, spreading myself wide, stretching my arms straight out in front and behind myself. She tried and failed not to trace the long lines of my body, her gaze snagging on several tattoos before settling on the very visible bulge in my shorts. I knew it. She may not have wanted to know me but she definitely wanted to *know* me. It was a start.

She blinked twice, her throat bobbing before she turned her gaze studiously to the front of the room.

But I didn't have the same restraint. I watched slender muscle harden and contract over the unblemished skin between the waistband of her skin tight yoga pants and sports bra. She had some tone to her, that was for sure. But I worried about her food intake. When she lifted her arms high, I could see the ridges of her lower rib cage pushing through her skin.

"And dance your forward arm back into peaceful warrior," the instructor breathed, and I nearly collapsed onto my ass trying to replicate the ridiculous pose. Giving up, I settled back into the first posture instead, watching Becca move her arms into the shape with ease.

It was clear she wasn't going to continue the conversation unless I pulled every word from her, so I might as well get to the point.

"Anyway, there was, *uh*, something in your purse that I took out before I gave it back to you and I need to know if you have any ene—"

"I knew you swiped my joint," she spat in a venomous whisper, moving out of her powerful warrior stance to stand tall, glaring at me. "It was my last one, so you better replace it."

She bent with a low growl to retrieve her mat from the floor, rolling it messily into a bundle she threw under her arm.

"Shit, sorry!" she hissed, tripping over the girl next to her in her haste to leave.

*Well, that shit went swimmingly.*

I ground my teeth, thinking of the texts from Dad no doubt piling up on my phone in the men's locker room. But fuck that. I wasn't going to give up that easily.

This girl had haunted my dreams all week. I was off my game and stumbling. But I knew how I could get back on my feet.

I ditched the mat and water, following behind Becca only a minute after she left. The cooler air outside the studio felt easier to breathe and I listened for her, swinging my head to either side of the hall. Across from me, in the women's changing room, I heard the creak of a knob twisting and water spurting over tile. I grinned.

The changing room I entered was identical to the men's one, except this one was stuffed full of yoga bags and water bottles and clothing neatly hung on hooks and folded on the benches.

Steam rose from the back of the space, where two banks of three showers with curtained doors filled a tiled area. The curtains were all open save for one.

The stall at the very back.

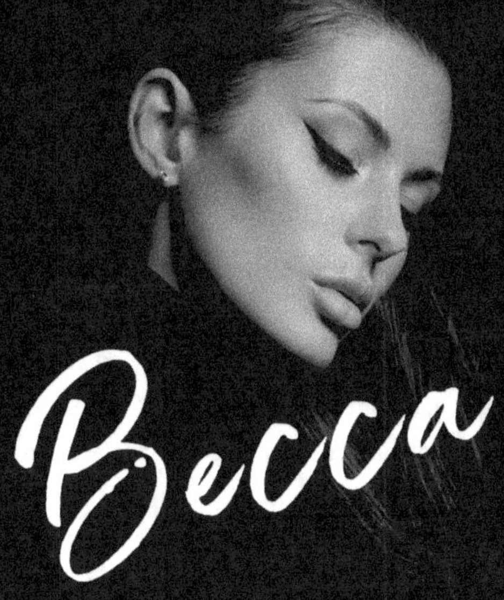

# Becca

## THIRTEEN

What was it about dangerous criminals?

Is it the cocky smirks? The tattoos? The confidence? The fact that they knew their way around a vast amount of weaponry?

Or was it just the unfiltered *rawness* of them?

Whatever it was, it managed to make Kaleb St. Vincent both one of the most frustrating men I'd ever met, but also one of the hottest. Like panty melting, dripping through two layers of skin tight fabric hot.

I drew the shower curtain closed in the empty change room, stripping down naked to find the evidence of my arousal lining the seamless thong I was wearing beneath my yoga pants.

My greedy cunt throbbed as the air hit it and I bit back a groan, roughly tugging everything else off, tearing my hair from its high ponytail to let it cascade around my

151

shoulders. I flicked the tap on, twisting it to the highest heat setting it would allow, as if I could wash the Saint off with nothing more than scalding water and thoughts of polo wearing, messenger bag toting, good boys.

There was one other thing I could do to banish him from my thoughts, though. My thighs pressed together as I bent my head and entered the stream of hot water, letting it plaster my hair to my face. Class wouldn't be over for another twenty minutes at least. I chewed my lower lip, water slipping over my closed eyelids as my hand snaked low, finding my warm, slippery clit.

I clenched my teeth, breathing through them as I began to swirl my fingers, turning to lean my back against the wall. All images of college frat boys with crew cuts and loafers fled, replaced with imagery that had me holding back moans.

A bicep flexing with a long sleeve shirt tucked into the crease of an elbow.

Wicked sneers on sharply bowed lips.

Tattoos arcing over eyebrows.

…running down toned waists to vanish beneath dark wash jeans.

Sun-kissed brown hair and the scent of spiced rum and cherry cigars.

…of leather and warm amber.

A four leaf clover charm pressed between white teeth.

The taste of whiskey and honey on my tongue.

I let out a little gasp, circling my clit faster, dipping my fingers into myself like an artist wetting a brush, ready to paint a fucking masterpiece.

I shuddered against the wall, my breaths coming short and shallow as my core tightened and I braced my other hand against the wall, spreading my legs wider.

The *shhh* of plastic rushing along a metal bar snapped me back to the present. I opened my eyes to a waterlogged view of Kaleb standing with his fist clenched in the shower curtain, a ravenous hunger in his stare as he took in every inch of me.

I opened my mouth to tell him to get the fuck out, but no words evicted themselves, stubbornly squatting there behind my lips like the little traitors they were.

My chest heaved, and his gaze caught on my pebbled nipples. He let out a low sounding breath, his cheekbones flaring.

"Kaleb," I started, my bracing hand dropping from the wall to cover myself, to cover my scar, as he continued to stare.

He cleared the gap between us, putting himself beneath the stream of scalding water. In one quick movement he had my wrist wrapped in his right hand, torn away from my chest so he could continue to marvel at me. He leaned down, using his free hand to run the pad of his thumb gently along the underside of my breast, over the puckered flesh of the scar that hugged its curve. I shivered at his touch, expecting to find disgust in his stare, but finding something else instead.

Wonder.

And something else.

A sort of recognition that could only come from

someone who knew the same level of pain. Of fear for their own life.

He cupped my breast in his palm, his lips falling apart as he rubbed the nipple between the pads of his thumb and index finger, drawing a muted cry from my lips.

He smirked at that, his gray-blue eyes meeting mine in the steam with a challenge. "Thought you didn't want to know me."

"I don't," I gasped and he punished me with a tug on my nipple that sent fucking lightning bolts right down to my pussy.

"Is that so?"

He dipped his head before I could reply, sucking the opposite nipple into his mouth while he continued stroking the other one with tortuous slowness.

My back arched into him, and I could feel his smug smile against the mound of my breast as he lashed my nipple with his tongue, but I didn't care.

I could go back to ignoring him in ten minutes.

Maybe fifteen.

Okay, twenty.

I cried out as he bit down with his teeth, my cunt aching with need. I tried to reach for his hair, to tug him away, but he drew my wrists up, pinning them with one hand above my head against the shower tile as he continued to suck and lick and bite.

"Fuck," I cursed, my knees going weak, thinking if he just kept going I might be able to come from his nipple play alone.

That would be a damn first.

In a moment of clarity, I realized I knew why a good guy would never be enough. Good guys didn't touch you like bad guys did. They didn't push the limits. Hold you down. Make you insane with need. Make you scream.

No. Good guys poked you with their morning wood and told you to jump on.

Kaleb pressed into me and the feel of his erection hard and long through his shorts was enough for me to forgive him from stopping the downright charitable work he was doing with his tongue.

Lubricated enough from the water, I managed to tug a wrist free, shoving it down between us to get a better feel of what I was about to be working with. He jerked at my touch, gritting his teeth, his head tipped back with a groan.

When his chin dropped back down, his eyes were filled with a lust that bordered on madness.

I tugged my other hand free and ripped down his shorts, the *slap* of the wet material hitting the floor ringing in my ears as I marveled at what I was certain was close to nine inches of solid steel.

My mouth watered, wanting to taste him, to feel him at the back of my throat.

"What are you—"

His next word was choked off on a violent growl as I took him into my mouth. Kaleb's hand twisted in my hair, grasping it at the base of my skull. Salty precum hit my tongue, and I moaned, working his tip with my tongue.

"Holy fucking shit," he said on an exhale, and I smiled

around his length in my mouth. I knew I was good at this. *More* than good. I was the best.

I pumped his base as I sucked and flicked at his head with my tongue, focusing on that sensitive spot on the underside. Once his legs were shaking though, it was my turn. So to speak…

I wanted him deep. I wanted him to use me like a toy and fuck my throat like it owed him rent.

I gagged lightly as I pushed my head forward, his girth stretching my mouth to its limits as he tapped the back of my throat, a string of curses falling from his lips.

Kaleb's fist in my hair tightened, and I opened wider for him, urging him on. He obliged with slow purposeful thrusts into my mouth, each time testing the limit of how much I could take.

"*God damn*," he groaned, pulling free of my lips to allow me a gasping breath, appreciating the angle of me on my knees for him maybe a little too much. "Where the fuck have you been?"

I opened my mouth for him again, but he jerked me back up to standing, crushing his lips to mine instead, his tongue slipping in to taste himself on my tongue. I yelped into his mouth, my core tightening, flipping as if I dived off a cliff instead headfirst into him. The sensation scattered out into my limbs like the roll of thunder.

My hands went around his neck, and he lifted my legs from the ground, guiding them to wrap around his middle, his erection pressing flat against my soaked entrance.

"Please tell me you're on some kind of birth control,"

he muttered between vicious kisses that were leaving me without any air left in my lungs. Making me dizzy. Drunk off the feel of him.

"I am," I hiccupped, and he grimaced, his hips swaying back as he adjusted his angle. My lips parted on a surprised gasp just a second before he fully sheathed himself inside me, my back meeting the wall behind me with a wet thud.

The push of his cock was like a punch against the dam of my cervix. A hard breath gasped from my lips, and I clawed at his tatted back, my eyes rolling at the blissful fullness of him buried deep inside me. The sound of his own pleasure, loud in my ears, almost had me coming undone right there and then.

There was nothing and I meant fucking *nothing* hotter than a man who wasn't afraid to make some noise in the bedroom.

"You're so fucking wet for me, Becca," he crooned against my cheek, his stubble scraping along my jaw. I rolled my hips against him, begging him without words to *move*.

I needed him to fuck me hard. Fuck me raw. It'd been months. *Months* since I'd been with anyone, and fuck what I said about not needing more than a few toys to get me by. There was *nothing* better than this.

Kaleb wrapped his thick arms around me, gripping me hard to keep me in place for him against the wall as he straight up abused my pussy. He jackhammered my pussy, grunting with every thrust that somehow managed to hit deeper, better, than the last, reaching parts of me with nerve endings I didn't even know I had.

He shuddered, burying his face in my wet hair as he fucked me against the wall, his breathing becoming stilted. Ragged. Signaling that he was close.

He growled, dropping my legs to let them fall before jerking out of me only to spin me around, pressing my chest flat against the wall as he entered me again from behind.

My breath fogged the tile as he gripped my hips, bending at his knees to get the perfect angle to buck up into me with hard, quick strokes. *"Fuck me,"* he choked out, his breaths becoming labored, signaling that he was close.

*"Harder,"* I urged him, pushing my ass into his lower abdomen, arching my back to help him push up deeper.

Kaleb pushed a hand between my stomach and the wall, dragging rough fingers low to grab me by the cunt. My fingernails dug into the grooves in the tile as he rubbed my clit hard and fast, his fingers gliding back and forth through my slippery wetness as he continued to fuck me from behind.

"Come on, Becca," he pleaded. "Come for me."

The strain in his voice twisted something in my chest, wringing my orgasm from me ready or not as he settled on the perfect pressure and rhythm with both his fingertips and his cock.

"Fuck!" I shouted against the wall as my core tightened, gushing for him as his voice rose to meet mine in rough panting groans, growing higher and higher until…

I *detonated,* screaming my release as my vision splintered into a thousand broken pieces, my pussy tightening around him as he poured into me. My heart beat a violent rhythm in my chest, skipping beats as every muscle tensed, burning brightly. Aching so fucking sweetly my eyes watered with the force of it.

And just as swiftly, my body went limp against the wall, knees giving out, legs refusing to hold me up as I struggled to gulp air into my lungs, my body trembling from the aftershocks. Kaleb pulled me to him as he slid down against the wall, and I could do little more than fall with him, my head lolling back against his chest, our feet splayed out past the shower curtain.

"That was…" Kaleb trailed off, dropping his cheek against my head.

"Never going to happen again," I finished between panting breaths, trying unsuccessfully to regather my strength. Pull away.

I felt his chest rumble beneath me with quiet laughter and my irritation came crashing back with a vengeance.

"Fuck you," I shoved him without any real strength behind it, using his beefy chest to push myself up from the floor. "And your stupid fat cock."

His lips pulled to one side, exposing that single dimple in his cheek as the water rushed over his head in a steady stream. He peered up at me through one slitted eye as he opened his mouth to gulp down some water.

"You just did," he teased, and heat rushed up my neck.

I reached over, twisting the shower knob to frigid bitch temperature with a smirk of my own before drawing the curtain back shut and rushing out of the changing room. I threw a towel around myself, the sound of his curses following me all the way out of the yoga studio.

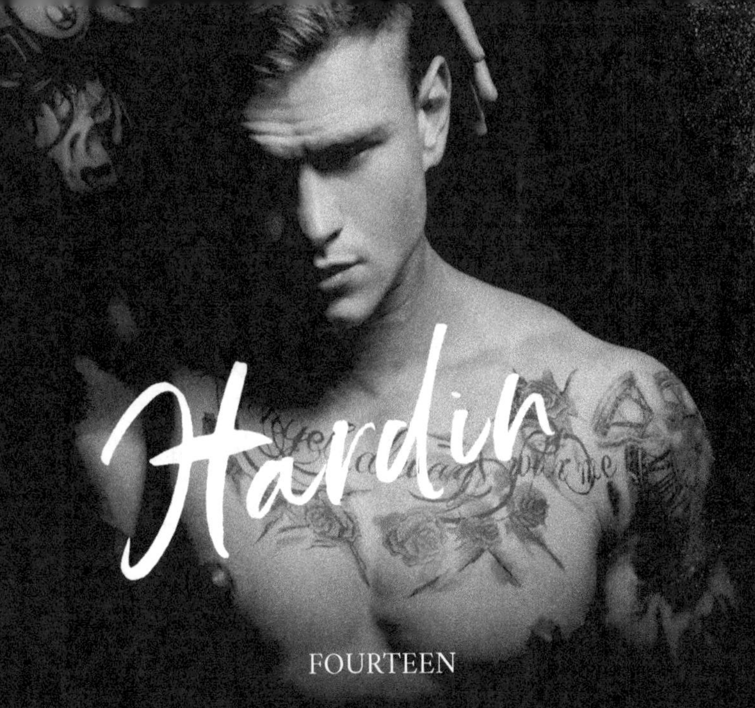

# FOURTEEN

"My boys!" Ma crooned, ushering us into the house. It smelled of her famous brown sugar meatballs and mashed potatoes and for the first time in days I actually felt hungry.

"Come on, you're late," she chided, dragging Kaleb along by the wrist. "Dinner's going to get cold. Help me bring everything to the table, would you?"

"Where's Dad?" Kaleb asked, letting her lead him off to the kitchen while I went in search of Dad myself.

My stomach growled, panging painfully and I cleared my throat, fighting the urge to maintain an upright position. After the shit that went down at the meet with The Warden out in the canyon, I couldn't focus on anything but finding these fuckers.

Well, that and my ever fucking persistent fascination with Rebecca Hart. I thought after she told me off the other night that would be it, but no. I still had to exert massive amounts of control to stay away from her. Every time I drove past Death Before Decaf—and I drove by way too fucking often—it was a study in resistance not to drive right through the front of the building and...

I exhaled heavily, banishing the thoughts from my mind.

I figured Becca was like a bad habit. All I needed to do was resist her long enough and I'd be free.

~~I didn't want to be free.~~

I needed to be free.

"Dad?" I called, pushing through the door to his study where I found him on the phone, talking in hushed whispers to someone on the other line as he poured over documents scattered over the surface of his desk.

He held up a finger, telling me to hold on as his face began to redden, his knuckles turning white as he collapsed the phone to his ear. "Fucking put me through, Teresa. I need to speak with him. It's urgent."

Dad stood, swiping a palm down his face, listening to something Teresa was saying on the other end of the call.

I leaned against the wall, crossing my arms to wait, trying to hear what she was saying on the other end of the call. Teresa was Senator Murphy's assistant and he'd been in our pocket ever since Dad started bank rolling his campaigns more than eight years ago.

"Bullshit!" Dad shouted down the line, pounding the side of a clenched fist down on his desk, making several pens roll to the floor. "Teresa, you listen good, if he..."

Dad trailed off, pulling the phone from his ear to stare

at the screen incredulously. "The bitch hung up on me," he sneered, chucking his phone across his office before falling down into his chair, putting his face in his hands.

"Ma'll have your balls if she finds you in here." I sniffed, shaking my head at the ridiculousness of it. Here we were practically at war but if Dad went against his words to reserve Friday evenings for 'family time' Ma would literally have his balls. Or his head. Depending on her mood.

"Yeah, well we have bigger fucking problems, Son."

"We've lost Senator Murphy?"

He lifted his head, rubbing at the scruff along his jaw with a solemn nod. "Looks that way. Costa isn't taking my calls, either."

My stomach soured.

"The mayor, too? Jesus fucking Christ. It's them, isn't it? The Sons. It has to be."

Dad lifted his slate gray gaze to the ceiling, thinking. "It can't be. There's no way some foreign fucks can just walk in here and undo years' worth of loyal partnerships."

"But they did," I argued. "The Warden admitted as much."

"But the Senator? Mayor Costa?" He shook his head again. "I don't buy it. I need to speak to them myself. In person. They won't take my calls, but I'd like to see them try to stop me from kicking down their pristine office doors."

I lifted a brow. "Let me know if you want company for that. Any leads on where they're holding up?"

Pushing off the wall, I went to his desk, bracing my

knuckles on the edge as I stared down at all the maps and documents spread out over the worn wood.

"We think it's possible they're in Pasadena. I have the guys on it but every other potential location has turned out to be a bust."

"What about our inventory situation?"

We'd taken all the guns and ammo The Warden and his men brought with them to the meet, but it was nowhere near enough to replenish the stock that was confiscated from us in the raid.

"Working on it. Might have another supplier. A Mexican cartel Diesel worked with when they were dealing with the Aces up north."

"And the other gangs?"

His jaw clenched at the mention of them.

My Dad had no less than five lower level gangs operating in this territory and all of them operated only with his express permission. They all paid tribute *to him*. And in a couple weeks, it would be time to collect their monthly dues.

"They've been useless," he replied eventually. "Not a single one has any intel that's proved useful."

"I find that hard to believe."

His stony gaze met mine. "So do I."

"Dinner!" Ma called from somewhere near the dining room and Dad shot to his feet.

"*Out*," he hissed, rushing around his desk to shove me from his study and into the dining room just in time for Ma to round the corner, a hot oven dish between her mitted hands.

She set it down in the center of the long cherry table, her blue eyes flicking up to meet Dad's with cold fire in their depths. Ma rose, putting her mitted hands on her hips as Kaleb entered behind her, juggling three other serving dishes piled high with potatoes, corn, and salad.

Ma cocked her head at Dad, a lethal warning hiding behind the tight smile she wore. "You weren't working, were you, dear?"

"No, my love." He cleared his throat, coming around the table to take the mitts from her hands and lay a light kiss on her right cheek. "Of course not. What can I help with?"

She lifted a brow at him before shaking her head with a deep, rumbling laugh that started in her belly, stealing the mitts back from him to swat him with them. "What is it with men? Always asking if there's anything they can help with *after* the work is done. You can help your sons with clean up, Damien. Oh! And go get the scotch from the bar. You know the one."

"Right," Dad said, his voice tight as he left the room in search of Ma's good scotch.

"Well, go on, sit." Ma flicked her wrists, gesturing to the chairs at the table. I noticed there was one setting too many, and narrowed my gaze at her as I sat down like I was told.

It was hard to rectify the woman before me with the one I knew as a child. The sad housewife who ran on autopilot, barely making it through each day, with the formidable woman who took a bullet for her husband and ruled the Saints at his side for years before she decided she'd had enough of bloodshed and bullets to last a lifetime.

There was no one I respected more.

"Who's that for?" Kaleb asked, indicating the place setting next to his own, still standing behind his chair, hands gripping the back.

"We have company tonight," Ma announced, sliding into her seat at the head of the table, laying her napkin over her lap just as Dad came back with her scotch and a glass. He filled it with two fingers of the golden liquid and set the decanter down next to her cup, passing out a few beers to me and Hardin. We'd take our scotch after dinner. Well, Kaleb would. Leaving me to drive his inebriated ass home.

"What do you mean, *company*?" Kaleb asked, his jaw ticking.

"I invited the DeLuca girl. She should be here any—"

The doorbell rang and Kaleb pulled his fingers from the chairback, eyes darkening.

"I'll get it, Kaleb," Ma said, seemingly oblivious to Kaleb's sudden mood shift.

"No, Ma," Kaleb said, putting a palm on her shoulder to keep her seated before he left the dining room. "Allow me."

He came home with that *just fucked* glow that told me he'd finally gotten himself laid after a near week sabbatical and he'd been chipper as all hell ever since. But now...?

I mean, Gillian DeLuca was more annoying than a

gnat on a good day, but he never let her get to him before. I was missing something.

Dad took his seat across from Ma, lifting a brow in question at Kaleb's behavior. I shrugged.

"Load me up, would you, Hardin?"

Ma passed me her plate, and I began piling it high with meatballs. I tried to pass it back, but she shook her head. "What? Am I on a diet?"

I put another two scoops onto her plate until she was satisfied. Down the hall, I could hear my brother and Gillian whispering harshly. Not loud enough to make out what they were saying, but loud enough to know it wasn't a pleasant exchange.

"What is going on over there?" Ma asked, lifting her napkin from her lap. I put my hand atop hers on the table and shook my head.

"Leave it, Ma."

"Is this because of *her?*" Gillian's nasally voice rose above the din of Kaleb's angry whispering. "That stupid slut!"

The crack of flesh hitting flesh rang out through the house, and I would've told you my brother would never hit a woman, but right now, I couldn't be sure if Gillian hit him or if it was the other way around.

Because I knew exactly which *her* Gillian was referring to and hearing the fucking cunt call Becca a slut had me gripping the underside of the table to keep seated. Heat flushed through my stomach and my skin bristled with it.

*Not your problem, Hardin.*

"Get the fuck out, Gill," Kaleb said, clear as crystal, the

five words given creed with the sharp slam of the door behind them.

My brother stormed back into the dining room, dragging his chair noisily from the table to sit down.

"What has gotten into—"

"*Ma,*" Kaleb cut her off. "Don't."

Ma reeled back from his words, her eyes widening with insult. "Excuse me? I invite someone to dinner and you think you can just—"

"I don't want her here, Ma," Kaleb cut her off again.

"Kaleb," Dad warned. "Respect your mother."

Kaleb inhaled through his nose, turning to face Ma with a forced expression of calm. "Ma," he started. "I would appreciate it if you did not invite Gill to our *family* dinners or bring her to my house. She is not welcome there, and I don't want anything to do with her. She's a fucking—*sorry.*" He cleared his throat and tried again.

"She's not a good person and I'm pretty sure if I ever fucked her, which is clearly what you're going for—I'd end up with crabs or something worse. I'm not interested, and I do not like her. Besides, Ma, why the hell would you invite her to dinner? You know Hardin won't say a damn word if she's here. Did you think about that? Hmm?"

Ma frowned, she might've disagreed with everything Kale said, until that last part. She turned her eyes on me, the fury that'd been there a moment before snuffed out by guilt. "Sorry, Hardin, your brother's right."

Then she turned back to Kaleb. "But regardless, you know better than to treat a woman that way."

"If you can call that a woman."

"Kaleb!"

"All right, all right," Dad said, lifting his hands in a gesture of finality as he cut Kaleb a glare. "That's enough. Stop it before your Ma busts out the garden shears, yeah?"

Kaleb slumped in his seat, running his index finger down the condensation on his beer bottle before drawing it up for a long swallow. "Sorry, Ma," he said when he pulled it away from his lips, rubbing the back of his hand across them.

Ma nodded triumphantly with a huff, reaching over to slap Kaleb's forearm with her knuckles. "Pass the potatoes."

"How's Archer?" I asked Dad, popping a meatball in my mouth and immediately following it up with a second one.

*Fuck, that's good.*

I pushed in a third for good measure, my mouth watering at the sweet browned meat.

"You know Arch," Dad replied, swirling his beer bottle. "One of the toughest sons of bitches I know. He's already on his feet even though I told him to stay laid up for a bit."

"Mmm."

There still wasn't a single motherfucker I wasn't considering a potential leak, shot in the stomach or not, Archer could still be it.

"Have you heard from Maggie yet?" Ma asked Dad, and Kaleb coughed uncomfortably, shifting in his seat. He always was an absolute shit liar.

Dad watched Kaleb as he answered Ma. "No. She still won't take my calls."

"I've brought her a few casseroles too but she never invites me in and I don't want to push, you know? I just feel so bad for her. The Chief was a good man. A good husband. A good father. Taken too soon."

"Kaleb?" Dad pried, setting his fork down against his plate with a clatter to fold his fingers together over his unfinished dinner. "You wouldn't happen to know how Maggie's doing, would you?"

Kaleb busied himself spearing a couple meatballs with his dinner knife to pop into his mouth. "Nope," he said around the mouthful, but his gaze flicked up to me, giving his ass away.

Fuck, Kale.

Dad turned to me, waiting.

"Fine," I sighed, tossing my fork down onto my empty plate that'd been overloaded only a few minutes before. "We went to see her."

"And she let you in?" Ma asked, surprised.

Kaleb scratched the back of his neck. "Didn't really give her a choice."

"Boys!"

Ma put a hand to her chest. "Maggie is grieving, how could you just barge in on her at a time like this."

"We heard a scream," Kaleb was quick to defend us. "Turned out it was just Maggie, *uh*, crying in her bedroom, but…"

Dad pinched the bridge of his nose with a sigh.

"It's a good thing we went," I added, skipping over the bits that didn't fucking matter. "She told us Chief Andrews *didn't* die of a heart attack."

Dad jerked his head up, his slate eyes boring into me. "What? What'd she say?"

"Not much. She was worried about her son. Clearly they threatened her. But she did admit that *someone* killed the Chief, and said that if she ever saw who it was again, she'd recognize them."

Dad sat back in his seat, his gaze shifting over the table as he considered this new information.

It was Ma's muffled curse that broke the silence, and when I turned to her, it was to find her flipping her dinner knife around between her fingers, breathing heavily. The spark of the rage I'd inherited from both my parents alight in her eyes. Fucking *dancing*.

"Sloane?" Dad asked hesitantly as Ma slammed to her feet, reeling her arm back to impale the dining table with the knife.

"This is those bastards trying to claim your turf, isn't it?"

Apparently, her rule of no work talk during dinner was being tossed. Good. As much as Mom wanted to remain ignorant to the worst of it these days, she needed to know this. She needed to be aware and wary.

Dad couldn't look her in the eyes when he replied. "It's likely. Yes."

Ma threw her hands up.

"Come on, Sloane, sit down," Dad urged. "We're handling it."

"If you were *handling it,* Chief Andrews wouldn't..." She trailed off, losing her steam. She wouldn't finish the sentence, but we all knew what she was about to say. She regretted it before she could even get the words out of her mouth. "Well, clearly, you could use a little help."

Dad shook his head, lifting a hand in a halting gesture. "Sloane, I'm not asking for you to—"

"You don't have to," she interrupted him. "Maggie's *my friend.* Dave Andrews, too. These assholes are on *our land.* Messing with *our people*. It's more serious than you were letting on, Damien."

"Fuck, Slo, I didn't want to worry you. Like I said, we're handling it."

She put her hands on her hips. "Yes," she agreed. "*We are.*"

Ma sank back into her seat and picked up her scotch, downing it in one, baring her teeth at the burn when she was through.

I didn't think there was a damn thing that would ever make her pick up her gun again, but apparently I was wrong.

Ma yanked her dinner knife from the table, wiping it on her napkin before proceeding to hack through the rest of her meatballs.

"Eat your fuckin' dinner."

The sound of cutlery scraping porcelain was the only thing that broke the silence for the rest of dinner.

# *Kaleb*

FIFTEEN

Hardin and I tried to excuse ourselves after supper but like fuck that was happening.

"*Ah ah*!" Ma chided, catching us by the front door. "Where do you think you're going?"

"Thought maybe you and Dad would want to talk, you know, alone."

She shook her head, her long graying black hair swaying with the motion. "Nice try, smartass."

I rolled my eyes at Hardin, kicking my shoes back off to trudge to the kitchen.

"You too," Ma snapped at Hardin behind me. "Your Dad's already in there, and he seems hellbent on breaking the good china."

He grunted, following me back into the heart of the house, the pair of us following the sound of clattering porcelain the whole way.

Ma wasn't wrong. Dad was there, elbow deep in soapy water at the farmhouse style sink, scrubbing the dinner plates like they owed him money.

Side note: you did *not* want to owe my dad money.

He muttered to himself as he worked, a dish towel slung over his shoulder. The formidable Damien St. Vincent reduced to the role of house husband for the next thirty minutes while we cleaned Ma's kitchen spotless.

"Thought you'd make a break for it, eh, boys?" Dad joked without any mirth as Ma strolled through the kitchen toward the sitting room where she'd watch her soaps until everything was to her satisfaction.

Or maybe not. Ma continued through the sitting room and went straight for the side door to the garage.

…and the gun safe Dad had installed below where he parked his truck. She wasn't messing around.

Ma stopped leading the gang with Dad before we were properly inducted. I'd never seen her operate in that capacity. No more than smelling lead and copper on her clothes when she came in late to kiss us goodnight.

"Tried," I said with a shrug, elbowing Dad out of the way to take over washing before he actually did bust up Ma's china and she had all our asses. "Failed."

"'the hell you doing?"

"You're going to break shit. Go wipe down the stove or something."

Hardin nicked the dish towel from Dad's shoulder and started drying the dishes in the rack with a knot between his brows. I knew he was in Dad's study with him while I helped Ma get the food ready and wondered what he'd learned.

Clearly, it wasn't anything good.

…and the shit pile just kept fucking growing.

"I want you boys to stick together," Dad said once he was done scrubbing the grease splatter from the top of the stove. "I said it before, but I'll say it again now. You don't go anywhere alone. You're never unarmed. You got that? Not until we find these bastards and deal with them."

"Daddy didn't raise no fools," I said, trying to lighten the mood, but Dad just stared at me deadpan. Totally unimpressed. As if I wasn't the comedic genius I was.

Tough fucking crowd.

I coughed. "Right. Yeah, Dad. We're not fuckin' teenagers anymore. I mean, hell, Hardin'll be twenty-four next month. That's the age you were when you split off from Uncle Diesel and Uncle Ransom to run your own gang."

Dad nodded to himself. "I know. I know."

I didn't mention to Dad that Hardin and I were decidedly *not* sticking together lately. When he wasn't holed up in his room doing god knew what on his computers he was driving around the streets of Santa Clarita. The Row in particular. And I had a pretty good idea why. Or rather… *who.*

*I stuck my dick in it so it's mine.*

My fucking childish brain knew no bounds.

I wasn't any better than my big bro, though. Between making sure my baby was ready for the race this weekend and stalking Becca at the yoga studio… safe to say I was a little distracted. And also at times, entirely unarmed.

My brother's gaze met mine, and an unspoken agreement passed between us. Dad was right. We needed to watch each other's backs.

No more distractions. Not until this was handled.

"So, who's the girl?" Dad asked, not so smoothly changing the subject as he leaned against the counter, letting me and Hardin finish the rest of the cleaning without him as he sipped his scotch.

Where the fuck was mine?

"What girl?" I asked, shaking soapy water from my hands as the sink drained. I fingered a glass from the cupboard and filled it with a fourth of scotch, hopping up onto the counter to get off my feet.

Dad lowered the scotch from his lips with a disbelieving smirk. "Whatever girl has Gillian DeLuca about ready to tear your face off."

I sipped the golden liquid, letting it mellow in my mouth, burning out the taste of the cherry cigar I had after dinner before swallowing it. "Oh, that girl."

"Yeah. *That girl.* Sounds like more than a lay. That's not like you."

He was doing a shit job of pretending to be not all that interested when in fact, I knew that he'd give me grandma's old wedding ring in a heartbeat if it meant I'd stop sticking my dick in anything with a decent pair of tits.

The man thought I didn't have standards. Fuck that. I *had* standards, and I was careful to always use a condom.

Well, except for my afternoon delight with Becca yesterday. I wasn't an idiot. I wasn't about to get some bitch pregnant or wind up with an STD.

And lately, my standards had only gotten higher.

I'd hit my peak and now no other pair of tits would ever measure up.

Hardin slammed the pantry shut and stomped out to the garage with Ma, his body coiled like a viper. Good thing Ma knew how to charm that snake, or I'd worry for her immediate safety.

This house was one of the only places I rarely saw Hardin get angry, and a good deal of that had to do with Ma. Her presence just... released him somehow.

But not right now.

"I don't know what she is," I admitted. "But I can't stop thinking about her."

"Do I know her?"

I pursed my lips, shaking my head. "Don't think so. She's new here. Moved up from Thorn Valley."

"*What?*" Dad snapped, his easy tone dropped in an instant. I twisted to meet his stare, finding him pale faced. A vein protruding in his temple.

"Dad?"

"Who is she?" he demanded, setting his scotch down with a hard knock on the counter. Cocking his head at me. "What's her name?"

My brows furrowed. "Why?"

"*Her name,* Kaleb." He closed the gap between us, all but barking in my face even though I had an entire head on him sitting up high on the counter like I was.

"Christ, okay," I hissed, leaning back from the spittle that was no doubt about to start flying from his feral mouth. "Her name's Rebecca. Rebecca Hart. She's that girl that's friends with Ava Jade. The one who got—"

"I know who she is," Dad sneered, his upper lip curling as he stepped back, throwing a hand through his hair.

"You do?"

Stupid question. Of course he did. He went up there to check on Diesel and his shit with the Aces right around the time Becca was shot. I was sure he heard about it. But why was he so damn upset?

Why did it matter if I was seeing her?

Fuck.

*Seeing her?*

What, was I about to go fucking steady now?

*Jesus.*

"Yeah, I know her," Dad said, his voice sounding far away. He muttered something I didn't catch under his breath before he managed to smooth out the sharp lines in his face. "And you'll stay away from her, do you hear me?"

"What? Why?"

"It doesn't matter why," he snapped, pointing toward me with two ringed fingers. "You stay away from that girl. That's an order."

"But Dad—"

"*Stay away from her.* I don't want her involved with you. Involved with any of this shit. You leave her the fuck out of it."

An irrational anger simmered in my gut, laced with

something like guilt. I didn't want to stay away from her. Quite the opposite, but Dad was right about one thing; with all the heat on us right now it would be stupid of me to get close to anyone, let alone a girl who I actually…

Shit, I was a fucking goner.

*"Kaleb."*

"All right! Fuck, Dad. Yeah. I heard you."

I understood what he was saying, but what I didn't understand was *why* he was saying it. Why did Dad give two shits about some chick from Thorn Valley?

I was about to open my yap and ask him just that when he snatched the bottle of scotch and his glass from the counter and left the kitchen, crossing the house to shut himself into his study.

My phone vibrated in my pocket after the house finished rattling from his slamming the door of his study shut behind him.

**Clay: Becca's working 11-4 tomorrow. Then she has plans to go shopping with her roommate. The gay one.**

**Kaleb: His name's Toby, dickhead.**

**Clay: Right. Toby. Sorry. Sounds like they might be going to the race tomorrow night, too.**

I bit the inside of my cheek, knowing that her being there would make my avoiding her fucking impossible. There was no way I had enough self-control to stay away if she was right there. I was a Saint, but I wasn't a damn celibate priest.

**Kaleb: All right, just keep tabs on her for me, would you?**

**Clay: You got it.**

I pulled up the tracking app on my phone. The one that received a GPS ping from the device I planted in her purse. Exchanged for the one that'd already been there. She was at home now. 82 Carlton Street. And if Clay's sleuthing skills were to be trusted, she was in apartment five, the one at the very top of the building.

### SIXTEEN

"I feel like I'm naked," I groaned. "Is this really necessary?"

I tugged at the tight little short shorts Toby dressed me up in. Paired with the tit squishing tank top that resembled something closer to a bra and the heels with the strappy laces that went up to my knees, I looked good. But good in the way a high priced hooker looked good.

Not exactly the vibe I was trying to push out into the universe.

…even if I wasn't exactly *fasting* anymore.

"Yeah, Tobes," Katie agreed, removing the little neon mesh top he gave her in favor of a baggy t-shirt in a light blue color. "I don't know about that top. It was way too pink."

"It's race night!" Toby argued, leaning over the bathroom counter to rub a dark charcoal liner over the rims of his eyes. His trademark look. "Nothing is too slutty or too pink for race night."

"If Kate gets to wear that baggy ass t-shirt, then I'm changing," I decided, but Toby caught me before I could leave the bathroom.

"Girl, you look hot as hell. Literally, *I'd* fuck you and I'm not even straight, okay."

I preened a little at the compliment, but still, this outfit screamed trouble, and I was trying my very best to stay far away from that. Whether or not I was succeeding was beside the point.

"Fine," I acquiesced. "But I'm putting a sweater over it."

"*Nuh uh*," Toby disagreed. "Don't you dare coat that sinful delight in cashmere. Use my jean jacket. It's hung up by the door. Fits the whole…" He gestured to all of me with pride-filled eyes at his monstrous creation. "*Vibe.*"

I gave my eyes a roll but I did what he said, dragging my ass to the front room, where a jean jacket was hung by the door. The one side in the front was almost entirely covered in enamel pins. There had to be at least nine different animated fandoms represented and several others I didn't recognize.

At least we shared the same taste in music and TV so I wouldn't mind repping his faves tonight.

Outside the door, I heard the shuffle of feet over the music playing low from Kate's Bluetooth speaker in the bathroom. I frowned, pressing my eye to the peephole in time to see what I thought was someone going down the stairs.

I didn't think much of it until I remembered ours was the only apartment on the top floor and all of us were home. Hardin's stupid face popped into my head, as it tended to do lately, and I ripped open the door, calling down the stairwell.

"Hello? Is someone there? Hardin, if that's you, I swear to…"

I let the words trail off, unclenching my fists, closing my eyes to take a deep breath and shut the door.

I wasn't even sure I saw someone.

And just because Hardin liked to sit in the cafe and drink coffee for three hours and stare down other guys who dared speak to me didn't mean he was *stalking* me. That was a bit of a jump, no?

*Unless he found out what you did with his brother two days ago...*

I chewed my lip. At least then he would really leave me alone, right? Who would want their brother's sloppy seconds?

Even though I hadn't seen Hardin in the cafe since that Thursday, it didn't mean I hadn't *seen* him.

I'd had to scrap three abstract paintings and counting because somehow they all wound up looking kind of sort of like *him*. Well, save for the one that wound up looking suspiciously like his brother's fat cock, but…

Yeah. I was fucked.

The denim felt a bit stiff as I slid my arms into the sleeves and shrugged it on, folding the collar flat instead of leaving it popped up like Toby usually did. I thought for sure I'd be swimming in it with Toby being so tall, but when I went to check in the bathroom mirror, I found, as usual, Toby was right.

It did fit the *vibe*.

"You have absolutely no right to look better in my jacket than I do," Toby said with a mock sigh. "But I guess I'll forgive you."

A little laugh bubbled up my throat, and I found myself smiling at my reflection. The jacket made my shoulders appear wider, stronger, more… intimidating. And the fact that it was just a bit longer on me than it should've been meant that if I wanted it to, it would cover the bulk of the sex kitten outfit Toby stuffed me into.

With my usually straight hair teased up into a mass of voluminous curls—the transformation a la Sandy in Grease—I felt like a real race queen. All I needed was a cigarette and the look would be complete. But since this bitch didn't do tobacco, a joint would have to do.

"Go on, say it," Toby said, looking at me smugly through the mirror as he finished with his eyeliner.

I sighed.

"*Say it.*"

"You were right, Tobes. There, you happy?"

"Yes! God, I will literally never tire of hearing that."

Toby tapped his phone and shrieked, tossing his eyeliner on the counter. He snatched my hand, his freshly polished nails glistening on the opposite hand as he swatted Kate's behind. "Come on, sexy ladies, Uber's here. It's go time!"

A thrill went through me as Toby dragged us from the apartment. The anticipation of *something* coming like a sixth sense I couldn't shake. It made my heart thud hard and fast against the wall of my ribs. Made my skin prickle with something halfway between anxiety and excitement. Like I was balancing on a tightrope, and if I wasn't careful, it would snap beneath my feet.

We had the Uber drop us off a solid half mile from where the race was. It was a rule, apparently. You needed to come in on foot.

If it was a matter of not letting the Uber drivers know where you were going or what was going on way out in the canyon, then I really didn't see the point.

The instant we stepped out of the Uber, the thump of bass could be heard even at this distance. And over the ridge of the canyon to the east, lights flashed up toward the sky in blue and pink and green. Cars were littered along the access road, abandoned like used condoms in the dirt.

We used our phones for flashlights as we tripped our way down the winding cracked pavement, our threesome growing the deeper in we got. Everyone on their way to the race grouping up in the dark, that pack mentality, safety in numbers, taking over.

My blisters had blisters by the time we made it over the hill and were able to look down on the insanity below, but I found I didn't care. Standing there atop the hill looking down on all the tiny-looking people crowded in the valley below, I felt excited and powerful. Ready to take on the world.

It also could've been the whiskey I drank during the walk. Or the joint I shared with Toby. But that wasn't important.

"Holy shit," I found myself saying, the words no more than an exhalation of hot air as the lights below danced over us high above.

I wasn't sure what I expected, maybe a Bluetooth speaker and a bonfire in a barrel. But this?

This was *insane.*

Huge speakers were set up all around the road on both sides, the music ricocheting all around the canyon, rising to meet us, thumping in my chest. At least two hundred people filled the valley floor, broken off into groups. Dancing, drinking, hollering, smoking.

Neon and leather.

The smell of good weed and even better booze.

"Right?" Toby said, leaning in to rub my shoulder with his. "Nobody misses Race Night, baby girl. You'd be a fool to."

"Come on!" Kate squealed, snagging my hand from my side to drag me down the hill. Her excitement seemed to be contagious because the large group of us who'd walked most of the distance together, whooped and hollered, all but running down the hill to the valley floor in a wave. Bodies jostled me on both sides, laughter filled my ears.

I reached out a hand in search of Toby, afraid to lose him or that he'd be trampled by the stampede, but his fingers twisted with mine, and he let out a wolfish howl as we all hit the bottom of the hill and scattered, our group merging with the whole.

And just when I thought I couldn't get any more pumped, I saw a shock of black hair over near a truck bed on the side of the road. Tattooed fingers slid through the inky locks, and I would know him anywhere.

"Oh my god!" I shouted, releasing Toby and Kate. "I'll be right back!"

I pushed through the throng, the pulse of the music in my ears carrying me forward. The smile on my lips wide and genuine. "Rook!" I called. "Rook!"

I basically tackled him from behind, wrapping my arms around his upper back.

"Shit," he cursed, all but flinging me off him. I almost fell on my ass, but he caught me when he whirled around, recognition flaring in his dark eyes. "Becca?"

"In the flesh! Fuck, it's good to see a familiar face."

Even if the sight of him brought back some not so pleasant memories.

Rook leaned back to look me up and down, a slow, devious grin spreading on his lips. "*Damn.* I hardly recognized your scrawny ass." He lifted his hand, hollering over the music. "Hey! Grey, get your ass over here."

Grey?

My lips pulled even wider as the crowd parted for Greyson Winters. His dirty blonde hair had been cut shorter since I'd last seen him and it made me glad to see he wasn't using it to hide his eye anymore.

He wore his patch tonight as opposed to the glass eye

Ava Jade and the guys got him last Christmas, and it gave him an added air of danger and mystery.

If he was here too then maybe…

I lifted myself up on my toes, my heart in my throat as I scanned the crowd for my best friend. "Is Aves here?"

Grey pulled me into a hug, and I let him, even though I was still peering over his shoulder in search of Ava Jade.

"*Nah*," Rook answered, leaning in to shout in my ear as Grey pulled away. "She's still on tour."

I tried not to look too disappointed. I really was happy to see them both. When I turned back to face Rook, I found *my* flask in his tatted hand. He winked at me as he took a swig from it and passed it back. I hadn't even felt him take it. The sneaky bastard.

I took another sip too even though I was already feeling the effects of the whiskey. I offered it to Grey next, but he shook his head.

"I'm driving," he said and I cocked my head at him.

He didn't mean…

"Just *couldn't* stay away, could you?" The familiarly frustrating sound of Kaleb St. Vincent's voice boomed above the sound of the music and I had just enough time to step out of his path as he crashed into the area where we all stood. Hardin was hot on his heels and Toby and Kate were making their way over, too. Toby's haughty stare fixed on Kaleb's perfectly sculpted ass.

Kaleb drew Grey into a massive man hug, thumping his back with a palm before turning to slap Rook's hand, drawing him in for a quick side hug. Hardin did the same, leaning in for half hugs with each of them.

I should've known they'd be here. It was race night in SoCal and they were the self-proclaimed Kings of the land. I resisted the urge to roll my eyes.

Grey's dark blue eye flashed with mischief as he fixed his stare on Kaleb. "How could I deny the chance to leave your ass in the dust?"

"*Oh*," Kaleb said, drawing out the sound. "Okay, big talker. Want to put some money down?"

"I'm in," Rook said, fingering a rolled bundle of hundreds from the inside of his leather jacket. I noticed the ghost tattoo on his knuckle and smiled at the tribute to my best friend. "I've got ten grand on Grey."

Holy fuck.

Kate and Toby flanked me on both sides, the three of us standing on the sidelines of the exchange as they all placed their bets. Apparently, Grey was going to race Kaleb, and I couldn't fucking wait to see Grey absolutely destroy him. Even with only one eye, I'd never met a driver better than Grey.

He was unbeatable. There was just no way.

Lifting my chin, a coy smile pulled at my lips as I pulled the four hundred dollars Toby had gotten me earlier tonight from the lining of my bra. It was no ten grand, but it would make my point.

"Four hundred on Grey."

Kaleb's back stiffened. He turned on his heel, taking me in as if he didn't even know I was there. I supposed, like Rook, he probably didn't recognize me at first. With the wild curls in my hair and the long jacket over the slutty outfit I never would've chosen for myself but was now glad I'd agreed to wear.

Kaleb lapped up every inch of me, his eyes narrowing hungrily as I stuffed the four hundred dollar bills into his hand. His lips twisted as he looked down at the cash and back up at me.

"Betting against me, Vixen?"

"There's no way you'll beat Grey."

Kaleb lifted a brow, and behind him I saw Hardin's lips twitch up into a smile, like he knew something I didn't. It made me irrationally angry, my cold hands clenching into fists as he watched me wordlessly from where he stood next to Rook.

"What?" I snapped at him. "You got something you want to say, St. Vincent?"

His jaw twitched, teeth clenching behind no longer smirking lips.

"Didn't think so," I added for good measure, the whiskey giving me a confidence boost, stroking the fire in my belly with its acid stain.

Kaleb winced, as if offended on his brother's behalf, or maybe he was worried his brother was going to do something about my smart mouth. But something told me he wouldn't. He was big and tough and oh so fucking scary with his whole silent act, but he wouldn't hurt me. I just knew it.

"I take it you know each other," Rook said, running his tongue over his teeth, the skin around his eyes crinkling as his sharp gaze slid back and forth between Hardin, Kaleb, and me.

When none of us answered, Rook let out a low dangerous chuckle, his eyes flicking to my roommates on either side of me. "Who're your friends, Becks?"

I blinked, the hot irritation in my stomach fading in an instant. "Fuck. Right. Uh, this is Toby, and this is Kate. They're my roommates. Well, and my co-workers. Kate, Toby, this is Greyson Winters and Rook Clayton—*er—sorry.* I guess you're both St. Crows, now."

I forgot they finally made the name change legal over the summer.

Toby was eager as hell to take the opportunity to introduce himself to them, wrapped Rook's hand up in both of his to shake with a too-wide smile.

I cleared my throat, dragging him back by the back of his jacket. "Not gay," I whispered in his ear. "And he's dating my best friend."

"What about mister eye patch over there?"

"Also dating my best friend."

"The same one?"

Toby lifted a brow at me, and I half sighed, half laughed. "I'll explain later."

"Please do. I am hella curious."

Kate blushed as she shook hands with both Grey and Rook, her fingers wringing the hem of her shirt as she rushed back to stand with us on the outer edge of the group.

"So, who do I collect my payout from when you lose?" I asked Kaleb sweetly.

He considered me for a second and then something

sparked in his gray sky eyes. Something that made my toes curl and all the breath rush from my lungs.

"You won't be collecting anything, Vixen. I never lose. In fact…" he paused for dramatic effect, peeling his gaze from me to scan the crowd as he raised his hands high in the air and roared loudly for all to hear.

"Let's have a round of fucking applause for tonight's *Race Queen.*"

Oh no.

I tried to back away, vanish, disappear, go invisible in the crowd, but Toby and Kate cheered in my ears, their hands clapping on my back, stopping me from going anywhere. All around me whoops and cheers erupted. Drinks sloshed over the red brown dirt at our feet. The lights pulsed, strobing until every movement of Kaleb's appeared stilted and broken as he fisted a hand in the jacket I wore, pulling my face close to his.

"Now you'll have a front row seat when I win. Hold on to your tits, Vixen, it's going to be a wild fucking ride."

He released me and shouldered past, his spiced rum and cherry cigar scent filling my nose until I was dizzy with it.

"Oh my god!" Toby was saying while Kate jumped up and down, proclaiming me the luckiest bitch in the universe as he tugged at my arm. But my attention was being held hostage elsewhere. Hardin watched me darkly from where he stood, hulking next to Rook, his expression betraying nothing. He looked away first, breaking the spell, the line of his jaw and cheekbones even more pronounced in the strobing lights.

He stalked toward me, each step seeming to bring him two steps closer as the lights continued to strobe. I stood my ground, waiting for the inevitable fallout I'd earned for taunting a King, but he walked right past me, following Kaleb's path away from the group. Away from me.

My brows knitted together, confused at the feelings of disappointment hollowing out my gut. I filled the empty void with another long swallow of whiskey, twisting the cap back on the flask to toss it to Rook, who caught it easily from the air with one hand, lifting it in a salute.

"Girl, you must have horseshoes up your ass or something," Toby was saying. "Your first time at race night and you're already chosen to ride shotty as tonight's Queen! *Ugh*, so unfair."

The gravity of it hit me like a wall of bricks, and I spread my arms out, looking for something to hold on to as I almost lost my footing. Grey steadied me, a look of concern drawing the brow over his left eye down. "Becca, you all right?"

I shook my head, coming back to myself all at once, my limbs heavy and heart pounding against my ribcage. "No one's ever crashed, right?"

Was I really going to do this?

Did I want to get into a goddamned *race car* with Kaleb St. Vincent?

I could run. If I left now he wouldn't be able to catch up to me.

Grey patted my back in a gesture that was meant to be comforting but only made me bristle even more.

"Don't worry, Becks. Kale's a good driver," Rook hollered, still nursing my whiskey.

"He fucking should be," Grey added with a wink, his hand slipping from my back. "Who do you think taught him everything he knows?"

I lifted my brows and Grey nodded, pointing both thumbs at himself. "That's right. This guy. And your money's safe. The student isn't beating the master tonight."

That brought a little smirk to my lips, but it wasn't lost on me that neither of them had answered my question.

I bit my lower lip, still seriously considering making for the hills.

"Maybe don't tell Aves," I said with a wince. "She'd kill me if she knew I was going to do this."

"Fuck that," Rook barked. "She'd be right there in the backseat with you."

I knew he was right. The image of her with that glint of insanity in her eyes, the same slant of light that often gleamed on Rook's dark eyes, made me miss her even more.

Primal Ethos' Lodi show couldn't come fast enough. I needed to see my girl.

Somewhere in the distance, the throaty roar of an engine revving sent a wave of cheers through the crowd.

"Starting already?" Grey mused to himself, his low voice almost inaudible over the music, but somewhere, whoever was controlling the dials was already turning down. The crackle of a microphone scratched at my ears through the surround sound and I grimaced, squinting an eye as I took whatever dregs of whiskey remained in my flask back from Rook.

He made a point of pouting at me, but I was going to need the additional liquid courage if anyone actually expected me to get into what was basically a metal deathtrap with Kaleb.

I shook off my nerves as Grey jerked his head at Rook. "Show time," he said before turning to me with the sort of warm smile only Grey could give. "See you at the finish line. Watch for my tail lights."

"Good luck!" I called after him even though I knew he wouldn't need it. "Actually, wait!"

He paused.

"Who's racing with you?"

He jabbed a thumb at Rook.

"Could you maybe take one of my friends?"

The pair of them screeched noisily behind me.

Grey snorted a laugh. "Sure."

Rook threw up a hand like I'd ruined all his fun, and I gave him an apologetic, pained smile.

"Rock, paper, scissors?" Toby said behind me as an announcer came on over the speakers and they repeated the words in unison.

Toby slammed his hand down, his fingers spread wide, indicating paper, while Kate's hand remained in a balled fist. Paper beats rock.

"Yes!" Toby fist bumped the air and Kate really only seemed upset for half a second before she gave Toby a high five and told him she wanted to hear about every fucking minute or she would disown his ass.

"Next race is yours," I promised her, knowing somehow that I would be able to make good on that promise before pushing Toby toward Grey and mouthing *thank you* to my friend from Thorn Valley.

"All right, all right!" The announcer was saying, his voice loud enough to deafen, echoing around the canyon. "Racers to your vehicles! Looks like we're starting the party early tonight, folks!"

"Go!" Kate urged, pushing me through the crowd toward the road, where the angry growl of a second engine rose to meet the first, getting closer as they crept toward the starting line. Kate shoved me through the line of cheering race babes, out onto the road. "Just don't die, 'kay?"

Yeah. I would fucking try not to.

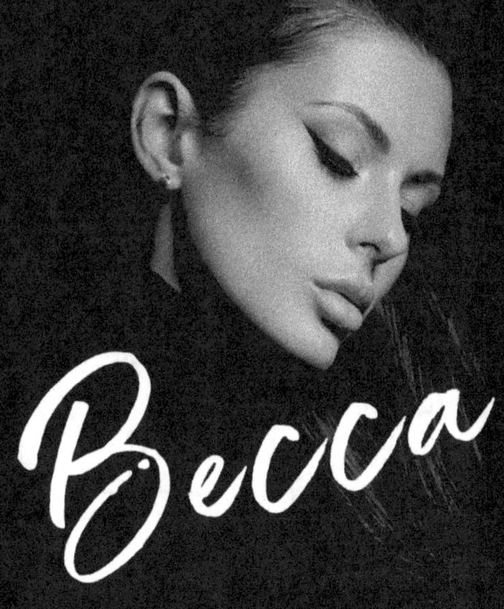

# Becca

## SEVENTEEN

Grey stepped out of his sleek lime green car to open the door for Toby, but I got no such welcome. Kaleb sat behind the wheel of his white race car, revving the engine lightly, his hard stare fixed on the road ahead as I walked around to the passenger side.

It appeared I'd struck a nerve. Good.

I slipped open the door, a hiccup in my throat as I folded myself into the low riding seat, my eyes catching on the series of simplistic—almost dated looking—gas gauges and speed dials. Between us, in the space where an armrest should have been, a large scratched up silver bullet rested in a red cage, a tube protruding out the front to disappear into the dark beneath the dashboard. A little metal flipswitch glinted in the lights outside. NOS.

They were using fucking NOS. What was this, Fast and the Furious?

"Buckle up," Kaleb ordered in an even tone, his chin lifted as he adjusted his position in his seat, eyes fixed on the road ahead of us.

I fumbled with the seat belt as a girl in a sheer dress with literally *nothing* on underneath stepped out onto the road and Toby and Grey in the car beside us slowly crept right up to the starting line.

The girl put herself in front of the cars, just between them, and I cursed, the seatbelt sticking in its holster, unable to be pulled any further.

"Shit. Shit *Shit.*"

Fuck. Shouldn't there be like a fucking harness or something? I looked at the flimsy strip of woven nylon and shuddered as the girl lifted her arms in the air to cheers from the crowd.

My heart lurched in my throat, pulling uselessly on the seatbelt.

"Fuck," Kaleb muttered, releasing the wheel to lean over me. My pulse jumped. He knocked my hands away and easily drew the belt across my lap, latching it before pulling roughly on the top strap, making sure it was good and secure. His gunmetal eyes flicked up to mine, his face barely an inch away.

"Thanks," I muttered, my hands curling on the underside of the seat. His lips pulled to one side in a smirk, and I got the sense he was getting off on the fear evident in my eyes. Like he could smell it beneath my designer perfume.

He reached up to draw the pad of his index finger

down the line of my jaw, his teeth skimming over his lower lip. "Hold on tight."

A horn blared, and I let out a little yelp, squeezing my eyes shut, but the car didn't jolt forward like I thought it would.

Kaleb settled in his seat, throwing his head back in a rumbling belly laugh as the horn blared a second time and everyone outside shouted *TWO*.

The girl standing between the cars went up onto the balls of her bare feet, her eyes alight with excitement that bordered on hysteria.

The horn blasted the third time, the voices of the crowd around us shouting *ONE* swallowed up by the deafening roar of the engines and the peel of tires on the asphalt as I was sucked back in my seat, a girlish squeal ripping from my chest.

My vision blurred, unrecognizable faces whizzing by in a menagerie of color until there were no more faces, no more lights, just dark and dirt and sky and the road vanishing beneath Kaleb's car.

He shifted gears again, and again, *and again*. The thud of his heavy boot on the gas pedal the same rhythm of my own heartbeat loud in my ears.

I strained to turn my head, the g-force keeping me plastered back into my seat, but I wanted to see where Grey and Toby were. There were no tail-lights ahead, which had to mean they were behind us.

I jerked back as Grey's lime green car sped up alongside us, the whine of his engine like the warning snarl of an apex predator.

"Fuck!" I shouted uselessly, my stomach twisting. Grey was too close. His car only inches from Kaleb's. Jesus fucking Christ. They all had a damn death wish.

I gripped the underside of the seat, straining my nails to the breaking point. Wanting to squeeze my eyes shut but being wholly unable to as I watched the road blur and speed ahead. Breaths sawed in and out between my clenched teeth, my lungs on the verge of collapse.

"Fuck," Kaleb's gruff curse somehow reached me through the cacophony of sound, and I flinched as his thumb and forefinger gripped my chin, screaming when I knew that meant he'd taken his hand off the wheel, until he drew my gaze to his face, knotted with intense concentration. His eyes met mine off and on as he jerked his gaze between my face and the road. "Eyes on me," he ordered in a stern voice that had me paying sharp attention.

"Eyes on me, Vixen. Breathe."

I did as I was told. Took a long shaky inhale even though it felt like the weight of the whole vehicle was on my chest. He released my chin and it was a challenge not to immediately look away, watch the road ahead, wait for what I assumed would be a fiery death, but somehow I managed to keep my eyes on him.

On his intent focus. The calm, reassuring way he slouched in his seat. His quick, sure movements as I was sucked into the passenger door as we whipped around a sharp curve in the road. My pulse evened out, still pounding fast, but steadily. The chaos in my head narrowed to a single pinpoint of uncertainty and then vanished entirely.

I blinked, feeling the vibrations of the strong engine. The solid steel boxing me in. The man next to me, warm and safe. He wouldn't let anything happen to me.

When I was sure I had control again, I leaned the back of my head against the seat, giving in to the rush, closing my eyes. A euphoric ripple started somewhere in my belly, racing up my spine like an electrical current until it came tumbling from my lips in a broken laugh.

Kaleb looked at me like I'd grown two heads. I released my death grip on the bottom of the seat, letting that feeling grow until it was spilling over. My body a live wire, shooting sparks from every nerve ending.

Feeling bold, I rolled down the window and air gushed into the cabin, drawing another string of curses from Kaleb as I wolf howled out into the dark, the sound eaten up by the rushing wind.

Kaleb used the controls on his side of the car to roll the window back up, and I watched Grey pull ahead of us, cutting Kaleb off, making him tap the brakes to avoid hitting their bumper.

Reflexively, I gripped the holy shit handle above my window, using it to anchor myself, my skin prickling with goosebumps. "Go!" I shouted, slapping Kaleb's thigh. "Go, go, *go*, they're getting ahead of us!"

That made him smile, and I realized too late what I'd done. The admission that I wanted Kaleb to win, wanted *us* to win evident in my demand.

"Not so keen on losing now, are you, Vixen?"

I clenched my teeth, but I didn't take it back, studying that dimple in Kaleb's cheek. Tracing it to his strong jaw and the vein in his neck, running straight down to disappear into the collar of his black t-shirt. I bit the inside of my cheek, feeling hot and cold all over as Kaleb pushed the car to its limits, trying to catch up.

I realized what I was doing a second too late, clenching my thighs together to stop the ache that'd started between them.

*It's just the adrenaline.*

We whipped around two more corners before setting into a long, winding turn and something told me we were coming back around the loop. It couldn't be much further until we were back on the road we started on, and through the same starting line where we began.

That had to be the finish line.

"How much farther?"

The words were lost to the growl of an engine and my brows pinched, confused since it sounded like it was coming from behind us.

What the fuck?

White lights filled the rearview and I gasped. "Kaleb!"

"*Oh shit,*" Kaleb shouted, careening to the left to get out of the way as a third car joined the race, bullying its way past us like a black shadow.

Kaleb righted the car and shifted gears, shouting at the other driver as he fell into line behind it.

"What the fuck, man? Get off the damn road! Who the fuck does this clown think he is?"

My heart lurched into my throat, recognizing the long rectangular tail lights. Not the kind you'd find on a car meant for street racing. The kind you'd find on a vintage Chevy Impala. My chest rose and fell heavily as I caught a flip of blond hair through the back windshield, sitting in the front seat.

*Oh god.*

What was he *doing?*

Did he want to die?

Kaleb's grip flexed on the steering wheel and his upper lip curled back over his teeth as he raced to catch up with both the new driver and Grey's car farther ahead.

Aodhán was gaining speed on Grey *fast.* I pressed my lips closed to hold in a sound of surprise as I watched him completely overtake Grey in a maneuver that almost sent Grey into a tailspin, making him press on the brakes.

Kaleb pulled up next to Grey and they shared a look through the car windows.

*Who is that?* I could see the words form on Grey's lips.

"I don't fucking know!" Kaleb shouted, spit flying from his mouth. "But he's fucking *dead*."

Kaleb floored it, the car's engine whining in protest as he quite literally put pedal to metal. A thrill went through me as Kaleb released his right hand's grip on the steering wheel, his palm hovering over the flipswitch for the NOS, fingers twitching and at the ready.

Every muscle in my body clenched, bracing as we drove up a slowly inclining hill, chasing those slim rectangular headlights that only seemed to get further and further ahead.

"How the hell is that bastard beating us in his fucking," Kaleb hit the steering wheel. "Grandma's." He hit it again. "Car!" Again. "Fuck!"

Lights flashed overhead as we neared the crest of the hill, and I knew this was it. The home stretch.

"Hold on, Vixen!"

We hit the top of the hill, and I inhaled sharply as the tires left the pavement and we soared in the air for a blissful second before crashing back down onto the cracked asphalt. The jarring motion made my head spin, and I held on for dear life as the crowd came into view ahead. Just a mile or two down the hill, across a flat stretch of road then there they were.

The finish line was in reach and it looked like Aodhán was going to be the winner. Could he even *do* that?

"Come on, *come on*," Kaleb cried, his fingers curling ever closer to that tiny silver switch as we hit the base of the hill and put tires down on the long straightaway that would lead directly to the finish.

Aodhán was almost there. He was going to fucking win.

"Press it, Kaleb!" I cried. "He's winning!"

"No, he's not!"

Grey, beside us a split second ago, sped out ahead, flames shooting from his exhaust as he engaged his Nitrous.

"Kaleb!"

"Too fucking soon," he shouted after Grey, finger on the pulse as he fucking *closed his eyes* and then flicked our switch.

A high pitched cry died in my chest before I could even get it out of my throat, smothered to nothing from the pressure on my chest as he rocketed forward. All I could do was sit there, wide eyed, trying to hold in the sudden violent urge to pee as tears bled from the corners of my eyes and we caught up with Grey.

Shit.

Kaleb was right. He had pressed it too soon.

We were going to get ahead.

The space between us and Aodhán depleted by the millisecond until we were right on his ass, and I held my breath, terrified we'd get close enough for Kaleb to see his face.

We edged alongside Aodhán's rear as the finish line appeared in a checkered blur ahead.

Oh god. *Oh god.*

Kaleb's arms flexed hard, shaking with determination. "Come on, baby!"

The NOS started to wane, slowing the car a second before it would've pushed him the extra few yards he would've needed to win.

Kaleb gasped as the black Impala crossed the finish line, unmistakably beating us by a negligible amount.

"I'm going to kill that fucker!" he shouted in a display of rage I'd never seen from him before. Didn't even knew he possessed. I recoiled from him in the seat, forced to brace myself on the dash as he hit the brakes, sending us skidding to a slow stop, the smell of burning rubber strong in my nose as it filled the cabin.

Grey braked next to us, but my gaze was still fixed on

the car ahead, specifically, on its faintly glowing red tail lights as it continued to drive down the road, away from the valley. Away into the night.

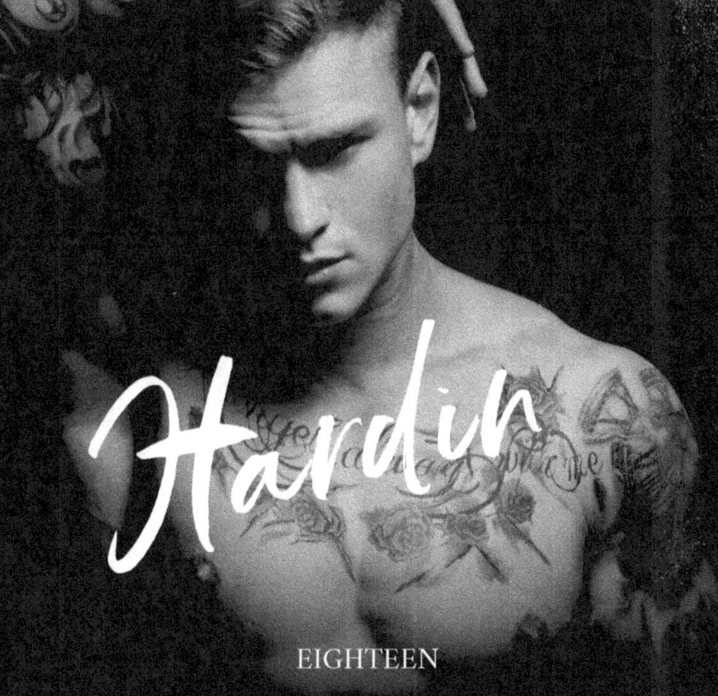

# Hardin



It felt like sleepwalking.

Leaving the house to go to the shed, tearing through the shelves in the dark to find what I was looking for. Jacking Kaleb's bike and riding into the city, past the sleeping streets of the shopping district and out to The Row.

Kaleb was practically fucking inconsolable last night after the race. The crowd cheered for him, but it was without the same mirth as was usual for a win. They also whispered. Talking animatedly about the black car that sped through the finish line only half a second before Kaleb did, with Grey right behind him.

We still had no idea who the bastard was. I'd been quick to check the plates as he barreled down the straightaway, my hand around the butt of my gun, ready to jerk it from the waistband of my jeans if I needed to. I'd only managed to catch the first three digits. ANR.

So of course Kaleb spent the night making calls, trying to find the son of a bitch who stole his glory and ruined the one night a month Kaleb truly looked forward to.

While he fumed and drank himself into a rage in his bedroom until finally passing out, it seemed I would have no such reprieve.

Sleep eluded me as it had for the last four days. Every time I closed my goddamned eyes, there she was. And after tonight?

Becca was *still* pissed at me for what happened last Sunday night, when I pulled her into my den, ready to have my way with her. And it was starting to tickle something at the back of my mind. The only reason she'd still be this openly angry about it, instead of just ignoring me, was because she *cared*.

If she didn't, she'd forget about the whole thing. Move on.

But she wasn't.

She was dead set on getting an apology from me, something I rarely gave, even to fucking blood. And yet here I was, about to give her what I refused everyone else.

Why?

Because I couldn't fucking stand it anymore.

Couldn't stand watching the way she smiled when she was with her roommates. The coy way she regarded my brother, like she wanted to fuck him and hit him over the head with a brick at the same time.

The gleam of adrenaline in her eyes when she stepped

out of my brother's Mitsubishi, her cheeks stained pink, hair a windblown mess that I wanted to tangle my fingers in, use to hold her down while I—

I gritted my teeth, towing the kickstand down from Kaleb's bike as I pulled up alongside Death Before Decaf, the sack on my back heavy with my loot from the shed. The cafe wouldn't open for another couple hours, and I had it on good authority from Kaleb's little rat that she wasn't in until the late morning shift anyway. Plenty of time.

*This level of obsession is unhealthy, Hardin,* my old psychotherapist's voice replayed in my mind. *You know how you get when you latch on like this. It can become... unsafe for those around you.*

My skin bristled, but I shut out the voice, stuffing it in a box, burying it down deep, throwing away the key. I *would* have Rebecca Hart. It was only a matter of time. She could either come willingly or—

*...and especially dangerous for those you try to latch on to.*

"*Fuck,*" I hissed to myself, covering my mouth as a shuddering sigh escaped.

No.

It wouldn't be like that this time. Not with her.

And besides, she could take it. She could take *me.*

I could see it in her. That same twisted broken thing that craved the dark, yearned to be close to it, to get right up alongside it, stroke its sharp edges.

Becca Hart was mine. She just didn't know it yet.

I swept the empty streets, checking for any signs of life

before I emptied the sack onto the concrete sidewalk, metal cans clattering against the ground.

My nostrils flared, the part of me that craved solitude wondering just what the fuck it was we were doing. Before I could stop myself though, I threw off my jacket and knelt on the sidewalk, ready to start my work.

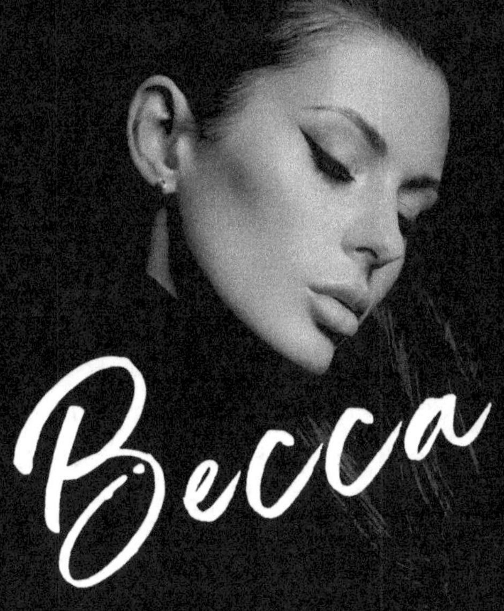

# Becca

## NINETEEN

"Oh my god, is that a Marni Trunk?"

I shoved past Toby, making a beeline for the rack of purses near the back of the thrift shop. My fingers brushed supple leather and I could have purred as I flipped up the front and peered inside the satin lined interior for the maker's mark. *It was a Marni Trunk.*

"Cool your tush," Toby whispered harshly. "If the shop attendants see you jumping up and down they're going to take that bag from you faster than you can say 'bye, bye, Marni.'"

I swallowed, schooling my face into a neutral expression as I carelessly dropped the bag into the shopping cart as if it was worth the twenty dollar price tag stickered on the back instead of the twelve hundred bucks I knew it was worth.

"Can I keep it?" I asked Toby, and he scoffed at me.

"If you must. Though I really don't see why you need it since you refused to let me sell half your available purse inventory. The ROI on that baby could pay your rent this month."

"But you've already sold enough of my wardrobe to pay my rent for the next six months," I argued.

He pursed his lips. "Touché. Fine, keep it. It's a good find. Nice to shop with someone who knows what to look for. Kate tries but she thinks Tommy Hilfiger is high fashion, so…"

I laughed a little at that, putting myself opposite him to flick through the racks of used clothing. I'd managed to convince Toby to get up early with me to go shopping for new clothes before our late morning shift at the cafe. But I hadn't expected him to take me here.

To a fucking thrift shop.

For the first five minutes I couldn't bring myself to touch a thing. But then I found a pair of Chanel heels and almost had an aneurysm at the price tag. Even without Dad's black Amex card, I would still be able to afford to dress the way I wanted, even if it was in last season's styles.

And the new and improved Rebecca Hart wasn't against that.

It helped knowing I had enough money stashed away in my nightstand that I could keep ignoring Dad's text messages, which were almost daily now.

*You're just as pigheaded as your mother was,* he said. *I received an invite to fashion week in Paris, it could be yours if you give up this juvenile obsession with defying me,* he said. *A job at a coffee shop? Really? You're better than that,* he said.

He wasn't doing himself any favors to win my forgiveness for cutting me off to pursue my own future. I figured he would change his tune eventually, though. As soon as he realized I wasn't going to come crawling back home and beg him to give me back my allowance and inheritance.

I didn't want to lose my only remaining parent, but I wasn't about to conform to his idea of what I *should* be. Not anymore.

I breathed in the cheap detergent and mothball scent of the thrift shop. This is what freedom smelled like and you know what? It wasn't half bad. I could get used to it.

"So," Toby said, drawing out the 'o' in that way he had that told me he was about to drag all the tea out of me. My back stiffened.

I'd been trying to come up with the best way to tell him about what happened between Kaleb and me, but every time I thought I had it figured out, it was like a physical block would form in my throat, stopping me.

I liked Toby. A lot. I didn't want to risk alienating one of my only friends in this place. Especially not one I lived with and worked with.

"So?" I repeated, trying to sound nonchalant.

"There was an awful lot of tension between you and Kaleb last night. What was that about?"

*"Um..."* I pretended to be studiously checking all the seams on a short Fendi dress that was definitely at least

three seasons old and too worn to merit buying. "I don't know what you mean."

Toby snatched the dress from me, shoving it back onto the rack with the others with a knowing look in his eyes. "You totally fucked, just admit it. Kaleb St. Vincent is a known man whore."

I winced, and he gasped, clearly his accusation was meant to draw the truth out of me and that's exactly what it did.

"Oh my god, you did fuck him!"

"Okay, you can't be mad at me. Who got you a passenger seat ride last night?"

He rolled his eyes.

"You only said it was, like, the best night of your entire existence."

He shrugged.

"Ugh. Fine. I'm sorry, Tobes. If it makes you hate me any less, I did ask him if there was any chance he was gay, first."

He swatted my arm. "You did not!"

"I did."

He pursed his lips again, crossing his arms to consider me. "Well then, I guess I forgive you, but *only* if you tell me in detail what I'm missing out on. I want length, girth, shape, veiny, not-veiny, cut, uncut?"

I blushed and Toby snapped his fingers, indicating that he wanted this information right now, in the middle of the thrift store.

My phone chimed in my pocket and I thanked my

lucky fucking stars for the interruption, drawing it from my purse.

"If that's Kaleb…"

I frowned, looking at the messages on the screen. Two from Ava Jade demanding I accept the three tickets to the Primal Ethos concert she emailed me—even though I tried to tell her I wanted to buy them myself—and one from *Unknown*. My hackles immediately rose seeing the white text on the screen beneath the sender.

**Unknown: Liar.**

"Becca, what is it? You look like you've seen a ghost."

I swallowed hard, tapping the message with shaking fingers, a hundred bad memories rising to the surface. My bestie, Ava Jade, had a stalker. He used to send her messages just like this one. Taunting. Vague. Until they were less taunts and more action.

Until those messages almost got everyone she cared about killed.

The razorblades in my throat cut sharply as I tapped the message, my chest tight as I typed out a reply.

**Becca: Who is this?**

But at the same time the message sent another one was received.

**Unknown: Your friend told me you're a solo act.**

What?

**Unknown: I'll give you a hint. It starts with A and ends with you agreeing to a date with me.**

*Aodhán?*

"Did you give my number to anyone?"

Toby winced.

"Oh my god, Tobes, what the fuck?"

He held up his hands. "Okay, in my defense he said that you'd written it down for him on a napkin and he lost it. And really, Becks, have you seen the guy? Tres hot. Like, angels would weep at his Irish beauty. I did you a favor."

I sighed, going back to my phone screen to grudgingly add Aodhán to my contacts, because I totally needed to be talking to another tattooed Adonis right now.

**Becca: Tricking my friend to get my number? Classy. Also, you must have a death wish pulling the stunt you pulled last night. What the hell were you thinking?**

**Aodhán: I was thinking you might take me up on that date if I won.**

**Becca: Wrong.**

**Aodhán: Time will tell. You didn't tell them it was me even though you knew, did you?**

My thumbs rested just atop the screen, fumbling for a reply.

He was right. I didn't tell them. I could've. But unlike he assumed, it wasn't because of some crush I had on him, it was born of a desire to not have his blood on my hands.

Instead of replying, I slid the phone back into my purse. "Kaleb had an amazing dick," I told Toby, no longer sorry. Friends didn't give out friend's numbers to total fucking strangers. I wasn't angry with him, how could I be with that stupid loveable face, but I could still get my shot in.

"It was long and fat and glorious and circumcised."

Toby pouted. "That's cruel."

"You asked," I reminded him, smiling sweetly.

"Fine," he groused. "I deserved that."

"Yes, you did."

He cleared his throat. "Can I ask you something else?"

"Shoot."

"Hardin…"

He let the name hang there in the air between us for a moment.

"I saw him watching you last night, too. Like, *intensely* watching you. Did you…"

I shook my head quickly. "No," I said, and wondered if Toby had an answer to the question that'd been eating at me since I first met Hardin St. Vincent. "Do you know why he never talks?"

Toby licked his lips, tipping his head this way and that. "No one really knows for sure, but I do know some really bad shit went down when he and Kaleb were younger. Have you seen all Hardin's scars?"

I frowned, shaking my head.

"Well look closer next time, they're hidden in all his ink, but there are a *lot* of them. Round ones that look like they're from cigar burns. Long jagged slashes. Even patches that look like the skin was carved straight off his bones."

Bile rose in my throat.

"Yeah," Toby said, agreeing with my expression. "It's gruesome. They don't talk about it, but it must've been bad, whatever happened to them. Kaleb doesn't have scars like his brother, but every once in a while he goes off on these drinking binges. Sometimes for days. Gets so wasted he can barely stand and Hardin has to come hunt down his ass at the Copper Crown or the club over on ninth. I had to call Hardin once to come get him because I was pretty sure he was going to get himself killed, picking fights with people at the club."

"*Oh.*"

"Anyway, I'm guessing that's why he doesn't talk. It's, like, a symptom of his trauma."

So, basically, I was an asshole.

*Awesome.*

"He's still a total dick though," Toby added. "And vicious as fuck if anyone messes with his brother."

Another sigh. "Doesn't mean he isn't hot as hell, though. Maybe even more so than Kaleb, but you have to be careful with that one, babe."

"What is that supposed to mean?"

Toby lifted a shoulder. "It's mostly rumors, you know, but I heard he strangled a girl to death while doing the deed last year and they buried the body out in the canyons."

"*What?*"

"Hey, I seriously doubt that's true," he amended, completely oblivious to how my pulse was racing in my ears. "*But* he is known to have some very particular tastes in the bedroom, if you get my meaning."

I shook my head, unsure I did catch his meaning. Or maybe just wanting to know.

"Well that one chick he's been boning for a couple months now—I think her name is Felicia—she always wears one of those little flight attendant looking scarves for a few days after Sunday nights at their place."

A stone sunk heavily in my gut and I didn't understand why the mention of her made me bristle with something that was definitely *not* jealousy. That would be stupid. Not to mention *insane* if what Toby was telling me had any truth to it.

"I've noticed ligature marks on her wrists, too."

My traitorous cunt throbbed, imagining my own wrists bound tightly, lifted high over my head as Hardin ravished me.

"Hardin scares the shit out of me," Toby continued, snapping me out of it. "But I can't say I wouldn't let him tie me up and have his way with me if he were so inclined."

Toby sighed before linking an arm with mine, using his other hand to guide our near full cart toward the front of the store. "Why are all the hot ones straight?"

I pushed down the lump in my throat and shook off the flutters vying for dominion in my belly. Leaning into Toby, I bumped my shoulder with his. "Not *all* the hot ones."

Toby smiled at the compliment. "Have I told you I love you today?"

"It won't hurt to remind me."

"Love you, boo."

I laughed, hurrying him to the checkout line that seemed to have only grown in the last five minutes. "If we're late for the morning rush, Kate's going to double our rent."

Outside of Death Before Decaf, a group of students crowded the entrance, whispering and talking animatedly among themselves.

"Shit. The morning rush started hella early today," Toby was saying, towing me along as we rushed down the street. "You got the espresso machine? I'll do the smoothie station and sandwiches."

We hit the densely crowded ring of students and Toby began to shove them from our path. "*Move people*, if you want your coffee we need to get through here."

I apologized, knocking into several shoulders as we squeezed our way through and stopped dead once we were inside the ring.

"It's her," someone said behind me, but everything else after that faded into background noise as I stared down at the thing that had everyone gathering outside the cafe. They weren't lined up to go inside at all. They were spectators at an art gallery.

Bold colorful lines slashed the sidewalk at my feet and I stepped back, recognizing long dark hair and light brown eyes. She stared up at me from the cement, a graffiti version of myself surrounded in strokes of neon blue and purple and green.

The Becca painted on the cement had a dangerous glint to her hard stare. Her jawline was sharper. Her lips downturned, but not in an unattractive way. Just in the way they always were. But there was no mistaking who it was.

Below the portrait, curving around the base of my neck like a collar were two words.

*Forgive me?*

And off to the side, just below the question mark, was a symbol I recognized. It was the same symbol tattooed into my best friend's back, running along the line of her spine. The Saint emblem. A fleur des lis with the tip elongated to make a dagger.

My hand flew to my mouth as something in my chest twisted.

*Hardin* drew this.

Numbly, I knelt to the cement, putting my hand to the paint. It was dry, but still tacky. He'd probably stayed up half the night to paint it. And after I teased him for not talking to me. For not apologizing.

I wasn't sure if he was the asshole here anymore. Or if I was.

"Ho-ly shit," Toby was saying. "Was this who I think it was?"

When I lifted my watery gaze to Toby's, he shook his head. "All right, that's enough," he shouted at everyone standing around the cafe's entrance. "You're all in violation of the fire code. Unless you want coffee, go the fuck about your business, yeah? Go on, scat."

I kept my eyes cast downward, feeling way too many eyes on me as the crowd slowly dispersed and Toby dragged me inside.

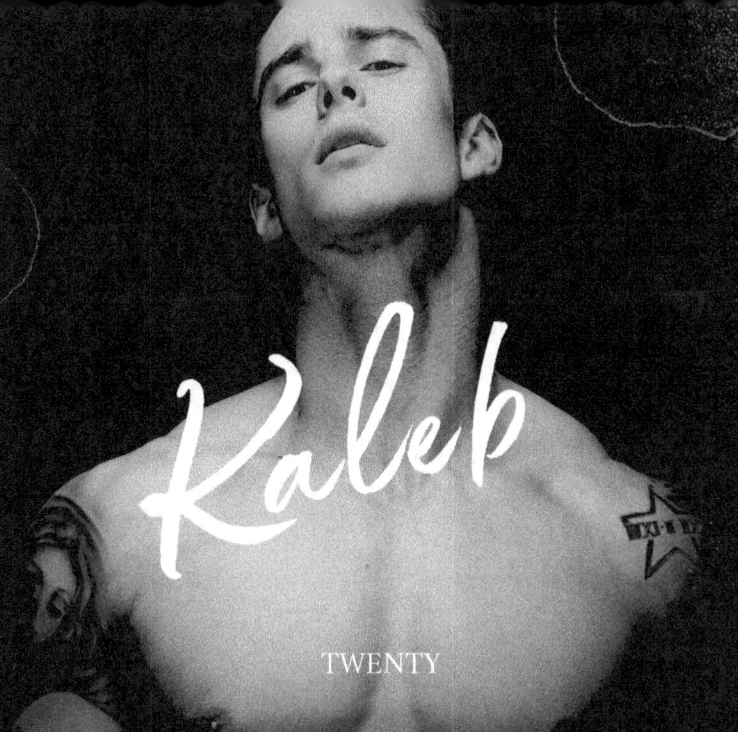

# Kaleb

## TWENTY

It would be the first Sunday 'mass' in almost a year to be canceled, but when the assholes you were hunting sent a direct message to your leader, it was time to make sacrifices.

Pope shut down Saint's Autobody early so even he could attend the meet. But he wasn't the only irregular face to take a seat at the table. For the first time in years, Ma took her place at the other end, across from Dad.

The other Saints were still welcoming her back to the fold when Hardin and I showed up. I went straight to Pope, a few seats down from where I'd sit next to Dad, sliding into the empty chair next to him. "You find anything?"

He sucked his teeth. "Sorry, Kale. I got jack shit. There isn't a single '67 Impala with a license plate starting with those letters. Not registered in Cali. I've got a list of plates with partial matches though. Going through registrations as soon as we're done here. I'll flag any that seem sus."

"Good. And broaden the search," I retorted, maybe too harshly. "I want him found."

Pope's lips turned down as he reached over to grip my shoulder. "I'll find him, Kale. I will. But don't you think we've got bigger fish to fuckin' fry right now?"

He was right, and I hated it.

But there was something about that car, about its driver, that set my teeth on edge. It wasn't just that he'd won. It was the blatant disrespect. Disrespect for a fucking King of Kilborn. A *Saint*.

I couldn't let it stand.

Grudgingly, I nodded, swallowing down the bitter acid filling my mouth. "Yeah."

Pope squeezed my shoulder again before dropping his hand. He'd always been like family. A younger uncle or maybe a cousin. When Hardin and I decided to open the autobody shop, I knew I wanted Pope to run it. His attention to detail and knowledge about all things cars and bikes was unparalleled. And I hadn't been wrong in my choice to hand him the reins.

He ran the shop like it was his own and took care of my baby for me. She was in desperate need of a tune-up after the race. I'd pushed her too hard to try to beat that motherfucker. Nearly blew a belt.

"What's with your brother?" Pope asked.

"The usual," I quipped. "A general disdain for the entire human race. Nothing new."

Hardin sat silent and brooding as usual, but there was an added darkness clinging to him like a bad aura.

As far as Pope or anyone else was concerned, it was likely to do with this shit with the Sons, but I knew better. And honestly? I wasn't sure I wanted to think about the reasons why he painted a fucking mural to the girl *I* couldn't stop thinking about lately. The one I jerked off to once a day like that might keep my cravings for her at bay.

Okay fine. Twice a day.

And three times on Sundays.

His message said *forgive me,* but when I asked him what it was about, he just said super fucking cryptically *she was supposed to be Fee,* and refused to say anything more, leaving me to imagine about a hundred different scenarios, at least half of which involved his cock and each one of her tight holes.

"Kaleb," Dad's gruff growl caught my attention, and I looked up to find everyone else taking their seats as he called the meeting to order with a knock of his knuckles against the table. I rose, giving Jimmy Boy back his seat as I moved to slide into the chair to Dad's left, between him and Archer, banishing thoughts of Rebecca Hart. At least for now.

Pope was right, we had bigger problems than whether or not the new girl in town wanted to fuck me or my brother on the reg.

"Lookin' good, Arch."

He nodded, patting his stomach. "It'll take more than a single bullet to put me down."

I snorted, and Dad rolled his eyes at the exchange,

leaning over the table with a sigh. "You all know why I called this meet. Our *friends* from Ireland have sent a message."

A few whispers rose from Saint lips, quieted by my Dad's sharp gaze. "Sloane, if you will," Dad said, passing the reins.

Ma rose from her seat at the other end of the table and my lips parted in surprise seeing the piece strapped to her thigh. She wore it like it was a part of her, and I remembered the smell of copper and lead. The feel of her lips as she brushed a kiss on my temple in the middle of the night.

...only to wake up in the morning to find smears of crimson on my bedsheets from where her fingers touched them.

Sometimes I forgot she was the OG badass. The first woman ever to be inducted into the southern arm of Saints.

"We received this in the mail, at our home address."

Ma tossed what looked like a postcard down the middle of the long table. Hardin and I both reached for it, but I was quicker, fingering it from the worn wood to inspect both sides.

One side was a photo of the canyons. The other had a couple lines of numbers scrawled in smudged black ink.

10-01-22

1100

It was a date and a time. And below was a symbol I assumed stood for Sons of O'Sullivan. The mark two jagged S's, one perched above the other with a slashed O between them.

S

Ø

S

"They want to meet," Ma reiterated for everyone else as Hardin reached across Dad to steal the notecard from my grasp. He looked at it for all of two seconds before tossing it back on the table with a popped eyebrow.

I knew what he was wondering.

I sat back in my seat. "There's a date and a time, but no location."

"Isn't it obvious?" Ma asked, pointing to the postcard photo. "That shot was taken from the valley floor of the canyons way out past the equestrian center on the canyon road. Look at the peaks. Four of them, each one larger than the one before it."

I recognized the spot now, remembering Ma taking us on a ride that way. She'd pointed to the ridges and said, *look, it's us. There's you, Hardin,* she'd pointed to the third largest after the ones she considered to be the mama and papa peaks. *And there's you, baby,* she told me, pointing to the smallest of the four. The one with all the crags in its tawny face, the sun lighting up the purple and yellow bruises on her face.

But that was *before...*

There was no way the Sons could know about that ride. It was only a coincidence, but still, the memory made the muscle around my mouth twitch with disgust.

"That's the location," she added, and the room fell silent, all eyes glancing between Ma and Dad.

The skin between Dad's eyes knotted as he stared wordlessly down at the postcard.

"What?" I snorted. "You're not seriously considering this, are you? It's probably a trap."

No one said anything in agreement, but no one spoke to the contrary either because they all knew damn well I was right. "And even if it isn't, *we* didn't set this meet. This is a location of their choice. A time of their choice. A date of *their choice*. That's not how we operate. Meets happen when we fucking say they—"

"Enough, Kaleb," Dad sighed, pinching the bridge of his nose. "Of fucking course we aren't going to go wandering out into the desert on their terms."

My ears heated, and I crossed my arms over my chest, adjusting my position in my seat, feeling sufficiently put back in my place. "Well, good. Just making sure."

I wiped an imaginary leak from my nose and sniffed, waiting for the attention to shift. There was a reason when Dad suggested I could take over for him someday, I'd turned down the offer, telling him Hardin would make a far better leader, despite his silence. He was the oldest, it made more sense.

I wasn't fit for leadership. Too slow to catch on. Too thick in the head; the idiot son who went and got himself lost in the canyons at ten years old for eleven days and almost died.

Everyone knew it.

I could see the judgment. The shame of it hot on my face.

Just Kaleb pointing out the obvious again.

"That said," Dad fucking mercifully continued. "We need to be ready for them to make a move. If we don't show up, there's no telling how they'll react and we still don't know their goal here. We don't know their numbers, but intel leads me to believe they are at least in the same ballpark as us, putting on semi-even ground."

"But we got home field advantage," Zade argued. "We have the mayor. The senator. All the smaller fish pay tribute to the Shark of SoCal." I watched my Dad's face tick with unease before his mask was back in place.

So, he hadn't told them about the Mayor or the Senator, but I knew damn well they were aware of the small gangs in the area being more than a little uncooperative lately. Everyone was on edge for tribune collection day, which was barely two weeks away now, on the last day of September.

"There's something you all need to know," Dad started, and I braced myself, tapping my fingers on the table. "Neither Senator Murphy or Mayor Costa are taking my calls. I tried to go to their offices yesterday but neither was there. Their assistants were slinging some bullshit about them being sick and working remotely. But they weren't at home, either."

Whispers rose from the group of high ranking Saints and I didn't need to hear exactly what they were saying to know that the general consensus was that this was bad. Like, set your tits on fire bad.

Somehow, hearing it directly from Dad rather than second hand from Hardin was a real punch to the gut. Like a nightmare made real.

Shit was getting dark around here real quick.

Ma tapped the table. "We have to start considering the possibility that they've turned on us."

The voices of every Saint in attendance rose, echoing noisily around the room as they argued over what to do. Wasting more time.

"That isn't all," Ma added, shouting to be heard over the others, forcing them back to quiet. "We've confirmed Chief Andrews' death wasn't from natural causes. Maggie isn't talking, and we won't force her, but we can assume his death is on the hands of these *Sons* as well."

"We can't let this shit go on," Archer spat, his face reddening as he gestured wildly, throwing a hand into the air. "We can't just let these clowns come onto our turf like they fuckin' own it. They can't just take what's ours."

"Yeah!" Jimmy Boy shouted in agreement.

"We need to teach these *Sons* a lesson. One they won't soon forget," Zade added, a lick of malice in his eyes.

"Yeah!" the others echoed, and I resisted the urge to roll my eyes.

I might have been thick headed, but even I knew the end goal was the blood of the Sons. Getting to said goal was the fucking problem.

"I think you're all forgetting that no one in this godforsaken city seems to know where they are," I growled. "They're like... like ghosts, just floating in and taking what's ours and throwing more shit in our laps and then vanishing as if they were never here."

The vibe in the room shifted right quick, a few grumbles sounding from the men as they quieted.

"Kaleb's right," Dad said, and I felt my lips tug up into a grin I tried to hide from the others. "The Sons of O'Sullivan will pay for everything they've done, but first we have to find them."

Dad lifted the postcard from the table, tapping the date on the back. "And this is our deadline. I want every man on this. Use force if needed. Kaleb, Hardin, you, too. Tear apart Santa Clarita if that's what it takes. We find these fuckers *before this date.*"

"No one goes out alone," Ma added. "Break off into groups of two or three and always be in communication with at least two other groups regularly. I'm talking *hourly,* updating with your current position. If anything happens..." She let the men fill in the gap there, her meaning clear, if any of the groups got taken out then... "At least we'll be able to narrow down the time and place and we can work from there to trace them. Capiche?"

Nods all around.

I stood from the table, already trying to come up with the best route. The best plan of attack. Wondering where we should start. "Let's move, Bro," I told Hardin, but Dad stepped into my path, stopping me from leaving the meeting room.

"I need a word with you boys," he said, his thick eyebrows lowering dangerously over his eyes.

Like I said, shit was getting grim.

*What now?*

If there was even more that he didn't want the others to hear, then it had to be really bad.

Hardin's chair scraped the polished cement floor as he stood, shouldering past me on his way out. Eventually, we were going to have to talk about it—about *her*—but for now I was content to let him listen to the rumors. The jackass manning the counter at the Yoga studio wasn't able to keep his mouth shut after all.

The Yoga room itself might have been soundproofed, but the change rooms weren't. They didn't even have doors. And the sounds of her moans definitely carried.

Her fleeing in a towel would've only confirmed any suspicion.

It probably didn't help that I ran out of the change room after her buck naked. I'd turned around, gone back for my gun and clothes, but not after the dude at the front got more of an eyeful than he bargained for.

I knew Hardin knew what happened between me and Becca.

Just like I knew there was something he wasn't telling me about her.

One of them was bound to break if I kept pushing buttons. I wondered who.

The door to the room we used regularly for gang meetings swung shut behind us, and Dad pulled out ahead, making us follow him across the shop. He shoved the door open to the garage, where the scents of grease, metal, and gasoline filled the air, and walked through.

Hardin and I shared a look, but followed.

Dad leaned against an older model Porsche Pope was working on, crossing his arms over his chest as he fixed us each with a hard stare before his gaze settled squarely on me. "I thought I told you to stay away from the girl."

I was sure my face betrayed my surprise, but really, I shouldn't have been surprised at all. I'd done the exact opposite of his orders to stay away from her, and of course he had someone checking up to make sure I listened because *spoiler alert,* I never listened.

"And I thought it was pretty damn obvious that the orders applied to both of you." Dad turned to Hardin. "I'm guessing your brother didn't even bother telling you I'd ordered him to keep his distance from the Matthews girl."

"Hart," I corrected. "Her name's Rebecca *Hart.* Not Matthews."

Maybe this was all a mix up? Was he getting his panties in a twist because he thought she was someone else?

Dad pinched the bridge of his nose. "Same shit," he said. "Doesn't matter. The point is I asked you to keep your distance and you didn't listen, did you?"

I forced myself to stand my ground. "I can protect her," I said, but as soon as the words were out of my mouth, I questioned the validity of them. I could hardly protect myself half the time. Could I protect Becca? Really? Could I be responsible for someone other than myself? My brother?

"Oh, you can, can you?" Dad snapped.

"Dad," Hardin warned, giving his head a barely perceptible shake.

Dad huffed heavily. "Since neither of you can seem to leave the girl alone, effectively putting her at risk, she needs to be brought in."

"Brought in?" Hardin asked, a muscle flexing in his jaw.

Dad nodded, a shadow falling across his eyes. "You'll bring her for dinner this Friday. Ma's making lasagna."

"But Dad—"

"Until then," he interrupted sharply. "I expect you to keep your fucking distance. We have no idea where the Sons have eyes and unless you want this girl hurt or worse you'll steer clear. Do you both understand?"

"What is it about this girl?" I asked. "Why do you care?"

He pushed to his feet, his shoulders flexing, a show of power. "I do not need to explain myself, Son. You'd do well to remember that. Remember who you're talking to."

"*Yes, sir,*" I scoffed.

Dad nodded, turning his attention back to Hardin, who nodded gravely. At least this bullshit meant he wouldn't be getting near her, either. Not for a while, anyway.

"Good, now that's settled, on the night of the intended meet, I'll want you boys at the house. Ma won't have it any other way."

"Can't," I argued. "We promised the Crows we'd go to the Lodi show."

Dad cocked his head. "Primal Ethos," I reminded him. "They're playing in Lodi the same night the Sons proposed for the meet."

"But if you need us here, then we'll stay," Hardin said, ever the ruiner of all the fun. I bought the tickets for the Lodi show months ago. It was practically carved in stone that we were going.

Dad thought about it and shook his head. "No. No, that's good, actually. I like the idea of you both being out of town. Just in case. Me and the guys can handle locking down the area. Then your Ma and I will hole up with the others. Yeah. That's a better plan. Go to your show. Maybe stay the night in Lodi if you can, but pay cash. No paper trail."

"What are we, rookies?"

Dad rolled his eyes. "Now get out of here, the both of you. When you're not in class, your asses are on the streets looking for these vermin. Together. And if I hear you've come within five hundred feet of the girl, I'll tan both your damn hides."

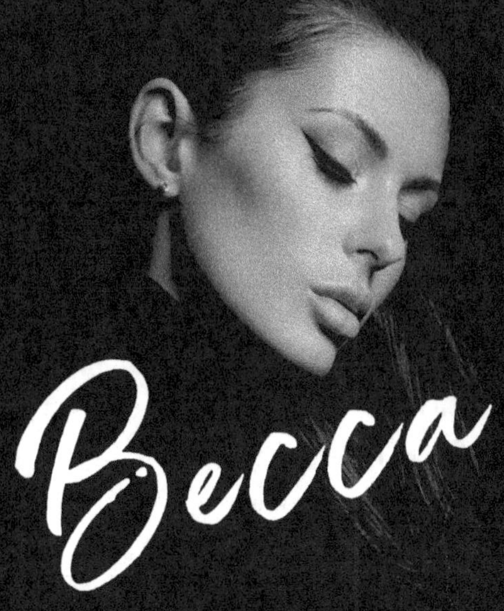

# Becca

## TWENTY-ONE

"I still can't believe you're friends with The Bone Man," Kate squealed, bouncing in Toby's backseat.

"Hey, don't forget about my girl, Ava Jade. I mean, yes, Primal Ethos was already dope before she came along, but she totally pushed them to the next level."

"Preach!" Toby sang out from the front seat, turning up the crackly sound system loud enough to drown out Kate and me in the backseat while he drummed the steering wheel, rocking out to one of their newer singles. Switchblade Smile. Which was quickly becoming one of my favorite songs of all time.

Kate giggled to herself, not needing even an ounce of alcohol or puff of a joint to be totally high on life right now. To be honest, neither did I.

I'd spent way too long without seeing my best friend. If she was in Thorn Valley, just a few hours' drive away, there'd be no excuse, but seeing as she was on tour I suppose I'd forgive her.

I missed the shit out of her these past months and really hoped she liked Toby and Kate. If she didn't, one of them might leave with a few less fingers than when they arrived.

A text from the woman herself lit up my phone screen, and I smiled widely as I opened it.

**Ava Jade: Your secret password is Carnage. Don't ask, Rook chose it. Give the password to any of the security team after the show and they'll escort you backstage. We have a whole studio set up with drinks and snacks and all the goodies for us to catch up once the curtains close.**

**Ava Jade: Oh, your roommates are invited, too. In case that wasn't obvious. I want to meet them.**

"You guys good for a little backstage party after the show?" I shouted over the music, and Toby swerved a little on the highway, earning himself a blaring honk from the car next to us before he cranked the volume down, twisting in his seat to look back at me with wide eyes.

"You're not serious?"

"Dead serious."

"Is that even a question?" Kate asked in a high pitched shout, shaking the back of the driver's seat. "This is going to be the best night ever!"

I laughed, thumbing a reply to Ava Jade.

**Becca: Count us in!**

Toby howled as he turned the music back up, he and

Becca singing along to one of Primal Ethos' older hits. Gravedigger.

I chewed my lower lip, unable to stop myself from wondering if Hardin and Kaleb would be at the show tonight. If they were, would I see them? Would they also be invited backstage after the show?

After the very public apology from Hardin and spending last Saturday night barreling down the canyon roads with Kaleb in his race car, I thought…

I didn't know what I thought, but I definitely didn't expect for them to go totally MIA.

Neither of them had come into DBD for coffee this past week. Not when I was working or when the others were on shift, either. I asked.

The closest I'd come to seeing them at all was watching their baby blue Ford Bronco prowl the streets of The Row, finding it parked in various places around campus, sans the men themselves.

I was starting to wonder if they both finally took the hint and were backing off like I asked them to. Except, now that they had…

"*Ow,*" I muttered to myself, tasting copper on my tongue from biting my lower lip too hard. I put my fingers to the corner of my mouth and they came away red. *Shit.*

I tugged a tissue from a box Toby had on the floor in the backseat and dabbed the blood away, hoping it didn't ruin my makeup. Since we had to leave pretty much right after our evening shift at DBD, I didn't have a lot of time to make sure everything set properly. But at least my inky black liner wings were sharp, painted with precision only someone with a very stable hand could achieve.

As much as Toby tried to get me into something with color tonight, I won out, winding up in my signature shade: black. The dress I wore was from a mid-tier designer I wasn't super familiar with, but for the thirty dollar price tag at the thrift shop, this baby was worth every penny.

Brand new, with a cut out back that extended downward to hug around my waist, only a thin strip of fabric running down the middle from my breasts held the thing together. It was sexy as sin and hugged my curves like a glove. Way better than the yellow number Toby was trying to force on me. I mean, *yellow*? Did the guy know me at all?

I wadded up the bloody tissue and stuffed it into my clutch, digging for the lip stain I brought to try to hide the fresh cut.

My phone vibrated again as I swiped it over my lips, the cherry red color doing its job to cover the broken skin even better than I thought it would.

I traded the lip stain for my phone, finding a message there from Aodhán. We'd been texting back and forth for the last week. Even though I'd managed to keep him at arms' length so far, the guy was persistent. He came in for coffee daily now, using any excuse to hang around the front counter and chat until I inevitably excused myself to get back to work.

**Aodhán: Enjoy the concert tonight.**

My lips turned upward as I tapped the message to

thumb out a reply, but hesitated. Wait. Had I told him I was going to the show tonight? I flicked back through a couple days of messages but found nothing about the show. *Huh.* I must've mentioned it to him when he came in for coffee.

"We're here!" Kate said, tugging her little jacket off to leave in Toby's car. She wouldn't need it in there. With floor tickets, we were going to be hot as hell, crushed in with all the other fans.

Out the window, twin lights scissored back and forth, crossing each other in the sky as Toby joined the line of cars trying to get into the main parking lot. They were at a dead stop, brake lights painting all of us in shades of crimson.

The show was going to start in ten minutes. We'd miss the intro.

"Awe, what the shit is this!" Toby groused, slapping the steering wheel.

"Wait, go that way," I told him, tapping his shoulder, pointing to the other route to the left. The one marked with a 'no entry' sign.

"Uh, last time I checked, no-entry meant *no-entry*, babe."

A security guard patrolled the blocked road and I rolled down the stiff backseat window, shouting over the thudding base from inside the stadium and the horns blaring outside. "Hey! Hey you, come here!"

The security guard, seeming more than a little perturbed, slowly made his way to us as we inched forward in the long line.

"Can I help you?" he asked in a gruff voice, hooking a thumb on his tactical belt.

"Carnage," I said and his brows lowered.

"Carnage," I repeated. "I'm a friend of the performers. Can we—"

"I'm sending the package through to the private lot," the security guard spoke into the radio on his shoulder.

"Ten four," the crackly voice said on the other end. "Send her through."

The security guard dropped his hand and waved for us to turn onto the closed road. "Follow this road around the rear of the building and the other security officers will show you where to park and escort you to the rear entrance."

"Thanks!" I called out to him as he rushed ahead of us to move the sign blocking the road and wave us through.

"I'm so freaking glad you moved in with us," Kate said, knocking into my side for a tight hug.

I laughed, and Toby whooped, pulling out of the main line and onto the vacant access road. "VIP route, here we come!"

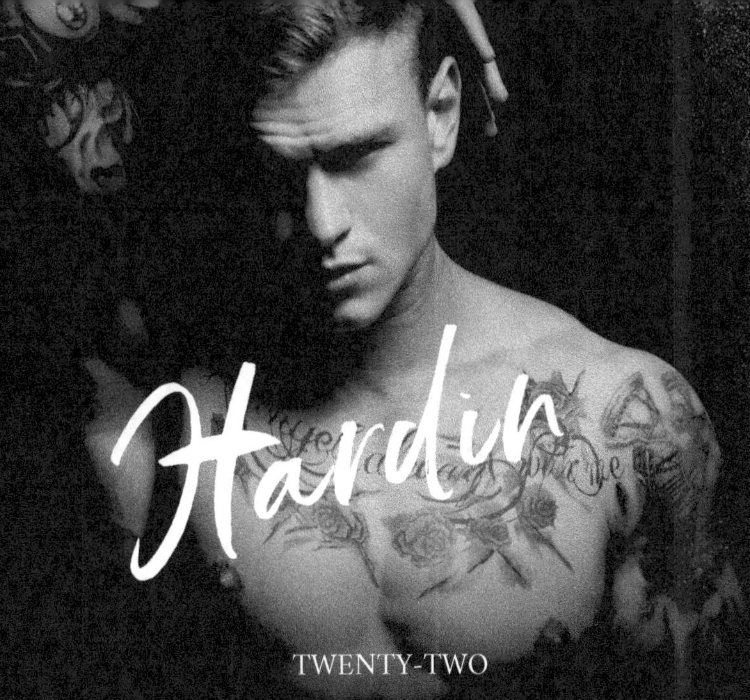


## TWENTY-TWO

"This shit doesn't feel right," I said as Kaleb pulled into the back lot of the concert venue in Lodi.

"Is that Toby's car?" Kaleb asked, ignoring me completely as he jerked his chin in the direction of the old Toyota parked at the rear entrance, a few spots down from Primal Ethos' tour bus.

My jaw flexed, recognizing the rusty yellow color and the dent in the rear fender.

Fucker.

We already knew from our eyes and ears around campus that they were going to the show tonight, but seeing Toby's shitbox here confirmed it. If it weren't for Dad's order to scour every inch of Santa Clarita keeping us busy, staying away would've been impossible.

Becca didn't know it, but I was there when she first saw my apology letter, written in the form of graffiti on cement. Watching from the front window of the Copper Crown while Sam dozed on the sofa after a long night spent tending to patrons. I'd watched as her back hitched up. How she'd stopped in place. Stock still, staring down at the message with trembling hands.

*Look up,* I thought. *Look up.*

But she didn't. She lifted her face and looked at Toby instead, and when he saw whatever expression resided there he'd told off everyone else gathered to speculate about the mural. He wrapped his arm around her and coerced her inside. The pair of them vanished beneath the awning before I'd even had a chance to properly see her face.

There were only a handful of people who'd know it was me who painted it. My brother among them. I hadn't touched a can of spray paint in years. I left the tagging days behind in my teens, but my artwork still clung to brick and cement and train car metal all around SoCal from those days.

I'd managed to get most of it off my hands by now, but idiot that I was, I hadn't bothered with gloves when I painted it and there were still bits of spatter caught in the hair on my arms. I couldn't be bothered to scrub it all out, not when at the end of each day and even longer night of interrogations and endless searching I'd wind up face down on my mattress, the blankets kicked to the floor.

"We should've stayed back," I growled as Kaleb put the Bronco in park and checked his hair in the rearview. "That meet with the Sons is supposed to be in a couple hours. If we leave now, we can make it back. We should stay with the others."

"Can you not be a buzzkill for five fucking minutes," Kaleb hissed, pocketing the keys as he stepped out of the car, holding the door open. "Dad wanted us *here*. His orders were to stay in Lodi. So, we're staying in Lodi. He has shit handled back home."

Heat rolled down my back, but I said nothing, shoving out of the Bronco into the tepid night air outside the concert arena. Inside, background music played for the gathered fans as the space filled for the show.

At least tonight would be an opportunity to warn The Crows about the potential threat down south. Dad may not like it, but we'd stepped up for them when they needed us, and I knew Diesel St. Crow would do the same if it came to that.

I was with my Dad when it came to asking for any form of help from our northern and eastern counterparts. It wasn't something I would do lightly, but they should at least know what's going on, in case the fight bled over into their territory.

It was also possible that they could secure us the firepower we fucking desperately needed right now since every one of Dad's contacts seemed unable to step up. The Mexicans were a strong contender for the sale, but they couldn't get us what we needed for another month.

I had a feeling we wouldn't be here that long without getting the shit we needed.

There was only so much that could be done with brute force and pure rage.

I slammed the passenger door shut and followed Kaleb to the rear entrance, the smell of cherry cigars wafting in his wake as he pounded twice on the black painted metal.

The door swung open and music flooded out into the private parking area.

Kaleb flicked the only half smoked cigar into the sand bucket against the wall and slid past the security guard, following the long, narrow corridor toward the main stadium. My skin bristled as the music rushed over me in a wave, the undercurrent of animated excitement from the crowds further ahead setting my teeth on edge.

I fucking hated crowds.

Loathed being boxed in and brushed against by total strangers, any of which could be carrying a weapon. Could be trying to slide greedy fingers into your pockets. I kept my jacket on despite the heat in the building, planning to park myself firmly near the back bar that ran along the back of the concert hall. It was set on an incline, up a handful of stairs from the main floor, and would give me a view of the majority of the area.

From there I'd be able to watch Kaleb. Make sure the girls who would inevitably brush up on him, grinding their asses into his groin as they flashed barely covered tits in front of his eyes, only wanted to fuck him. If I'd learned anything from Ma and watching Ava Jade rise to become an influential member of the Saints, it was that chicks were not to be dismissed.

They could just as easily gut you as any man could. The difference? They'd have your guts on the floor before you even knew it was coming.

Kaleb went straight for the bar, shouting to order a drink from the bartender with a raised arm. His shirt pulled up, putting his piece on full display where he still had it tucked in the back of his waistband. I rolled my eyes, stepping behind him to conceal my movements in the dark as I tugged it free.

He whirled on me, ready to pummel whoever touched his gun, giving me an annoyed look with a held out hand when he saw it was me.

I shook my head.

He could have it back after the show. We didn't need everyone in here losing their damn minds if someone saw it. While everyone else in attendance needed to go through front security, walking through metal detectors, we were not in the same category.

But that didn't mean we had to fucking flaunt it. What if someone got the cheeky idea to grab it from him while he was busy with some pair of tits?

Nah. He knew the damn rules. At these kinds of things our pieces needed to be properly concealed, which was why mine was securely strapped just above my ankle. Along with no less than three other concealed weapons in the forms of my favorite switchblade, the pocket knife Dad gifted me a few years back, and a boning knife on my other ankle because you just never knew when you might need to break down a body.

I had a feeling in my gut it might become one of those nights. Hoped to fuck I was wrong.

Kaleb rolled his eyes at me but didn't fight it, taking his drink from the bartender without paying and shouldering past me to find a good spot on the floor. I clenched my teeth hard, checking to make sure the safety was still on his Sig before sliding it into the front of my waistband and pulling my shirt over it. No risk of anyone touching that shit if I stayed right the fuck where I was.

"Drink?" The bartender hollered over the music, cupping his ear for my reply. I shook my head, taking up a bank of three bar stools since it seemed no one wanted to get any closer to me than that.

I watched Kaleb's head bob as he sliced a path through the steadily growing mass of fans gathered on the floor, keeping track of his movements in case I needed to get to him quickly.

I didn't know what exactly his problem was, but I could guess. With each table we turned in search of the Sons, finding nothing, he grew more irritable. But something told me it was more to do with what that meant for him and his pursuit of Becca Hart than anything else.

The longer it took to deal with this, the longer he'd have to stay away from her.

But my little brother had surprised me this week. Exhausted or not, he hadn't brought a single pair of legs home to fuck since I heard about the yoga studio. Specifically what the entire campus was saying they'd done in the showers there.

That familiar heat rushed through my core, and I parted my lips to let out the steam, my brows knotting as I watched Kaleb drink his whiskey Coke. Alternating between putting it to his lips and lifting it high in the air above his head to prevent it from spilling as the crowd jostled him from all sides. Each one vying to get closer to the stage as the lights there dimmed to nothing, signaling the start of the show.

I leaned back against the bar, threading my fingers together as I settled in to watch.

Black lighting hidden in the rafters above the stage ignited, giving the black abyss on stage an ultraviolet hue.

The crowd cheered, screaming their hearts out as a spec of white appeared in the dark, growing as Corvus James walked slowly to the front of the stage. His white skull makeup glowed bright beneath the lights, giving him a menacing quality.

Even though for the first couple years the makeup served its purpose of keeping his true identity hidden from everyone who came to see his shows, he'd kept it going even now. When everyone had stopped speculating online whether he was a serial killer or a foreign prince or an escaped inmate.

Ava Jade came out of the shadows behind him, her matching skeleton makeup lighting up in the pitch dark to a raucous barrage of even louder cheering.

Primal Ethos had already been great, but her addition only made them even better, rocketing them from their status as underground indie into stardom. They hit one of the spots on some top ten list last month. But unlike the others on the list, PE didn't bend or shift to make their music more to market, trying to reach even higher.

No.

If anything they went darker, more violent. Openly

lyricizing about meticulously planned executions, the words lost on anyone who didn't know what they did for a living.

The metaphors not really metaphors at all as the tabloids would suggest.

"Can I get two rye and gingers?"

The voice cut through all thought as Becca Hart shouted her order to the bartender not five yards from where I stood, twisting around to cheer and shout with the others as Corvus James—aka The Bone Man— took the mic from its stand at the head of the stage.

"Lodi!" he shouted, his rich voice carrying to all corners of the arena. "You beautiful bastards, how the fuck are you?"

Screams erupted from the throng.

"Can't hear you," Ava Jade egged on the crowd, putting a painted hand to her ear for dramatic effect.

The volume went even louder and Becca rose up on her tiptoes, cupping her delicate hands around her mouth to call out to her best friend on stage. The pride lighting up her eyes struck something buried deep inside and my breathing turned heavy and shallow as I continued to watch her.

Her lips spread wide into the truest form of a smile as Primal Ethos finished riling up the crowd and a familiar beat pulsed through the air as they began the first song.

Switchblade Smile.

My favorite one.

The bartender yelled something at Becca and she turned to throw some money down on the bar before lifting her drink to her lips for a sip through the tiny straw. Her brow wrinkled, and I immediately stood upright, searching the people around her, checking for any unsavories. If anyone put something in her drink they were fucking dead.

Not just dead. I'd fucking smash them into the earth until they were nothing but human pulp.

But an instant later, she plucked the too tiny straw from her drink and threw it down on the bar like it offended her, and I knew the only thing that had her making that face was that she couldn't mainline her booze fast enough.

She scooped the second cup up from the bar, lifting both of them high overhead as she wove her way back through the crowds of people now all pushing to the front. I tracked her movements, something in my gut pulling me forward like the force of a human sized fucking magnet.

Just because no one drugged her drink at the bar didn't mean someone wouldn't on the dance floor. And wearing that fucking dress she was wearing I didn't doubt every brickheaded asshat in attendance wanted in her pants.

I cursed to myself before leaving my perch at the bar, the crowd parting for me as I stalked down the stairs, trying not to lose sight of her. I'd stay close to both her and my brother. Out of sight. On the sidelines. Close enough to make sure they were both out of harm's way since neither seemed capable of doing it themselves.

I almost lost her as I found my way to the center of the

floor and had to bowl through another twenty people before I found her, their bodies knocking into mine. Shoulders brushing arms. Bumping into my back. Suffocating in their nearness.

But there she was, her and her two roommates lifting their heads to sing along with the lyrics to Switchblade Smile. If they knew they were recounting the story of when Rook fucking Clayton carved a literal joker smile into an asshole who's only offence was giving his Ghost dirty looks.

Turned out the bastard had some roofies in his pocket, so the others didn't give him too much hassle after the deed was done.

I widened my stance, pushing my elbow out to keep everyone around me at a breathable distance as I tried to find my brother's face in the clusterfuck of people.

No dice, though.

*Shit.*

I pushed myself higher, thinking I could see him near the railing at the very front. He lifted his arm, and I could just make out the blur of ink over the front of his forearm. The Saint symbol worked into the wooden handle of a Viking ax giving him away.

When I narrowed my focus back to Becca, satisfied he was within view of the stage and security, my blood lit in my veins like it was gasoline.

Her gaze locked on mine, the match striking flame.

Becca was the picture of stillness in an ever-changing world, as immobile as a statue as her friends bounced on their feet, bodies swaying with the beat as they sang their hearts out.

Her lips parted as she took me in, something like pain in her eyes making me want to rip the universe to shreds just to make it *go*.

In a move I didn't see coming, Becca moved toward me, squeezing through the bodies between us, all of them oblivious to her, their attention squarely ahead as Primal Ethos finished the song to deafening applause.

Another song kicked up where Switchblade Smile left off, this one starting with a hollow beat that I could feel like a reverberation from my head down to my feet. The *thud thud, thud thud* of the intro to Fuckface like the sound of my own heartbeat in my ears as Becca stopped right in front of me.

She looked up at me, a wicked defiance knotting the pale skin between her eyes, twisting her mouth. But in her eyes there was only that haunting touch of pain that I would do anything to erase.

Becca extended her hand to me, and I looked down at it between us. At her long fingers, each one circled various golden rings. Her nails, sharpened to points made me ache to know what they would feel like if they pierced my skin.

I stepped back, shaking my head, but she stepped forward, disobedient as she slipped her hand into mine and squeezed, pulling me closer.

Becca pivoted on her feet, pulling my hand around her waist as she pressed into my chest with her back, swaying to the music.

Her head brushed against my chin, her buttery soft hair filling my nose with the scent of her. Distinctly floral, but not sweet like most girls smelled to me. No, her scent was heady, full-bodied, and warm. Sharp jasmine and smooth smoldering sandalwood.

I inhaled deeply, my grip on her waist tightening as she pressed her peachy ass into my groin, making me growl into her hair, my teeth bared behind my lips.

Was this…

…her accepting my apology?

Becca moved with the grace of a lioness, swaying perfectly in tune with the beat. Her bare back rubbed against my chest and I brought my other hand to her opposite hip, guiding her nearer.

My fingers brushed bare skin, and she shivered in my hands.

*Jesus… fuck.*

The cutouts in her dress made it easy to slip my hands beneath the soft fabric, the pads of my fingers skating across her middle, touching, feeling, grabbing.

She leaned back against me, her head tipped up in ecstasy, eyes closed to reveal two mean slashes of black liner across her lids. She reached up, curling a hand around my neck.

I dipped my head closer to her cheek as I allowed my fingers to search lower, tracing a straight line down from her belly button beneath the dress she wore.

Becca's breath caught, and I watched her suck air in between her teeth as I brought my teeth to her throat, biting down on the supple flesh at the nape of her neck.

She bucked against me, arching her back, but my hands, now firmly wrapped around her middle, pressed flat against her lower abdomen, keeping her plastered to me as I tasted her.

The song ended, but I didn't let her go, holding her there as I breathed her in, my hot breath fanning over the back of her neck as my cock twitched hungrily in my jeans.

"H-Hardin," she choked out, her hands gripping mine through her dress, but not pulling. Not stopping me as I pressed the fingers of my right hand below the waistband of her thin silky panties, brushing the mound of her sweet cunt and the next song began, bodies shuffling all around us.

I looked up in time to see her friends gawking at us through the crowd, but I didn't care. My upper lip twitched into a snarl, warning them to stay away as I dragged Becca back, pulling us deeper into the throng of screaming fans.

They didn't know.

They wouldn't see.

I pushed my face back into her hair, and her grip on my forearms through her dress tightened as I slid my first two fingers down onto her slippery clit.

I grunted into her ear, every inch of my skin on fire.

She was so damn wet for me already.

Becca let out a loud moan that was swallowed up by a hundred singing voices and the boom of the base through the loudspeakers. I held her in place with my one hand still firmly gripped on her hip while I circled her greedy little cunt with my other fingers, rubbing her until she was shaking against me, her eyes squeezed tight with pleasure.

She came like a fucking hurricane, a vicious cry tearing from her throat as those sharp claws of hers bit down into my forearms. Her thighs pressed tight, trying to push me out, but I stayed, pushing her to the edge of how much pleasure she could handle until she threw her body forward, breaking contact.

Becca stumbled, catching herself on some chick with a rushed apology before she turned, looking back at me through eyes filled with surprise. Filled with fear. As if she just realized what she'd done. What she'd allowed to happen right here on the fucking dance floor of a stadium filled with well over five thousand people.

I grinned wickedly at her, my cock thick and throbbing between my legs, pressed tight against my thigh. The slightest brush of it against my boxers was making me even harder.

*Run,* I mouthed to her and her brows shot up. Sweet, beautiful terror hung as a tangible force in the air between us before she turned tail and took off, shoving past everyone in her way.

I smiled wider, rolling my shoulders back, taking a long inhale through my nose, readying myself for the hunt.

She could run all she liked, but she couldn't hide.

Three...

Two...

One.

I darted forward, heedless of the meat sacks in my path as I hurtled in the direction she headed, my predator's gaze in hunting for long, dark hair. Long, lean legs. A black dress with cutouts in the sides and an open back revealing smooth, pale skin.

A whip of black hair and I parried left, grabbing her by the arm. A face I didn't recognize twisted to face me, draining of all color. I let her go, lifting myself high in time to catch a flash of her as she slung herself around the corner into the hallway leading to the bathrooms.

*Got you.*

I knocked several faceless bodies to the ground as I marched out from the cluster of fans and into the corridor, picking up my pace. Her scent filled the air, and I zeroed in on it with the sort of focus only I could achieve, passing door after door, my back lifting with each great inhale as I tracked her further. Deeper into the areas of the building not meant for fans.

A security guard stood at the end of the long hall. He lifted his chin, recognizing me. I pointed down deeper into the building with an arched brow. He nodded.

She went in there.

I gestured for him to block the way, no one in or out, and he fell into place behind me as I ventured into the shadowy passageway that I knew for a fact led to nothing more than an old equipment and instrument storage area with only one exit. One exit that the owners locked from the outside on concert nights so no one without a ticket could get in.

The music from the main stadium was reduced to

nothing more than background noise from here. Loud enough to block out most sound, but not clear enough to make out most of the words Ava Jade and Corvus were singing.

As if on fucking cue, the rattle of chains broke through the distant synth and base, and I whipped my head to the right, making for the exit doors.

The area around it was packed with shelves and old speakers that were even taller than me, left to collect dust.

The chains rattled louder, and I shoved the speaker to my right, sending it toppling to the ground with a muted *thud*.

Becca let out a short scream.

I pushed the next one from my path.

*Thud.*

And the next.

*Thud.*

The shelf standing between us went down in a symphony of broken glass and clattering metal and Becca finally gave up her attempt at escape, turning to press her back flat against the metal door. Her chest rose and fell rapidly as she watched me approach.

I stopped just shy of grabbing her and making her mine in ways she would never fucking forget, giving her this one chance. This one second to walk away. To tell me *no.* If she didn't take it now, I wouldn't offer it again.

Swallowing hard, I steadied my breaths and opened my mouth to speak. I just needed two words. One warning.

"One chance," I told her, and her eyes widened at the

sound of my voice, loud enough to be heard above the pounding music. Her lips parted, expression softening, opening like a fucking flower for me to steal her soul.

I flicked my eyes to the left, where there was a clear path for her escape, and back to her. I let the full weight of my true meaning show in my eyes, wanting her to see the animal that would be unleashed if she didn't take this one chance to run. Because if I touched her again there would be no restraint. No holding back.

I'd get lost in her. In her smell. In the feel of her. In the sounds she would make as I pummeled her sweet cunt until she couldn't walk straight for fucking days.

No amount of fight would stop me once I'd started.

Becca looked left. Looked back. Didn't move.

My core tightened, coiling for the strike.

*Time's up.*

I rushed forward and she let out a wordless exclamation as I pushed a fist into her hair, pulling tight against her scalp to angle her face upward. Her hands pressed against my chest, wide eyes slamming shut as I dove into her gasping mouth with my tongue, ravishing her. Becca moaned into my mouth as I bit down on her lower lip, running my teeth along the perfectly pillowed swell until I tasted the tang of copper on my tongue.

That only made me kiss her harder, take her deeper, until her little panting moans turned frantic. She arched her back, pushing her tits up against my chest as she reached between us, trying to find my cock.

I curled my fingers around her wrist, jerking it away as I pulled my mouth from hers and spun her around.

I snatched a fistful of dress and yanked it up, revealing the ass that didn't even come close to the version in my wettest fucking dreams. She arched her back again and I reeled back, my palm cracking against her left cheek, leaving a handprint I could see even in the dark as Becca hiccupped against the door, letting out a gush of air.

I spanked her again, harder, and a small sound, something between a moan and a sob lifted from her lungs.

She needed to be punished for denying me on the dancefloor. For running. She was *mine.*

She had her chance to run, and she didn't take it. I punished her for every glare she'd cast my way since we met. Every harsh word spoken. Every moment she spent denying the connection between us, fighting it.

And when I was done and she shuddered against the door, I dropped to one knee, ready to take all the pain away. Needing to taste her. Needing to *feast* on my prize.

She let out a yelp as I released my hold on her hair and spun her again. I threw her right leg over my shoulder and jerked up her dress, mouthing her sweet, sweet pussy through the damp fabric of her panties until she was trembling.

I bit down on the thin fabric and tore, jerking my head sharply right until her cunt was laid bare for me. She pushed it into me as I dove in with my tongue, licking along her slit. A possessive growl vibrated in my chest as I savored every drop, licking and sucking and nibbling as she fisted her hands in my hair. Holding tighter. Not fighting it.

Not fighting *me*.

Becca cried out as her orgasm started to crest, her thighs squeezing on either side of my head, her hands in my hair pulling frantically.

I shoved her legs back open, forcing her to wring every drop of pleasure she could, but still she fought, screaming, pushing, kicking.

In one fluid movement, I drew the gun from the front of my waistband and pushed it against her inner thigh. She gasped, forcing her legs open, holding them that way while I ate her fucking senseless, until she was gushing on my tongue and couldn't breathe. Her body trembling against the barrel of the gun.

I kept her there while I lapped up her release, knowing there wasn't a damn thing in this cruel world powerful enough to stop me from fucking her now.

Her eyes were still glazed, half rolled back as I dropped the weapon and let her leg fall from my shoulder, but not before biting hard into her thigh, right where the barrel of the gun had been pressed—hard enough to break the skin, leaving my mark there for anyone who dared trespass on my turf.

Becca screamed, pushing at my head, but when I pulled my mouth away, teeth stained with red, her now focused stare flitted between my mouth and the mark in her thigh I prayed would scar, remaining there forever as a reminder of my claim.

Fear made her face pale, and I knew a second before

she made her move what she was going to do. I grabbed her ankle at the same moment she tried to make a run for it, sending her tripping to her knees on the concrete floor with a cry.

I was on her in an instant, tossing the gun aside, holding her down with my weight alone, her chest pressed flat against the floor, her arms reaching and grasping uselessly for anything, finding nothing but bits of broken glass further away to her left.

I tugged her hands back from the shattered remains of the fallen shelf, pinning them behind her back, both of them fitting easily into one of my hands as I used the other to unbuckle my belt. My cock pulsed against the wall of denim, begging for release. I rolled my hips, shoving my jeans down low enough to free it as Becca continued to struggle beneath me, only adding fuel to the fire.

Palming her dress away from her bare ass, I took a split second to marvel at the artwork my hands had left there before gripping the base of my cock and thrusting between those perfect cheeks, making the fight go out of her as a cry of absolute ecstasy poured from her chest. I buried myself deep in her cunt, all nine inches of me sheathed in warm flesh. In utter perfection.

I choked out a groan at the vicious pleasure running through me as pure and unfiltered as an electrical current. Her gorgeous cunt squeezed around me, tight and so fucking *warm*.

Her cry trailed off into a whimper as I slid out from

her only to slam back inside, her whole body moving with the force of my thrust.

Testing a theory, I released her wrists and her palms fell flat against the cement to either side of her body. I traced the line of her back, watching her muscle flex in a wave as she used the leverage of her hands to lift her hips, arching her back for me as I drove into her again, *harder*, earning myself another choked off cry.

She wanted this.

She *wanted* to be dominated. Wanted to be *used*.

My vision narrowed to pinpricks, that all-encompassing obsession I'd been fighting against for weeks anchoring itself in me in a way that I knew could never be pulled up, pulled out.

I curled my fingers around her hips, jerking her up onto all fours.

She let out a sound like a fucking snarl as I began to move faster, fucking her like a man possessed. My thighs slammed against hers as I drilled into her, pumping between her legs until I was sure I was going to splinter into a thousand pieces and be blown away by the fucking wind.

A throaty cry hit my ears, and I realized with a stomach turning certainty that it'd come from my own mouth. I slammed my lips shut, holding in the sounds of my hedonism as Becca's cries began to reach a crescendo.

This time, when she came, I went with her, pouring into her with a feral roar, uncaring if she heard me as we both collapsed on the cool floor. I pulled her to me, wrapping my arms around her to bury my face in her neck, feeling her pulse against my lips.

She stayed there, perfectly still, as if suspended in time. Until whatever spell the music and the dark had cast was broken. She shrugged out of my grip, and I let her go, watched her push shakily to her feet, stumble in her heels. Watched her collect her dignity, straighten her dress. Her hair. Discard her torn panties and lift her little black purse from the floor.

Then she spun to face me, her face concealed in shadow as her arms swung and her foot connected with my gut, forcing the air from my lungs. I laughed darkly, quietly, goosebumps rising on my flesh at the purity of the pain hitting deep in my solar plexus. She kicked again and I let her, opening my arms wide as the toe of her heel hit bone and the hit ricocheted up my rib cage.

She tripped to the side, catching herself on a still standing speaker, her face twisted in pain. Letting me know she'd hurt herself far more than she hurt me with her little show of strength. I watched her, felt my lips twitch up into half a smile.

*You loved every raw second*, I challenged her.

"Fuck you!" she hissed, and I pushed up onto my side, looking up at her with a cocked head, letting the smile fall, understanding that she needed this. She needed time to accept that she liked every dirty, wrong thing I did to her tonight. That she craved it more than she would ever crave anything else.

It was no easy thing, bowing to the dark.

*It's okay.*

*"I-I hate you!"*

*It's okay.*

Her chin quivered, and she squeezed her eyes shut, shaking her head violently as she turned on her heel and left. This time, I wouldn't chase her because I knew, one way or another, she'd come back all on her own.

# Kaleb

TWENTY-THREE

"There you are."

About time he decided to grace me with his presence. I went looking for my brother after the second encore song to find his spot at the bar lacking its usual occupant. It would've been one thing for him to ditch me, but to refuse to answer any of my text messages and leave me without a piece was just a dick move. Especially given the current circumstances.

"Where the hell you been?" I asked him. "I went out to the car, checked the perimeter. I thought you fucked off."

He came into the backstage area The Crows already had set up for a late night of overtime debauchery. The fridge was stocked with good booze and a mountain of snacks covered the long bar top counter running the length of the space against the back wall.

Something about the disheveled look of him made me pause. Reassess.

*Oh shit.*

I knew that look. It was the Hardin-just-ate-a-fucking-soul glow he only got after a particularly good lay. And fuck if this wasn't the perfect place for him to find that. What with the type of music Primal Ethos slung. I bet he found a good little freak to take the edge off. If only I could do the same, but this wood only seemed to stand at attention for one girl these days.

"Clearly I missed a good time," I said, with a lot more bitterness than intended. "But next time pick up your phone and text me back. It's that little rectangular thing you keep in your pocket. Has tiny little buttons to make messages."

He lifted his gaze to mine as he fell into one of the three long black sofas set up in a fucked up triangle formation around an artfully misshapen coffee table. But even though my brother was looking at me, he wasn't seeing me. There was a faraway quality to his stare that told me he was anywhere but here right now.

"Everything good, Bro?" I asked, unable to be pissed at him anymore. Not when he was looking so damn… haunted. Hardin St. Vincent always had his shit in check. Nothing ruffled him. Nothing shook him.

He was solid. Made of cold iron from his head to his fucking toes.

"Yeah," he muttered, reaching into his waistband for my piece. He held it out to me and I took it with a wary eye, finding claw marks over his forearms. Down the right side of his neck.

"Hardin…"

He swallowed, looking through me again.

"The girl you fucked. She still breathing?"

His brow wrinkled in confusion and then he was back, the twist of anger warping his mouth into a sneer, his black eyes narrowing.

I lifted my hands in a placating gesture. "Right. Stupid question."

"Hey, fuckers!" Rook called, a bottle of Jack in his hand as he strolled into the room with Grey behind him. He made a show of looking around before lifting a brow. "They still not out?"

It took me a full second to register he was talking about Ava Jade and Corvus, all my brain cells focusing their functionality on the issue of my brother having potentially murdered someone tonight.

"Nah, haven't seen them yet," I told Rook, and he and Grey shared a knowing look, both of them letting out little laughs.

Oh my god, they were fucking. That's what was taking so long.

I was reminded again of my cousins' arrangement or rather their shared relationship with Ava Jade. Neither Grey nor Rook seemed even a little perturbed that their adoptive brother was getting his rumored to be massive cock all up in their girl right now.

"What's with the face?" Grey asked, sliding onto the

sofa next to where I stood. Rook fell to his ass on the other side, putting his Jack to his lips.

He held it out in offer to me, giving the brown liquid inside the glass bottle a swirl, but in a totally unforeseen turn of events, I realized I didn't want a drink. I'd barely finished the one I had on the dance floor earlier.

I shook my head and sat down between my cousins just as Ava Jade–aka the Saint's Dagger—and Corvus James—aka The Bone Man—entered the room. They knocked into each other's shoulders, AJ with a flush to her cheeks and Corvus still sporting a half chub through his pants. Not that I was trying to look, he was just that big, making it hard to fucking miss, especially in sweatpants.

"Kind of you to join your own party," Grey joked, rising to wrap AJ up in a big hug, pressing his lips to her neck. "Amazing show, AJ," he whispered to her and then smacked her ass. "Not that I'd expect anything less."

Hardin and Corvus caught up with each other near the drink fridge, chatting in hushed tones, no doubt about the threat further south. I just hoped he wasn't saying shit Dad wouldn't want him to. There was a fine line between warning our sister chapter of the Saints and getting them involved in something that wasn't rightfully their problem.

"Hey," Rook chided AJ when she tried to make for the snacks, snagging her wrist to look her intently in the eyes. "Best concert I've ever been to, Ghost."

AJ leaned down to whisper something in Rook's ear that made his Adam's apple bob in his throat. Then she skipped to the snacks.

I couldn't help a small smile at their fucked up love rectangle. Or square or whatever. It really seemed to work for them.

"Can I ask you something?" I posed the question to both my cousins.

"Shoot," Rook said, sighing as he pulled a coin from his inside jacket pocket, flipping it edge over edge over his knuckles.

I rubbed the back of my neck, unsure exactly how to phrase what I wanted to know. "This, *uh*, thing, whatever it is, with you guys and Ava Jade…"

Grey smirked as if he already knew where this was headed.

"How does it work?" I blurted out before I could change my mind, my gaze lifting to my brother in the makeshift kitchen area. If his little mural of Becca Hart told me anything, it was that he was a lot more interested in the girl than I originally thought.

And since I'd decided she was going to be *mine*, that posed a bit of an issue.

"How does what work?" Grey asked, enjoying this way too much. "You mean, do we each get a hole, or…"

I shoved him. "Don't fucking tease. I'm serious."

Grey sobered at the sincerity in my tone. I genuinely wanted to know. No. I *needed* to know.

"All right man, sorry. The truth is I don't really know how it works, just that it… does."

"Rook?" I hedged, curious if he had a different answer. Anything that would be even remotely helpful. Because the truth was I hadn't only noticed the attention my brother was paying Becca, but also the attention she was paying him. Namely, the way she looked at him whenever he was near her.

When he wasn't paying attention: like she wanted to unravel him.

And when he was: like she would like nothing more than to douse him in gasoline and set him on fire.

Rook pursed his lips, shifting a bit in his seat as he considered it and then clicked his tongue. "I got nothing."

"Seriously?"

He leaned forward over his knees, knocking the bottle of Jack onto the weird ass coffee table as he turned to me. "It just happened naturally, man. It was clear from the start that we all liked her. We all wanted her. And in some fucked up twist of fate she also happened to want all of us. You know, after she was done pretending she hated our asses."

"That's it?"

"Pretty much," Grey answered for Rook. "It never felt wrong. Not really. And we never asked her to choose, which I think made it easier for her to accept."

"And you never got jealous of each other?"

They shared a look. "Not enough for it to matter," Grey said.

"I know where Ghost and I stand. That's all I need."

That shit was not helpful.

"Why are you asking all this, bro?" Rook asked, nudging me with a knee. "Is there someone you and Hardin—" He cut himself off abruptly, stiffening beside me, and I knew he'd already figured it out. People said

Corvus was the super perceptive one, but I didn't think he had anything on Rook. "Shit. Becca?"

"*No*," Grey said, drawing out the 'o.' "We asked you to watch over her, not fuck her. AJ's going to slit our throats in our sleep. Scratch that, she'll slit *yours*."

Rook laughed darkly to himself, still flipping that damn coin over his knuckles. "Nah. Don't worry about Ghost. Becca's a big girl, and we already knew she had a thing for the bad ones. Besides, she's not as helpless as she pretends to be. That girl has fire, she just hasn't figured out how to wield it, yet."

What the shit was that supposed to mean?

As if on cue, Becca, Toby, and their other roommate— shit, what the fuck was her name? Katelyn? Katie?— walked into the room.

Becca looked paler than the Ghost her best friend was nicknamed for as she stumbled into the low lit area, her long legs shaky in her heels even though she was holding her head high, her eyes searching for her friend, finding me instead.

Her throat bobbed and her gaze immediately flicked to where Hardin stood, watching her with a predator's gaze. She broke eye contact with him the instant her eyes met his, and I felt something crumple in my gut.

Oh fuck. No. Not her.

*Really, Hardin?*

I remembered the scratch marks on his arms and neck and shut my eyes against a rush of something close to jealousy. My brother would never force a girl he thought was unwilling, which had to mean that she *was* willing. Proving my theory of their shared connection true.

"Becks!"

I looked up in time to see Ava Jade throwing her arms around Becca, knocking both of them off their feet. They landed in a heap on the vacant sofa opposite us and Ava Jade laid kiss after kiss all over Becca's face as her friend laughed.

Becca managed to extricate herself long enough to catch a breath, a very real, but still tainted looking smile pulling at her lips. "I fucking missed you, bitch," she told Ava Jade, her brown eyes glistening.

Ava Jade hugged her again, tighter this time. "Missed you, too. I promise, no more tours until next year, okay?"

"Okay."

Toby and Kate hovered awkwardly across the room. Grey lifted his hand to give Toby a wave, and I remembered he'd let him ride shotty last weekend at the race. Her other roomie gave a little wave, too, the pair of them still absolutely jacked from the concert, their cheeks pink.

"Oh fuck, sorry," Becca said, standing from the sofa to introduce Ava Jade to her roommates. I didn't miss the way AJ assessed them. Like a butcher might assess a cut of meat before deciding whether or not to package it up or throw it in with a chuck to grind into pulp.

I waited for them to finish their moment, Becca introducing her friends to Corvus as well, before interrupting, unable to keep my big mouth shut. "No hello for us, Vixen?"

Tension lined her forehead as she settled onto the Sofa with her friends and glared at me. "Hi, Kaleb."

"Hi?"

She rolled her eyes, and I didn't miss how she completely ignored my brother. No hello for him.

"Wait," Ava Jade said, her brows lowering as she looked between her friend and me. "You know each other?"

Becca looked guilty as fuck, and I flashed Ava Jade my most innocent smile. The one that got me out of even the worst kinds of shit I'd managed to walk my ass into.

She gave me a cheeky sneer and then laughed, the loud sound of it bordering on a cackle as she set a hand on Becca's knee and wiped a tear from her eyes. "What am I even saying? Of course, you know each other. Leave it to Becks to find the biggest, baddest fuckers on campus and make friends. Right, Becks?" She elbowed Becca, who let out a strained laugh as Ava Jade wiped another tear from her eye. "Priceless. I'll have to get that story later, for now I want to hear all about your new place and your job and everything I've missed since you moved away."

Toby cleared his throat, biting his lip as he tugged something from his pocket with two fingers. The tiny baggy he shook held four round, all-white pills. "Before we launch into the magnificent tale of how Becca basically swindled herself a job at DBD and made me her shop bitch in a matter of twenty-four-hours, how about we kick this shindig up a notch, hmmm?"

Rook shifted uncomfortably beside me, and I had to admit, the feeling was mutual. It'd been a few years since I got clean and my 'problem' wasn't nearly as severe as

Rook's. At least when I got high, all I wanted to do was stare into space while I chain fed a never ending parade of pizza into my face. When he got high, he was liable to murder anyone in his vicinity with his bare hands.

"I don't think—" I started, but Becca was already taking a pill from the baggy and popping it into her mouth. Something passed between her and my brother, and I watched his nostrils flare angrily as she swallowed the pill dry.

Toby took the next one and offered the bag to Kate—*that's her name*—who shook her head. "Someone's gotta drive us home, Tobes."

"Shit!"

"No, it's good." She waved him off. "You know I don't do that shit, anyway."

Toby offered his drugs to AJ, but she declined. "No one else," he asked.

I swallowed. "I could—"

"The fuck you are," Grey said, and I remembered the shithead also knew about my past issues with everything under the sun from E to MDMA. "Give it here."

Toby tossed the bag to Grey, who popped the last two pills in his own mouth before either me or Rook could make a play for them.

I felt a cold sort of relief once they were all gone and Rook, shaken from his reverie, went right back to rolling that coin over his knuckles, taking another pull from his Jack.

"All right, let's get this party started!"

Becca launched into a redacted tale of how her first

few weeks were going in Santa Clarita. She was careful to focus on her schoolwork and her roommates, the topics that would involve me or my brother glazed over at best.

Trying to eavesdrop on her conversation made it hella hard to keep up my own with the guys, and within thirty minutes, all semblance of proper conversation came to an abrupt end.

Grey nuzzled against Rook, humming blissfully to himself while Rook gave him shit for getting nacho powder on his jacket, but made no move to stop him.

Toby danced in front of the open refrigerator, pulling out the ingredients for what he called a lazy man's margarita while Kate chatted with Ava Jade about the merits of drip versus french press coffee. Kate, I might add, on her *second* cup of glorified tequila and lime juice. There was no way I was letting either of Becca's roommates drive her anywhere.

And Becca? Becca did not seem to be having the same kind of trip as the others. Her dark eyes kept shifting about the room, the tension in her shoulders getting tighter and tighter until I could hardly stand to look at her anymore, my stomach in knots on her behalf.

I shook my head, extricating myself from the conversation with Rook and Corvus as I stood from the sofa, grabbed a bottle of water from the counter, and went to kneel in front of Becca. I held out the bottle like a peace offering, no longer caring that she might've fucked my brother a few hours ago.

She didn't look good. Not at all.

"Drink this," I ordered her, and she tried to paw it away.

Ava Jade, tuning back in to her best friend, held up a hand to Kate to silence her, shifting back over to where Becca sat hunched over herself, her eyelids drooping.

"When was the last time she ate or drank anything?" Ava Jade asked Kate as I finally won out in our silent battle, getting Becca to take the bottle and drink.

"*Uh*, I don't know. We came straight from work and I... *shit*. I don't think she took her last break, and I didn't see her eat or drink anything but a few americanos."

The way Ava Jade looked at Kate could've curdled dairy, but shockingly, Kate didn't cower, she jumped to her feet and went in search of food.

"Hey, Becks? You okay, babe?" AJ was asking her friend, rubbing reassuring circles into her back.

"Tired," Becca said on a sigh. "So tired."

Hardin's phone rang loud in the room, cutting through the low music and the buzzing in my head. Distantly, I watched him answer the call and excuse himself to the far wall. He wouldn't take a call right now unless it was...

Ah fuck. Not now.

"I need you to drink some more," I told Becca, helping her tip the bottle up to get more past her lips. Some spilled down her front, and she groaned weakly to herself.

Hardin jerked his chin to me, and I shook my head, not wanting to leave Becca's side. She looked fucking white. "What was that shit?" I asked Kate as she came back with an armload of snacks.

"It's just Molly," she said.

"Where did he get it?"

Kate blanched. "Um, some guy called Minty, I think."

I clenched my teeth, wanting to ring the fucker's neck, but at least that meant one good thing. "I know him," I assured Ava Jade. "He's a fucking tool, but his shit is as clean as it gets. She'll be okay, just needs to sleep it off."

On cue, Becca keeled over, laying her head on the armrest of the sofa, tucking her legs up into her chest.

"*Kaleb*," my brother hissed, earning himself a little chirp from Kate as he grabbed me by the back of my shirt and hauled me to my feet. I twisted from his grip.

"What the hell, man?"

He inclined his head for me to follow him back to the edge of the room, and I suppressed a growl as I stormed after him. "What?"

"There's a problem."

"What kind of problem?"

"The kind that has Dad calling me at two in the morning. What the fuck do you think?"

My face pinched, and my piece weighed heavily in the back of my jeans as a bolt of unease drove up my spine. The Sons.

We didn't know.

And they made their move.

"What happened?" I asked.

Hardin ran a flat palm over his mouth, his face a menagerie of fury and an unsettling amount of uncertainty. "I don't know. He wasn't exactly forthcoming, Kale. He said to get our asses back to SoCal. Now. We're supposed to meet him at the house."

*Fuuuuuck.*

I turned my attention back to Becca, who was currently being babied by her friend. Ava Jade brushed her long dark hair from her face and pressed the back of her palm against her pale forehead.

"I'm not leaving her," I decided.

Hardin's jaw flexed. "Agreed."

At least we did on something.

I cleared my throat. "We have to peace," I announced, hurrying back across the room. I lifted Becca's clutch from the coffee table and slipped it into my back pocket. "We'll drive her back to Santa Clarita. Make sure she gets tucked in."

Hardin brushed past me, already lifting Becca from the couch, tucking her tight against his chest despite her muted protests.

"Wait, maybe she should stay," Ava Jade argued.

Kate nodded. "Yeah, I don't think she should be alone in the apartment right now. She can–"

"We've got her," Hardin said, speaking for the second time in front of Becca and her roommates, surprising the hell out of me.

Ava Jade and Kate fell silent, but Toby returned to the living room and had to have his two cents. "We're leaving soon anyway. Let us drive—"

"Look, Toby, I've got no beef with you or your roommate, but you're high and she's had two... whatever that is... in the last forty minutes. Neither of you should be driving. Not until you sober up a bit. We'll get her back safe, and we'll stay with her until you guys get back, yeah?"

I had no idea whether or not I could actually make that happen, depending on what kind of shit we were dealing with back home, but we'd figure it out once we were there. I just knew I wasn't leaving her. Not in that condition.

"O-okay. If you're sure."

"I am."

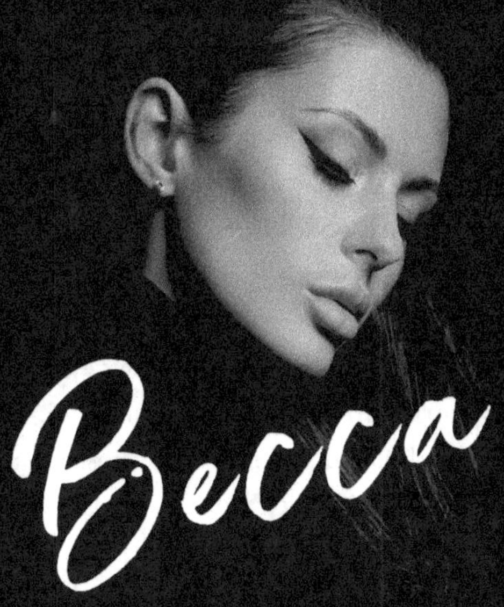

# Becca

## TWENTY-FOUR

"Can you drive?" Hardin's rumbling voice vibrated against my side and I fought for a sense of focus, of alertness that seemed just out of reach, making everything come through foggy and muddled. Like I was hearing through ears filled with cotton. Moving through mud. Trying to speak through a mouth thick with a numb tongue.

I did know one thing, though. I liked the feel of him. I liked the sound he made when he finally opened that beautiful mouth to speak.

I couldn't remember why, but I was meant to be angry with him. I wanted to be. But every time I tried to latch onto those feelings, they slipped through my fingers like sand.

A small sound came from my throat, something like a moan or a whimper. I just wanted him to keep talking. For that rumbling voice to lull me back to sleep.

Soft leather brushed against my cheek with each step, and I tried to reach for it, wanting to feel it under my fingers. It smelled so good. *He* smelled so good. Like warm amber and musk and wood and *Hardin*.

"Yeah," I heard Kaleb reply, and the sound of something jingling had me trying to peel my eyelids back only to see a blurry, streaky mess of dark colors that appeared discombobulated. Like one of those paintings where everything was backward and upside down, purposefully distorted.

I caught black eyes, hooded and shadowed. A bright sliver of moon and the close darkness of the inside of a vehicle.

Something bumped my feet, and I jolted, jostled from the other end as I was pulled onto a lap, rough fingers pushing my hair out of my face.

"She okay?" Kaleb asked.

Hardin didn't reply, not audibly, but I could picture him nodding to Kaleb in the rearview, the imagined image pockmarked with blooming lights, coming into and out of focus.

Something pulled the hem of my dress, covering me, and I sucked in a breath as something grazed my ass. The lightest touch sent a ripple of fire coursing up my body. Like pain, but also, not.

Why did it hurt?

A vivid image of a hand clapping down on my skin, punishing me, stole through my mind, and I shuddered at the drug-tainted memory, my thighs pressing together.

It came back in waves, my body bowing and clenching

as I relived every rough touch, every fevered kiss, all of it tinted with an air of delusion. Making me question whether it happened at all.

"Mmm," I moaned against Hardin's lap, the space between my legs aching but on fire again anyway. I twisted my hand sloppily in my dress, trying to put the fire out, my hand finding wet, sensitive skin. The light touch of my own fingers sent a jolt through me, and I moaned, grinding against the slippery touch of my fingers.

A hand grabbed my wrist roughly, prying my fingers away, making me whimper.

"*Don't,*" a savage growl echoed somewhere above me and I tried to find him in the broken dark as the car moved beneath us. I found a jaw that seemed set in stone. Eyes that flashed with physical pain as light passed over the face of a fallen angel, illuminating him only for an instant before he was plunged back to darkness.

I blinked, a moment of clarity taking me as I remembered taking a pill from Toby. Realized that I was high. And in the backseat of Kaleb and Hardin's Bronco. How the hell did I get here?

Why did I take that pill?

Oh yeah... because I didn't want to think about the fact that I...

Kaleb was sort of beautiful from this angle.

I mean, he was always beautiful, but with both hands on the wheel as he propelled us god knew where, I could see the cut of his jaw, the perfect angle of his nose. The way his lips were evenly sized. The strong protrusion of his cheekbone.

I blinked, and he was a statue, carved of marble. Blinked again and he was marble made flesh.

"Whoa," I said on a breath, reaching out a hand as if I could touch him, but he was just out of reach and there was still something holding me back, shackling my arm to the seat.

I tugged it free and sighed heavily into rough denim, letting my heavy arm drop.

"Vixen, you with us?" Kaleb asked, and I got the feeling we were moving very, very fast even though I couldn't see out the windows. It felt like I was flying, and I let out a little giggle.

"Yeah," I replied, my voice sounding sluggish to my own ears.

"See if you can get some more water into her," Kaleb said, and I gulped as the lip of a bottle was pushed to my lips, the cool liquid slithering down both my throat and the side of my face, feeling like silk.

A thumb brushed over my lips when I was finished, and I pulled it into my mouth with a short moan, sucking greedily, feeling something hard push against the back of my neck.

"*Becca*," that perfect voice groaned, more of a plea now as he jerked his hand free of my mouth and I licked my lips, tasting salt.

He brushed his hand up and down my back, and I felt my eyelids drooping as a sense of ease slipped over me like a warm blanket.

I couldn't be sure how long I was out, but I knew from the ache in my neck that it must've been a while when I jerked awake at the sound of a ringing phone blasting through loud speakers.

My exhausted mind struggled to catch up to the present, feeling movement beneath me. Trying to stretch out my legs and finding I couldn't, the cramped space not affording me the option of luxury.

"Where the fuck are you?" An unfamiliar voice spoke through the speakers, making my head throb. I tried to cover my ears, wanting nothing more than to close my eyes and go back to sleep, even though colorful starbursts kept exploding like fireworks over the backs of my eyelids.

"Almost there," Kaleb replied. "We just have one stop to make and then–"

"No stops," the other voice shouted. "Get here *now*. I don't want the others to see this shit. We need to clean it up before they come looking."

"What?"

"I'm sending you the coordinates. Don't stop for anything, that's a fucking order."

"I thought you were at the house?"

"Not anymore."

The line went dead, and the soft sound of radio music filtered back through the cabin.

"What the fuck? What does he mean, clean what up?"

I could feel the tension in the car, the discomfort of it making me squirm, making my stomach turn, but despite the lingering feeling of dread, I could already feel myself slipping away again. My soul leaving my body to go someplace softer for a while. A place where there were no worries and I could drift on a cloud into oblivion.

"She's out," a familiar voice rumbled distantly as my body sagged back down into the seat.

"We can't take her with us."

"We can't leave her, either."

The next time I woke, my head felt heavy, like it'd been filled with bricks, and I couldn't lift it from where it lay. I blinked away the gluey substance in my eyes, and I squinted into a light that was too bright, recoiling with eyes squeezed shut.

Except... what was that?

I opened them again, slower this time, the bright light making searing pain arc over my skull, but still I tried to force myself to see.

My palms pushed uselessly on the soft fabric beneath me, trying to push myself up only to lie more heavily once I was spent.

My sluggish mind tried to comprehend the distorted image through the windshield, partially blocked by the seats in front of me. High above the ground, bright white lights were tilted against a flat surface.

...a... a billboard, my tired mind supplied.

And there, in the center of the rectangle of purest white was something red.

My chin quivered as I started to make out shapes. An arm. A leg. A torso. All parts of a whole that no longer was whole. Dismembered pieces of a man were pinned to the white surface like an entomologist might pin insects to a peg board. The limbs were bent at odd angles. Lined up toes over fingers. Thigh over torso.

I squeezed my eyes shut, a rolling wave of nausea threatening to bring up acid from my stomach, until I remembered.

The chalky taste of the pill on my tongue, the difficulty of swallowing it dry. Molly.

I was on Molly.

*Chill, Becks. You're just trippin'.*

I wasn't sure how long I held my eyes shut, praying that what I thought I saw tacked onto the billboard wasn't really there.

But when I opened my eyes again, my body heaved with a sigh, finding a smooth white billboard with an artistic red smear over the middle that looked almost like a maple leaf. No body parts. No carnage. Just white and red.

Like a Canadian flag.

Peaceful.

My lips twitched into something close to a smile as I allowed my eyes to close again, praying that I would be sober again the next time I opened my eyes.

A door opened. Something rocked the car. A door closed.

An odd smell filled my nose, made it wrinkle. Acrid like bleach. Tangy like a copper penny.

Was I asleep? Or awake?

I wasn't sure.

"What the fuck is she doing back there?" That angry voice from earlier asked in a haughty, accusing tone.

The voices grew more and more distant until they were gone again.

The empty abyss of my sleeping mind shifted, the sound of it opening up like a shovel in dirt. But the tape was skipping.

Rewinding.

Fast forwarding.

The shovel sound played again and again. The *shhhk* of steel burying into dry dirt followed by a *thump*, the looping soundtrack of my existence, until finally, blissfully… silence.

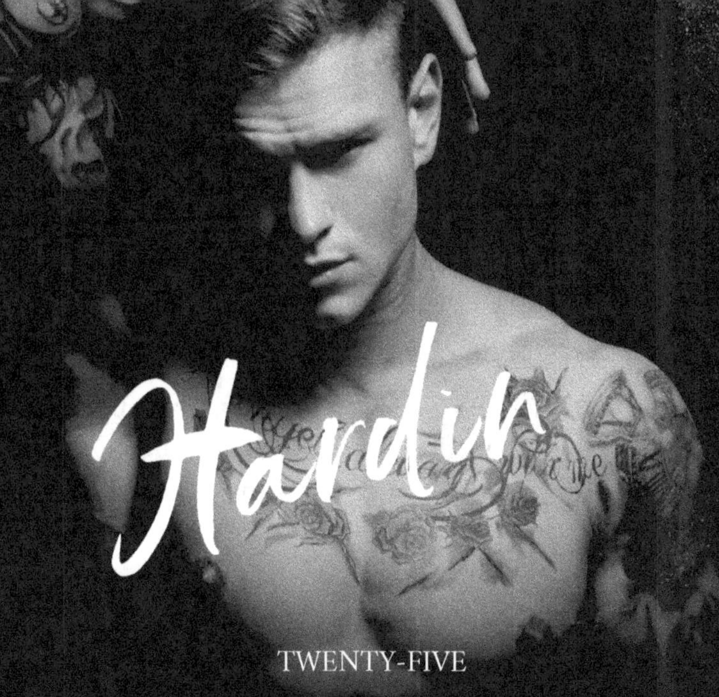

# TWENTY-FIVE

I quietly turned Becca's key in the lock, only to find the door to Becca's shared apartment already unlocked.

*Idiots.*

I adjusted her limp body in my arms and clenched my teeth, a shiver of anger ratcheting up my back. Even if Toby and Kate hadn't spent the better part of the night taking a hacked up body down from a fucking billboard and burying it six feet under, they couldn't be naive enough to think leaving their door unlocked this close to The Row on a Saturday night was a good idea.

I exhaled low through my nose as I pushed inside, finding the apartment dark save for a blue-screened television humming in the living room.

In front of it, Toby was passed out half on and half off the couch. Kate's shoes were discarded in the middle of the floor, and I assumed the door that was ajar across the living room was hers.

Becca sighed to herself in her sleep, pushing her small nose into my chest as I carried her toward the other door, but I knew without even turning on the light that it was Toby's. It smelled of his cologne.

I left his door open as I carried Becca down the hall instead, to the only other bedroom. I used the toe of my boot to push the door open, finding a sparse room bathed in the warring cold and warm hues of the moon and sun still sleeping beneath the horizon line, its light seeping into the pre-dawn sky.

I set her down on top of the covers, turning to leave, but being unable to.

My phone vibrated in my pocket, and I lifted it out, seeing a message on the dirt-streaked screen from Kaleb.

**Kaleb: What the fuck is taking so long? Tuck sleeping beauty in and get back down here. We need to figure out our next move.**

I ignored the message, sliding the device back in my pocket as I folded myself into a seat at the end of Becca's bed, studying her face in the moonlight.

Fuck, she was perfect. Maybe not in the traditional sense. With her permanent scowl and her dark, thick eyebrows. But to me…

There would never be anything more beautiful.

I undid the laces on her heels, lifting her legs one at a time to unwind them from her calves and slip the shoes from her feet. She stretched out her legs and her dress rode up, revealing the angry bite mark on her thigh. My cock twitched at the sight of it, but I buried the urge to take her again.

*Not now.*

*Not yet.*

I stalked to the kitchen, washing my dirt caked hands in the sink before finding a glass and filling it with water. I carried it back to her room, setting it on her nightstand. I took her phone from her little purse and plugged it in, frowning when I saw a message light up her screen. The content blocked from view, but the name was decidedly fucking male.

Decidedly… *Irish.*

Aodhán.

I stored that information for another day, trying to tell myself there were hundreds of immigrants in SoCal and three times as many with Irish ancestry. It was only a name. And as soon as I had a free fucking minute after the shit was done hitting the fan, I would find out exactly who this fool was. Make sure his name never crossed her phone screen again.

Ibuprofen. She would need some when she woke up. I fingered the nightstand drawer open, my lips parting in surprise at the fucking vault of sex toys filling the small space. I glanced between her and the fucking treasure trove, tugging out a flogger, unable to keep a smile from pulling my lips wide.

"Such a bad little mouse."

I dropped the flogger back in the drawer, satisfied that I was at least an inch bigger than any of the silicone cocks in her arsenal and found a bottle of ibuprofen tucked in the corner. I put it next to the water and leaned down to kiss her temple before I realized what I was doing.

An uncomfortable weight settled in my gut as I pulled my lips away from her skin and forced myself to tear my gaze from her sleeping face.

My phone buzzed again in my pocket, and I growled quietly to myself as I rose, the bed springs creaking.

I lifted the phone to my ear. "I'm coming," I whisper-snarled down the line, trying not to rouse Becca as I crossed the room to check her windows, making sure they were locked. I shut her door behind me and checked every other window in the apartment before I felt comfortable enough to leave.

I closed the front door behind me and dropped to one knee, pulling a pin and hook from my wallet to engage the lock on the door from the outside.

"What, did you sing her a fucking lullaby?" Kaleb asked as I shoved back out onto the street a block away from The Row, where he and Dad waited for me to get Becca inside.

I gave Kaleb a warning glare.

"She going to be all right?" Dad asked, working his jaw, and I narrowed my eyes at him.

"Yeah."

He nodded before jerking his head in the direction of The Row. "I don't know about you two, but I need a fucking drink. Where's that shitty little bar you guys always talk about?"

"The Copper Crown?" Kaleb asked.

"Yeah, that one."

"Shouldn't we head back to the house? It's just Pope and Ma there alone."

"I sent Arch and Zade over while you two buried him. Besides, the bastards already made their point. No doubt they've crawled back into whatever hole they've been hiding in by now."

Dad's back rose with a long, shaky inhale, an attempt to subdue his rage.

"This way." Kaleb led the way to the Crown, pounding on the door until Sam came down wrapped in a bathrobe that was hanging open over a pair of Simpsons boxers.

His eyes widened when he saw our father with us, and he rushed to pull the robe closed and stand up straighter. No doubt he'd been about to tell us he was all closed up for the night, but now he wouldn't dare speak a word other than...

"Damien," he rushed to say. "It's a pleasure to—"

"Yeah, yeah," our Dad said, brushing past Sam to head up the stairwell. "Skip the pleasantries and show us where you keep the good scotch."

"Of course."

Within minutes we were all seated at the freshly cleaned bar, each of us with three fingers of Sam's top shelf booze, listening to his go-to Spotify playlist. A mix of classic rock from the seventies and eighties.

Sam excused himself, giving us our privacy as dawn crept over Santa Clarita, pouring amber onto the bar floor.

"What the fuck am I going to tell the others," Dad said,

breaking the silence only after he'd finished half his scotch.

It was a good question, and usually, I'd already have several answers for him. Typically, I'd be enraged that someone took something—in this case, *someone*—who belonged to us and broke them.

Jimmy Boy was good shit. He didn't deserve to go down like that. And I was angry, but my thirst for the deaths of our enemies simmered with the calm certainty of knowing my hands would eventually be stained with their blood. The inner chaos that made my rage spike into an uncontrollable swinging ax seemed numbly absent.

I swirled the scotch in my glass, frowning at the golden liquid before taking a swallow.

Neither of my father's sons seemed to have a good idea. I was blaming my lack of a single functioning brain cell on what'd happened earlier tonight.

My cock thickened in my jeans as I remembered the slippery feel of her against my sharp tongue. One taste and I knew she would be an addiction from which there would be no return. No hope of ever getting clean. Not that I wanted that anymore.

No.

I'd gladly stay high on her for the rest of my miserable life, aching for my next fix.

"You should tell them the truth," Kaleb said finally, and I noticed he hadn't so much as touched his scotch. Instead, he just stared at it like he might find the answers to every question he'd ever had but didn't actually want the answers to somewhere at the bottom of the glass. "They deserve to know."

"This never should've happened."

My back tensed, muscles flexing with annoyance. "Jimmy Boy didn't deserve to go like that, but he didn't follow orders."

Dad had told us everything he knew when we met him beneath the billboard out on the canyon road. He was an idiot for going there himself after getting the tip from a beat cop still loyal to the Saints.

Dad shook his head.

"Hardin's right," Kaleb added. "You told Jimmy to hole up at the shop like everyone else. He's the idiot who didn't listen."

"He had kids for fuck's sake." Dad seethed, his grip on his now empty glass tightening. He rarely drank, for the same reason I didn't. People tended to die when we weren't in control of our emotions and other than rage, I was in full control of the rest of mine.

"Two little girls," he added, pouring more scotch into his glass. "His wife…" He trailed off.

"They'll be taken care of," Kaleb said. "Like always."

Dad sagged on his barstool. "Hush money in exchange for growing up without a father."

"Riley knew what she was signing up for when she married him," Kaleb argued. "She was a Saint's Sinner for fuck's sake."

"It won't make telling her any easier."

Kaleb threw a hand through his messy hair, scattering

dirt over the bar, getting some in his scotch. "Do we even know if she and the kids are all right?"

"They seem to be. I had that beat cop go 'round to check on them. He said lights were out, no signs of forced entry, and he could see Riley asleep on the couch inside. No doubt Jimmy was on his way to the shop when they grabbed him."

Were we really not going to address the elephant in the room? I wasn't up at five in the fucking morning to talk about how to tell Jimmy's wife, or even how to tell the other guys.

"Does it really matter how the fuck you tell her?" I all but snapped, the simmer of rage in my gut was already turning up the heat, rolling into a boil again. So much for my short-lived sense of calm. It was nice while it lasted. "What we need to be talking about is what we're going to *do* about it."

Kaleb took the first sip of his scotch, grimacing. "We can't let the Son's get away with this. If they were willing to make a move this fucking ballsy just because we didn't show up for their meet, what's going to be next? Maybe Riley? Her and Jimmy's little girls. I mean, fuck, did you *see* what they did to him?"

I'd seen my fair share of gruesome shit in my time with the Saints, but what they did to Jimmy was on another level. If it weren't for the ink on his skin, we wouldn't even have been able to identify him seeing as his head was missing.

They'd artfully arranged his body parts into their gang tag, arms and legs bent at opposing angles to make S's. His torso, missing all limbs and a head made a macabre 'O.' His own blood slashed over his pale chest to make a strike through it.

We'd just seen Jimmy two days ago. While he operated directly under my father, he lived in Santa Clarita. In fact, the fucker lived barely five blocks from our place.

The idea of some scum being so close to *our place,* on *our turf,* taking *our men* right out from under our noses, made my fucking skin itch.

I shoved away the last swallow of my scotch, not trusting myself not to go ape on the first person who didn't share blood with me. I enjoyed taking money from the preppy fuckheads who thought they could beat me at pool or darts here too much to like the idea of Sam dead.

"Good talk," I sneered sarcastically when no one answered me, pushing the stool out from the bar, ready to leave them both to wallow without any help from me.

"Sit the fuck down," Dad hissed.

I cut him a glare.

"What exactly are you proposing, Son?" he demanded, his eyes getting that crazed glint I knew all too well, but my father wouldn't lift a finger to harm us, no matter how much we pissed him off. Ma would literally kill him. Instead, I had the pleasure of watching his face turn red and his eyes bulge.

He wasn't really angry at me, anyway. He was angry at himself.

"Hmm?" he pressed, leaning in close, unblinking. "Do you know something I don't? Something like, I don't know, where these bastards are hiding out? Because we're flying blind here. We got nothing. *Zip.*"

I cast my fury away from him, staring at my glass atop the bar instead, my teeth grinding. He was right. We still didn't know where they were, which would make retribution all but impossible, but they had to fuck up sometime. And somewhere out there, someone had to know something, we just hadn't found that motherfucker yet.

"There has to be something we can use," Kaleb interjected. "We just haven't found it yet. What about the rest of The Warden's men? Maybe they'll talk."

"To the gang leader who killed their head honcho?" Dad lobbied back, raising a skeptical brow. "I don't fucking think so."

"Then we don't give them a choice," I said plainly, giving Kaleb a nod. He was on to something. The only person we knew for certain had actually had any facetime with these new players was The Warden. And if the Sons had wanted to make a spectacle, which clearly they fucking did, they'd have made sure every one of The Warden's men was there to see their warning. Their brutality. They'd want a full and rapt audience while they killed The Warden's nephew.

Dad's brows furrowed, but I saw the moment he realized what I was proposing. Not our usual mode of operation but desperate times…

"Yeah," he said, his gaze darkening, a shadow passing over his eyes as he bowed his head, coming to terms with the only viable option he'd had placed in front of him since the Sons invaded our turf. "I'll get Arch and Zade on it."

"Let us—"

"No," Dad interrupted. "I need you here with your ears to the ground and your eyes fixed to Rebecca Matthews."

"*Hart*," Kaleb corrected him, shaking his head. "I'm guessing inviting her for Friday night dinner is a no go now?"

Relief flooded my veins.

But our Dad looked at Kaleb like he wanted to push his head through a wall. "Are you shitting me?"

I cocked my head at him.

"You put that girl even more at risk than she already was. You made her a goddamned accessory to murder tonight. I don't even like the idea of her locked up tight in her apartment right now without a set of Saint eyes to watch over her. Since you've both proven you can't follow orders where she's concerned, she needs to be brought into the fold, if only temporarily. Don't look at me like that," he snapped at the pair of us.

"Dad—"

"Shut it, Kaleb. If you two knuckleheads had just listened to me, this wouldn't be happening. She'll come to dinner and that's it. I don't care what you need to do to get her there, just get it done."

He polished off his scotch and got up from his stool. "Now come on, I need a ride back to my damn car."

We followed Dad back to the house just in case, but when we got there, I didn't like the idea of leaving, heading back to Santa Clarita.

Our smaller SC crew, mostly initiates from Kilborn, were all at the ready. They'd patrol the area around our house and Becca's apartment at all hours if we just gave the word, but...

After seeing what they did to Jimmy Boy, I wanted to see Ma with my own eyes. Make sure she and the others were still whole. Besides, it was already dawn and we needed to figure out our next move. No fucking point in going home just to come back here or to the shop for a meet in a couple hours.

"Thought you were headed back to yours," Dad hollered, getting out of his truck as we parked behind him.

"We'll stay," I replied. "We need to fill Zade and Arch in on what happened. Send them out to Stockton to see The Warden's crew."

Our Dad nodded gravely.

"What the fuck is that?"

Kaleb pointed at something at the edge of the flagstone footpath that curved up to the front door. It looked like a weird ass tiki torch. I squinted into the bright dawn light and felt my blood chill in my veins.

"Is that..." Kaleb trailed off, and I had my gun up, the safety off, finger next to the trigger before he could finish his question because I already had my answer.

It was Jimmy Boy. Well, his head. On a fucking spike. On our fucking lawn.

"Ma!" Kaleb shouted, and I'd never moved so fast in my life. I was up the path, ready to put a Hardin shaped hole in the front door when I saw what was tagged to it.

I was too far gone to read the words written in blood on the single sheet of white paper pinned to the door with a blade.

"*Ma,*" I bellowed into the house as the door flew open with one swift kick of my boot. I swept the front entry, moving swiftly farther into the house. Blood pumped noisily in my ears, and my eyes burned hot.

"*Sloane!*" Dad roared behind me, and I all but raced forward, not properly sweeping the area anymore as I pushed deeper into the house.

My vision ebbed with black spots and I felt my stomach hollow and drop out through my toes.

"*Ma!*"

The sound of the pocket door to dad's office slipped open, and I slung myself around the wall in the dining room, ready to rain hell on whoever exited when I saw the business end of a familiar Beretta poking through the dark on the other side.

"Hardin?"

"Christ, Ma," I hissed, lowering my weapon to rush forward and crush her against my chest.

She hammered on my back, but I refused to let her go, my hands still shaking. "What in the hell is going on?"

"Sloane, *thank god.*"

Her rigid body went soft in my arms as she seemed to realize why we were coming in so hot. She stopped pounding on my back and started rubbing wide circles there instead. "Okay," she said, giving me a pat. "Okay, calm down. What's all this about?"

"Is there heat outside?" I heard Zade ask, his gun trained low as he pushed out of the office behind Ma. I let her go, clearing my throat, and she gave my arm a squeeze, nodding to tell me she was all right.

Dad and Kaleb crowded her.

"*Boss,*" Zade hissed.

Dad planted a kiss on Ma's forehead. "No. Not exactly."

He passed the slip of paper from the door to Zade, who hesitantly clicked his safety back on before taking it.

Ma stole it from Zade's hands before he could have possibly had a chance to read it.

The adrenaline in my veins was quickly turning to fucking sludge, and I fought against the exhaustion making my bones tremble in its wake.

"Where was this?" Ma asked, and I shook my head, fighting to clear the still ever present need to rip someone's head off. I stared down at what I thought was just a piece of paper but was actually a postcard.

Ma flipped it back and forth in her hands. It was the same picturesque view on one side as last time. The four ridges of the canyon lit up with warm sun. On the flipside the message was a familiar one. Except this time the date had changed. And it was written in blood.

10-08-22

1100

S

Ø

S

"It was pinned to the front door with that," Dad said, tossing a blood-coated blade on the dinner room table.

Ma fingered the blood they used for ink.

"Whose blood is this, Damien?"

Dad tapped his gun against his head, grimacing, and then sighing. "It's Jimmy Boy's," he admitted.

Ma gasped.

"Me and the boys just finished pulling what was left of him off a billboard out on the Canyon road."

"Not all of him," Kaleb said, kicking at the carpet, and I remembered the little gift the Sons had left on our goddamned doorstep.

Ma's face pinched and she cocked her head at Kaleb.

"His, *uh*, his head's outside. On a spike."

"Oh my god."

"Zade, Arch," Dad said without looking up, likely not ready to see the haunted expression both his oldest companions were wearing right now. Jimmy Boy wasn't part of the original crew, but that didn't mean the guys would miss him any less. "Clean up our boy and then come back inside."

He plucked the postcard from Ma, whose shock was quickly warping into something far more dangerous.

"This can't stand," she hissed as Dad fell into his seat at the dinner table, getting dirt all over the carpet.

"I know."

"There has to be retaliation."

*"I know, Sloane."*

Dad tapped the postcard against the table, and I knew

he was thinking the same thing I was. If we weren't there a second time, someone else was going to die. Hell, maybe more than one someone. Even if we had everyone brought in on that date. The sisters, brothers, cousins, children, and wives of every single Saint, there was no guarantee they wouldn't just strike the next day, instead.

When we least expected them to.

We had no choice. We were going to that meet. The Sons may've had the advantage of choice location and time, but they were playing on our turf. There was no telling whether home field advantage would be enough, but then again, I'd never needed much to get a job done.

"We go," I said, echoing my Dad's thoughts. "We go there, and we kill every last one of them."

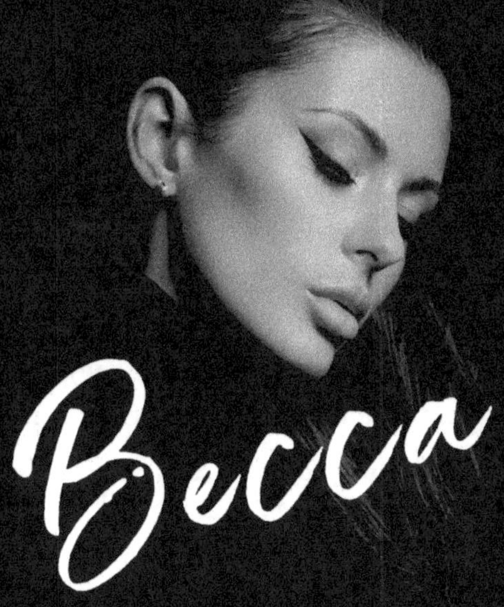

# Becca

## TWENTY-SIX

I woke up with a sandpaper throat and limbs that felt like they'd run a fucking marathon last night. My head pounded, and I squeezed my eyes against the warm sunlight trying to burn out my corneas.

"*Ughhhh*," I groaned to myself, rolling over to feel the surface of my nightstand, searching for anything to make the scratchy burn in my throat go away. I knocked my phone to the floor with a clatter and couldn't be bothered to pick it up as I slitted my eyes open, finding a full glass of water and a bottle of pills.

*Fuck. Yes.*

Clearly somebody loved me.

Even though it hurt, I somehow managed to prop myself half up and twist the cap from the bottle of pills. I dumped several directly into my mouth and swallowed them down with three greedy gulps of water that drained the glass dry before flopping back onto my pillow.

"No more drugs," I promised myself and any gods who might take pity on me and get rid of this damn hangover. What the hell happened last night.

I lay there, eyes shut, arm draped across my forehead as I tried to piece it all back together. I remembered seeing Ava Jade and bits and pieces of the concert, but it was like I wasn't really seeing it. Like it happened to someone else.

And oh my god, was there dirt on my blankets? What the fuck?

Shit. I needed to check my messages. Oh! And my camera roll. That should jog my memory. I rolled back onto my side, reaching my fingertips to the floor, but the stretch made a sharp pain bloom on my inner thigh, and I cursed, forgetting the phone entirely as I shot up.

My breath caught in my throat seeing the unmistakable ring of teeth marks in my flesh. The tiny scabs were surrounded by purpling skin. What the...

It all came rushing back and my vision doubled, my head spinning as a barrage of illicit images bombarded my mind, playing in a compilation of sin across the backs of my eyelids.

Hardin.

His mouth on mine. On my body. His hand fisted in my hair. His fucking *gun*... pressed to my thigh, forcing me to keep my legs open as he brought me to the absolute precipice of pleasure, not allowing me to forfeit a single second of the rush.

And then after, the feel of him on top of me. Holding me down.

Except... was he? Was he really?

I remembered the cruel way he thrust into me from behind. The insane way he seemed to fill me up perfectly, not in a way I'd ever felt before. I remembered him releasing my arms, dragging me to my knees.

Me... rocking into him, pushing my hips into each of his brutal thrusts, wanting him harder, deeper, *more.*

I covered my mouth with a hand to stifle the strangled sound that tried to escape because the truth was... the truth was...

I'd never felt more alive.

...how broken did that make me?

Hot tears burned in my eyes, but I refused to let them fall, jerking the fabric of my black dress down to cover the mark on my leg I would probably need cosmetic surgery to remove. Cosmetic surgery that I couldn't afford.

A knock at the door had me jumping out of my skin, digging under my pillow for the taser I hid there, an image from a vivid drug induced dream slingshotting into my head. Of amputated limbs, twisted and coated in crimson.

"Holy shit, is that a taser?" Toby asked, spry as a fucking summer daisy, and I dropped it to my lap, breathing heavily as I shook the macabre images from my head. "Can I see?"

"What the hell did you give me last night, Tobes?" I asked him, the pain returning to my head with a vengeance.

He shrugged as he sat on the edge of my bed and tugged the taser from my hands, pressing down the button with a sound of glee. "It was just Molly. Bad trip?"

I pressed my palms into my eyes. "You have no idea."

"Well, I hate to be the bearer of bad news," he sing-songed. "But your shift at the cafe starts in, like, fifteen minutes."

I groaned, remembering I picked this shift up *for him* because he had a choreography rehearsal this afternoon.

"Toby…" I trailed off, pleading, giving him my best puppy eyes. "Look at me, I'm a mess, I can't go anywhere like this."

He pushed out his lower lip. "Oh, hunny, I'm sorry you had a bad trip and I promise never to share my drugs with you again—scouts honor—but I have to go to this rehearsal. It's worth a third of my final grade or some shit. Now come on, get up."

He tugged me out of bed, and I wobbled unsteadily on my legs, clutching the bed rail for support. Toby winced. "Okay, we can fix this. You go put your sad self in the shower, and I'll make you my famous hangover smoothie. You can drink it on the way."

It was kind of difficult to eradicate all thoughts of Hardin and Kaleb St. Vincent—erotic or otherwise—from my mind when they seemed to be taking turns brooding in the cafe. All week, they were there from the moment I started my shifts to the moment I finished them. Hardin was just as quiet as ever, maybe even quieter, which made it easier to ignore his presence and pretend whatever happened between us was all just a figment of my apparently very vivid imagination.

Kaleb was a different story, though. He kept pestering me about having dinner with them *and their parents.* As if I wanted to share a meal with the most dangerous man in all of SoCal who also not-so-coincidentally happened to be the man who inadvertently got my mother killed, and his two twisted sons.

After everything that'd happened in Thorn Valley, I'd learned through personal experience and from watching my bestie, that it wasn't really Damien St. Vincent's fault. Not really. And I'd put those ragey feelings aside, for the most part, but that didn't mean I wanted to be face to face with the man.

Share fucking lasagna and laughs.

No, thank you.

But by Tuesday night, I was ready to beat Kaleb senseless with the cash register if he didn't shut up about it.

And then on Wednesday, I just didn't have the energy anymore and my resolve was fading. I started to wonder what Damien St. Vincent was like. Why my mom was ever drawn to him in the first place. Why she couldn't seem to stay away from him despite the danger she knowingly put herself in by remaining close at his side.

By Thursday, I decided I would do literally anything if Kaleb would just shut the fuck up about it. That day coincidentally, was also the day he casually reminded me that it was him and his brother who got me home safe after the concert.

I wasn't sure about the 'safe' part, but I definitely woke up in my own bed. Apparently, I'd been put there by none other than Hardin.

Hardin, who'd removed my shoes and tucked me in.

Hardin, who set water and ibuprofen next to the bed and plugged in my phone on the nightstand.

Hardin, who somehow managed to lock the apartment door on his way out.

How could that man be the same man who told me to *run* that night at the concert? The same man who was now giving me the silent treatment every day at the cafe, sitting there drinking his drip coffee, brooding at nothing. Like he was waiting patiently for me to come to him, like he knew he didn't have to chase me anymore. Back to being my Mr. Dark and Gloomy.

No.

Not *my.*

Never mine.

Anyway, by the time my morning shift arrived today and Kaleb showed up at six a.m. sharp, ready to ask me the same question he asked me every day, I finally, grudgingly, gave in. On one condition—I wanted a St. Vincent free day. An entire shift without seeing either of their faces on pain of hot coffee thrown directly into their smug faces.

Now, though?

I was regretting the choices of pre-coffee Becca.

That bitch was a train wreck and not to be trusted.

Look where she got us.

I plucked up whatever remaining pride I had, hefting the expensive bottle of wine I brought with me because that was what you did when you were invited to dinner, right? Right? …and rang the doorbell at 89 Poppy Lane.

In hindsight, I should've accepted Kaleb's offer of a ride, the Uber from my apartment to here ran me almost eighty bucks.

What the fuck was I doing here?

Was I completely insane—

The door opened and a woman with long, graying dark hair blinked at me. At first I thought I had the wrong house, but then whatever had been holding her face hostage released her and her lips curved into a welcoming smile. "You must be Becca."

"Um, yeah. I am," I held out a hand to her. "And you must be Kaleb and Hardin's mom?" Aka the woman Damien St. Vincent married barely a couple years after my mom was buried six feet under.

She looked quizzically at my hand before shaking it, her grip strong as she nodded. "Sloane," she told me. "It's nice to meet you. You know, it's not often my boys invite anyone to dinner, especially not a girl."

Should I have been flattered? Kaleb didn't really give me a choice.

I pasted on a smile as Sloane pulled me gently into the front foyer and closed the door behind me. My throat went dry as I caught sight of the gun openly strapped to her thigh. In her own house. Why was she armed in her own house?

*Jesus fucking Christ.*

Maybe I should've brought my taser.

I cleared my throat as a man came around the corner from a different room, his wide frame filling the space. His hair was jet black with a lick of silver cutting through one side. A well-groomed salt and pepper beard covered his jaw, contrasting with his tan face. Even though I knew Diesel St. Crow and Damien St. Vincent weren't actual brothers, I could see how easy they'd be to mistake for it.

Even with Diesel's much fairer hair and complexion, they both had the same atmosphere surrounding them. A miasmal sense of foreboding that had my stomach turning even though he'd done nothing threatening and in fact, seemed to be smiling, however tight of a smile it was.

"This is my husband, Kale and Hardin's Dad, Damien," Sloane was quick to make the introduction and I awkwardly thrust the bottle of wine between myself and Damien as he approached, stopping him before he could get too close.

I scrutinized every inch of him, trying to imagine my mother with this rough, intimidating man. Failing.

"Thanks for having me," I blurted and Damien lifted a thick black brow, taking the bottle of wine from my hand, tilting it into the light so he could read the label, his amusement obvious.

"Hunny, we don't really drink grape juice in this house."

"That's a fifty dollar bottle," I scoffed, the words

coming out before I could stop them. My latent hatred for this man coming out despite trying to see past it.

"*Damien*," Sloane chided, taking the bottle from him with a glare that actually had the man cringing.

He coughed. "Right. My apologies. It looks… great."

"It is great," I agreed. "That's one of the best pinot noirs made in this region." I was rambling, but I couldn't seem to stop. "And that year, 2018, was the best harvest at that vineyard. I'm surprised I even found a bottle of it at the liquor shop on The Row. Probably only did because none of the students know a thing about wine."

Damien's lips pursed, and I got the sense he was holding back laughter, which made my cheeks heat.

"Clearly, at least one student does," he replied.

I crossed my arms over my chest, holding them tight against myself, wondering if it was considered a shootable offense in this house to take off before the first course. "My dad taught me," I muttered almost inaudibly.

"Oh, he did, did he?"

His obvious disdain for Gregory Hart shone through his words without him needing to speak a single ill word against my father. There was definitely still some animosity there, because ultimately, my mother chose Gregory Hart over the revered Damien St. Vincent. She chose security over chaos. Light over dark.

Not that it did her any good in the end.

I wondered if he saw my father when he looked at me the way that I saw my mother in a casket when I looked at him.

"*Damien*," Sloane warned again. "Why don't you go put this in the fridge."

I tried not to roll my eyes. It was *red wine*.

Obviously Damien wasn't lying when he said they didn't drink wine in this house.

"Sure thing, love," Damien said, taking the bottle back from her while laying a kiss on her cheek. He lifted his gaze back to mine before leaving. "Can I get you a drink?"

"*Um*, yeah. Thanks," I replied, praying whatever it was had booze in it. That was about the only way I was going to make it through this dinner.

When Damien was gone and I could breathe, I leaned forward to try to peer around the corner of the room to the right. "Are your sons here yet?"

I was sure they said six and the Uber had already been late.

"They should be here any minute." Sloane assured me. "No matter how many times I threaten to withhold dessert they're always late."

I hung my purse and jacket on a hook by the door and followed Sloane deeper into the St. Vincent home.

She ushered me through the dining room, already set up for dinner, and into a warm living room where music filtered low from an old record player. Castle Walls by the Styx filled the room and somehow, that seemed so... unthreatening... that I relaxed a little as I sat down on the sofa, pressing my hands between my knees.

Damien came back with three short glasses filled with golden liquid, distributing one first to his wife and then to me.

He must've sensed my confusion because he stood above me, cocking his head. "Do you prefer yours with ice?"

"*Uh...*"

I looked down into the glass, the acrid, peaty smell of scotch tickling my nose.

"There's beer in the fridge if you'd prefer," Damien offered, but there was an unmistakable challenge in his stare. And fuck if I didn't want to *win*, show him I wasn't the spoiled little rich girl he so clearly saw me as.

"No, this is fine."

"Not a whiskey girl, I take it?"

He fell onto the cushion next to his wife, on the loveseat that ran perpendicular to the one I sat on.

I lifted my chin. "Actually, I prefer it to wine. But I'm more of a rye girl as opposed to whiskey or scotch."

"Is that so?"

Smug bastard.

"Yes," I said, plastering on a sweet smile. "Crown Royal is my favorite."

Damien dipped his head appreciatively. "A good everyday drinker," he agreed. "But it pales in comparison to a good scotch. That there is a single malt. Aged 16 years. Give it a try."

I put the glass grudgingly to my lips as the front door opened and I heard Kaleb shout, "Ma, we're here!"

But Damien's haughty stare never wavered, waiting for me to try his fancy ass scotch. I took a tentative sip and let it mellow in my mouth. At first there was only the hard bite of malty alcohol, but within a few seconds other flavors started to show themselves. That peatiness I'd smelled when he first handed me the glass. But also smoke and vanilla.

I felt my brows rise as I swallowed it down, relishing the burn and the non totally unpleasant after taste.

"That beats grape juice any day of the week."

"Hey, Dad. Ma," Kaleb said as he entered the living room. "Any sign of—*Becca*."

His hazel eyes stuck on me. "You're here."

"You sound surprised."

"I wasn't sure you'd make it."

Hardin leaned against the door frame behind his brother, his hands pushed deep into his pockets. I was careful not to meet his eyes, once again mentally kicking myself for agreeing to this.

"You didn't really give me much choice," I replied curtly, taking another sip of my drink.

In the kitchen, which I'd briefly glimpsed opposite the main hallway, something chimed and Sloane tapped Damien's thigh as she rose from the sofa. "Come give me a hand bringing everything to the table."

They left and Kaleb came to sit next to me on the sofa, stealing the glass from my hand for a sip. He seemed on edge. But that wasn't anything new. This week at the cafe he and Hardin could've tied for first place in the brooding Olympics.

Kaleb alternated between tapping angrily on his laptop and taking calls in nook number nine, thinking nobody could hear him hissing down the line at whoever was on the other end.

Hardin just sat there and brooded even more heavily than he usually did. Occasionally, someone would come in and whisper something to him or he would check messages on his phone.

One thing was clear, there was something going on.

I knew that sort of tension. I'd felt it when shit was going down back in Thorn Valley. Something was definitely up, and I wasn't sure I wanted to know what.

"Your mom seems nice."

Hardin snorted from where he still leaned nonchalantly across the room and Kaleb straight up laughed. "That's because you don't know her yet."

*Awesome.*

"Dinner!" Damien called from the adjoining dining room, and the smell of melty cheese and tomato sauce filled my nose, making my mouth water. Between school and work and homework and attempting to have something of a social life, eating proper meals didn't really fit into the schedule most days.

If Dad knew, he'd flip shit, but I wasn't starving myself. It wasn't like before. Not at all.

I swallowed, deciding I could wait until *after* I ate to attempt to excuse myself. And if I needed to leave in a rush, I'd taken note of the gas station and convenience store the Uber passed only a few blocks away from here. I could just go there and wait for an Uber. Piece of fucking pie.

I followed Kaleb into the dining room, finding Sloane at one end of the food-laden table and Damien at the other. My stomach flipped uneasily and I stole my glass back from Kaleb to take another small swallow of scotch to calm my nerves.

Kaleb sat down, and I went for the seat beside him, where there was another place setting.

Hardin got there first. I muttered an apology, thinking I'd been about to take his seat, but he dragged the chair from the table for me, waiting for me to sit down.

He inclined his head.

I swallowed. Sat down. He easily lifted and pushed the chair until I was snuggly against the table, Kaleb seated next to me.

I studiously ignored Hardin as he made his way around the table and sat down exactly opposite me, which would make ignoring him even harder. Fuck my life.

Surface level conversation went up around the table as we all filled our plates with homemade lasagna, Caesar salad, and breadsticks. Sloane asked some harmless questions about what classes I was taking at CalArts and alluded to her eldest son being something of an artist himself, if you counted illegal tagging an artform.

I was starting to wonder if this was the point of the meal. Was this a 'get to know you' thing? Did Kaleb, or worse, *Hardin,* tell their parents that I was dating them or something? Were they just trying to get to know their son's girlfriend?

Which one of them had the brilliant idea to introduce me to ma and pop?

A clammy sweat coated my palms as I did my best to smile politely at the right times and answered their questions to the best of my ability, trying to keep the conversation light.

Hardin's stare bored into me across the table the whole time, making me squirm as I took tiny bites of food. Suddenly, not very hungry anymore.

"Eat," Kaleb whispered next to me while Sloane and Damien reminisced about their own college experiences.

"What?" I lifted a brow at Kaleb, my fork hovering over my plate.

"You've barely touched your dinner," he said in a low tone, piling more breadsticks onto his already cleared plate. "You need to take better care of yourself, Vixen."

"So," Damien said, with an air of finality as he wiped his mouth with a blood red napkin and pushed his cleaned plate to one side. "I'm guessing my sons haven't shared with you the reason I invited you to dinner tonight?"

The reason *he* invited me?

I thought...

"I can see I guessed right," Damien said before I could formulate a reply. He swirled the remaining scotch in his glass, lifting from his comfortable slouch in his seat to lean his elbows onto the table.

I kicked Kaleb under the table and he jerked, mouthing *ow* as he reached down to rub the sore spot. "What exactly were you supposed to tell me?" I whispered at him harshly.

He sighed, rolling a reply around in his mouth before opening it to speak. "There's some shit going down."

"That's a hell of an understatement," Sloane said,

tossing her napkin down even though her second helping of lasagna wasn't even half finished.

My face screwed up as my gaze shifted to each of them in turn. "I'm sorry, I'm confused. Are you talking about what I think you're talking about? What would your *business* have to do with me?"

"Nothing, under normal circumstances," Damien answered. "But my two pigheaded sons have decided to completely ignore my orders to stay away from you."

I glared at each of them in turn. Not only were they completely ignoring my protests that I wanted nothing to do with them over the last few weeks, but they were also ignoring direct orders from one of the most renowned gang leaders this side of the USA. Awesome.

But... I still wasn't following. "But why does that—"

"It means," Damien interrupted me. "That by associating with you in the capacity that they have, they've knowingly put you at risk."

"Dad, come on," Kaleb argued, but without any real fire, proving that he knew his father was right.

Something cold slithered in my stomach and made a home there. I'd been so good since moving to Santa Clarita. Or at least since moving in with Toby and Kate. Those old feelings of dread, of paranoia that anyone could be a monster in the skin of an innocent. That at any minute I could go from being safe in my bed, to shot through the chest, came rushing back.

*They've put you at risk.*

What did that mean, exactly?

I shuddered, gripping the underside of the table to use

it as an anchor. Breathing became difficult as a wave of panic washed over me, fighting to drag me under.

I'd had an entire month of panic attacks after I was discharged from the hospital, and Ava Jade was there, holding my hand through each one, telling me the same thing over and over and over again.

*Let the panic consume you,* she would say. *Accept it or else it'll never let you go. And then remember, you are stronger than you think you are.*

But Aves wasn't here to hold my hand right now.

"Hey," Kaleb said, and I gasped as his hand found mine, balled in my lap beneath the table, and squeezed it tight. "We're not going to let anything happen to you. I promise."

"Don't make promises you don't know you can keep," Damien said, his voice rough with anger.

*Let the panic consume you.*

*Accept it.*

*And then remember, you are stronger than you think you are.*

*I am stronger than I think I am.*

I exhaled, the tremor in my core stabilizing. And I hated to admit it, but Kaleb's warm hand wrapped around mine beneath the table was helping, providing me with something sturdy to hold on to.

Once I got the lump out of my throat, I found my voice again, warmth returning to my limbs. "What did you mean?"

I posed the question to Damien.

"About them putting me at risk. What kind of risk?"

"There are insurgents in our territory," Sloane replied for him. "The *Sons*. They've all but declared war and right now, we're waiting for them to make their next move. As I know you're aware, there can be a certain amount of... *collateral damage* when these things happen."

My heart squeezed painfully in my chest, remembering Mom.

She'd been *collateral damage*.

...because of the Saints.

And like an idiot I went and followed directly in her footsteps, walking the path that on some level I knew could and very likely *would* lead me directly to an early grave. No passing go. No collecting two hundred dollars. Just six feet of earth that I could already feel like a physical weight on my chest.

"Okay," I said, chewing my lower lip. "But why would you have any reason to believe that *I'm* at risk? What if I just—"

Damien shook his head. "It's too late for that."

"But—"

"I'm sorry, but I made a promise and I don't intend to break it."

"What's that supposed to mean?" Kaleb slung the question at his Dad and, *um*, yeah, what *did* that mean? A promise to whom?

"Until we get this situation sorted out with the Sons," Damien said, ignoring his son, pointing two fingers in my direction. "You'll be under Saint protection. Now, since you're in Santa Clarita, the majority of the time that'll mean sticking with Hardin and Kaleb. But if they aren't available, I've asked Pope to be your shadow. He's a good guy and you won't even know he's there. Now, have you ever shot a gun? We can get you—"

"Whoa," I said, a laugh bubbling hysterically from my lips. "Hold on a fucking second. I didn't agree to anything here. What if I don't want your 'protection?' " I asked, putting air quotes around the word, barking a hollow laugh. "What? Like that does anyone any good? Why don't we dig up my mom and ask her what she thinks?"

It was a low blow, and I knew it, but I couldn't help it, I was seething. The indignant anger burning away whatever remained of the panic trying to claw its way up my throat and suffocate me.

Damien's face went a shade of red, a vein in his temple throbbing.

"What is she talking about?" Kaleb asked.

Damien sucked his teeth, breaking his staring battle with me to sigh at the table, the red shade bleaching from his face as he scrubbed his hands over it and then dropped them back to the table with a defeated thud.

"She's talking about Eden Matthews," he replied, and just hearing her name come from his vile mouth had me both wanting to cut his tongue out and cry at the same time.

"Matthews?" Kaleb asked, the look on his face like he was finally putting something together. I guessed his Daddy dearest never told him about the woman he tried to steal away from a perfectly happy marriage? The one he got killed when her daughter was barely five years old.

It didn't matter that supposedly he was crushed by her

death. Or that the whole reason the Saints separated was because he couldn't stand to live on the same streets where she once walked. It didn't change the fact that if she'd never met him, she'd still be alive.

"I'm sorry, am I missing something?" Kaleb asked.

Damien sighed again and the tension at the table ratcheted up a notch. Sloane looked between me and her husband murderously. Hardin looked like he was gut punched, like he knew something the rest of us didn't. But Damien? Damien looked very suddenly like a man on death row and he had no right to look so damn hurt.

"I'm out of here," I announced in a huff, shoving out from the table, but Damien rose with me, his expression daring me to defy him.

"Sit down, Rebecca."

I moved to leave, but Kaleb's hand, still holding mine, stopped me. I tugged on my arm, but he wouldn't let go. "You can't leave, Vixen. Not without us. Not until this is over."

"Ugh," I growled, ripping my hand from his. "I don't want your protection. And I don't fucking need it."

"You do," Kaleb argued and something in his eyes kept me rooted in place. "Even without all this fucking bullshit going on with the Sons, there's more." He shared a look with Hardin, who nodded. "We didn't want to freak you out," Kaleb continued. "But I found a tracking device in your purse."

And cue freak out in three...

Two...

"It was hidden in the lining. We thought at first that it might've been planted there by—"

"*You idiots*," Damien said, pinching the bridge of his nose, drawing attention back to him. "I thought *she* found it herself and destroyed it. *Jesus*."

"Wait…" Kaleb said, and I was beyond all ability to comprehend what exactly was happening here anymore. Kaleb glared at his old man. "It was *yours*? You planted a tracker on her? Why?"

I'm sorry, *what?*

Damien's cheekbones flared. His slate eyes flitted to mine before they landed with an apology on his wife. "Because she's my daughter."

I snorted, doubling over in with a cruel laugh on my lips. Tears burned in my eyes and my sides squeezed as I downright fucking cackled. "*Oh fuck*," I said through the laughter and the tears. "*Wow*. You all look so serious."

And they did. Every face around the table watched me in muted horror as the laughter started to die on my lips. My gaze connected with Sloane's, and I watched her scan my face, fixing on every curve and dimple, before she got up from the table, her chair scraping loudly against the floor, and left.

"It's true," Damien said. "I've had my suspicions your whole life, ever since the moment your Mom asked me to watch out for you should anything ever happen to her.

"But when the hospital notified me of your injuries and I came to see you in the hospital in Thorn Valley, those suspicions were confirmed. You have a very rare blood type,

Rebecca. You needed a blood transfusion and the hospital was having a hard time getting the amount you needed from the blood bank. Gregory Hart came to me, begging *me* to save your life. He wasn't a match, Rebecca, but *I* was."

"No."

"*Yes.*"

"He would've told me."

"Would he?"

The question echoed in a loop through my mind. Would he?

If my Dad knew I was fathered by someone else, would he want me to know that? Or would he keep it to himself? Do everything in his power to steer me away from the Saints and anything even remotely connected to them. Denying my biological connection, trying to erase it with his own morals. His own expectations.

"I had absolutely no intention of barging into your life, Rebecca. None. I'd planned to continue to do what I've always done, keep an eye on you from a distance, to keep my promise to your mother."

But then his sons fucked that right up for him, didn't they? If they'd just stayed away then I never would've had to know this. I didn't want to know this.

Wouldn't accept it, not without cold hard proof that I could see with my own fucking eyes.

Was this why my father was so against me going to school here? Because he knew it would put me closer to Damien?

My lungs couldn't seem to get enough air and when I looked up they stopped working completely, because when I looked at Damien St. Vincent, I saw what his wife must've seen before she left.

The bow shape to his lips, mostly hidden beneath his short beard. The wicked curve of his jaw. His wide cheekbones. His inky black hair. The shape of his eyes.

All things that reminded me of my own reflection.

My stomach twisted.

Wait a second.

*His sons.*

His sons who I…

Bile rose in my throat. I couldn't even bring myself to look at them. I pressed a hand to my mouth, feeling my stomach heave as I almost tripped over my own chair rushing to find a toilet. "Fuck," I choked. "I'm going to be sick."

# Becca

## TWENTY-SEVEN

My hands shook as I locked myself into the bathroom and the dining room exploded with sound. Kaleb and his father were shouting at each other and after a minute I heard Sloane join in, too. But I was beyond hearing them as I clutched my stomach, spots crowding my vision as I fought to remain conscious.

*You didn't know, Becks,* I told myself. *You didn't know.*

*It's not fucking incest if you* didn't know.

*It might not even be true.*

*He could be lying.*

*He's a criminal. Criminals lie.*

But then why did everything in my bones whisper that it was the truth. It just made sense. I didn't *fit* with my Dad.

I *fit* with people like Ava Jade.

Like Hardin and Kaleb.

*Oh god.*

My sides squeezed, and I fell to my knees in front of the toilet, whatever meager amount of dinner I'd managed to consume coming up in waves until I had nothing left to throw up.

I swiped the back of my hand over my lips, getting shakily to my feet to splash icy cold water on my too-hot face. Soaking myself until my shirt was sodden and I could breathe without feeling lightheaded.

My phone rang, and I jumped, jerking it from my pocket bleary eyed. I saw the *A* and didn't even wait to read the rest. Ava Jade had been calling to check in a lot this week after the concert. She'd know what to do. She'd get me the hell out of this place.

"Aves," I croaked down the line, not knowing when I'd started crying.

"Becca?" a decidedly male voice asked, worry tainting his Irish accent. "What's happened? Are you all right?"

I blinked back more tears, a sob growing in my chest as I slumped back against the counter. "No."

"Okay, just breathe. Where are you? I'll come get you."

"I'm not in Santa Clarita. I'm... I'm in fucking Burbank."

"Where in Burbank?"

"I don't know, near a golf course and a... a gas station."

I sniffed, shaking my head as if he could see it. I didn't want him to come get me. I didn't want to see anyone right now. Wasn't sure I could face another human being without them somehow being able to see all my sins as if they were written in plain ink over my flesh.

"I'm going to need you to be more specific, love."

"No. I-I'm calling an Uber. Thanks though."

"Wait, Becca, just—"

I hung up the phone, unable to talk anymore. I just needed to get out of here. Right now. I needed to go bury myself in my bed and lock the door and… and…

I didn't know what else.

The argument outside the bathroom raged on like a war, which made it simple to slip out of the house unnoticed. I walked aimlessly, not knowing where to go. Who to call. I couldn't see my phone screen through my watery eyes to order an Uber. Couldn't seem to bring myself to care.

I walked until my feet started to hurt and the sun had fully set. Until I was so thirsty that I finally remembered leaving my purse hung by Damien St. Vincent's front door. I must've walked right by it when I left his house.

A horn honked behind me, and I moved further to the side of the road, getting out of the way, but they honked again.

Aodhán's Impala idled noisily as he pulled up alongside me and leaned over to shove open the passenger door. "Get in."

"I said I was good. I don't need your help. Just go."

"Becca, get in."

"Just go!"

My eyes burned like fucking hellfire as new, angry tears threatened on their rims.

"I'm not leaving until you get your ass in this car."

"What is it with you?" I all but screamed, trying to

stomp away. "Do you always try to force women into your car, *hmm?* You know, in most places that's called *kidnapping.*"

He had the fucking audacity to smirk at me, but something about it disarmed me. "Just get in, love. Let me take you home."

I stopped walking and my legs betrayed me, shaking, barely able to hold me up anymore.

"Why?" I croaked.

He thought about my question, and the answer seemed to surprise even himself as he replied, "Because I want to."

I sniffed.

Aodhán took a long breath, tugging his clover charm from his shirt to rub it between his fingers. "You don't even have to say anything. We can put the radio on and just drive."

My body sagged. One look at the comfortable leather seat and I was a goner.

I slid into the car and shut the door behind me, buckling myself in.

Aodhán reached into his pocket and pulled out a slip of discolored white fabric, passing it to me.

"Is this a fucking handkerchief? Are you kidding?"

"Nope. Not kidding."

I snorted, unable to produce a real laugh as I wiped my damp eyes and Aodhán pulled back onto the residential street where he found me. I wondered how long he'd had to drive around before he got to this place that seemed almost to be in the middle of nowhere.

"So, I know I said I wouldn't ask, and I'm not, exactly–"

"*Aodhán...*"

One more word and I was going to tuck and roll right up out of this car.

"I just want to know, did they hurt you?"

"Who?"

"You know who."

I didn't want to think about them, I closed my eyes, letting my heavy head fall back against the seat. My subconscious conjured an image of Hardin with his teeth in my thigh, and I clenched my teeth against it, swallowing back more bile. Hating how the thought of him there, touching me like that could still make my pussy throb, even now.

What sort of monster did that make me?

"Becca?"

"No," I managed. "They didn't hurt me."

I caught the furrow of his brows from the corner of my eyes, but he didn't push me again. And maybe that was what made me want to tell him.

Aodhán wasn't all twisted up in this mess. He was just some guy who gave me a ride home once. A guy who was nice to me. Showed interest in me. Didn't know my friends. Or my family.

A stranger.

"Have you ever had someone tell you something that you can't unhear? Something so fucked up that it makes you want to... to smash your fucking head against the wall just so that you won't have to think about it anymore?"

My chest ached.

I tried so hard to hate Hardin and Kaleb, but the truth was I didn't hate them at all. I wasn't sure I ever did. I just hated how they made me feel.

No. That wasn't right.

I hated how I *loved* how they made me feel.

"Yes," Aodhán replied darkly, his hands gripping the wheel tight. "Something like that."

I swallowed hard, needing to hear myself say it. "Damien St. Vincent is my father."

# *Kaleb*

## TWENTY-EIGHT

Pope stood outside Death Before Decaf, his steady gaze scanning every face, every inch of the street, in both directions on a loop. Ever the trusty watchdog.

Dad was right to assign him to keep an eye on Becca while we figured out the details of tonight's official meet with the Sons. Aka, motherfucking doomsday.

"Kaleb, what are you doing here? Thought orders were for me to watch the girl?"

"I'll take it from here, Pope."

Of course, he was right. Orders were for him to watch Becca. No one else on the crew knew her real connection to our family.

Dad told us to lay off her while she processed the shit he threw at her last night. The shit he threw at *all of us*.

I didn't blame Becca for taking off on us even if I kind

of wanted to shake her for being so stupid. Didn't she understand how serious this was?

She should. After the shit she went through in Thorn Valley.

Regardless, we found her at home and Toby and Becca refused to let us inside to see her. We could've forced our way in, but that wasn't about to earn us any fuckin' brownie points.

The crew though? They only knew what Dad told them. That she was an innocent Hardin and I had gotten all twisted up in our shit, making her a liability that he didn't want to see die an innocent casualty of gang war.

The lie would hold, for now, but it was only a matter of time before the truth got out and Becca went from being potentially threatened by association to actively hunted as an easy target.

"You sure?" Pope asked, his thick brows knitting together.

"Yeah, man. Go home, get some shut eye so you're fresh for tonight. I need to talk to her."

He gave me a pat on the shoulder and a sad smile. It wasn't the first one I'd gotten since I hauled my ass out of bed this morning, either. Everyone had that fucking solemn look to them this morning during the meet at the shop, when we went over the plan of attack for tonight.

Like they weren't sure any of us would be walking away from tonight alive, despite all the safeguards we had in place.

There was just one more piece of the pie. One more thing that needed to fall into place and then we were on.

Zade and Arch should have the intel we needed from The Warden's men within the hour. If there was intel to be gotten.

*Hey, God, it's me, Kaleb, if you were ever planning on doing me any favors, now would be the time.*

We could really use a fucking leg up on these guys.

I watched Pope walk away and scanned the street outside one more time before pushing into the cafe, the smell of coffee beans and freshly baked carrot muffins filling my nose.

Becca handed a takeout cup to a customer, looking like an actual ghost. The smile she wore looked like it pained her to make it. The dark, puffy half moons under her eyes told me she hadn't slept, and judging by the tremble in her hands, I didn't think she was in any shape to be at work right now.

I couldn't imagine what must be going through her head. To all of a sudden be told that your father is not your father. And then in the same breath to learn your father is actually the head of a gang and also coincidentally the man you blame for your mother's death.

I mean, shit, that was a lot to unpack. Pope also overheard her on the phone with her Dad—or, adoptive dad, I guess—who'd apparently grown a pair and fessed up so at least she could start to accept it, right?

Becca's eyes lifted to mine, and any remaining color drained from her face, turning her a sickly shade of green.

"You can't be here," she said, swallowing with a wince as she pressed a hand to her stomach and backed away from the counter like she'd erect an actual fucking wall between us if she could.

I flinched. "Well, I kind of have to be. Dad's order's, you know. You can't be without protection."

It was weird, realizing the implication, as if I was saying *our* Dad's orders. How messed up was that?

"Hey, babe," Toby called from down the line as he chopped a banana and filled a blender with the chunks. "You need me to take over the counter?"

Becca's red-veined eyes fell from mine, and she backed away another few feet. "Yeah. Please."

"Look, can we talk?" I tried again. "Please. Just five minutes."

She shook her head, her hand pressed to her stomach twisting in her apron now.

Why did she look so sick? Why didn't she want to talk to me? It wasn't my fault Dad decided to hide the fact that he may or may not have another kid running around out there in the world. That was his problem. One he was going to have to sort out with Mom, who'd made him sleep on the couch last night.

If it weren't for the Sons on the prowl, I was pretty sure she'd have kicked his ass out, burned all his shit on the lawn and keyed his truck too for keeping something so big from her.

Toby raced past Becca, getting all up in my face. "I don't know what the fuck you did, Kaleb, but you leave her alone, okay? If she says she doesn't want to talk to you, then she doesn't want to talk to you."

Brave words.

Even if my fists were clenching, ready to pummel the audacity out of Toby, I also kind of admired his willingness to quite literally put his life on the line to stick up for her. I didn't care what anybody said, Toby was okay in my books.

"Okay," I quipped, jumping the counter to shove past Toby. He made a grab for my arm, and I jerked to a stop, staring between his hands on my arm and his face. "Respectfully, Toby, if you don't remove your hands, I'll remove them for you and you won't like my methods."

He released me as if shocked. "Good choice."

"Kaleb, please," Becca said, her expression and posture betraying utter defeat. "Just go. You're going to get me fired."

"Nope," I argued. No one would dare fire her. Not if they wanted to still be breathing when it came time to collect the insurance money after this place burned to the ground.

I scooped her up before she could protest, throwing her over my shoulder as I pushed through the little flap in the counter.

The few customers still hanging around this late in the afternoon pretended not to notice as I hauled her through the entire place, down the long channel of cozy little nooks to the one in the very back.

The one that would give us at least the guise of privacy.

Becca didn't fight me at all, which honestly kind of fucking freaked me out. Where was my vixen? I swear I could break Dad's nose for just dropping that fucking bomb on her like that.

I set her down gently on the floor between the curved antique sofa and the oval coffee table in front of it. She didn't sit though, she just stood there, her jaw clenched almost as tightly as her fists at her sides.

I hated seeing her like this.

"Vixen," I whispered, reaching for her hand. "Talk to me."

She ripped her hand away before I could touch her. "Don't call me that."

She shuddered as if my touch revolted her and what the actual fuck?

I understood us not being her favorite people right now, but she couldn't deny this... whatever *this* was between us. There was no way she didn't feel it, too. This ran far deeper than any surface level attraction. And you know what? Even if she did like my brother, too, I could get over that. I could get used to it.

Whatever she wanted if she'd just stop looking at me like I kicked her fucking dog.

"Talk to me," I repeated, hating the itchy feeling crawling up my spine, gnawing at the back of my mind, whispering that this was always going to happen. Using a voice I thought I'd banished from my subconscious years ago.

*You're not good enough.*

*You're weak.*

*A scared little shit.*

*Useless.*

I clenched my teeth.

"Becca…"

"*What?*" she finally snapped, setting the full force of her stare on me, strong enough to damn near knock me off my feet. "What the hell do you want me to say, Kaleb? And why the fuck aren't you just as freaked out as I am?"

I frowned. "It's not the same thing. Finding out your dad isn't your dad isn't the same as finding out your dad has another kid. It's a fuckin' trip, but it's not the same thing."

Her eyes about bugged out of her head, and I pretty quickly gathered I was missing something here.

"You're right," she hissed loudly before lowering her voice, leaning in like she was afraid someone else might hear us. "It's not the same thing, and that shit would've been bad enough. But finding out you also…"

She grit her teeth, turning that sickly green again.

"Also what?"

"Finding out you also fucked both your brothers is a whole other level of fucked up."

"Stepbrothers," I corrected her. "I mean, sure, it's a little taboo, but that's not the same thing."

"What?"

Her eyes went wide and round, and I wanted to kick myself for not figuring out where her head was earlier. How could she think…? Oh dear god.

"Wait a sec," I said, inclining my head to her, feeling a twist in my own stomach at the thought. "You didn't think…"

She shook her head, blinking, confused.

Shit. Fuck. Balls.

"Becca, we are *not* related."

"But Damien—"

"Is our father in every way that counts… but not by blood. Think about it, we're, what? Three, four years older than you? How would that even be possible? He didn't even know Ma back then. I was eleven when they met. Hardin was twelve. When Damien and Ma got married, we took his last name, too."

"And your old man was okay with that?"

*That* was what she decided to focus on right now?

The mere mention of my sperm donor made a weight settle in my gut. "He didn't have much say seeing as we buried his ass out in the canyons."

Her lips parted in surprise at the admission, but she said nothing, just stared up at me silently until finally, it all sunk in. Her chin quivered, and her eyes went glassy. "So, we're not related? At all? Like, not even a little bit?"

"No, baby girl. Not at all."

I pulled her into my chest, holding her tight against me, feeling like an idiot for not coming to her sooner. I couldn't imagine what was going through her head all night, thinking that she…

Jesus.

I didn't even care that she full on admitted to fucking my brother right now. I just wanted her to stop shaking like a leaf in my arms. I pressed a kiss to her hair and rubbed hard circles in her back as she came to terms with all the new information. "I'm so sorry. I should've realized you would think that."

She shook her head against my chest, pulling back, but not away, just far enough so she could look up at me with those piercing hazel eyes of hers. "I've been in hell for the last twenty-four hours, Kaleb."

I couldn't help smirking, dropping my hand to her waist to squeeze tight. "Then let me take you back to heaven where you belong."

"Oh god." She snorted, teasing me for the line that was so cheesy I was surprised she didn't offer me wine and crackers to go with it.

I crashed my mouth onto hers, swallowing her laughter, loving how I could turn it into a moan at the drop of a dime.

She roughly pulled her lips from mine, her breathing lower, but at least the color was back in her cheeks. If she just gave me five minutes, I was sure I could take her from Wednesday Addams to Megan Fox, windblown hair and all.

"Wait, wait, wait," she gushed.

"What?"

"This is still weird. You're my…"

"Vixen, you fucked my brother."

She had the decency to look guilty at my accusation, but she wasn't denying it.

"Assuming that was something you were a willing party for, I'd have to say you're into shit that's far more taboo than a little stepbro romance."

She bit her bottom lip, making me want to bite it, too, needing to hear her moan *my* name to erase the image in my head of her with my brother.

I shifted my hand down her lower back, parking it on her ass, grabbing myself a good handful in a way that had her face crumpling with need. But still, there was a fight going on behind her eyes.

"Look, I wasn't going to say anything because, fuck, you'd probably be better off if we all kicked the bucket tonight, but—"

Becca went stiff in my arms. "What do you mean?"

"We're going to—how do I put this—*negotiate terms* with the Sons tonight. I have to meet Dad and Hardin in a few hours to head out to the canyons."

"You're going to kill them, aren't you?"

I wasn't sure if she wanted the truth here, but she was going to get it from me anyway. I figured she'd probably had enough of people lying to her to last a while, and she needed to know what she was getting into here, because I was getting dangerously close to considering monogamy as a full-time gig.

"Yes," I told her with a nod.

She blinked up at me, for once those eyes weren't set on me with anger. With a taunt or a glare or anything else she tried to use as a shield to hide from me how she really felt. Her doe-like expression had me high-key worried that I might not come back from this in one piece if only because it would mean never seeing this face again.

Shit. Look at me. I was turning into a goddamned tragedy. What was next? Asking her to go steady?

"So you're saying that you might not be back."

I'd be lying if I didn't admit that the fear in her eyes at that idea made my stomach flip, just a little.

I pulled her so close that I could feel her breath against my lips. "What I'm saying, *lil' sis*, is the last person I wanted to see before Armageddon is you. Unless… unless there's someone else you'd rather see."

Like say, my older brother.

She surprised me with a rare smile, the playful kind that made her eyes light up like fucking Christmas morning. "You idiot."

This time when I kissed her, she didn't hold back. My little vixen buckled in my arms, curving into the contour of my body as I pried her lips apart with my tongue.

She opened for me like a good girl, letting me sweep in to taste her as I moved us closer to the couch. My foot hooked on the coffee table and I tripped forward, pitching us both onto the curved sofa.

Real fucking smooth, Kaleb.

She let out a surprised sound that I swallowed up with my mouth before moving to her cheek, marking a path with my lips down to her jaw. Her neck. The swell of her tits that past Kaleb might've said were too small. That dickwad could shove it, though, because they were perfect.

I palmed them through her work apron, feeling the start of what I was sure would be an absolutely raging hard-on press against the seam of my jeans.

A soft groan escaped my lips, and she hushed me sharply, making me remember where we were. As if I'd care. Hell, I wanted every Tom, Dick, and fucking Sally in this joint to hear her scream my name. I wanted them to hear her and to know it was *me* who made her shatter under my touch. Me who she couldn't get enough of.

*Me* who she belonged to.

I reached behind her on the velvet cushions to pry off her apron and she lifted her head for me, helping me get it off her, her eyes greedy and lust-filled. She needed this almost as badly as I did.

To erase all the ugly thoughts that were no doubt still raging in her pretty head. She needed me to escape what happened. I needed her to escape the thought of what might happen.

And fuck if I wasn't high-key so fucking down to be her human eraser. Let me scrub away all that pain, baby. Wipe it clean.

I barely got the apron all the way off before she was working on my belt, jerking me forward to try and rip the thing off. I watched her work furiously to get to her prize, with a little knot of concentration in her brow.

"You're so fucking beautiful."

"And your belt is about three seconds from being shredded to ribbons."

I laughed, helping her get it undone. My cock pushed free into her hand and she started jerking me, as if I wasn't already the hardest I'd ever been. I shuddered against her, falling from my hands to my elbows on either side of her.

"Holy... *Jesus*..."

I thrusted into her palm, practically seeing stars already and my dick was drier than the goddamned Sahara. As if she knew what was lacking, she brought her hand to her mouth, sucking each one of her fingers with a devious look in her eyes before going back to doing God's good work downstairs, this time, with natural fucking lube, baby.

"Fuck, careful there, Vixen, or you're going to have a mess on your hands real quick and we haven't even got to the fun part yet."

She hushed me sharply again, and I groaned, squeezing my eyes shut as my balls began to tighten with each stroke of her hand. The slippery minx was fucking enjoying this.

Determined *not* to come prematurely all over the girl I fully intended to be bedding on the regular, I slipped my dick out of her hands. Really, I should win an award for that shit.

"My turn."

I shifted down the sofa, tugging her yoga pants down with me. She looked over my shoulder, apprehension in her eyes. She was worried someone would walk around the corner, find us in a—shall we say—compromised position.

She still hadn't learned, as long as she was with us, no one could touch her. No one would say a word against her or I'd have their tongues and fuck... I was turning into my goddamned brother over this girl.

But I would quite literally kill for her.

I ran my hand up her thigh, my fingers brushing something that made her wince. I frowned, looking down between us to the unmistakable ring of bite marks on her inner thigh, the skin around the nearly healed scabs stained with shades of purple that was already turning yellow with age.

He'd fucking marked her.

I ran my finger over the ridge of raised skin that I was certain would scar and felt strangely…glad. He deserved to have this, too. And as long as Hardin cared for her, she would be safe from him. Safe from anyone else, too.

"Please," my Vixen moaned, trying to inch lower on the sofa and I chastised myself for making my lady wait.

She was so wet for me already, and I clenched my teeth as I slid two fingers around her clit before sticking those same two fingers inside her. She clutched onto me at the quick thrust of my arm with a gasp in my ear. I hooked my fingers inside her warm cunt, using my thumb to rub her clit until she was thrashing beneath me, moving her hips in tandem with my movements.

"You're going to make me—"

She bit down on her own hand to keep from shouting as she came apart beneath me, the walls of her sweet pussy contracting against my fingers with the force of her orgasm.

I kissed her nose, not giving her any time to mourn the loss of my fingers before I got my cock inside her, covering her surprised groan with my mouth.

I let myself settle there, locked in her pussy, my cock so hard I could feel my heart beating through it inside her, wondered if she could feel it, too.

Her hands went to my hips, urging me to move as I kissed her. I groaned against her lips, and she shivered as I began to move. This encounter not like the hot, angry claiming in the showers at the yoga studio. I wanted to take my time with her. Feel her.

I rolled my hips, fucking her deep and slow, making sure every thrust hit the good spots, the ones I knew would make her see stars. Her hands gripped the back of my biceps, needing something to hold onto.

She let out a cry, tipping her head back, arching into me to press her clit harder to the base of my cock as I fucked her.

"You like that cock buried deep inside you, Vixen?" I purred into her ear and she clenched her teeth.

"Yes. Oh fuck. *Don't stop.* Just like that."

I kept the exact pressure and pace going, knowing that it would drive me to my own end any second. I needed her to come. Now. Her little moans were driving me to the brink of insanity.

My breaths came out in stuttered bursts, my own moans growing louder, matching the rhythm of hers.

"That's it, Vixen," I urged her, bending up her right leg, pushing it down against her torso to get even deeper as I continued rolling my hips into her. "Take it. Take it all."

She opened her mouth in a silent scream as her orgasm started to take her, and I hooked a thumb into her mouth. She clamped down on it, sucking on the digit until I fucking detonated with her, pumping my seed deep into her belly with a muted roar, my balls so tight it was a damn miracle they didn't break off.

Becca put a hand in my hair as I laid my face against her tits, wanting to savor the moment, if only for a second. Her heart beat erratically in her chest as her fingers ran through my hair, both of us struggling to catch our breath.

"Come back, okay?"

The reminder of what awaited me when I left the cafe had me shutting my eyes against her tits.

"I will," I promised her in a whisper, pulling her hand to my lips to brush them over her knuckles. "Do me a favor, Vixen, and stick close to Pope. He's going to take you to one of our safehouses with the other families. Do not leave his sight. I need your word."

Her breathing hitched, and I hated that she needed to be scared, even knowing it would be worse if she wasn't.

"Vixen?"

"Okay. You have my word."

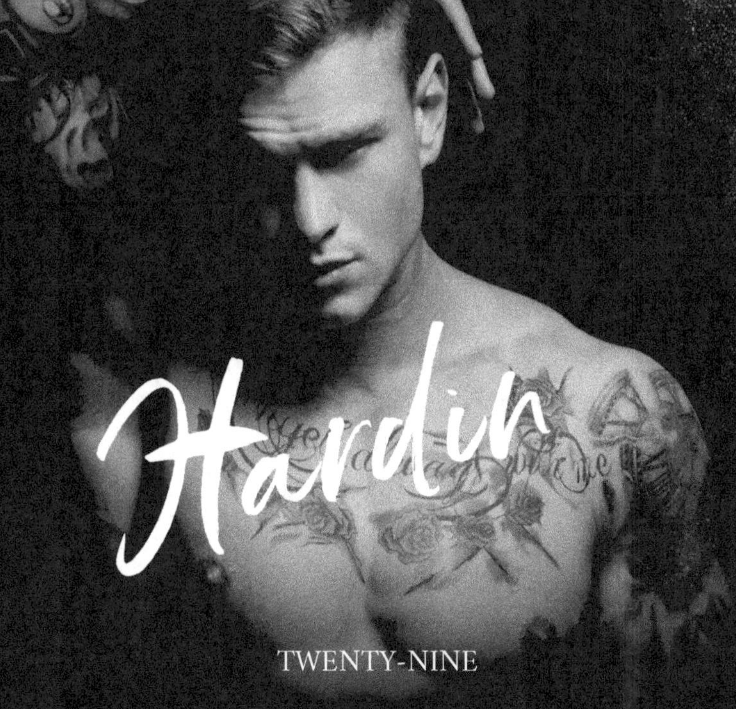


## TWENTY-NINE

"Where the fuck are Arch and Zade?"

Dad paced back and forth, kicking up red dirt in his wake.

We were just a few miles out from our intended meeting point with the Sons with only minutes to spare before we needed to be there.

Dad picked up his phone and called Arch again, but the line just rang and rang.

"You missed me," Archer's recorded voice came loudly through Dad's phone. "I don't check this shit so try again in a few."

He hung up furiously, calling Zade only to get a similar voicemail message after seven rings.

"They know where we're going to be," Kaleb said. "They'll be at the meeting point. We have to go. Time's running out."

"I don't fucking like this," Dad was saying, rubbing a thumb over the stubble on his jaw. "Something isn't right."

"We got their intel before they went radio silent," I reminded him, keeping my voice low while every other able-bodied available Saint armed up around us. Our vehicles idled in the dark valley where we would hold until the last possible second, filling the air with the smell of diesel exhaust.

"We have them by the balls," Kaleb agreed. "If they don't play ball, you make the call to Tanner and he blows their storehouse sky high."

The Warden's men gave Arch and Zade the location where they delivered the last arms order. An old storehouse way out near Five Points, hidden in the mountains. Tanner—our resident explosives expert—and a small team were already there.

The building wasn't guarded, but this fucker that led the Sons seemed the cocky type. I wouldn't put it past him to think himself untouchable. Besides, Tanner said the structure was well hidden and locked up tight.

The guns that were inside were already loaded up into one of our vans. Tanner had the charges set, waiting for a signal from Damien to blow what remained—a few crates of coke and H—into oblivion.

Dad would use that and the weapons to force the leader of the Sons to bend the knee, but we didn't intend to let him live regardless.

There was a line, and this fucker crossed it when he killed Jimmy Boy. I'd make sure he was hacked into just as many pieces, putting his head on a sharpened spike to mark the edge of our land in case anyone else thought they'd try their luck killing a Saint.

Our revenge would be swift and merciless.

Dad pulled his lips back over his teeth, shaking his head. He had every fucking reason to worry about Zade and Arch.

They could both be the source of the leak for all we knew.

And if this bastard had them, we could kiss our bargaining chip goodbye unless Dad was willing to sacrifice his two best men besides me and Kaleb. His two best friends.

It would be a bloodbath of epic proportions if that happened and the sadist in me craved it like a starving man craved his next meal. No one fucked with my family. No one touched my Ma's house.

If it came to a firefight, I had no doubt we'd lose some of our own, but it was a sacrifice I was willing to make if it meant burying the threat once and for all.

"Everyone's ready," Ma said, coming up behind me.

She had her hair pulled back in a long ponytail that made her look years younger as she leveled a hard stare on Dad. They were speaking now, after the shit that happened on Friday at dinner, but that was about it.

I checked my phone for another status update from Pope, and it was there, right on schedule.

**Pope: At the safehouse now. The girl's safe. Picking at a pack of peanut M&Ms.**

He followed it up with a picture of her for proof. Becca sat in the corner of one of the couches, her knees pulled tight to her chest, a big blue M&M between her fingers. Beyond her, I could see the other family members lounging about. Some huddled together, worry making lines in their faces, but even more were at ease, laughing, treating this as an excuse for a social gathering.

They had that much trust in Damien, in their husbands, brothers, and sons, to know that everything would be all right.

"You wearing your vest," Dad asked Ma, and she jerked the collar of her black long sleeve shirt down to show him that she was.

"Boys?"

Kaleb opened one side of his jacket to show his.

"It's time to move out," I said gruffly before Dad could demand to see the vest I wasn't wearing. That shit would just slow me down, make it harder to move, and I had a feeling I was going to need a full range of fucking movement before the night was through.

Dad straightened his spine, checking his phone one last time for word from Zade or Arch. He lifted a hand in the air, whistling the crew he'd pulled in from every corner of our territory. "Move out!"

Near eighty men piled back into their vehicles, ready to follow Dad's truck to the meet point. Kaleb slid into the driver's side of our Bronco, and I jumped to sit atop the roll bar, twisting the rifle slung across my back to my front.

"You ready, Bro?"

"Let's just get this shit over with."

I stared down at my brother as he pulled in line to

follow Dad, great clouds of fine sand tinted red from his tail lights. The better question was, was *he* ready?

Unlike me, Kaleb preferred using a tactical approach as opposed to brute strength and savagery, and there was no telling which way this was about to go down.

But I knew, with Ma there and with me and Dad there, he could be every bit as merciless as I could if it meant the difference between all of us getting out alive or winding up dead.

The drive to the canyons was silent save for the occasional chirp of the CB radio we rarely had occasion to switch on. Other gang members sounded off with every mile marker.

*Clear. Clear. Clear.*

The hills were eerily quiet as we made our way down into the crater-like floor of the valley where a twelve year old version of myself helped Ma bury our deranged father.

Where were they?

Tension stretched across my back, and I slipped down into the seat next to Kaleb. "It's too quiet," I growled over the roar of thirty engines and tires crunching over sand.

"No shit. We're almost there."

I squinted to see into the dark, through the mist-like spray of red sand, but couldn't see past Dad's tail lights.

Just as he hit the base of the decline, leveling out on the valley floor, bright lights flashed to life, drenching us in blinding white, making Dad slam on his breaks and Kaleb have to carve the wheel left to avoid hitting him, skidding to a stop in the sand next to Dad's truck.

"What the fuck?" Kaleb grunted, jolting forward in his seat as the Bronco rocked and we both squinted to see into the light.

Behind us the rest of the cavalry came to a halt, and I heard doors open, our men marching forward to defend their leader as he stepped down from the driver's seat of his truck.

I shoved out from the Bronco, thumbing the safety off on my rifle.

"Welcome," came a man's voice loud over a megaphone and my gut twisted, filling with heat. *Great. A fucking showman.*

"Step right up," he called, his voice deep with a definite accent. "Let's have a look at you, shall we?"

Once my eyes finally adjusted to the brightness, I made out what looked like a parked truck; a man stood in the raised bed, no more than a silhouette against the lights behind him.

But where was everyone else?

A crew of four men stood in front of the back bumper of the truck, rifles held across their chests, at the ready.

Four?

This lunatic brought four men as backup to the meet? I wasn't buying it. I whistled low to Dad and the others, making a circular motion with my finger to indicate that they needed to watch our surroundings.

We had a small team of sharp shooters on their way up the canyon wall to watch our backs, and we'd checked all roads before moving to the holding location, but that didn't mean they couldn't have driven up behind us, trying to box us in.

We'd anticipated something like that could happen, which was why we'd rolled spikes across three of the four entry point roads and covered them over with sand.

It would slow them down, but it wouldn't stop them.

"Are the lights necessary?" Dad bellowed across the divide of sand between our rival gangs.

"Paul," the man on the truck bed said, and the massive rectangular light panels set up on either side of the truck dimmed enough to make out the bastard's features.

A twisted smile curved his lips upward, mismatched eyes, one lightest blue and the other darkest brown stared with cruel glee down at our gathering. As if we were all guests at a surprise party he was throwing for himself.

"Who am I speaking to?" Dad asked as Mom took her place beside him. Kaleb and I boxed them in on either side, me next to Ma, him next to Dad.

"Where are my manners?"

The man tossed the megaphone down into the bed of the truck behind him and jumped down, crossing the gap between his group and ours with his hand outstretched.

Twin pistols strapped over his chest moved with each one of his long strides.

"Name's Séamas ó Súilleabháin."

Kaleb and I stepped in front of Dad before he could get any closer.

His malicious gaze caught on first my brother and then me before settling on our father behind us. "I see," he said, looking down his nose at Dad.

The fucker was tall and built wide through the shoulders, but a well-placed bullet could end him now. My finger twitched near the trigger of my rifle, but I wouldn't make the move until Dad gave the order. Or until there was no other choice.

"I'd been hoping to keep things civil between us given that we'll be seeing quite a lot of each other from now on," the Irishman said, and I spat at his feet, thinking of Jimmy Boy's head on the spike in my front lawn.

He looked down at the darkened dirt and back up at me. "Your son, I presume. Charming."

"Hardin, stand down," Dad said, and I took a step back but didn't take my eyes off him for a second.

Dad adjusted his stance, rolling his shoulders back. "I think the time for civil conversation has passed, don't you?"

Séamas' eyes narrowed to slits, but the smile never left his lips, as if he'd been expecting that response. Waiting for it. I recognized the glint of insanity in his eyes. It was the same look my father gave me right before he butted a cigar out on my back. Or as he stalked toward me with a knife, ready to take an inch of flesh in payment for a perceived slight against him.

We weren't dealing with the regular type, here. This wasn't some cocky idiot jacked up on a power trip. This was a loose cannon and we were standing under fire.

"Very well." Séamas dipped his head. "Then let's get right down to it, shall we?"

"You killed one of my—"

"*Uh,*" Séamas cut him off, lifting his finger to silence

Dad as if I wasn't considering cutting it clean off his hand with one strong arc of my blade. "Wasn't finished. Me first, then you, yes?"

The Irishman took a long breath, cocking his head at Dad as he threaded his fingers together behind his back as if he were having a chat with an old friend instead of a man who wanted to see his head swiftly removed from his shoulders.

"So," Séamas started. "I have an offer to make you that I think you'll find quite fair."

I fucking doubted that.

"Twenty percent."

Dad lifted a brow. He usually only asked for fifteen percent of the take from the gangs who operated on his territory. If it wasn't our plan to kill this bastard and his men here and now, it'd be a tempting offer to consider.

"I—"

"And a life of your choosing," Séamas offered. "I'll make it quick and painless."

Wait. This fucker wasn't offering up one of his men in exchange for having killed ours. He wasn't offering Dad twenty percent of his gang's take. He was demanding both.

Dad seemed to come to the realization at the same time and laughed, aiming his rifle at Séamas ó Súilleabháin with a dark chuckle. "Tempting," he slung back sarcastically. "But I have a counter offer."

Séamas grinned.

"You and your men bend the knee here and now and I'll think about letting you walk out of this canyon alive."

"I always lead with my best offer, Damien," Séamas taunted. "Take it or suffer the consequences."

Dad clicked off the safety on his rifle and fire ignited down my spine, ready for a fight, even if the odds were stacked against Séamas and his tiny ass crew of four.

"*Ah, ah,*" Séamas warned, moving slowly as he unbuttoned the leather vest he was wearing to reveal enough C4 strapped to his chest to blow us all to kingdom come.

I snarled, taking a step back.

"Hold your fire!" Damien roared as every gun behind us clicked with the sounds of safeties being switched off, hammers being cocked back.

"If my heart stops, it detonates. So does the bomb my crew placed at your safehouse."

Becca's face snapped into my mind, the M&M pressed between her fingers, poised just before putting it in her mouth. Up in fucking flames that burned so hot they tinted my vision red.

"You're bluffing," Kaleb growled.

"What was that address, Pauly?" Séamas called back to one of his four men.

"1322 Hightower Street."

"1322 Hightower Street," Séamas repeated as if we didn't hear his man ourselves.

My grip tightened on the butt of my rifle, and it took every ounce of my willpower to stay rooted to the spot and not gut this bastard where he stood.

I didn't think it was possible for his men to have rigged the safehouse with explosives without our noticing but there was no way to be certain. "I will end you," I hissed and the Irishman cocked his head at me.

"No, son, you won't."

My nostrils flared, and an aching heat fanned over my back, bathing my chest in a cold sweat. I'd never wanted to kill someone as badly as I did right now.

"Don't hurt them." It was Ma who spoke this time. "Those people at the safe house are innocent. They have nothing to do with this."

"You let your woman speak for your crew?" Séamas asked, completely ignoring Ma.

Dad bristled. "*She's my wife,*" he snarled. "And she has bigger balls than any man I've ever met."

"That so? Then maybe she'll do the choosing for us. I'm assuming you've reconsidered my generous offer? Twenty percent of your take, payable to the Sons on the first and fifteenth day of every month. I'll need to take one life now—call it a deposit—and another every time you fail to comply."

"Hardin," I heard Ma whisper low, almost inaudible, her voice pulling me back from the edge. How did I get my knife in my hand?

I let out a shaky breath and stepped back in line next to Ma, sheathing it as Séamas squared off with Dad.

"Or," Dad said. "We can call your bluff, destroy your storehouse and everything in it, and kill the men you brought with you."

Séamas leaned in conspiratorially. "I never much liked those four anyway," he said. "So go on, have your boy, what's his name? Tanner?"

Fuck.

"Yeah, have him blow up my storehouse out in the mountains. I'll be sure to let the cartel know who to come to to collect for all the drugs they were storing in there."

Double fuck.

"And one thing you should know about me, Damien, is I *never* bluff."

"What do you want?" Dad said through bared teeth.

"I already told you—"

"No. Why *here?*"

Séamas waved an arm all around him, at the dry canyons where we stood. "I was getting tired of all the rain."

He lifted an arm to casually look at his watch before clapping his hands together. "Well, time's up, I'm afraid."

"*No,*" Ma gasped. "Wait."

"Is she always this dramatic?" Séamas asked Dad, jabbing a thumb in Ma's direction.

I was going to feed him his own dick and watch him choke on it.

Maybe not right now, but very fucking soon.

Séamas turned to his men, waving an impatient hand. "Pauly, bring 'em out."

Two of Séamas' men went to the cab of the truck, and the thud of boots hitting the ground was background noise to the static in my head as they dragged two men in the dirt, forcing them to their knees a few yards behind where Séamas stood.

They pulled the black bags from their heads at the same time, but I already knew who they were.

Zade and Archer. Their faces swollen damn near beyond recognition.

We'd lost.

I racked my brain, rifling through every possible outcome, every possible solution.

Our sharpshooters up high in the hills? No good. If they shot him, we'd all die.

A diversion? If I just started shooting up the other four it might provide the cover we needed to get Zade and Archer and get out of here.

…unless he wasn't bluffing about having explosives at the safehouse. What would stop him from detonating them if we didn't cooperate.

I knew this bastard's type. I could see it in his eyes, he would lose no sleep over killing a warehouse full of innocent people.

*Think, Hardin. Fucking think.*

There was always a way. There had to be a way out of this.

"Heard you paid a visit to The Warden's men. That's really too bad. I'd intended to let them all live, but alas, they couldn't be trusted."

The Warden had over forty men on his crew, but judging by the looks on Archer and Zade's faces I could tell the Irishman wasn't lying. He'd slaughtered them all.

"That's enough." Dad seethed, his fingers flexing on the stock of his rifle. "Let them go and I'll agree to your terms. Twenty percent. It's yours."

He spat each word like they were poisonous, filled

with a venom so potent that he was shaking. A king reduced to the role of jester in his own court.

This guy had no idea what kind of monster he'd woken here tonight.

"Done," Séamas said, whirling with a violent gleam in his eyes, pulling one of his pistols from its holster. The gunshot echoed back to us from the canyon walls, boomeranging until it faded like thunder.

"Oh Christ," Ma gasped, hurrying to pull the rifle from Dad's hands as Archer keeled over to one side, the hole in his head still smoking as blood pooled around him.

"*Arch*," Zade cried out, his voice loud, broken, and raw, grating enough to make my skin crawl. "*Archer!*"

Dad stormed forward, his neck thick, face red, eyes bulging as he went straight for Séamas, his knife raised.

*Damnit.*

I stepped in front of him, disarming him with one quick twist of my arm, pulling him in tight to hold him back as he tried to push past me with a string of pained curses on his lips.

I felt his pain as if it were my own, knowing Archer was a brother to him, feeling guilty as fuck for ever having thought he could betray us.

"It's done," I hissed in Dad's ear, fighting him back with everything I had. "He's gone. He's gone."

Kaleb came to help me while Séamas laughed behind us.

"This is what he wants," Kaleb whispered harshly, and I knew he was right. If Dad attacked him now, it would only get worse. Séamas could kill as many of us as he wanted right now and we wouldn't be able to stop him. Not until we knew Becca, and the people in the safehouse were free.

"Don't give it to him."

The fight went out of him all at once and he threw us off him, standing on his own.

"I knew you'd see the big picture," Séamas said, his laughter dying out as he put his pistol back in its holster and lifted his arm, making a motion with his hands. His four men left their stations, three piling into the back of the truck while one went for the driver's seat, starting the ignition.

"It's been a pleasure doing business with you. Shall we say, same place, same time on the 15th of the month?"

Séamas backed away, stepping through Archer's blood to leave a gory trail behind him as he hopped up into the back of the truck with his crew and pounded a closed fist on the side of the wheel well.

The truck drove off into the night, leaving us standing under the spotlights with our fucking dicks in our hands… and another dead Saint to bury.

# Aodhan



## THIRTY

The safehouse at 1322 Hightower Street held enough souls to make the good lord work overtime and enough explosives rigged into its walls to shake the foundations of the earth.

I should know, since I was the one who placed them, burying each one tenderly beneath brick and mortar.

*But she wasn't supposed to be there.*

When the one called Pope brought Becca in to join the others, something in my chest crumpled like cheap wrapping. I sat heavily on the upturned stool from the fifth-floor window in the apartment building where I watched at a safe distance.

*Damn it all to hell.*

*She wasn't supposed to be there.*

I balled my hand into a fist, pressing it into my teeth

until I tasted blood. Until I felt the sting of it like air on a fresh cut from Da's whip. I spat onto the carpeted floor, rising despite the lightness in my head and kicked the bucket into the wall with a roar.

"Fuck!"

I could fix this. I could.

There was a chance Da wouldn't blow it. If Damien St. Vincent just bent the knee, he would let them live. But if Damien refused...

I snatched my phone from the windowsill, tapping out a message to Becca.

**Aodhán: Meet me for coffee?**

**Becca: It's almost eleven at night**

**Aodhán: Since when has that stopped you?**

*Come on.*

**Becca: Can't tonight**

*You can, mo mhuirnín.*

**Aodhán: I can come pick you up**

*Come on, Becca...*

I waited for what felt like a lifetime for her to reply before realizing I wasn't going to get one, clutching my phone hard enough to split the skin on my knuckles even further. Droplets of brightest crimson pelted the carpet as I paced the congested living room, considering making a choice there would be no return from.

But what other option did I have?

If I did nothing, she would burn with the others.

No one out at the canyon would be able to get a cell signal to warn them—that was part of what made it all work—but *I* could warn them. Warn *her*.

I could already feel the crack and shred of Da's whip on my skin. Could taste the blood in my mouth. Feel the echo of the pain I would be forced to endure in all the scars, healed and still healing across my torso like the web of a twisted spider.

She didn't deserve to burn.

Fuck that.

Da didn't need to know it was me. He wouldn't know. Not if I did it right.

My runners chirped against the linoleum stairs as I threw myself down them, foregoing the wait for an elevator. There was no time. Like Becca said, it was almost eleven.

I sprinted down the darkened streets, past parked cars and humming streetlights and an empty community pool. The building on Hightower lay ahead, a long flat building, white, with a brown roof that would soon be painted in shades of glowing orange and red.

Diving into the thorny bushes on the side of the road to avoid being seen, I lowered to a crouch and made my way silently to the rear of the Saint safehouse. A flashlight beam stole over the yellowed grass of the back lawn, and I waited for the patrol to pass before darting across.

*What the fuck am I doing?*

I cursed under my breath, mentally kicking myself as I twisted the loose screw in the rusted old newspaper carrier affixed to the brick wall, and popped off the front panel.

A red light glowed like a pulse in the dark cavity of the box, and I reached in—around the signal beacon Da could trigger any moment—to the bulky length of wires behind it. I only had minutes before the Saint patrol came back around and only one wire would give me the result I wanted.

I fumbled my phone in the dark, my back aching in anticipation of Da's retribution. Sweat beaded at my brow as I worked my phone into the rusty box and clicked on the screen to see.

*Aodhán, don't,* Mum's voice whispered in my mind, trying to save me from myself. Like she had so many times before.

My fingers shook as I pulled apart the wiring, having to hold my phone between my teeth to keep the light where I needed it as I worked.

The shuffle of feet coming around the building urged me to work faster as I plucked the connector free from the cord and went for the blade fixed to the belt at my waist.

"Hey!" A voice roughly called and the distinct sound of a weapon slipping from a rigid leather holster had me moving faster than I could think. I dropped to the ground, the heel of my boot twisting in the dry lawn as I locked my eyes on the threat and loosed the blade between my fingers.

It whistled through the air for a fraction of a second before embedding in the neck of the Saint. His flashlight dropped to the grass, its light squarely on me as I darted forward, kicking it to the bushes as the Saint fell.

Blood erupted from his mouth in a choked gurgle as all the color drained from his face.

"*Shhh,*" I hissed, lowering him down easily, silently, before tugging my blade free of his thick neck, letting his blood feed the starving grass.

I wiped my blade clean on his vest, sucking a frustrated breath in through my teeth as he breathed his last. I reached over to shut his eyes, painting the backs of his eyelids with nature's red paint. Hating the missed opportunity to add his demise to my little film collection, but there was no time.

"Better you than her," I told his corpse, patting him on the shoulder before rushing back to the box and the wire that I still needed to cut.

I pinched it between my fingers, hearing my own blood rushing in my ears as I held the blade to it.

*Don't.*

I shook my head, trying to rid myself of her voice, speaking through clenched teeth. "*But she's in there.*"

Movement inside the building spurred me to complete my task, and I sucked in a sharp breath as I clipped the wire in two and the pulsing red light blinked out.

*I was a dead man walking.*

I hurried to place the front of the old box back into place, the metal scraping loudly as I hooked it into the latches and twisted the screw back in to hold it together.

The thorny bushes welcomed me back with claws and fucking teeth as I flattened myself against the earth just as two more Saints rounded the corner of the building, their flashlights scanning the yard.

I lay there perfectly still, patient as a patron saint, as they discovered their fallen comrade. As they searched the area, working their way into the street. As they shouted over radios and started up engines, the idiots completely unaware that the man they were hunting just saved all of their miserable lives.

Back at the apartment, I bleached my blood out of the white carpet and scrubbed myself clean in the shower before putting everything back just the way I found it. The owners, away in Spain, wouldn't even know I was here when they returned.

With the borrowed towel around my waist, I took up the binoculars in the living room and watched the Saints' nearest and dearest exit the building into the slowly growing dawn. But there was only one face I wanted to see.

Becca followed Pope from the front door, the pair of them making for Pope's old Chevy truck, when a familiar vehicle approached the building.

Hardin St. Vincent was up and through the roll bars of the Bronco before it'd even stopped. Kaleb left the vehicle idling in the street as they both closed in on Becca. My grip tightened on the binoculars.

Hardin gripped her chin, jerking her face toward the light before Kaleb shoved him off and pulled her into his chest, burying his face in her hair.

Were they behaving as though the building should have blown? Or were they only worried my Da might have blown it regardless?

The only way I was getting away with the sin I'd committed against my father was if he didn't detonate it. Because if he did and he returned to find the building still standing, all its occupants still whole instead of turned to ash, there would be no one to blame but me.

Kaleb threaded his fingers into Becca's hair, crushing his mouth to hers while Hardin appeared to still be checking her own for damage. As if either of them had the capacity to *love*.

I'd done my homework on them like Da wanted. I knew who they were. *What* they were.

They were about as likely to love her as a lion would be to love a mouse.

I snorted, lowering the binoculars with a clenched jaw. Da'd been debating whether to take one of Damien's sons as his sacrifice, but it seemed he'd decided against that idea. Smart, really. He didn't want to go making any martyrs, only to sow enough fear to gain control.

A sharp rap at the door preceded Da's return, and I set the binoculars down, rearranging my face when he entered the way I'd learned as a boy.

He took in the towel hanging low around my hips with a raised brow. "Enjoying your accommodations, fuil mo chuid fola?"

The Gaelic nickname, *blood of my blood*, sank into my ears like quicksand, the weight of it heavy in the face of what I'd done.

How I'd betrayed him.

"Da, you let them live?"

The attempt to sound surprised may have been too obvious and my throat tightened, blocking me from saying anything else that might give me away.

Da's lips curled up on one side as he approached the

window, staring out into the pink hued streets to watch the Saints and their kin disperse like rats from a sewer. No doubt they were all just informed of the explosives.

"Look at them run," Da mused, a king overseeing his new kingdom as he removed his armor. First, his pistol belts and next his vest, revealing bricks of C4 strapped to his torso.

"Da?" I asked, uneasy as I watched him pull a metal pin connected to a wire from one of the bricks, disconnecting a device that also connected to two round tabs stuck to his chest. This… whatever this was, was not part of the plan.

"A failsafe," he explained, tattooed fingers peeling the little discs from his bare chest. "I wasn't certain you'd help with this one."

He set the last of the bricks of C4 down on the windowsill and turned to face me. "Now, I'm not so sure."

I kept my expression neutral as he moved to the dining area in the next room and folded himself into one of the seats, gesturing to the one opposite him.

Without missing a beat, I slid into the seat he offered, sitting up straight, my gaze never wavering. Any indication of doubt or weakness would be met with suspicion.

"Sure of what?" I asked with a steady tone, resting my hand on the table.

"Your loyalty."

I made my brows wrinkle. "You are fuil mo chuid fola," I echoed back to him, hating myself as I spoke each word because he was blood of my blood.

The man who made me. Who molded me into someone who could never be hurt. Never be tricked. Never be used. Who could kill without remorse, to whatever ends I deemed worthy. Being reborn as something stronger than a mere mortal took pain. Patience.

Da looked into me, and I knew he was seeing everything I wanted to hide from him just as I saw everything Becca tried to hide from me when I looked into her eyes.

My face pinched, feeling guilt for every moment I spent with her, for the freedom I felt when I let my mask slip, showing her parts of me I thought died under Da's whip years ago.

That guilt only grew, twisted into something far more potent when I recalled the sight of Becca with Kaleb St. Vincent's lips on hers. With Hardin St. Vincent's eyes roaming her glorious body. Guilt *and shame* because I was naively trying to protect a thing that could never be mine.

My fist clenched beneath the table.

I'd been a fool.

I could see that now.

"I would never betray you."

Da inclined his head to me, his light hair turning to fire as dawn broke the horizon, painting him in shades of copper. "Then, tell me, who is the girl?"

I felt the twitch in my jaw the same time Da saw it, and I knew he had me. At least he seemed unaware of my work at the Safehouse. For the moment. I'd have to come up with a good excuse for that body I left behind.

There was no sense in trying to lie now. If Da wanted to know, he would know. With or without my help.

"Has my son grown back his heart?"

Now it was my turn to smirk.

"No."

"Then why all this time spent with the girl?"

A vaporous heat filled my core, and I restrained the urge to demand to know why he was having me watched when he'd tasked *me* with doing the watching.

*Don't give it to him.*

I fingered my Ma's four-leaf clover charm, rubbing it between my fingers, unable to understand what she was trying to tell me from the grave. I shut my eyes against the gut instinct to lie to my Da twice in one night, knowing this time, it was wrong.

"You're withholding something, fuil mo chuid fola, and I will have it. *Now.*"

Becca wasn't mine to have.

"...before my patience wears thin."

Nor mine to protect.

Da pounded his fist on the table, and I jerked my chin up to see his face twist, his eyes glinting with fury. "If this girl is nothing to you then—"

"She's the daughter of Damien St. Vincent."

His snarling mouth slackened, his fist unfurled, and a slow smile spread his lips wide over two rows of white teeth.

"*Ha ha!*" he exclaimed, jolting from his seat to pace the floor with single minded focus that had his mismatched eyes shifting over the floor. He knelt in front of me, drawing my hand roughly to his mouth for a kiss. "I never should have doubted you, fuil mo chuid fola. You have given me a great weapon."

Then why did I feel like I'd given him my soul, instead?